The Second Path

A Selkie Moon Mystery

VIRGINIA KING

Be sure to visit www.selkiemoon.com for insider information, character bios and author updates. Subscribe to *Myth & Mystery* for exclusive news and events.

Books By Virginia King

Selkie Moon Mystery Series:
The First Lie
The Second Path
Book Three (Coming Soon)
Laying Ghosts (www.selkiemoon.com)

The Second Path

A Selkie Moon Mystery

VIRGINIA KING

Celestial Hedgehog

For more information or to book an event or interview, contact the author at www.selkiemoon.com

Printed in the United States of America

First Printing, 2015
ISBN 978-0-9924870-9-6
www.selkiemoon.com

Glossary

Selkie – sea creature from Celtic folklore that takes the form of a seal in water but can take human form on land.

Serendip – former name of Sri Lanka; in a Persian fairytale the three princes of Serendip have the ability to discover desirable but unexpected things.

Hawaiian words

Aloha – traditional greeting meaning welcome and goodbye.
Aumakua – a shape-shifting spirit guide that takes animal form.
Hiwa – type of kava root.
Ho'ohihi – interconnectedness.
Kahuna – wise person, sorcerer.
Lanai – veranda.
Lei – garland of flowers or shells, worn around the neck.
Lolo – crazy.
Mahalo – thank you.
Mo'o – lizard; water spirit; animal spirit guide.
Muu-muu – long loose-fitting dress.
Pele – volcano goddess.
Pau hana – happy hour.
Portagee – Portuguese.
Shaka – welcoming hand gesture with the three middle fingers folded down.
Shape-shifta (pidgin) – supernatural being that can change form.
Talk story (pidgin) – catch up, chat.
Tutu – grandma.

French words

Anglophone (m or f) – English-speaker.
Atelier (m) – studio, workshop.
Avocat (m) – lawyer.
Bien sûr – of course.
Bijoux (pl) – jewellery.
Brocante (f) – bric-a-brac, second-hand goods.
Cacahuètes (pl) – roasted peanuts.
Château (m) – castle.
Chercher – to look for.
Cherchez la femme – look for the woman.
Chéri(e) – dear, darling; cherished, beloved.
Clouer – to nail.
Cuillère (f) – spoon.
D'accord; Dac! – OK; I agree.
Déesse (f) – goddess.
Dépôt-vente – sale of second-hand goods on consignment.
De rien – don't mention it; no worries.
De rigueur – obligatory; the done thing.
Désolé(e) – sorry.
École (f) – school.
Escargot (m) – snail.
Franglais – pidgin French/English.
Frites (pl) – French fries.
Guinguette (f) – outdoor drinking and dance event.
Histoire (f) – story; history.
Joie de vivre – joy of living
Liberté (f) – freedom.
Lit (m) – bed.
Mon dieu – my God; my goodness.
Mer (f) – sea.
Merde (f) – shit.

N'est-ce pas? – isn't it?

Pas disponible – not available.

Pied-à-terre – an occasional home.

Salon (m) – living room.

Salut – hi, bye; cheers.

Séminaire (m) – seminar.

Son et lumière – sound and light show.

Soupçon (m) – a hint of, a suspicion of.

Sympa – warm and likeable.

Tête-à-tête – a cosy chat.

Trajectoire (f) – trajectory.

Troglodytique – troglodytic, cave-dwelling.

Trompe-l'oeil – a painting technique using perspective to make objects appear real.

Vide – empty.

Vin rouge (m) – red wine.

The light was both livid and shifting, but it cut me off from the universe, and doubled the darkness of the surrounding night.

Travels with a Donkey in the Cevennes
–Robert Louis Stevenson

CHAPTER
One

I wake on the beach and discover I'm naked.

What?

Unless it's my mind, playing tricks.

I'm afraid to look, but my other senses are screaming. The waves shushing at my eardrums. The ground hugging my body. The breeze stroking my skin. I move my legs and sand slips from my inner thighs like icing sugar from cupcakes, the freedom of it suddenly delicious as I stretch and wriggle my toes.

The sensation flips to panic when I open my eyes. In the low light, my bare limbs sprawl away from me, white and vulnerable like a stranded mermaid's. *Mermaid.* The word is like a message. The word my mother always used.

"Because you're a mermaid," she said whenever anything magical happened. Not that I remember her, but I hear her voice in my heart. My imperfect, selfish, dead mother. This is all her fault.

Snatches of memory invade my consciousness. Moonlight. Singing. The touch of rough hands.

I squint against the pale light, trying to scan the beach, wondering if I'm alone. Hoping. Because I don't know why I'm here. Or who the hands belonged to. Was I taken by force? Drugged? Or did I go willingly, duped by beguiling music? The sirens used music to lure the gullible into watery graves. Does that mean I'm already dead?

My fingers reach up and find the cowry shell, its cord tied around my neck. Not totally naked then. I brush sand off my belly and discover a drop of moisture in my navel, but the rest of my skin is dry. Just one drop. Another message.

The implication's lost when someone calls my name.

"Selkie," he screams against the sound of the surf. "Selkie, it's you. My God, it's really you."

A man with unruly dark hair is racing towards me, kicking up sand. Derek. He falls over and gets up again. When he finally reaches me and collapses at my side I see he's crying. Sobbing.

"I knew we'd find you," he gasps, "but it's been so long. Where did you come from? One minute the beach is empty, the next minute you're lying here. Like you've never been gone. God, if you don't tell me everything I swear I'll kill myself." He notices my nakedness. "Where are your clothes? What's happened to you?"

I try to speak but nothing comes out. Have I lost the power of speech? Then a primal croak, followed by words. "Stop that, DD." Another croak. "I'm...fine."

At least I think I am. If I'd been raped I'd feel it, wouldn't I? There'd be bruises, dried blood. An overwhelming sense of violation. Of shame. The first dark stirrings of revenge. Instead I'm strangely bemused by the situation.

Derek gazes at me, tears coursing down his face. He hasn't shaved for a day or two and his usual sharp jawline has sagged. He looks exhausted.

"Is it morning...or evening?" I manage.

"Morning." He wipes his eyes with the back of his hand and sand catches in the stubble on his cheek. "But that's the wrong question, Selkie."

"Why?"

"It's...Monday."

Monday. I remember now. I came to the cemetery on...Sunday. I climbed down the cliff. I...took off my dress. My dress. Where the hell is my dress?

"You've been missing for two weeks," he says. "We've been looking for you for fourteen days. Even the police."

"The police?" Two weeks? I try to get my head around this. Where have I been? And what's happened to my dress?

"Alister just left," Derek adds. "I took over from him. Then a moment later you...materialised."

"Alister." I haven't forgotten him. Alister Sloane, the seminar tycoon with a crush on me. "He was here? At Bantry's Bluff?"

At least I know where I am. The cliffs are unmistakeable.

"All weekend," he says. "We've been doing shifts since you disappeared. Nigel too. Looking, waiting. Praying. We camped on the beach." He points to a silver tent just visible below the cliff.

"Watching for me?"

"Yeah." Suddenly he's grinning. "The cops said we were wasting our time. They found the car near the cemetery gate and assumed the worst. They searched the rocks and the shore but there was no sign of you. They waited a couple of days for the sea to bring your body back, then gave up."

My head is spinning. And I'm suddenly cold. Freezing.

"You're shivering," Derek says. "I've got blankets in the tent. Can you stand up? Here, wear my shirt."

He starts on the buttons, but I shake my head. I just want the blanket. My nakedness isn't an issue. Derek's always been the big sister I never had.

He helps me sit up and the world tilts, as if I've been prone for two weeks. Now I'm shuddering and Derek pulls me up and wraps me in a bear hug.

"Are you sure you're not injured?" He runs his eyes over my limbs.

"Blanket," I croak. "Food."

"In the tent. Lean on me."

He puts his arm around my waist and together we hobble across the sand. My legs don't feel stiff exactly, more like rusty – doing something they haven't done for a while. Two weeks?

Soon I'm wrapped in a woollen cocoon and sipping hot coffee, after Derek made me drink a gallon of water. He's stoking the tiny campfire and throwing eggs and bacon and bananas into a pan.

"So you guys didn't starve," I say.

He gives me a sideways glare. "We wouldn't be much good to you if we weren't prepared. We just weren't expecting it to take this long."

I think about their devotion, and it confounds me like it always does.

"There are clothes in there." He nods towards the tent. "From Wanda. And warm water for washing when you're ready."

"*Mahalo*, DD." I don't know what else to say.

"Don't thank me, just tell me what the hell happened."

But I don't remember. After I got to the beach and took off my dress, apart from a few vague images I'm blank. I've been here before, to the blank place. When I've been scared. When I've seen something I don't want to remember.

"I don't know," I say. "And now you're telling me I've been gone all this time. I've got no idea what I've been doing."

Except that tiny glimmer. The hands. The voices. Something I must remember. Something important. I try to hold it but it dives into darkness.

Derek's shoulders slump. "Amnesia only happens in bad movies."

"It's not amnesia. I know who I am." That feels important.

"If I put this scenario in one of my stories, my editor would call it *convenient*."

"This isn't a story."

"Isn't it? You're living out your own fairytale, Selkie. Disappearing for two weeks, then turning up in the same place everyone's looked a hundred times, with no memory of where you've been, naked and without even a scratch."

"Would it help if I was injured?"

"Of course not."

My guardian angel is burdened with so many emotions he can barely do 'pleased to see me'. Not yet. He's done in. And he's angry. Angry with me for putting him through so much worry. He's also right about the story. My mother named me after the mythical seal-people before I almost drowned in the sea, then thirty-five years later I wake up on this beach stranded like a baby whale.

"I must have gone somewhere," I say. Somewhere time stood still. Just like a fairytale.

"Yeah. Whisked away on a magic beach towel."

We sit in silence while he finishes the fry-up and the aromas work their own magic on my salivary glands. Then he hands me a fork and I eat straight from the pan. Like I haven't eaten for two weeks.

After breakfast, I drink more water and more coffee and huddle by the fire, trying to get my memory working, going over what I do remember about that Sunday and hoping the chain of events gets my synapses sparking. I know something happened on this beach. Something shocking.

And amazing. I ran to the edge of the cliff thinking I was going to die. I was even ready for it. Then everything flipped and I was descending Bantry's Bluff.

While I worry away at my memory and fret about my missing dress, Derek wanders off. When he returns, he sits down and watches my face, as if keeping me under surveillance will trigger a light-bulb moment.

"You've furrowed your brow enough," he says. "Give it up. A surprise will jump-start your memory while you're thinking about something else."

It turns out he's engineered a surprise. About thirty minutes later, a figure appears crossing the sand, his energy barely contained, as if he wants to run but is holding himself back. The sun has risen and I squint against its glare, but his light-brown curls, backlit like a halo, give away his identity. Alister. The sight of him sets my body tingling.

He stops a few feet away and blinks a couple of times.

"I'm not a ghost," I say, my voice almost back to normal.

"Can I come closer and make sure?"

"As long as you don't prod me." I blush, remembering I'm naked under the blanket. In front of Derek is one thing, but not Alister. I never did face up to why he affects me so much.

"Derek said you turned up in your birthday suit."

Birthday suit. That Sunday was my birthday. Two weeks ago. I'm now officially the same age as my mother was when she died.

Alister flops onto the sand opposite me. "Welcome back." His eyes are enormous and I realise he's fighting back tears.

"I hear you've been watching out for me. A vigil. Thank you."

"Derek organised it. He's responsible for all this." He points to the tent. "Until he got in touch I didn't even know you were missing."

Missing. A strange word. Missing from where? Wherever I was, I was there. I was only missing from here. And from my memory.

"Well, I'm back. All in one piece."

But if my memory stays blank, then I've lost that piece of myself. Along with my dress.

"Thank God," Alister says. He hasn't taken his eyes off me. "The police were sure you were dead, you know."

"Yeah. But you guys didn't agree with them."

"We all felt it," Derek says. "Felt that you weren't dead."

He hasn't moved. He summoned Alister but he's not going to leave me alone with him. Not if I'm about to remember something.

"How long were you going to wait?" I ask.

They look at each other. "Till the next full moon."

The full moon spilling a path across the sea...the image flashes by, then disappears.

Soon Nigel is striding across the tiny beach. The sun bounces off his shiny head and doubles the early morning glare. Without ceremony, he walks right up and bends over to punch me on the arm.

"Here's looking at you, kid."

"Sorry to be such a drama queen, Nige."

"You disappeared deliberately, just to get attention?"

"I...don't think so."

"So don't apologise." He drops to the sand beside Alister.

"I don't know what I would have done if DD hadn't been here," I say. Or if Alister had been here instead. "I don't think I could have climbed the cliff and walked to the main road. Tried to hitch a ride. Hungry and naked."

"And made some motorist's day," Alister murmurs.

"The drivers might have thought I was Pele and left me standing there." The volcano goddess. I remember she caused a landslide on the Pali Highway because nobody would give her a ride.

"Are you sure you're not Pele?" Nigel jokes. "She's good at disappearing. And coming back."

"I'm not sure of anything at the moment. I don't even know where I've been."

Nigel nods. "Would you like me to give you the once-over? Or a massage?"

Nigel's a nurse. He works with dementia patients. People who've forgotten who they are.

"Thanks, but I feel fine. Normal." It used to be my favourite word but now I'm not so sure. "And it's time I got dressed."

As I get up and step into the tent, they're giving each other looks.

The sand comes off with a sponge and warm water from a thermos – Derek has thought of everything. But my bare skin reminds me of my little black dress and the sense of loss is overwhelming. I've never had a garment that's expressed my essence so...totally. And now it's gone, taking something precious and intangible with it.

With a heavy heart, I unfold the bundle of clothes and one of Wanda's fish-cards falls out. Vibrant in turquoise and yellow with beady black eyes and crimson lips, at least the fish doesn't look like anyone I know. I read her spidery handwriting.

If you're reading this you're back, right? But 'back' doesn't mean 'the same'.

Hope the gear fits. I went with your old size figuring if

you're bigger it's probably on the inside.

Wanda xx

I turn to the clothes. There weren't many of my things left in the flat we share, so she's picked up some pre-loved stuff. It's just like what she wears herself – cut-off cargos and a top that says *Magic Happens*. She'll be as inquisitive as Derek and I'll have to disappoint her.

As I pull on the gear, a memory comes rushing at me. Something to do with peeling off my dress, wearing nothing but the cowry shell, then...?

I sigh and wrap the blanket over my new clothes before emerging into bright daylight.

"Let us know when you're ready," Nigel says, "and we'll dismantle the tent."

"Ready for what?"

"Going home."

That's the word that triggers it. In a rush I'm doused by an overwhelming sense of loss. It's where I've been for two weeks. And I'm not there any more.

Home.

Alister wants to take me to my other home. The tiny flat in Waikiki that I shared with Wanda until two weeks ago.

Festooned with camping gear, the four of us scramble up Bantry's Bluff. Up the path to the cemetery that holds too many memories for me to deal with right now. When we reach the top, the silent gravestones are just the same, rising at angles from ragged grass, glinting under an early sun, accompanied by the pounding waves. What happened here that Sunday after I climbed down to the beach? I don't do beaches - not since a wave nearly drowned me as a toddler.

The others pass my mother's grave without comment, sensing their questions would elicit the same answer: 'I don't remember'. But I stop and wait, hoping to feel her presence, hear her voice. Does she know where I've been?

Nothing.

The moment isn't right - too many onlookers. And I want it too much. The fantasy of being a child again, of having a mother who'd explain away all the strangeness.

When we reach the cars, Alister makes his pitch to play chauffeur and Derek lets him win. As we bump down the track in his BMW, I blow kisses to the boys, who are bundling the gear into their cars. Soon we're at the crossroads above Kailua, then hitting the Pali Highway and crossing the range.

"What's the latest on Genevieve?" I ask, to deflect the focus from my antics and recapture two weeks of news. I've never met Alister's ex, but last I heard he'd ended their relationship and was trying to diffuse her fury with a trust fund for her twins.

"She's sacked her lawyer and gone to ground."

"She accepted your offer?"

"I thought so. Now her silence feels...ominous."

"Why would she be up to something? She wants the money, doesn't she?"

"Unless...it's not enough."

I sense it too: a cloud hanging over him. It kills further conversation as we descend into Honolulu and arrive at police headquarters, so I can break the good news.

Detective Watkins frowns. He isn't as pleased to see me as my friends are.

"We could charge you with wasting police time, Miss Moon. A whole team of officers combing that beach. Where have you been for the last..." He looks at my file. "Fourteen days?"

Home, but I don't say it. It's crazy.

"I don't know. It's like I've woken up from a deep sleep." He gives me a sceptical look as I press on. "I didn't even know I was missing, let alone for that long."

"Very convenient." Derek's word. "Turning up in the very same place without even a bruise."

Alister interrupts. "Derek Delaney and I are prepared to make statements. The beach was empty, the tide was exceptionally low. One minute she wasn't there, then she was."

"A good swimmer, are you?" Watkins asks me.

"No." Derek must have told him about my phobia. "I'm afraid of the sea and everything in it."

Watkins shrugs. He doesn't want the paperwork.

The police found my tote bag in the cemetery. After

signing for it, I peer inside and find my dead phone, my money purse and my keys. My ballet flats too – they were where I left them on the cliff edge – but there's been no sign of my little black dress.

Alister guides me through the throng in the foyer. Monday morning after a weekend of alcohol and crime. People of varied origins, queuing and waiting, pushing and arguing, slumped in chairs, while an officer at a counter tries to keep the peace. As we make our way to the front door, the closeness of so many bodies brings back the sensation of 'others'. Then we're outside, being blinded by the morning glare, when an enormous camera is pushed in our faces.

"What the –" Alister's arm goes up. He shoves the camera aside, along with the man behind it, but I'm glued to the pavement.

"Welcome back, *Selkie*," the guy says, wielding my name like a slap. "Anything you'd like to say about your...vanishing act?"

Words are forming in my mouth, when Alister pushes my head down and rushes me towards the car.

"And what about you, Mr Sloane?" the man yells after our retreating backs. "Taking the missing mermaid back to your penthouse for a little *reunion?*"

In seconds Alister has unlocked his car, bundled me inside and exited the parking lot on two wheels, as if the journalist is in hot pursuit. But surely the guy's got everything he wants? Only a few lines of fabricated copy needed to caption our startled faces and he's got his 'story', something juicy for the online tabloids – *Missing Mermaid Meets Millionaire.*

Alister's got history with the paparazzi and while relief is washing over me – no nude photos of my surfside arrival –

he's negotiating a maze of backstreets like a man possessed.

On Ala Moana Boulevard, the traffic slows him down and I know we're both thinking the same thing. How did the guy know? Derek and Nigel wouldn't squeal. One of the detectives? After we presented ourselves to Detective Watkins, a quick text from one of the others would do it. Or there was Derek's text to Alister. Has the media hacked Alister's phone? Then there's the guy's last question. Will I be going back to Alister's? Our fledgling relationship, if you could call it that, is not public knowledge. Only a handful of close friends know. People I trust.

"Did you tip him off?" Alister asks.

"What?" I don't believe this. "Why on earth would I do that?" Not to mention *how*.

It's been a morning of emotions and I add livid to the list. If Alister thinks I'm capable of this, then the pedestal he put me on hasn't taken long to topple. I remember the last time we spoke in private – our smoky looks and suppressed passion, while he murmured promises to take me away. Now there's a barrier between us in spite of his two-week vigil. Or because of it. The barrier of my unexplained reappearance. After hearing about my aquaphobia, was he already doubting the story before the journalist turned up?

Convenient. A splash of free publicity to kickstart my quirky business seminar – a seminar inspired by seals.

I open my mouth to defend myself but nothing comes out. Stuff it. I don't have energy for this. Alister's sudden infatuation has always terrified me. Let Genevieve and the twins have him back.

***

He drops me in Koa Avenue and doesn't offer to walk me to my door. At night it isn't safe around here for single females – not without a pimp – but it's broad daylight and parking's a chore, so he lets me go. Suits me. The journo's unlikely to know where I live, since Wanda's the one who's listed. I get out of the BMW and slam the door without a backward glance.

The humble enclave of old flats are just a few blocks from Waikiki but the built-up environment feels alien and claustrophobic. Passers-by ignore me as I gaze up at the retro mosaic wall that marks the front of our building. Along each walkway towels and surfboards adorn the iron railings like urban art. When I lower my eyes to basement level, the usual racks of health foods cluster around the doorway of Hi-Fibes, Wanda's favourite store. Three flights up in our fridge, bags of chia and almond meal and pepitas, each clipped shut with a clothes peg, always dwarf the remnants of my Chinese takeaways.

I buy a bag of cashews and begin to climb, the cooking smells of several nationalities assaulting my nostrils, my senses heightened ever since I woke up. Then I'm knocking on Wanda's door, even though my key is in my bag, hoping she got Derek's text, hoping she's home, feeling a sudden hankering to hide in this humble refuge.

As the door flies open, she almost knocks me over. "Selkie," she screams, as if she's seen a ghost.

"I'm back," I say unnecessarily.

"I can see that. First Coral. Now you."

Coral. The *kahuna* who lives in the bus shelter and gives out one-word prophecies. Her name is practically an anagram of oracle. Coral took off before I did – on the back of a turtle according to the grapevine – leaving her checked bag to mind her favourite spot. Just like I left my tote bag near the edge of the cliff.

"Did you see her just now?" Wanda asks.

"Coral? No, Alister dropped me." Like a hot potato.

"She said you'd be back."

How did Coral know that, since I didn't even know it myself? But Coral knows everything.

I give Wanda the cashews and step over the threshold. The walls are covered with painted resin fish, who size me up with their usual suspicion. From the bookcase the four-faced Buddha is beaming out his smile, and the nuts-and-bolts parrot from Goodwill is silently shouting *talk story?* via a balloon wedged in his beak. At the end of Wanda's bed, Doris the shop mannequin is sporting a fresh *lei*, carelessly tossed around her headless neck.

Wanda grabs it and drops it over my head. "*Aloha*," she says and my eyes go moist.

She's gone to some trouble to welcome me back, and the familiar surroundings are just what I need to try to make sense of what's happened. But when I glance at my Shona sculpture at the head of my bed, I see it's buried under a sunhat. Not my hat. And Wanda would never do that to Shona. Now I'm seeing other changes. The small crucifix on the wall, the cat curled up on my pillow, the suitcases under my bed. The space I vacated two weeks ago on a compulsion to go to the cemetery and the cliff is a space I no longer inhabit.

I turn to Wanda and wait for the explanation.

Her smile falters. "I trust Coral's predictions so I knew you'd turn up. I just didn't know when."

"So you hawked my bed to someone else?" I'm shouting but I don't care. My legs have started to wobble. "Shit, Wanda. How could you?"

She puts her hands on her hips and looms over me.

"Rent is rent, right? It's still got to be paid, Selkie. Especially while you're sailing off to Serendip in a fucking cowry shell."

Serendip – where the unexpected happens. It explains my absence as well as anything, but not my sense of home.

"She's my cousin," Wanda is saying. "Myrna. A good kid really, if a little *literal*. And way too attached to that cat. A favour to my aunt. It's only for a few weeks."

A few weeks?

"So where am I going to sleep?" Not at Alister's, in spite of the journo's prediction. "This is my *home*, Wanda. I understand about the rent, I know I left you with a problem. But I've got nowhere to go."

"And it's still your home. It's just till Myrna finishes her training. You can stay with Derek. Or Davina. Can't you?"

Sleep in their spare beds like a vagrant. Sure, I've done it before but the thought brings on a sinking feeling. Where do I belong?

There's an uncomfortable silence while we face each other off. But there's nothing I can do. It's always been Wanda's flat and I was camping here. Now Myrna is. Maybe this was never my home, but it's been a haven. Until now.

I take a deep breath. "Where are my things?"

"Davina had most of them."

True. My Irish friend Davina Kennedy, dress designer and clairvoyant. I was staying with her when I left that Sunday. She lent me her car and I parked it outside the cemetery for the police to find.

"Except Shona," Wanda adds, looking towards the sculpture.

"Now Myrna's hatstand."

Wanda strides across the room, startling the cat. She whips off the sunhat and the sight of Shona's profile floods me with warmth. She occupies the space with a fierce sense of belonging. Shona's grounded wherever she is.

"I told Myrna not to do that," Wanda says. "She tried it with my Buddha first. She's not really into...spiritual stuff. She thinks a lump of rock is a...lump of rock. Unless it's the Virgin."

Until I moved to Honolulu, I wasn't into spiritual stuff either. Now I'm the one who's been 'sailing to Serendip in a cowry shell'.

"Isn't she Tutu's granddaughter too?" I ask.

Wanda's grandmother was a *kahuna*. She saw visions in our bathroom mirror. Then I saw one.

"Nope. Myrna's from my father's side. *Portagee*, Catholic."

Wanda has a touch of almost every nationality – Portuguese, German, Irish, Japanese, Filipino, Hawaiian. It gives her skin an all-year tan and makes her worldview as patchwork as my memory.

We sit at the tiny table like old times, eating the cashews and sipping herb tea as if I haven't just been tossed out onto the street. Wanda grows her own herbs on the windowsill – tiny forests for the cockroaches to explore. Unless the cat's been earning its keep. The tea tastes like nothing much but it's soothing, and my anger about Myrna softens. Wanda's an art student who supports herself by painting casts of dead fish then selling them at the markets, so without paying her rent in advance I left her no alternative.

"What's it like, Serendip?" Her tone is wistful.

"I don't know where I've been, Wanda. Or who with. It's a bloody mystery."

She's used to my mysteries. "But you were with...someone?"

"I think so. And I went...somewhere."

She swallows. "Did they hurt you?"

"No."

"So you're...bigger? On the inside?"

That again. "I don't know what you mean."

"An expanded consciousness. A bigger heart."

I think about what I've returned to. "More like a bigger headache."

She pulls a face. "You're not holding out on me? Because of Myrna?"

"Of course not."

Just like Alister, she's misjudging me. Together with losing my bed, it's too much. I burst into tears.

Wanda's a big girl and her bear hugs are the best. She holds me till I'm wiping my eyes, then she makes another round of tea.

Myrna's traineeship goes from nine to five, so she's not around and I'm glad. Seeing her sitting on my bed stroking that cat would make me feel even more jilted. I call Derek to invite myself to stay for a while and he's ecstatic. He can stake out my bedroom until my memory comes back. And Nigel has already picked up my things from Davina.

"What else don't you know?" Wanda asks.

I shrug. It seems less important now. "Why I'm not dead."

She thinks about this. "You thought you were going to die, right? But you might have been in the sea for two weeks and you're alive."

"I wasn't in the sea. I can't swim."

"That's thinking literally, Selkie. You've got to look back with your soul eyes."

Meaning peep in her grandmother's mirror again. "I won't look in Tutu's mirror, Wanda. Don't try to make me."

She knows these concepts are still new to me, so she doesn't say any more. With a *kahuna* for a grandmother, she grew up with the paranormal, while on the other side of the world my stepmother, Stella, was bolting all the psychic doors and windows and leaving my spirit out in the cold. It's how I'm feeling now.

Wanda offers me her shower, but that would bring me face to face with the mirror. It's propped up at the end of the bath, poised to interfere.

She sees me staring at the bathroom doorway. "It's only a mirror, Selkie." I know she doesn't believe that. "Unless you're psychic."

Until I moved to Honolulu, I definitely wasn't psychic.

"Yeah, so it won't be bothering Myrna," I say.

"Nope. And it doesn't bother me either."

In spite of Tutu's wish to pass on her powers, Wanda hasn't got the gift. Lucky her, but I don't say it because Wanda would even eat meat just to have one vision.

I go into the toilet cubicle and urinate a bucketload but not two weeks' worth. Did I eat while I was missing? Did I go to the toilet?

Then I toss a towel over the mirror – a trick that worked in the past. The shower is divine. Hot for a change. But when I'm reaching for the towel I forget about the mirror and there I am.

Someone I hardly know.

I can't look away, but it's not my appearance that's changed. It's definitely me. Spiky black hair with silver streaks. A little thinner but the same face that's been aging little by little since childhood. No, it's my eyes. In the past they had a desperate look – an unrequited longing that attracted Alister. Now they look...what?

Did the others see it? When they shared a look outside the tent, they'd noticed something. I thought it was just my Lady Godiva impersonation - without the hair and the horse - but now I wonder. Is it the real reason Alister got scared off, the journalist just giving him an excuse? Because Alister got hooked by my longing look, enough to break off with Genevieve. He thought he could satisfy it, fill my empty spaces with his passion. But now my eyes look...deep.

Tutu's mirror - it's done it again. I stare at my eyes, unable to avert my gaze, and that's when it happens: a kind of knowingness washes through my bones. My mind still doesn't know what happened to me, but deep inside I know. I'm a blend of my experiences, remembered and forgotten. The awareness brings a touch of comfort for the first time today.

***

Wanda's got a hula class and it's time to go. But there's still the problem of Shona. She should come with me, but she's heavy and I told Derek I'd meet him at the office, which means catching the bus downtown. That decides me to leave her behind - to claim the space for my return. It feels like the right decision as I rub my hand over her cool knobbly head and silently apologise for her 'undercover' role as hatstand.

"How long is Myrna staying?" I ask as we hug goodbye.

"Not as long as it sounds," Wanda says.

"Out with it."

"Three months."

"You owe me, Wanda."

"Yeah, I know." She breaks into her most radiant smile. "I'll teach you how to hula, honey."

In her home in the bus shelter, Coral is vast in a new *muu-muu* – orange and black like sunrise, with splashes of purple and white. Her checked bag doubles as a footstool. When she sees me across the street, her face disappears behind a gaping toothless grin. I'm afraid to approach in case she's got a prediction, but Coral and I are kindred spirits – disappearing in the same week. She doesn't speak English and I don't speak Hawaiian or pidgin, so we communicate with signs unless Wanda's around to translate. Today she lifts her hand in what I expect to be a *shaka* greeting, but instead she flaps it in a traditional goodbye. As if I'm going somewhere.

Bloody hell.

I cross Kuhio Avenue and walk right up to her, until she's pressing her outstretched feet against my thighs. It's how she 'reads' things – sole to soul – and I wait impatiently while she does her thing, closing her eyes, humming a few notes, then waiting for a vision to come.

When she finally speaks, it's a one-word pronouncement. "*Ala.*"

She looks pleased when I nod, even though I don't understand. Does she mean…God? I'm going to meet my maker after all?

Panic grips me until the bus arrives and I'm flopping in a seat and texting Wanda.

Path, she texts back. *Ala means path. You're on some kind of journey.*

But I just got back.

So you're not done. You're 'passing through'.

It's one of Wanda's phrases about the spirits in Tutu's mirror – passing through this world into the next. I recall the cliff, just how close I came to taking a short cut to the hereafter. If I'm passing through, it explains why I don't need a bed, but am I meant to go right back to where I've come from? Home? Until I can remember, the whole escapade is unfinished business.

Outside, sunlight is glinting on the glass panels of the buildings downtown, strobing me into a dreamlike state. I reach for the cowry shell and put it to my ear, hoping for some oceanic wisdom, but its emptiness matches my own.

CHAPTER
Three

When the bus drops me into the bustle of Honolulu, I still feel out of place. As if I belong beyond this melange of commerce and craving. It matches the message about passing through, but when I turn into Merchant Street, the sight of my building grounds me with its red-brick incongruity. I even remember to check the street for journalists.

Upstairs, Derek is keeping an ear out. Before I reach my door, he's out of his. He's been holding the fort while I've been missing.

"Thanks for everything, DD. Now I just need some time alone."

In my office. The only space that's still mine.

"Sure. But there's something you need to know."

"What?"

"Don't freak out. You're about to have...a visitor."

"Not a journo."

"No. I've sent one guy away with a flea in his ear. What a nerve."

"Who?"

"I don't know her name."

"You sent the journo away, but you told a strange woman I'd see her - after I've just crawled out of the sea and look like it - without finding out what she wants?"

He sighs. "It's complicated." He bustles me into his cubicle and drops his voice. "She turned up here the day after you left, said she wanted to see you. I told her you were away and I couldn't say when you'd be back, so she asked if she could wait."

"Wait?"

"I put a chair outside your office. She waits from one till two every weekday. Her lunch hour, I guess."

A shiver of something makes me suddenly cold. It could be a blast from Derek's dodgy aircon, but since arriving in Hawaii I've been forced to pay attention to these 'feelings' that my stepmother spent my childhood suppressing.

"What time is it now?" I ask.

"Twelve fifty."

"Shit, DD, I need some time in my office. Alone. A meeting with this woman is out of the question."

"Tell her you'll meet her tomorrow."

"Waiting every day...it's creepy. I might not want to see her at all."

"What if she's a client?"

He's right. After two weeks without an income, I could use a few of those.

"What does she look like?"

Derek thinks. "Thirties. Attractive but not beautiful. Spends time on her hair and makeup. Inexpensive clothes but her style's good."

"What's your gut feeling about her?"

He's pleased to be asked and takes his time. "Not what she seems."

That makes two of us.

The prospect of meeting this mystery woman stifles me. I can't breathe. It's like Wanda's flat – an intruder in the space where I should be. There's a pattern here. And it's got everything to do with Coral's pronouncement. *Ala.* Nowhere to settle, nowhere to belong, nowhere to be normal after disappearing. Passing through.

Derek watches me as I try to decide what to do. Cringe in his armchair until the woman's gone? Flee down the back stairs and skulk back later? Or confront her and find out what the hell she wants?

He doesn't try to persuade me either way, but I still feel like a coward as I take the fire escape to the back lane. When I reach the corner of our building, a woman is opening the front door. It's just a glimpse, her image reflecting in the glass, but Derek's description is perfect. Soft brown hair twisted up with a comb. Low heels. A simple skirt and blouse, muted florals. An office worker would be my guess, well-groomed and unspectacular.

There's a sushi bar across the street – my regular lunchtime haunt. They're pleased to welcome back their best customer, so I take a table behind a potted palm and plug in my dead phone to charge. It's a great vantage point and two guys with cameras and predatory looks soon turn up, their eyes fixed on the entrance opposite.

After I've consumed an hour's worth of sushi, my visitor emerges right on cue and I'm ready for her.

Click.

When she's gone, air rushes into my lungs. Exhilaration. Relief. Running away wasn't cowardly. I've given myself some power. This woman knows who I am and I want the same advantage.

Her photo goes to everyone I know – Davina, Wanda, Derek, Nigel, Alister, Curtis at the coffee cart – with the message: *Who is this woman?*

***

The heat has driven the paparazzi away, but I return via the lane just in case. When I open my office door, I feel a rush of something like gratitude. A tiny space that's still mine. Immaculate, thanks to Derek, with the mail stacked in a basket and a vase of orchids on the windowsill. After I give him a hug, he leaves me alone with my laptop and the backlog of seminar requests.

Word has got around about Being Sleek – the seminar about seals that crept up on me and wrapped me in its spell – and I'm in danger of becoming an overnight success. There are so many queries I could fill a room twice over. It's what I've always dreamed of, making a name for myself on the seminar circuit. A dream that gave me the courage to try for a green card, to walk out on a bad marriage, leave Sydney and start a new life. Then Being Sleek presented itself and my future success looked assured. Now it's something to hold onto in the face of all the uncertainty.

As I reply to each enquiry and sign them up to my Moonshine blog, the rhythm of the work anchors me. Until the phone rings, and I almost jump out of my skin. It's a sound I haven't heard for a while and the last person I expect. Alister.

He reads, "*Siren's Seaside Striptease.*"

I hiss. "That journalist."

"You won't like the story either. Or the close-up." He reads out the lurid fantasy, which ends with me sprawled on a black sand beach wearing nothing but a girdle of seaweed.

"And you accused me of setting this up!" I say. "You keep telling me how well you know me – better than I know myself – and then you misjudge me like that."

"I was angry. Paparazzi bring out the worst in me."

"I wasn't too thrilled either. Not that I got the chance to say."

"I know. It was unforgivable."

"At least we agree on something."

He chuckles, then gets serious again. "I'm really ringing about Genevieve."

So his ex has broken her silence. "What's she done now?"

He misses a beat. "She's the woman in your photo."

Genevieve. The woman scorned. The woman for whom Alister's money isn't enough. Shit.

I tell him about how she's set up camp outside my door. "Do you know what she wants?"

"No, but I don't want you to meet her, Selkie. I saw her while you were...away." He didn't tell me that this morning. "We discussed the settlement...over dinner."

"And?"

"She was emotional in a way that shocked me. Angry. Bitter. She accused me of humiliating her, even though our relationship was so private no-one else knew. Waiting outside your door like that is completely out of character. I'm worried she might be...dangerous."

Bloody hell.

"You were with her for over a year, Alister. Didn't you notice what she was like?"

Alister, who could have any woman he wants. Except me. And so rich he can't trust anyone in case they're dazzled by the dollars instead of him.

"She was...unusual. Serious and quiet. She wasn't trying to schmooze me like so many other women I meet. She'd lost her husband, given birth to the twins on her own. I made allowances and didn't question why she was so...unemotional."

There's more, I can tell. I wait.

"She also craved privacy, which meant I could get away from the spotlight...and be with her kids."

There's the truth of it: the instant family. He told me

he'd never loved her enough. But he'd got in deep with her boys.

"Emotional or unemotional," I say, "without staying away from my office every lunchtime, I don't see how I can avoid her." At least she doesn't know where I'm staying. "I get the feeling she's a woman who doesn't give up."

His laugh is rueful.

"I need to sort this out," I add. "Hear what she has to say. For her sake and mine. I'll make sure Derek's around, OK?"

He doesn't like it but there's nothing he can do. After we hang up, he texts me the link to the news item, but I'm already all over the online bulletins. Then the calls begin.

After no-commenting three journalists, I turn off my phone. It must be a slow news day if my mystery dip in the Pacific is this newsworthy. I know from my PR training that you deal with adverse publicity by ignoring it. "This too will pass," the Buddhists say. It's the same for bad press.

Derek is standing in the doorway, staring at me in the mirror above my desk. I tell him about Genevieve.

"Does Alister know what she wants?" he asks.

"No, but it can't be good, can it? He's worried about her motives, thinks she's emotional, angry. He told me not to meet her, but this is a public building so she can loiter all she wants. And she's obviously the tenacious type."

"Are you going to tell her that you know who she is?"

"I'm not sure. It was good that I ducked out today. I'm better prepared knowing who she is. Are you around tomorrow at lunchtime?"

He grins. "If I cancel my table at Jimmy Ho's."

I grin back. Derek never eats at Honolulu's top restaurant.

***

He leaves me with my emails – offers for seminars in far-flung places have started coming in, from China, Europe, the UK. After an hour, my head is spinning and Derek suggests we call it a day.

"You need to sleep off the jetlag," he says. "You've been in another time zone, remember?"

We walk to his car and try to beat the rush hour. Once we exit the freeway and start snaking up the mountain to Makiki Heights, the energy of the city clears, the taro hedges give way to an expansive sky, then we're on top of the world.

Nigel greets us at the door and we follow him onto the deck of their white clapboard house. Honolulu spreads beneath us like a picnic rug covered in sprinkles. My fears about not belonging seep away as Derek fills Nigel in on my day.

First, Myrna.

"Stay as long as you need to, Selkie."

"Thanks, Nige." I don't mention Coral's prediction. "I'll buy Chinese once a week." The offer is out before I remember my bank account. Shit.

Then Genevieve.

"If Alister thinks she's a tad unbalanced," Nigel says, "then you need to be careful. If she blames you for being dumped – and she might have to demonise you, to preserve her opinion of Alister – she's had time to plan her attack."

The obsessiveness of that image ripples through the air.

"She might just want to vent," I say. "She'd lined Alister up for a lifetime of happy families, all that security and comfort. Now everything's ruined and she's left to bring up the twins on her own."

"Exactly. Revenge is an explosive emotion. You mustn't

meet her alone."

"DD's going to back me up."

Nigel looks at Derek, the big softy around here. He won't say it but he'd rather be there himself, all six foot six of him, with a black belt in aikido.

We start thinking about food. As usual I could eat a horse. They won't let me help in the kitchen, so I turn on my phone. While I was away, Derek was so confident I'd be back that he updated my timeline so people in Sydney wouldn't know I was missing. His posts are a little too eloquent, with a touch of the new-age and ever so slightly *gay*. Did anyone notice? But then I'd been borrowing much of my news from him these last few months, trying to give my mad dash for freedom a bit less madness and a bit more dash.

"I make a good virtual Selkie," he says.

"Only if Gretel fell for it." My sister. "She's got an inbuilt radar for fake."

He sniffs. "I'm not sure I'd like her."

"You'd adore her, DD. And she'd adore you."

Then I notice his emails to Andrew. My ex. For months Andrew's hounded me with daily texts to 'come home where you belong' and 'stop pretending to be someone'. Until he found Juliet.

"DD, a few fibs on Facebook are one thing, but you had no business writing to Andrew." As Derek ducks behind the breakfast bar, I understand why. "My God, you've negotiated a settlement on our house."

"Someone had to do it and I was dispassionate."

"You didn't sign anything, did you?"

"Forge your signature on a legal document? Puh-lease. I do have some standards."

I want to be angry but I'm laughing. And I haven't even

started on the wine.

I read out a couple of the email exchanges and Nigel looks shocked.

"If you don't agree to my terms, Andrew, I'm more than happy to wait for a property upturn. Then buying me out will cost you more."

Andrew fired back with some well-chosen expletives to which Derek replied: *"Forget the vocabulary, douchepants."*

"Douchepants?" I snort. "He'd have to know that wasn't me. *If you want me to sell now, you'll have to do better than 50/50.* Oh my God, he's offered me 55 per cent."

"His first offer," Derek says, looking smug. "You rejected that. We're up to 60/40."

That's when I smell a rat. My voice is shaking as I ask, "Whose valuation are you using, DD? On the house?"

He hesitates. "Andrew supplied it. From a certified valuer."

"But I engaged my own valuer. Just before I disappeared."

Derek hangs his head. "I didn't know."

When he tells me the valuation, it's what I feared.

"You don't know the Sydney property market, DD. He's been screwing you. I've got no idea where he found his valuer – no doubt for a hefty kickback – but you can't buy a tool shed in Sydney for that."

Derek pulls a face. "It was fun while it lasted."

He won't admit that he needed to pay Andrew back for the grief he's given me. Over the last few months, Derek's witnessed the daily abuse by text message and, if it wasn't for his support, I might have lost courage and crawled back to Andrew's bed of nails. Now Andrew's met Juliet, so there's only the house between us. Another home that's no longer mine.

The meal is vegetarian because the boys were hosting a *kirtan* tonight – a group from the ashram that chants in Sanskrit, before tucking into Himalayan-sized portions of meat-free food. They cancelled it when I asked Derek if they could put me up.

"The last thing you need," Nigel says, "is a bunch of blissed-out strangers quizzing you about Nirvana."

"Er, why would they do that?"

Nigel and Derek glance at each other.

"You've got the look, Selkie," Nigel says, "of one who *knows*."

It's what I saw in Wanda's mirror, what I felt in my bones. But what do I know?

"I'd have nothing to tell them, Nige. My head has never been emptier." It's true.

"Exactly," he says.

Beside me Derek mutters, "Those who say do not know...those who know do not say..."

"And those with empty heads," I say, "*eat*."

For the first time in several weeks, I get drunk. It numbs the reality of where I might have been and what I've returned to, and stops me from thinking about Coral's prediction.

The boys put me to bed in their spare room and I plunge into sleep.

***

In the moments just before waking, a familiar voice bounces off the bedroom walls: *Turn the tables on the troglodyte.*

Shit. It brings back the first message I ever heard: *Someone is trying to kill you.* It was soon after I arrived here, and it sent me on the journey that ended at Bantry's Bluff, looking for answers that I can't remember.

"Turn the tables on the troglodyte," Derek repeats over a late breakfast. "It's getting cryptic, that voice of yours."

"It's always been cryptic."

I took the killing message literally for a while, but the strange things that happened while I was missing can't have been literal. Or I'd be dead.

"What do you think it means?" Derek asks.

I sigh. "The only troglodyte I can think of...is Andrew."

Derek looks sheepish. "It fits but how can you turn the tables on him?"

"Upset his plans to undervalue the house. It was on my mind when I went to bed last night. Then I woke up with the message."

"Upset his plans by going back to Sydney?"

He's worried I might do something silly now I've been kicked out of Wanda's.

"No way." I don't want to cross paths with Andrew. Or his new woman, Juliet. "There must be a way to do it from here."

"Troglodyte," he says. "It's a weird word for the voice to choose."

"Not really. Andrew's behaved like a complete Neanderthal, but there's a literal meaning too. When I first met him, he used to take me on bushwalks that always ended at a secret cave. He called it our special place."

"That's what predators always say when they lure girls to secluded places."

"I wasn't really a girl. I was sixteen."

"But naive?"

I nod. "He wanted me so badly, it terrified me. But I felt powerless to run away."

"You didn't want him?"

"His obsession with me...freaked me out. Like he was crazy about some fantasy woman who wasn't me. He was almost twenty-one, good-looking, going to uni."

"Glamorous."

"Yeah. All my girlfriends would have gone with him in a heartbeat, but he wanted me."

"And you thought there was something wrong with you for not wanting him?"

It seems obvious now. "He said I just needed help with my...inhibitions. Until I gave in."

"Rape by attrition."

"Something like that." Then I married him.

"That makes him the troglodyte," Derek says, "in more ways than one."

"The whole chapter with Andrew would be finished if it wasn't for the house. And after your emails, DD, he thinks he's conned me. I know him - his smugness will make him complacent. Maybe I can get a fair property settlement while he's looking the other way. Then I'd be free."

But the word has an undercurrent. Freedom needs to be grounded, and right now I'm on shifting ground. How can I cut my ties with Sydney when I don't have a base I can rely on here? Ever since I woke up at Bantry's Bluff, a crack's been opening up beneath my feet - a chasm. If that's the path Coral's talking about, then I don't dare look down.

CHAPTER
Four

Derek usually gets to the office around midday. We could go later to avoid Genevieve, but I'm never going to feel braver than I do today. And there's work to do on the marketing plan for Being Sleek. As generous as the boys are, I can't stay with them forever so I've got to generate some living expenses. Fast.

After parking, we walk to Merchant Street, grabbing coffees at the cart.

"Don't hardly knows da mermaid wid her clothes on," Curtis jokes as he hands me a mug.

"I hope it's been good for business," I say. "Can I autograph a few napkins?"

"Don't bother. S'already blowin' over. You'll be back to nobody 'fore you can say...paparazzi suck."

I laugh. Curtis is a reformed alcoholic who lives in the Y, and those AA meetings have almost turned him into a mystic.

Next it's some sushi to eat at my desk until the woman-who-waits turns up. It's the only thing I can do to prepare for our encounter, except worry about what she'll accuse me of. Blame games push all my childhood buttons – every family drama was my fault – and I just can't think of any other reason why Genevieve would want to see me.

At exactly one o'clock, there's a knock on my door.

"I've read the papers," she calls. "I know you're back."

So she suspects me of hiding. I throw open the door and wave her in.

She takes a seat on the only chair, making me perch on my desk. It was an act of control on her part, but now I'm looming over her.

"Hello, Genevieve. I'm Selkie. Derek says you've been waiting for me."

We're looking each other over. She's wearing a matching skirt and blouse, brighter colours than yesterday. The tangerine and blue enhance her tan and light-brown hair. She knew I'd be here today so she's gone for more flair. By contrast, I couldn't face my red business suit so I'm looking my corporate best in jeans and a T-shirt.

"So you know who I am," she says, "and you're still prepared to face me. I suppose I should be impressed."

"Suit yourself."

"I thought you'd been avoiding me, but now I hear you've been –"

"Away."

"Missing, according to the news."

"Why shouldn't I face you?" I'm sounding more courageous than I feel.

"I've got a few home truths to deliver. You may not like what you hear."

"Well, you've had plenty of time to rehearse your lines. So start whenever you're ready."

To my surprise she laughs. "I have been rehearsing, but I'm not sure it'll make any difference."

When I say nothing, she gets up and tries to pace in the tiny cubicle. "You can't blame me for wanting to see what you're like, see why Alister's so...besotted. When you weren't here, I got angry. A little obsessed. I wanted someone to show me some respect. Then I thought your disappearing act might be a publicity stunt. Some of the papers think so and it's worked on Alister. The man's more hooked than ever."

I want to defend myself, say it wasn't a stunt, that Alister's actions are his own, but she's been waiting two weeks for this moment and she needs to let me have it.

"Let's get to the home truths," I say.

"Yes." She sits down. "I'm here for the twins, not for me. Although Alister's completely forgotten about me, about how I might...*feel*."

It's a glimpse into her emotional state.

"I like Alister," she says, "but I never pretended I loved him. Before we met, I lost the love of my life and I wasn't going to fall head over heels again. To his credit, Alister hasn't tried to replace him, but he's been like a father to the boys. We had an arrangement. It worked. He insisted on keeping our relationship secret, and that suited me. I got some intelligent company, a caring bedfellow. And Joel and Jake got a man in their lives." Pause. "Until you came along."

"None of this is my fault."

Genevieve has morphed into my stepmother.

"Doesn't matter," she says. "The outcome's the same. Because of you, the boys don't get Alister any more. They get...his money."

Her eyes flash and I see the anger that's just below the surface. Alister was right, but not in the way he thought. The money isn't enough because it's an insult. What she wants is a father for her boys.

"I'm sorry about what's happened," I say, "but I can't change it. The last time I looked, I wasn't in charge of Alister's heart."

"No, but you are in charge of your own."

"How does that work?"

"Do you love him?"

Even if I knew the answer to that one, I wouldn't tell her. For a start, it's none of her business. And it might make things worse if she thinks Alister's walked out on her for a woman who's as unsure as I am. I stare at her and say nothing.

"Because it's in your power," she says, "to give him space to make a choice. You don't know him. He adores the twins. He won't be happy without them."

She's nudging all my weak spots. There's a part of me that wants to make Alister happy. The part that tried to make Andrew happy – and almost killed me in the process.

"If you're not around to distract him," she says, "there's a chance he'll decide...to come back."

"What the hell are you asking me to do? Go missing again?"

Just passing through...

"You're Australian, aren't you?"

"Yes."

"Go *home*."

Shit. It's the wrong word. I was tolerating her criticism, trying not to blame myself, feeling compassion for her situation, till she said that.

"I didn't woo Alister away from your boys. And I'm *not* going back to Australia."

She purses her lips. "It's what I suspected. I can see it in your eyes."

My eyes? Can she see it too?

"You pretend you don't want him, but you do."

"I've got lots of reasons for not returning to Australia," I say. "Alister isn't one of them."

She waits, as if I'm going to tick the reasons off my fingers, then says, "I knew I'd never lose him to one of his ex-models. It was only ever going to be someone...complicated."

We sit in silence. Surely we're done here. She's delivered her lines, I've batted them back. Our five-minute relationship is over. It's been pretty civilised considering the context. Derek, hovering just outside, is probably disappointed.

I get off the desk but Genevieve doesn't move.

"Where were you? When you went missing?"

"Why do you want to know?"

Get a scoop, ring up the nearest journalist, create a teensy scandal and blow Alister's cover sky-high. But I don't think that's her style.

"They're calling you some kind of...sea sprite. A *shape-shifta* with magical powers. You've certainly bewitched Alister."

I pull a face. "That's just newspaper-speak. Don't let the truth get in the way of a sensational lie."

"But you were gone for two weeks. If you didn't fake it..."

I don't owe her an explanation, but I hear myself telling her anyway. "I don't know what happened, Genevieve. I went down to Bantry's Bluff and the rest is blank."

"Bantry's Bluff?" She's gone suddenly pale. "They didn't say it was Bantry's Bluff."

"It's an unofficial name, isn't it? Not on any maps."

"Didn't anyone warn you not to go there?"

"Why? What's wrong?"

The colour continues to drain from her face. "It's where Tony disappeared."

"Tony? Who's Tony?"

"My husband. Gaston Luce."

My skin is prickling. "What happened?"

Her tough demeanour has crumbled. She stares into

space, as if she's trapped in a revolving past. "One day he sailed in on a yacht and a month later we were married. It caught everyone's imagination - our romance - and overnight we were public property. So when Tony...disappeared, it was public too." She swallows down a lump in her throat. "He'd gone for a swim at Bantry's Bluff. We were living nearby." She still is, according to Alister. "He swam there every morning, but this time he didn't come back. I went down to the beach and ran up and down calling his name. By the time I phoned the police, I was frantic. They searched for days but he was nowhere. His body never turned up."

The resonance with my own disappearance is making me uncomfortable.

"I'd always hated that beach," she continues. "I thought it was treacherous. The strange tides. I was sure he'd had an accident, hit his head on an offshore rock...drowned. I was totally traumatised, but I showed up at work, held myself together, kept away from the press. The reporters were relentless. They wanted to make the most of the widow in her grief.

"Then after a couple of months, a policeman knocked on my door. He said he had news of Tony and I'd better sit down. When I asked if they'd found his body, the cop grinned and said they'd found him alive. In Hong Kong. Someone had applied for a passport in the name of Gaston Luce."

I try to imagine how shocking that must have been.

"I waited, but nothing happened. The weeks went by, with no more news. The man with Tony's passport had disappeared."

"That must have been worse than thinking he was dead."

She nods. "I'd lost him a second time. The news got out, and the papers twisted the passport story into a faked suicide to escape his marriage. They decided he'd arranged to be picked up offshore by sailing friends. It was terrible. I've never believed he'd leave me like that."

"Did he have reasons to run away?"

"Those last few weeks he'd been a little distant, even depressed. He wouldn't tell me why, but that's not a reason to fake your own death and leave your new wife destroyed and humiliated. I think his old sea captain used a photocopy of Tony's passport to help someone out, a refugee needing a new life. Miguel would do that, break the rules without a second thought. One night I braved the Bay Bar when Tony's old crew was ashore. Miguel was already drunk but he wouldn't tell me a thing."

I don't know what to say, so I put on the kettle and make tea. We sit over mugs while her story sinks in, how similar it is to my own. Disappearing from the same beach. A police search. No body. Then turning up in strange circumstances.

"I kept to myself after that," she says. "The papers lost interest, then the twins...came along."

"Did Tony know?"

"About the...pregnancy? I didn't know myself, until he'd gone. I never take the boys there, you know. Not even to make sandcastles. And here you are, coming into our lives then disappearing again from the same place."

"It's a coincidence."

But she's not listening.

"There's something...strange about that beach. I'm not superstitious, but the locals don't swim there. They say it's got an Irish curse."

We sip our tea in silence until Genevieve's hour is up.

She looks at her watch and goes to the door.

"You're not a conniving bitch with no scruples," she says. "Or the siren described in the papers. Disappearing like that makes you seem exceptional, but really you just strayed into cursed waters. Like Tony."

It's a theory that hasn't occurred to me. It's all about the beach.

"Otherwise, you're not complicated," she says. "You're *ordinary*."

"That's me." But her putdown packs a punch. It's the last thing I want to be and she knows it.

She turns to go, then turns back. "Tell Alister we'll take the money if it makes him feel better. But he can never see the twins. I'll only let him hurt them once."

"I understand but I won't be your go-between. You'll have to tell him yourself."

***

Soon Derek is sitting in the same chair. "What a story. Do you think it's true?"

"It's so strange, it could be."

"She's had two weeks to make it up."

"Why would she?"

"So you'll feel sorry for her and let Alister go."

"She knows it's not that simple, DD. And what about this story that Bantry's Bluff is blighted by an Irish curse?"

As long as it isn't deadly, Derek doesn't mind a little curse. "There's something surreal about that graveyard, but I didn't pick up any vibes when I was camping on the beach."

"What did you think of her?"

"She doesn't seem like the superstitious type. Too...*ordinary*."

We grin. He knows me so well.

"The curse makes her feel better," I say, "about losing Gaston like that. It confirms her belief that he didn't kill himself."

"If the passport story's true, he's alive and well somewhere."

"He was a sailor, French. He'd crewed on boats, and stopped in Hawaii. If someone picked him up on their yacht, he could crew his way back to France. That's possible, isn't it?"

"I suppose. But the police would know if he used the passport."

"If they followed it up. He hadn't committed a crime, he wasn't a US citizen. Would they care?" I'm remembering how Detective Watkins couldn't wait to be shot of me. "They put their energy into bad guys, DD."

We're silent, then Derek says, "She's got under your skin, hasn't she?"

"No. But Gaston has. We vanished from the same beach."

"Probably the curse." He grins. I know he's thinking it's *convenient*.

"It just makes me wonder, that's all. But I can hear Gretel saying, 'The simplest explanation is usually right'."

As if she's been listening, my sister chooses that moment to call. We haven't spoken since I flew back to Sydney a few weeks ago for the birth of my nephew, Gretel's first child. Does she know about my disappearing trick?

"Got time to talk, Selkie? Or do I need an appointment between press interviews?"

"Oh God. I was hoping no-one in Sydney would see all that crap."

"It's gone semi-viral. The 'naked mermaid' headline is

very clickable. I thought your posts were a bit suss lately so I did a search of your name. Does 'all that crap' mean you really did overdo the vanishing cream?"

How much do I tell her? She's just had baby Tyler and might be sleep-deprived and fragile. But I've never kept secrets from Gretel. As a kid, she always knew when I was holding out.

"People tell me I was missing," I say. "And the date on my phone's changed so it must be true. But my mind's blank. The police thought I was dead, I'd been gone so long, but my friends believed I'd come back."

"They say you were washed ashore." She knows how I feel about coastlines.

"Bizarre."

"Any clues?"

"Not really. I get a few flashbacks of something – memory or imagination – but I'm not sure they mean anything. Otherwise I'm in good shape, except" – the stab of loss comes out of the blue – "my dress is missing."

"So you were naked."

"Yeah. There aren't many facts and they got most of them right. They've just spun them into something sensational."

"And your name's a gift. The seal-maiden sheds her precious pelt."

I manage to laugh but my grief over my dress is acute. "Has my name ever done anything but cause trouble?"

"Never. But I'm delighted you're not dead. And I think you should read every one of these stories. I'll send you the links."

"I've been avoiding them. They make me mad."

"Well, I reckon that one of these fantasies might just nail what happened."

We say goodbye as a text arrives from Andrew. He's obviously read about my disappearance and put two and two together about Derek's emails over the house.

Girls who play games get hurt.

CHAPTER
Five

I pour myself into work. At least Being Sleek is something I can still call my own. Seminar space in a local hotel is unlikely any time soon, but I send off requests for their next available two-day slots. Then it's a post for the Moonshine blog about how seals adapt to changing conditions: *The Hawaiian monk seal has as much fat as its polar cousins, but it has adapted to its tropical habitat by sprawling on beaches most of the day and feeding at night when it's cooler. We can emulate this when business conditions change...* It's advice I should be taking myself.

Alister rings. Until Genevieve speaks to him herself I don't want to talk about her visit so I text him to call me tomorrow.

At the end of the day a Chinese takeaway beckons – to thank the boys for everything. My noodle bar of choice is always the Pearl, just a short walk from the office. Most nights I'd drop by for a bowl of noodles or a takeaway. If my mermaid story hasn't hit the Chinese headlines, Suzi and Eugene might be worried about me. Derek comes too. Downtown's slick high-rises and *pau hana* crowd give way to early diners in pho cafés where the fringes of Chinatown morph into Little Vietnam, then we're surrounded by humble shopfronts dotted with red lanterns. A rush of homesickness hits me. It's been ages since I've been here – even before I disappeared – and I'd forgotten how much it means to me. Chinatown has been my second home ever since my first day here. Feeling homeless and friendless, I sat down to a bowl of comfort food and found Wanda's leaflet for a room-mate lying at my feet.

The Pearl is buzzing – the usual mix of regulars holding melamine bowls to their chins, adventurous or lost tourists, and the backroom 'boys' playing mah jong. There's a lump in my throat as Derek takes my arm. Will Suzi and Eugene be pleased to see me?

Derek stands beside me in the queue at the counter, and when it's our turn Suzi looks up. For a moment I think she's going to scream, then her face breaks into a smile so warm I almost burst into tears. She rushes into the kitchen and in seconds Eugene emerges, his rolled-up sleeves revealing arms as chubby as his cheeks. He lifts the lid of the counter and comes through to put both hands on my shoulders.

"Old friend come back," he says.

"Yes," I say. "I've been on a few adventures, Eugene."

He beams. "Adventure good. More adventure, more better."

Does he sense I'm going somewhere too? If Coral's the oracle, Eugene's the sage. He certainly sees things others don't.

As he goes back to the kitchen, we place our order with Suzi, who can't tear her sparkling gaze away.

When our takeaway is ready, Eugene pops his head through the curtain of plastic strips. "On house." It would be insulting to protest – and my bank balance will be forever grateful – so I wave a thank you.

Derek picks up the food and, as we turn to leave, the fortune cookies on the counter catch my eye. I keep a jar of them on my desk, but I haven't seen it since I returned. Derek was no doubt consulting the universe every day about my fate. I never walk past a fortune cookie, and if I ever needed independent advice it's now. Suzi nods to take one.

Then we're outside and Derek is saying, "Open it, open it."

I gape at him with sudden fear. I'm remembering how often fortune cookies have got me into trouble. If it wasn't for a fortune cookie, I might still have a home with Andrew, I might not have moved to Honolulu and turned psychic, I might never have peeled off my dress at Bantry's Bluff, I might never have disappeared.

"You can't pick up a fortune cookie and not open it, Selkie. It's against the laws of nature."

"You open it, DD."

He might be tempted, but he's too much of a tragic to flout those laws.

"It's your fortune cookie," he says. "And you can't throw it in the trash either. That would be karmic suicide."

Bloody hell.

"I might just eat it, paper and all. Absorb it into my consciousness."

I go to stuff it in my mouth and we burst out laughing, but Derek won't let me off the hook.

With a sigh I crack it open, then shove the slip into my pocket. "No rule says I have to *read* it."

He shrugs, knowing he's beaten for now.

***

Nigel's been kayaking and arrives home soon after dark. Whenever he can, he paddles out to the Mokulua Islands and watches the mutton-birds return to their nests – good for the soul he says. Everyone's starving, so we rewarm the noodles and make green tea while Derek updates him on my latest conduct malfunction with the fortune cookie.

"It's her call," Nigel says. "She'll read it when she's good and ready."

When Derek might not see it – that's the real issue here. "Or leave it in her pocket," he says, "and put it through the wash."

If he wasn't being so pushy I might have read it, but now it's a battle of wills. I make a mental note to move it from my pocket before Derek offers to do my laundry.

"Have you ever been influenced by a fortune cookie?" Nigel asks him.

Derek takes a mouthful of noodles. "Back in my teens. I was trying to date girls and my dad told me if I couldn't *be* a man, at least try to *look* like one." Nigel nods. "It was just four words," Derek continues: "*Closets are for clothes.*"

We burst out laughing.

"How about you, Nige?" I ask.

"Mine was a bit more zen: *Water makes a pebble smooth.* For me it meant experience, and pain. They act on the soul like water on a pebble. You go through trials, you overcome obstacles, you get knocked about, your rough edges get rubbed off."

There's silence for a while and I wonder if Nigel's message also applies to me. Is that what Eugene meant by 'more adventure, more better'? I've got a few more trials to go through?

When I look up, four eyes meet mine.

"What?" I say, and they grin.

With a sigh, I pull out the paper strip and spread it on the table. Nigel keeps his eyes on me, but Derek can't help craning.

I look at it, then hold it up and they gasp.

"It must mean something," Derek says, as Nigel shakes his head. "Everything means something. But it's creepy."

The slip of paper is blank.

***

It had to happen eventually, after all the uncertainty I've returned to. A nightmare.

Doris, Wanda's shop dummy, is running a garage sale. She's strapped in a chair and surrounded by mattresses and junk. Strangely I'm not interested in the mountains of spare beds, but I want to buy a silver bucket. Doris is ignoring me, and when I shake her by the shoulder to get her attention her head falls off. Not because she's a dummy who doesn't need a head. Because she's dead.

I wake feeling angry and afraid. Not about Doris but what she represents. Dummies don't die, so who does?

When I look around, I'm confused. Then Derek is beside me, followed by Nigel. Did I call out? Then the light goes on and we're all in a state of shock.

"What the hell?" Nigel says.

I'm lying on the kitchen floor surrounded by scattered objects. I've brought the bed sheet with me – black satin – and I'm hugging it like a lover. Overturned beside me is their fruit bowl, fruit strewn across the floor. As I blink in the sudden brightness of the overhead light, I see a spoon, a lipstick, pieces of torn paper. And is that...a rock?

A moan escapes from my open mouth. "Sorry, guys. I've been walking in my sleep again."

"More than that," Derek says, looking gleeful. "You've been...collecting things."

It's my own junk sale.

"Before you ask, DD, I don't remember a thing." Almost true.

"Don't worry. You've written a message."

He picks up the ruined lipstick, crouches down and starts reading words smeared in red across the floor.

Glo tro on air quee

Shot shoe key zard lay shay share

"It doesn't make sense," I wail. "That would be way too helpful."

I start to get up, but Nigel stops me.

"We need to photograph the scene, Selkie. With you in it. Then we can revisit it, try to work out what it means."

I stay in place like an effigy of myself until he comes back with several devices. He clicks away, and when he's satisfied he helps me to my feet. That's when I feel the dirt. I lift up one foot, then the other.

"You've been outside," he says, "to get the rock."

"Coral says the feet are sentient," I murmur.

"The old *kahuna* in the bus shelter?" I nod. "Must mean something then."

That I'm on a path? Just passing through?

Meanwhile Derek is holding up the sheet. "Holes," he says. "Tiny holes."

Did I do that? To a perfectly good satin sheet? The nightmare comes back. Mattresses and sheets are symbols of my vagrant status. But holes? Doris wasn't making holes. Doris was dead.

Derek spreads the sheet across the white tiled floor while Nigel photographs the holes.

"Get a close-up of the message, Nige. And each of these objects too."

"Not the fruit." I didn't know I was going to say that. "It's not the fruit, it's the bowl."

Large, wooden and hand-carved locally, it's always at the end of the breakfast bar. Now I remember I've seen it before – in a hypnosis session where I was shedding some bad feelings.

"What does the bowl signify?" Derek asks, peering at it with new eyes.

I don't want to say it, but it pops out anyway. "Leaving. It can act like a...doorway. You put bad feelings into a virtual bowl and spin them away."

"You going somewhere, Selkie?" Nigel asks.

"I hope not." I tell them Coral's prediction.

"It fits with the rock," he says. "In the Pacific, when you're visiting another island you take a rock with you from your island to present to your hosts as a gift."

"I didn't know that."

"And you've worked pretty hard to dig this one up, look. Pulled it right out of the ground, judging by the soil on all sides. You must want to leave pretty badly."

I imagine digging furiously in Nigel's garden. My fingernails are broken and dirty and there's soil in the creases of my palms.

"Have I walked it across the carpet, Nige?" He's into white. Tiles and rugs. We always take our shoes off at the door.

"Nope, you've gone out the back. It's still unlocked."

A door I've never used before. Something about doorways...

Derek is looking at the torn pieces of paper while Nigel puts the kettle on.

"It's a page from a magazine," he says, rearranging them like a jigsaw. "That article you saved about mutton-birds, Nige."

"But how did I find it? I didn't know it was there."

"Your waking self was asleep," Nigel says, "while your sleeping self was wide awake. You went to the shelf and...browsed. Till you found what you wanted."

"Busy night," Derek says.

"So why did I go to the trouble of finding it just so I could tear it up?" Tears are threatening to spill.

"To make a jigsaw," Derek says. "It either represents a puzzle, or it's a puzzle in itself."

"The thing about mutton-birds," Nigel says, "is the way they leave the nest and return. If the message here is about travel."

"How do mutton-birds do it?" I ask with a sigh.

"Clumsily."

That makes us laugh as we take in the chaos.

"Just call me Selkie Mutton-bird."

We sit in our pyjamas over a very early snack of toast and coffee and try to figure out what the other things mean.

"The spoon's got me beat," Derek says, examining it. "It's in perfect shape so you weren't spoon-bending. And it doesn't fit with leaving."

"I always leave nothing on my plate, DD."

No-one laughs.

"The dish ran away with the spoon?" Nigel suggests. "Rhymes with Moon. And it's silver. I picked it up in a French flea market."

"And what about the holes?" Derek asks him.

"Do they make a pattern?"

We look at the sheet again, still spread out on the floor.

"Don't ask me," I say. "I just make the puzzles. I don't solve 'em."

"You do eventually."

"With lots of help from my friends. Then I promptly forget everything."

Nigel thinks about this. "What if that's what this is about, Selkie? The forgetting? You can't remember where you've been because your conscious mind blanked. This might not be about the future, it might be about the past. You left two weeks ago. You went somewhere, and your memory is still there, if you will. And now you've got to solve the mystery so your memory can come...home."

That word again.

"It would explain this nocturnal frenzy to grab all these things – to give your memory a jolt."

"Except I'm more confused than ever."

"Give it time."

Derek's caught between keeping a spotless kitchen and preserving my lipstick message to show the *kirtan* crowd. We take one last look at the strange words before he gets busy with detergent and paper towel.

"What's the name of the lipstick?" he asks me.

I shrug and look at the label on its base. "Moulin Rouge."

Derek and I exchange a look. Along with Nigel's spoon, it's the third reference to France in two days.

We huddle over the laptop as Derek googles Gaston Luce. An article comes up: *Disappearance of French Sailor*. Five years ago.

After their whirlwind courtship and marriage, Gaston (Tony) and Genevieve Luce were minor celebrities, living the perfect life. But earlier this week, the former French sailor, who landed on our shores only a year ago and met the woman of his dreams right here in Kailua Bay, disappeared during his morning swim. After an exhaustive search found no trace of him, police are waiting for further clues. Genevieve Luce (nee Davenport) was unavailable for comment, but sources close to her say she's distraught and asks the media to respect her privacy.

The story's accompanied by a grainy wedding photo showing a radiant Genevieve, but Gaston's hand is shading his eyes and obscuring his face.

"Doesn't match the story she told you," Derek says. "That he might have faked his own death."

"That came later, DD. There must be another article."

He finds it: *Sailor's Disappearance Takes Bizarre Twist*. It describes what Genevieve told me about the passport and goes on to surmise:

Police have closed the case. One officer told Island Eye *off the record, "Men leave their wives all the time. This one went to some trouble to cover his tracks. He must have wanted out real bad." But Genevieve is pleading for the police to take her seriously. "Tony wouldn't leave me," she told our reporter. "Especially not like this. He loved me. He must be dead."*

"Humiliating," Derek says. "She had to insist he was dead to save a shred of dignity."

"And now Alister's dumped her, she's humiliated all over again."

"No wonder she's been camping outside your door," Derek adds, showing more compassion after reading her story. "All that grief she's been sitting on...it's exploded into obsessiveness."

"Tony Luce," Nigel says, nodding. He's only hearing the story now.

"Did you know him?" I ask.

"A few years back – the Frenchman who drank at the Bay Bar." He chuckles. "He didn't like kayaks." Nigel keeps his kayak at Kailua Bay.

"Why?"

"He was a big yacht sailor – a big drinker too – and called kayaks 'toys'. He'd given up sailing for some reason. Don't think he ever said. But being landlocked made him antsy."

"Genevieve said something was bothering him before he disappeared."

We tidy up in silence, and Nigel puts the rock on a plate.

"It's not a lava rock," he tells me, "so your subconscious was looking after you. If you take a lava rock away from here, it rains curses down on you forever."

More curses. This place is full of them.

While I take a shower and scrub my hands and feet, Derek gets busy with sticky tape, and when I emerge he shows me a patched-together photograph of a mutton-bird leaving its nest. Its expression is very determined. I sigh. I've been warming to Nigel's theory that it's just my memory that's looking for home, but it's hard to argue with symbolism like this.

"It looks like I'm leaving," I say to Derek. "And I tore it up –"

"Because you don't want to go."

He throws his arms around me and I start to cry.

"You've got a home here, Selkie. For as long as you want."

"Thanks, DD."

But as I dry my eyes, I'm sure he's wrong.

CHAPTER
Six

To get another opinion about all these messages I call Davina. She's good at psychic stuff. She's busy intuiting a collection of designs for a New York fashion shoot, but she proposes a late lunch then a sleepover so we can catch up.

Does she know I've lost my home?

As I pack my meagre belongings and grieve for my missing dress, it feels like any kind of stable base I had here is slipping away. Without my dress, a part of my soul is missing. How can I go on without it?

Derek drops me at the bus stop. He'd love to drive me all the way to Davina's but he's got a deadline. As I wait for the bus, I'm acutely aware that although I'm surrounded by wonderful friends, I'm on my own.

***

In Kailua Bay, I walk past bungalows hidden behind lush vegetation. The day is particularly steamy and Derek's lent me one of his hats. When my phone rings and I see it's Alister, it feels good to talk about someone other than myself.

He hasn't heard from Genevieve yet but I give him the gist of our meeting.

"I don't like it, Selkie. Gennie's never told me that the police thought Gaston was alive. Her behaviour's been so out of character, she could be delusional. And even if the story's true, why is she dumping it on you like you're suddenly best friends?"

"She just needed to tell someone. She's still grieving for Gaston, and strangers make good listening posts."

He hasn't picked up on the link to my own disappearance. Good.

"I don't want you to see her again," he says. "Sorry, I've got no right to tell you that."

"No, you haven't."

"But it sounds like you're considering it."

No, I'm not.

When I say nothing, he changes the subject. "How about considering this? Dinner."

He's been trying to get me to have dinner with him since before I disappeared.

"I don't know, Alister. I don't think I'm ready."

I'm sure I'm not.

"Jump in the deep end, Selkie."

I sigh. He owes me after misjudging me. "You like Chinese?"

"Table for two at Jimmy Ho's?"

"The Pearl. Maunakea Street."

"Chinatown. Let me guess. Best *sang choy bow* this side of Nathan Road."

It's one of my lines and makes me I smile.

"Dress down," I say. To match his date. "Kung fu pants and *rubbah slippahs* are *de rigueur*." Why am I speaking French? "And leave the BMW at home."

He laughs and we agree on Friday night.

***

Davina opens the door of her turquoise house and gives me a hug. We haven't seen each other since I borrowed her car that fateful Sunday – my thirty-fifth birthday. She knew where I was going and seemed to know why, but I can't confirm whether her hunches were right until my memory comes back.

"Good to see you again, Selkie Moon."

"You too. Sorry...about the car and everything. And thanks for putting me up."

She waves her hand dismissively. "You eejit, Selkie. As if I give a toss about any of that. I got the car back. And now you're back."

If she was worried while I was missing, she doesn't say. Does she know where I was? I wouldn't put it past her, but she'd never tell.

I step into the coolness of her front-room 'shop' and we walk past walls draped in the 'tribal chic' garments that are her signature, through the bamboo curtain to the living room behind. With its crisp white walls and vibrant ethnic fabrics she's created an inspiring home. It gives me a pang.

"When Nigel called in for your clothes and things, he told me everything he knew. You've still got no inkling about what happened, where you've been?"

"No."

"It was so amazing that your mind can't fathom it, I'd say. That can blow your memory to the four winds." She pours two glasses of juice and uncovers a plate of sandwiches. "I've been catching up on what the press did with it. Quite a celebrity now, aren't you, girl?"

She laughs her tinkling laugh and for the first time I see the funny side.

"My sister sent me links to every story. She reckons the truth is buried in all the bullshit."

"Wise woman, your sister. But you haven't read them, have you?"

"Too salacious and ridiculous." Too distracted by messages about leaving.

"So you don't really want to know."

Davina always gets to the core of things.

I sigh. "Sounds like I've got some reading to do."

We sit on floor cushions at the coffee table, where we've shared a bottle of wine or two in the past.

"Except for my memory, I'm in one piece. But," my voice catches, "my dress is missing."

She stops eating. It's the dress she made for me, after she went into a trance and found the finished garment in her hands. "Did you look for it?"

"Where would I look? That beach was scoured by everyone. Even the police."

She snorts. "They wouldn't find it. It won't be lost for long, you'll see."

Her confidence comforts me like it always does. If I get the dress back, surely I'll feel less adrift. I move on to Myrna taking my bed, and the message from Coral. Then I tell her about the bizarre tableau of objects I collected last night in my sleep.

"You're a restless soul, that's for sure."

"But I don't want to go anywhere, Davina. I've just come back, and I want to settle down and get on with it."

"Get on with what? Getting your memory back? Memories don't take kindly to being pushed and shoved, you know. They clam up."

"My career. I know my memory will take its own good time. But I've got hot prospects for my seminar queuing ten deep around the block and I can't sign them up because I'm making holes in sheets."

"I can lend you a needle and thread," she says.

It's so bizarre we laugh.

"The bloody universe has pushed me out onto the street. That makes a girl restless."

"You haven't found 'home'."

"That's just it, Davina. It's the one word that resonates since my disappearance. I went 'home'. And ever since I've come back, I've lost it again. And it...hurts."

As my voice cracks, she tilts her head and her auburn curls tumble over her shoulders. "What kind of home?"

I shrug. "The place I...belong..."

"There are many different homes. Spiritual homes, ancestral homes, childhood homes, emotional homes... Which home was yours? Come on, say the first word you think of."

"Mythical."

She nods. "That makes sense."

"Just like the tabloids are saying? I turned into a seal and went to the bottom of the sea?"

"That's your head talking, but when you said 'mythical' it came from somewhere else."

It reminds me of Wanda's mirror. Davina listens to what I saw in it, the depth behind my eyes.

"It's grand that you've seen it. I didn't want to say." So she sees it too. Then she creases her forehead. "Part of you has that look you saw, that 'mythical home' look. Another part is homeless. That's a paradox. There's somewhere else you're meant to go, to complete whatever you've started."

"Lots of places to choose from, from Vladivostok to John O'Groats." I list the locations of my seminar invitations, grateful that Being Sleek is giving me something to cling to. If I have to go somewhere it will come with me.

"Sydney," Davina says. It wasn't on the list.

"I'm not going to Sydney."

Davina's got plenty to say about that. "It's where you're

meant to go, Selkie. The house you shared with Andrew is unfinished business. While it's unresolved, part of your soul is trapped there. That man siphoned off your essence and smeared it on the walls so you'd never leave."

Bloody hell. Just the image makes me weak.

"I'm not going to Sydney, Davina. I can manage the property settlement from here."

"The settlement's working, is it?"

"He's trying to rip me off."

She doesn't have to say it again. More siphoning.

"You've got away from him," she says, "but you'll never settle anywhere until you call back every last drop of yourself from that house."

"I lashed out at him once on the phone," I say, the sense of power from that call draining away at the thought of actually facing him. "So he's even more pissed off than when I left. Going to Sydney now will play right into his hands. If he's been siphoning off my essence, it'll happen again the moment he looks at me. Just the thought of it makes me feel impotent."

She drops her voice. "Because you ran away instead of standing up to him."

"That's easy for you to say."

"No, it isn't."

Shit. It's happened to her. She's told me nothing about her past but she's a runaway too. I turn her question back on her.

"What kind of home is Hawaii to you, Davina?"

I'm not saying another word until she answers.

She hesitates. "A refuge."

It's what I've been craving myself.

"There are worse places to settle than a refuge."

Her green eyes flash. "Listen to me, Selkie. Don't be

hankering after a refuge when it's a home you're wanting. I know what I'm talking about, girl. There's a big difference. A refuge is somewhere to hide. But a home is somewhere to...dance."

I *danced*. In the nude. In the moonlight. Then...

"While you were missing," she's saying. Did she see me dancing? "You tasted a *soupçon* of home. That's what you're remembering. I'm thinking your memory is holding that morsel of home safe until you're whole again."

"And I get whole by standing on a milk crate and eyeballing the arch-siphoner?" I've raised my voice. "Sorry, that was flippant."

"Look him in the eye and it's over, Selkie. It's the only way to turn the tables on a bully."

Turn the tables. On the troglodyte. Shit. But wait a minute, Davina's not talking from experience. She's another one who ran away.

When I say nothing, she nods. "Fine, fine, fine. That's decided. Now you just need your dress back. You can't be staring down bullies while it's lost." Pause. "Send Alister."

"To look for my dress? Where would he look?"

"You know where."

"Under a rock." It just pops out.

She's grinning, but it's taken me back to the selkie myth.

"In the myth," I say, "the man who wants the selkie steals her skin and hides it under a rock. So he can...capture her soul."

Andrew imprisoned me. Alister wants me. What if he gets my dress?

"She was powerless, that one," Davina says. "But you're rewriting your own myth. If you send Alister to get your dress back, that's the *reverse* of stealing. That's *retrieving*. At your request. Sometimes you've got to view things backwards to get a good look at the truth."

I'm not sure about any of this, and we've come right back to Bantry's Bluff. Davina needs to know what Genevieve said.

When she hears about Gaston Luce, she remembers when he went missing.

"There's more," I say. "The locals don't swim there because the beach is cursed. An Irish curse."

She laughs. "Because it's called after Bantry Bay? A few of my countrymen might be falling off the cliff from too much drink. That's an Irish curse."

"Genevieve thinks our disappearances are…linked."

"Does she now?" Davina pleats her forehead and sniffs. "Maybe there's something there. Some connection. What do you think yourself?"

"His story makes me uncomfortable. I don't know if that's a feeling I should pay attention to, or just my phobia talking."

"Time will tell," she says.

***

She suggests I spend the afternoon searching the news reports and let my mind join up some subconscious dots. The idea hasn't got any more appealing, but it's better than thinking about walls smeared with my essence or a floor scattered with objects. So while Davina gets back to her designs, I start on Gretel's links.

Dozens of stories about the 'shape-shifting selkie' and other descriptions that sound nothing like me. The art departments have gone crazy trawling the archives for illustrations from old books: mermaids and sirens, seal-women and water nymphs. One etching shows a mermaid brandishing a whip as she rides a seal bareback through the waves. In another, a stock-photo nude, chosen to look like me, right down to the spiky hair and painted Moulin Rouge lips, is draped across a stretch of black sand with scales airbrushed onto her lower limbs. They've syndicated that one. Others combine my face, stolen from my website, with semi-nude bodies in various poses from coy to seductive. Another favourite is the close-up of a startled me taken before Alister ran me to his car. The paparazzo's made more than a few bucks out of that one.

Nothing triggers a blinding flash of memory about 'home' or even evokes an emotion. I was expecting to feel anger or shame, even longing, but except for the dull ache for my dress, my main reaction is boredom.

When she opens a bottle of wine, Davina asks me what I've found.

I sigh. "My mother is always called a 'siren', and 'moonlight' and 'dancing' resonate, but that's just covering old ground."

"Nothing surprising at all?" Davina likes surprises.

"Something in French." I thought I'd better read that one. "It got a bit scrambled through the online translator and gave me a laugh." My only laugh.

I read out the headline: "*Curious Miss Siren.*"

Davina smiles. "The most truthful one for sure. Curious to know where your memory is hiding. Where home is. Anything else in that translation?"

"You could read the French, couldn't you?" It's one thing I know about her: she studied design in Paris.

"*Bien sûr*, but I like the sound of that scrambled translation. It's like looking backwards."

I read: "*When a girl disappears from the back of a seal, it is mysterious, then goes again two weeks later, we ask a Hawaiian empty beach, a crack did she swallow her?* Swallowed by a crack," I add. "It's the only article to suggest the waters parted."

"Then closed up again. Very mythical."

We move to the other thing that's strange – a tiny item from Gretel's search. On the morning after I disappeared, a dead monk seal washed up on Kailua beach.

"I researched monk seals for my seminar," I say. "They're endangered, and rarely found around the Oahu coastline. Mainly on the uninhabited islands further north."

"The morning after," Davina murmurs, her eyes misting.

"Don't go all mythical on me, Davina. This seal's got nothing to do with me."

"No?"

"It's too literal. I'm not reliving the selkie story. You said so yourself."

"Just a dead seal, is it?"

"Interesting but irrelevant."

"So why would we be talking about it?"

Shit.

CHAPTER
Seven

Over breakfast of fried fruit salad – pineapple and banana and mango – Davina tells me she's got a busy day ahead, so I thank her for putting me up and leave her to her designs.

As I walk to the bus stop, the decision I've got to make about 'leaving' oppresses me more than the clammy air. I don't mind Coral and her prediction. Or the waking message about a troglodyte. I don't even mind the blank fortune cookie message or the nocturnal treasure hunt. At least they're cryptic, leaving me to make my own choice. No, it's Davina that's pissed me off, her insistence that I've got to go to Sydney. I've stopped being good at doing what I'm told.

And in spite of her advice and the searing flashes of grief for my dress, I can't bring myself to ring Alister. He's more involved in my life than I ever wanted. His fantasy of the perfect woman has uncanny echoes of Andrew – a fantasy I can never live up to. A quest like the missing dress will only inspire him to more misplaced adoration and gallantry.

But the dress is unlikely to turn up any other way. Unless I return to Bantry's Bluff myself, and that feels impossible, thanks to the curse. Until I remember where I was, I can't risk disappearing again.

A sign catches my eye. Bay Bar. It's still early, but a guy is opening up and it looks cool inside, so I approach the empty bar and order a tomato juice. I've got no idea what I'm doing here. Do I think I'm going to stumble across the missing Gaston under a bar stool and make Genevieve forgive me for 'bewitching' Alister?

Feeling stupid for wasting money, I gulp my drink and turn to leave. But when I see the photos of boats lining the walls, I change my mind and cruise by the gallery, reading captions.

Amidst the kayaks and outriggers, a photo of an enormous yacht stands out, and when I get closer I see its name: *Déesse de Mer*. I recognise the French word *déesse*, pronounced 'day-ess'. Goddess. It's what my one lover since Andrew – a troublesome Englishman with a flat in Honolulu and a penchant for foreign phrases – used to call me. That affair didn't end well, so I shake off the memory and peer at the small print under the *Sea Goddess*. It's the list of crew members, and there he is in black and white: *Gaston Luce*.

Morphing into Curious Miss Siren, I work my way from left to right staring at each grainy face. What is it about Frenchmen that makes them look so...French? Gaston isn't good-looking exactly with his long nose, puppy-dog eyes and shaggy brown hair, but he's attractive in that dangerous Gallic way. They're all wearing windcheaters, and Gaston is looking nonchalantly at the camera with a cigarette dangling from lips that hint at a smile. Where is he now? Under the sea? Or living it up on his new passport in exile from his wife and sons? And why do I care?

For some reason I snap his image, but when the flash goes off the barman wanders over, wanting to know what I'm doing.

"Just a friend of a friend," I say. "Gaston...Tony Luce, did you know him?"

I'm his only customer and he might be the type to gossip.

"Sure. Tony practically lived here a few years back. Newly hitched, but he was here every night."

"Why?"

He thinks about it. "Something wasn't right about him. Or her. Then he disappeared into thin air."

"He drowned, didn't he?"

He shrugs. "She said he drowned, off Bantry's Bluff. But they never found his body, and the cops weren't saying much. Some of them drink in here and you can usually get them to let something slip. His old crew mates didn't want to talk about him either. Like...they all knew."

"Knew what?"

"That she'd murdered him. Or he'd beat it."

***

There's shade in the bus shelter, but the humidity clings. When the bus arrives, I settle gratefully into a seat and try to forget the barman's opinions. I shouldn't have gone in there. Genevieve's an unlikely murderer, but the rumours explain why she became a recluse.

I sigh. Gaston's fate is a giant distraction from my predicament. Wherever he is now, it's got nothing to do with me.

By the time I reach the office, Derek is there. He's busy at his keyboard so I settle down with my inbox, until a text from Andrew makes me jump.

Your emails commit you to 60/40. My valuation. Didn't mean it? Tough shit :-)

He thinks he can hold me to Derek's agreement. The smiley face almost makes me puke.

When Derek pokes his head in, I update him.

"Troglodyte on steroids," he says, still smarting from his

gullibility.

"Davina thinks I've got to confront him."

"What? Visit your old house and have a cosy *tête-à-tête* about a property settlement?"

"Bullies back down when they're eyeballed apparently."

Derek cheered when I stood up to Andrew on the phone, but now he shakes his head. "Not face to face, Selkie. Not if you're the person he's controlled since day one and you had the audacity to walk out on him."

True. I've humiliated Andrew big time and, in my fragile moments, my unease about his retribution envelops me like an old straightjacket. Andrew thought he had me in his thrall forever, and his communications since I packed my little red suitcase and took off have been loaded with incendiaries. I keep hoping that Juliet has made him mellow. Or indifferent. But his negotiations with Derek suggest the opposite – ruthless intransigence and a taste for payback. He's out to avenge his dented honour any way he can.

I've got to find a way to cut the ties – without getting screwed.

***

When Nigel appears at my office door, I know something's happened. He never comes by, and I perch on Derek's armchair for the news.

"Nothing...life-threatening," he reassures us. "Just my cousin, Rupert. I knew he was coming to stay but he's flown in three months early. I'm on my way to pick him up."

"But Selkie's got our spare room," Derek says, putting me first as always. "Why didn't he come at the agreed time? He can't just blow in and expect us to make room."

"He's English," Nigel says, as if that explains it. "On my mother's side. We got the dates mixed up. Rupert wrote 7/4 meaning April 7 and I read it as July 4. Stupid mistake. And I was so relieved it was three months away I didn't check. He even sent me a reminder last week and I still didn't notice."

"I can sleep on the sofa," I say, winding my vagrancy level up a notch. Next it'll be the bus shelter. Sharing a pizza with Coral.

"Thanks, Selkie," Nigel says. "Sorry to kick you out five minutes after you've moved in. I know you're between homes, so you're welcome to couch surf as long as you need to."

Between homes. Real-estate-speak for No Fixed Address.

"But first," Nigel adds, "you need to know...about Rupert."

***

In the car after work, Derek and I are silent. Nigel painted a vivid image of his English cousin and we're hoping he exaggerated, but that's not Nigel's style. Rupert's only flown in from Hong Kong – from another relative – so there's no point praying for jetlag.

Rupert's booming voice reaches us at the front door, and Nigel looks haggard around the edges when we find them in the kitchen. When Rupert sees us, he stops speaking and stands up. He's almost as tall as Nigel, but instead of a shaved head his hair is white. It went white almost overnight, Nigel told us when he explained Rupert's condition.

He shakes hands with an iron grip, then sits down and opens his mouth. "Charming to meet Nigel's friends. Got a knack with new people, me. A real raconteur, eh, Nigel?" He winks at his cousin then rushes on. "Not long back from the Afghan war, did he tell you? Royal Air Force."

He begins to list how many missions and how many troops have been sent to Afghanistan, then moves on to raid schedules, ammunition inventories, casualty statistics, climate data. He knows the acreage of the annual poppy crop, the weight of the opium haul. The man is a walking encyclopedia of facts and figures. Nigel slips away for a shower, and Derek starts preparing dinner. I sit opposite Rupert and try to interrupt the monologue with questions about life in a war zone.

Rupert stops. Blinks. Smiles a crooked smile. Tells me how charming it is to meet me. Then starts again with another onslaught of data.

When dinner's in the oven, Derek keeps Rupert company at the breakfast bar while I unpack my meagre possessions in a corner of the living room. There's no door between the kitchen and the sofa; the living area is open plan. Until Rupert runs out of steam, I won't be having any privacy. Or sleep.

"He's been known to keep going till 2am," Nigel told us. "Then start up again at six. Then there are the nightmares."

By midnight, Nigel has already sent Derek upstairs to bed. He takes Rupert's arm and coaxes him towards the spare room. "Time for some shut-eye, Roop. After your flight."

"Wide awake, Nigel. Flying's in the blood. Tried to get up to the pointy end, introduce myself to the captain, swap a few anecdotes. Chief steward wouldn't hear of it. I told him a thing or two about Afghanistan. That shut him up. Did I tell you about the operation up near the Swat Valley?

Top secret..."

As they move down the hall, I grab my chance to bunk down on the sofa, but I'm beyond sleep. I can hear Rupert talking to Nigel behind the spare-room door. Eventually I doze off, but my dreams are strange.

I'm walking through a grid of streets lined with narrow houses. It's an old city, and I pass a church. A man in a suit is walking behind me carrying a silver bucket. I take several sharp turns, trying to lose him, but to my dismay he stays right behind me. I start to run, but he maintains the same pace and the same distance. Gripped by panic I consider leaping into the sky, but the buildings lean towards each other, blocking my escape. Suddenly I'm confronted by a vintage street sign with arrows pointing in opposite directions. One sign says Paris, the other says Doris. In desperation I turn in the direction that's familiar and race into a garage, just as a deluge begins. It's the same garage where Doris the dummy had her sale, but now it's empty and I'm alone. A wall of water is cascading down the open doorway trapping me inside. I can't see through it, but when I look down, the silver bucket is at my feet, filling with water but never overflowing, and around it nothing else is wet.

***

When Derek and I drive down the mountain, we take Rupert with us. Derek has offered to show him over the Pearl Harbor exhibit – and give Nigel a break. They'll take each day as it comes, bring in some of their network as a fresh audience, spread Rupert around. On the weekend, Nigel's friends from the Marine Corps Base are hosting a barbecue at their beach house.

I've packed up my little red suitcase, hoping to find somewhere to stay that's better than a park bench but takes account of my bank balance. I feel bad about bailing out, but Nigel insisted.

"You can't spend another night like last night, Selkie. At least DD and I can take turns going to bed upstairs, but from the sofa you can't escape his voice. We can't even take him onto the balcony or the neighbours will complain."

At Makiki Heights people are big on peace and quiet. They'd be hearing Rupert streets away.

"He has to have an audience, poor guy. It doesn't matter who. He's had some therapy, but it hasn't worked, so the family is sharing him around for a while. It's a tough gig for his wife, doing 'till death us do part' with a guy who's fighting a war in his head."

In my office, I stare out the window at my glimpse of the mountains. Derek suggested searching a house-sitting site, in case someone local hasn't been able to find a sitter. I've turned on my laptop but I can't get Rupert out of my mind. Something about his predicament reminds me of my own and it's shaken me. His mind has latched onto a slice of his experience and expanded it to replace his whole being, while I've lost a two-week slice of my life and carried on without it. It confirms my decision not to go back to Bantry's Bluff. I can't risk losing any more of myself.

I make a cup of tea and close my eyes, taking myself back to that moment in front of Tutu's mirror when my body knew what had happened, even though my mind didn't. Into the emptiness an insight comes. The things I collected on Nigel's floor predicted I'd be leaving. So did Coral. They weren't symbols of a confused mind. They were right. Because of Rupert's arrival, I'm homeless again. My subconscious has its own psychic clarity.

What else did the objects predict?

For the first time I list them: the rock, the bowl, the mutton-bird, the spoon, the sheet with holes, the lipstick, the weird words. Seven symbols.

Has Derek noticed? He loves things that come in threes or sevens. Mythical.

The first three point to leaving. And I have left. Left Nigel's and Derek's. I'm sitting in my office with everything I own – my seminar and my little red suitcase. If I think about that I'll have a panic attack, so I rush on.

Where am I going next? Not Sydney. I won't be sucked into that vortex just because I'm desperate for a home.

What do the spoon, the pattern of holes, the lipstick and the words predict?

The lipstick and the spoon suggest something French. Am I meant to go to France? The sign in last night's dream pointed to Paris. But if the words were French I'd recognise the language even if I couldn't translate them. And what about the holes? Curse my subversive subconscious.

I google house-sitting sites.

There's one immediate placement that hasn't been snapped up. It's only for five days, and the home-owner's list of requirements has obviously limited the applicants, even though it's in the heart of downtown.

Single female. Tick.

Non-smoker. Tick.

No lovers. Sigh. Tick.

No parties. What are they? Tick.

Teetotaller preferred. Double sigh. Tick.

Must like reptiles. Shit.

Over the phone I try to sound like lizards are my thing. My Australian accent does the rest.

"It's top of my bucket list, a trip to Oz," she coos.

"You've got all my favourite snakes over there. And the goanna and the blue-tongue lizard."

Her name is Sylvie and she explains that all I have to do is stay in the same apartment as a dozen glass tanks and a dozen or so geckos. Just to 'keep an eye on things' overnight.

"What things?" I ask.

Sylvie only laughs as she arranges to meet me tomorrow afternoon.

CHAPTER
Eight

There's a fitness club in Bishop Street where I can shower and change before meeting Alister. Derek's got a pass and I borrow it from his desk drawer, feeling like a thief. Where I'm sleeping tonight doesn't bear thinking about. If Alister invites me back to his place after dinner, I'm in danger of accepting for all the wrong reasons.

My shopping trip this afternoon didn't work out as expected. Ignoring my bank balance, I cruised the Ala Moana Centre, thinking I'd find something on sale - a dress, simple and cool. But floral fabrics aren't my thing, and the monochromatic evening wear was way too sexy for the venue - and my budget. The whole excursion left me longing for my little black dress. Then I saw a cheongsam shirt in the window of a thrift shop. A bit Genevieve-esque, but the two-dollar price tag and the red-on-black pattern to team with my red pencil skirt clinched it.

Jostling at the mirror with the girls from the aerobics class is a very different preparation from the last time I tried to have dinner with Alister Sloane. Back then Derek and Nigel paced like fretting parents while I was terrified of being out of my depth with the rich guy. Tonight my anxiety is more grounded. Alister is way out of my league - especially now I'm a vagrant - but he doesn't *know* it. It's one thing to fear my own gaucheness, and quite another to fear his blind and burgeoning attention. Why did I agree to have dinner?

Someone bumps my elbow, smearing mascara across my

freshly blushed cheek. It takes a while to repair the damage. Then I walk along the same route Derek and I took a few nights ago, feeling both excited and afraid.

Alister is already waiting. Couldn't he play harder to get? He's found a table against one wall, and when he sees me he stands up and pulls out a chair. Then he takes a bottle from a cooler and pours something cold and white into tumblers.

"I can see why you like this place," he says. "Ambience in spades. And the menu's authentic. What do you recommend?"

"That we sit here for ten minutes. Sip some wine." Drink too much. "Once we order, it'll be here so fast we'll be in bed by eight o'clock."

"Your place or mine?"

Oops. I can't stop thinking about beds. And he's got that look again. Ardour 'in spades'. No wonder I'm slipping on my own Freudian banana skins.

"My place," I say, letting him think I'm staying with the boys. "Derek and Nigel can always find a sofa for a stray."

He grins. "Well-deflected. But you won't deflect me forever, you know."

"I'm going away," I say.

"Again? But I've only just got you back."

No, you haven't.

"Unfinished business." What do I mean by that?

He takes a sip of wine. "What's so unfinished that you've got to go away again so soon?"

"Is this why you asked me out – to quiz me about my private life? Because that's what it looks like."

"Sorry. I –"

"– care too much."

We sip in silence for a while.

"Is that so bad?" he asks. "Caring?"

"When it comes wrapped in too much attention, it is."

"You're comparing me with men who wanted you for the wrong reasons, Selkie. Control. Lust. Dressed up as love."

"So stop looking like them then."

He grins. "With that tongue of yours, how has any man ever got the better of you?"

Good question. I'm only tough around Alister. It feels like another message – a man who can't intimidate me. But it's Friday night and I refuse to decipher messages on the weekend.

"Back off a little," I say. "Give me some space."

"Only 'a little'. That's encouraging."

He's a hard man to dissuade, but he seems less intense and I relax.

Eugene comes out of the kitchen with bowls for another table. He gives me a cheery nod. Alister and I discuss the menu, scrawled on the wall with chalk. When I order at the counter for both of us, Suzi winks conspiratorially and I realise I'm comfortable being seen with Alister. It's an old trick my teenage girlfriends used to use to test if they really liked a guy – parade him down the main street. Another message?

Back at the table, Alister braves another question. "Will you tell me where you're going in such a hurry?"

"Paris."

I've just decided that I took the wrong turn in last night's dream.

"Not Sydney?"

"I may never go back to Sydney."

"So you don't call Sydney 'home'?"

That word is following me around like a stalker.

I shake my head. "It's where I grew up, where my father and stepmother and sister live, where I shared a house with my ex, but I know now that none of those places was 'home'."

He nods.

"I'm still figuring out what 'home' means," I add.

"The unfinished business?"

"Yes." It must be.

"And you'll find the answer in Paris?"

He's probing again, but the questions interest me. Three things are pointing me towards France. Nigel's spoon and the lipstick. Then the sign to Paris in my dream. Alister always does this to me, puts me in touch with something strong and clear. There's also a practical reason.

"A company in France has offered me a seminar tour," I say. "And Paris is the one place on earth I've always wanted to visit but was never able to. Being Sleek is about to...fly."

He grins. "A sojourn in the city of light will change your perspective on a lot of things."

"My perspective on...chocolate?"

He ignores the cheap joke. "The French don't just know how to live, Selkie. At their best, they know how to...*be*."

It's a word with a lot of meaning. Like 'home'.

When I say nothing, Alister adds, "Someone else I care about has gone to Sydney. Mia." His pet python.

I gasp. "Why?"

"It's against the law to keep snakes here, so they don't escape and kill the local fauna. When I brought her here, I didn't know."

"That's terrible." He adores Mia. "Couldn't you get a special permit?"

"Because I'm rich? Not my style. I found someone in Sydney – an astronomy student with blue hair. When he saw Mia's photo it was love at first sight. While you were disappearing, she was settling into her new home."

The steaming bowls arrive, and I push thoughts of Mia in Sydney from my mind.

"Will you go to France alone?" he asks.

It feels like a loaded question.

"I haven't firmed up the details yet."

I ask if he's planning any trips, and he tells me that he's flying to the UK in a couple of weeks to check out the scene for his seminar empire.

"Care to join me afterwards?" He sees my eyes widen and adds, "My *pied-à-terre* in Knightsbridge has *two* bedrooms."

"Did Genevieve ever travel with you?" I ask by way of deflection.

"She wouldn't leave the twins, and there was some problem about getting them passports."

Because Gaston isn't officially dead?

"Are you missing them very much?" I ask. "Joel and Jake."

"Better not go there, Selkie. I prefer not to weep in public."

"That bad."

He nods.

"Why did you let yourself get in so deep? Especially if you never loved Genevieve. Why not stay the carefree bachelor? All the tabloids think that's what you are."

"The millionaire playboy who changes his women more often than his socks. It's hard to keep up with that reputation. Luckily a new ex-model as my date at every social function satisfies them and they haven't dug any deeper."

"Into what?"

"Now who's doing the quizzing?"

"Sorry."

But he begins a story I wasn't expecting. About his wife and son.

"It was back in the eighties," he says. "In San Francisco. Our parents were dead against the match. They thought we were just naive, that the feelings would pass. Hoped they'd pass."

"Because you were too young?"

"Because Fleur was Chinese."

We look around the Pearl, at the groups tucking into steaming bowls, sharing conversations in noisy tonal discords. Alister knows this milieu. No wonder he's so comfortable here.

"We were desperate to be together so we ran away to Reno, tried to get hitched. But we were only sixteen, too young for a licence without permission from a guardian. By the time our parents caught up with us, Fleur was pregnant."

"Suddenly you were one big happy family."

He grins ruefully. "My parents were just as bad as hers. They didn't want a mixed-race grandchild either. Before we eloped, Dad pulled me aside every day to insist I give her up. Fleur and I even agreed not to see each other for three months, to date other people and test his theory that we'd forget each other. But the day the three months were up, we fell into each other's arms sobbing. The break backfired. It confirmed we were in love."

"So you eloped, and with Fleur pregnant, their worst fears were coming true."

"They made the best of it because of Fleur's condition. Gave us permission to marry. Both sides wanted us to live with them, but that was never going to work. I got a job as a gopher with a seminar company and we rented a tiny apartment."

"Poor but happy?"

His eyes are gleaming. "Delirious. We couldn't believe we were together – and it was legal. Fleur was so full of life and fun. She found old furniture and painted it wild colours, pinned up sheets for curtains, made a home out of nothing."

This story has all the hallmarks of a tragedy. He's using the past tense. Fleur is dead. Did she die in childbirth? Along with the baby?

"After Deshi was born," he continues, "Fleur went back to school part-time. If she'd stayed at home or got a job, she'd still be alive. And I'd still be Deshi's father."

I wait till he can go on.

"A guy with a gun. Angry about being suspended or something. He hit the campus as students were arriving. Shot seven people at random. Killed...Fleur."

Neither of us speaks. It's a long time ago but his emotions are raw. Grief does that to you. Gnaws away at your soul.

Eventually I whisper, "And your son?"

"He was only ten months old. Our mothers were sharing the babysitting while Fleur was at school. He was with Fleur's mother that day. Another twist of fate. In all the chaos, her parents hung onto Deshi. I was a mess, grateful for their support, but they weren't doing it for me. They were so devastated by Fleur's murder, they found a way to blame me. My grief didn't count. They waited about a month...then slipped out of the country back to China. With Deshi." He presses his palms to his eyes, then looks back at me. "He'll be almost thirty now."

Didn't he look for him? But how could he – a teenager with no resources? And there's no way anyone could track down a baby in China if his grandparents didn't want him to be found.

"He'll speak Chinese," Alister says, "and not even know I exist."

"Until he wants his birth certificate. His ticket to work in the US."

"They'll have got around that somehow. Bribed an official. Changed his name. Passed him off as their own. It was easier then."

We finish our noodles, even though they're gluggy and cold. Alister's loved before. His Chinese princess. Barely more than a child herself. Slender and beautiful, artistic and funny – her death cruel and senseless. The tragedy explains why he's never married again. Until he met Genevieve, and the twins stole his heart. In his mind Deshi is forever an infant. If the boys were with her when they met, Genevieve must have seen it. Did she exploit it? But if she wanted a steady man, the arrangement suited them both. Until Selkie Moon dropped a grenade into the pond. My stepmother would nod knowingly. Stella's always labelled me a troublemaker.

We leave the Pearl and walk in silence through Chinatown. Does he wonder if every passing Eurasian youth is Deshi? He's had twenty-nine years to get used to his loss, but it's clear there's a hole in his heart that's never healed. And now, because of me, he's lost the twins too.

Beside me, Alister has returned to the present. "I was hoping you'd wear your black dress tonight."

"I lost it. At Bantry's Bluff."

"Ah, the reason for the birthday suit. Get Davina to make you another one."

"She never makes the same dress twice. Anyway, she says it's out there somewhere. And I should send you to find it."

"Me?"

"She named you specifically."

"You think it's washed up with the tide? Like its owner?"

"I don't know. It could be anywhere or nowhere. You'd have to search for it."

"If it's been in the sea it'll be ruined, won't it?"

"I don't care. I want it back, whatever state it's in."

My passion is palpable and he understands. "I'd be honoured to look for it."

It's what I was afraid of but I don't feel alarmed. I've remembered that Davina made the dress for my first dinner with Alister. Maybe that means he'll find it.

"Where will you look?" I don't mention my own hunch. It feels important that he finds it himself.

"I've spent some time on that beach lately – I know where to look." Pause. "Come with me."

The thought of holding the dress makes me gasp. But do I want to go back to Bantry's Bluff with Alister? I don't really believe in the curse, but...

"I'm not sure I can go back right now. It's too soon. It's one of the reasons why you have to go."

He nods. "Come with me as far as Davina's. If I find the dress, you'll get it sooner."

***

As we wait for a cab we talk of other things. He doesn't mention London again. The seed's planted and it's enough. I'm still wary of getting more involved but my business brain is working on his offer. If I go on to London after Paris, I could follow up other invitations to present Being Sleek and establish some contacts of my own. Earn some good money and a reputation, and stop sleeping on park benches. Alister's experience could help me, if he stays professional and doesn't try to take over. And behind the thought of sharing his flat is the old cocktail of excitement and fear.

Alister is surprised when I don't get into the cab. It would be so easy to stay with him so we can make an early start. And with the night I'm about to face, I'd kill for a real bed, but I can't risk it. The opportunity to take a tumble just for fun passed weeks ago and the tension between us makes everything more serious.

As I climb the stairs to my office my footsteps echo. It's Friday night and there's not another soul here. After my first big break with my Moonshine business I had money in the bank, but I used it to pay back a loan from my father. So honourable – and so hasty. He wasn't in a hurry for it, but I was in a hurry to cut the family ties. Now I'm running on empty, living out of my suitcase and bunking down in my office. Thank God it's only for two nights.

Derek keeps a blanket in his filing cabinet for those days when his aircon is working on arctic. It will do to sleep on. I eye the armchair where he slept off many a hangover before he met Nigel, but I think I'll be more comfortable stretched out on my own floor. I take the cushion for a pillow.

The first noise has me on high alert before I've had time to fall asleep. A scraping sound. Followed by shuffling. There's someone in the building. Did a fellow vagrant chock open the fire door so he could gain access after hours? What if he comes up to this floor? The neon sign from the lounge bar opposite the alley is flashing an ugly light through my window, and there's only a thin curtain between me and the glass wall to the corridor. I'd feel safer in the dark. I stayed in my clothes in case I had to make a run for it, but now I'm sinking into the floor and holding my breath.

The shuffling fades and I breathe out. Can I hear snoring?

As I try to settle on the ever harder floor, unmistakeable shrieks and moans come from just below my window. I should have closed it but I wanted air. A working girl is giving her customer what he's paid for. Loudly. From the metallic banging, almost in rhythm with the flashing sign, they're doing it on the lid of the dumpster. It takes so long that one of them must be faking. When they're done, I weep with relief, but the alley comes alive with more creatures of the night. Tom cats. Drug dealers. I hear the click of cigarette lighters and whispered voices. Two guys going at each other with fists. Or I'm dreaming the dreams of the rough sleeper.

When I finally doze off, a fissure of light cleaves a dark place. The glare prevents me from seeing what's lurking in the shadows.

By the time sunlight wakes me my mind is made up. I'm going to do exactly what I told Alister. I'm going to trust my dream. Davina's talk of mythical homes feels too much like living out the Selkie myth. Another straightjacket, like my marriage. What I'm looking for is what I've always been looking for – a stable base to live a creative life. Sleeping in my office is about as far from that goal as I can get.

Ever since my mermaid act, Séminaires Tours has been making me offers. Their clients are English businesspeople attracted across the Channel by the promise of a seminar wrapped in a French holiday. After stashing the blanket and cleaning my teeth in the washroom, I run a wet comb through my hair to regain a scintilla of dignity and email them. Then I exit the building in the clothes I slept in and take a shower at the fitness club.

When I return, everything falls into place as if it's meant to be. Séminaires Tours emails back that they need a month to promote Being Sleek. They mention several dates for the tour and I agree to all of them.

In the blink of an eye, I've gone from being spooked by all the signs that I'm 'passing through' and living on the edge of homelessness to feeling energised. About Paris.

There's only one problem. Surviving till I go.

CHAPTER
Nine

Davina makes me breakfast as I pace. "He'll find it," she says. "I've never been so sure of anything, never."

"Are your hunches always right?"

After her insistence on Sydney when I'm so sure about Paris, her intuition feels unreliable.

She hesitates. "Sure, I'm not infallible, you know."

"When did you go wrong?"

I'm guessing it's linked to running away, and she doesn't want to tell me, so I know it was bad. It's what bothers me about my own intuitive hits: that they're nothing more than indigestion – not psychic, peptic – and that trusting them would be an act of folly.

"Since I've been here," Davina is saying, "everything's been fine, just fine."

I press her again. "If this place is your refuge, what were you running away from?"

For a moment I think she's going to tell me. Then she says, "Is that the phone?" just before it rings.

"Special delivery for Selkie Moon," Alister says when I pick up.

"So quickly." I try to keep breathing.

"I like to keep my promises."

Except his promise to Genevieve.

"Where did you find it?" I whisper.

"Wait till we're face to face. Be there in half an hour."

"Alister. Is it...ruined?"

"You'll see."

When I open the door, I don't know what the rush of elation is for - Alister or the dress. He stands there holding it, his blue eyes beaming out his own emotions. But he doesn't move a muscle. The first move is mine to make. He's a guy with a lot of self-control.

"I can't believe you found it," I gush, looking between him and the shiny bundle of fabric, trying not to snatch it.

"Can I come in?"

Davina's in the shower, so I take him out onto the *lanai*. Now I know the dress is back, I'm savouring the moment when I can touch it. It's always had the same effect on me. As precious as Gollum's ring. Soon I'll be pulling it on, no matter what state it's in.

We sit on floor cushions facing each other.

"It was under a rock," he says. "That cluster of boulders in the middle of the beach. Pushed deep into the sand, which is why we missed it when we were searching for you. But the police had dogs down there so I don't know why they didn't find it."

I'm not really listening. He's handed it over and my fingers are burrowing into the folds, while my mind is spinning through fragments of recollection. Something to do with a key. Was it in the pocket of the dress?

"It's not damaged at all that I can see," he's saying. "Just smells of sea water. And not a lot of that."

As I hold it to my nose, a sense of something wafts back. I remember peeling it off. Images strobe past, too fast to catch. Was that a candle flame?

I should be frustrated. This reunion might have come with answers, but just having the dress in my hands is enough.

At that moment, Davina emerges and I'm on my feet, racing past her into the bathroom. It takes only seconds to shimmy into the dress and step under the shower. I'm like a toddler who won't let his sleeping rug go. Showering in it was the only way it was going to get washed.

When I rejoin them, Davina has made coffee. I've dried my legs, but the dress is still wet and glistening. Alister stares as I kneel down in a patch of morning sun.

"Just as well the paparazzi aren't around," he says. "You'd make all those fantasies real."

His eyes are huge. It's the look that told Genevieve he'd met someone, just before she slammed her door in his face.

Davina fetches a bathrobe and throws it over my shoulders. "In case one of those paparazzi is hiding in the bushes, you know."

We giggle. Alister and I breathe out.

Davina's got a question for him. "How many places did you look?"

"Just one. I went straight to that outcrop of rocks."

"What made you start there?" she asks.

He looks at me. "A hunch. When Selkie asked me to look for it, I thought of those rocks."

"You'd looked there before, had you?"

"Yes, but the police had already searched so I didn't think of digging. And I was looking for evidence of Selkie herself. If I'd found her dress –" His voice catches.

"You might have thought she was dead."

He nods.

"Good that you didn't find it," Davina says. "Or you and the boys might have given up hope."

I sense that Davina wants to look at the dress – with her soul eyes – but the bathrobe was her idea, and the atmosphere between me and Alister is less charged since I covered up.

It's time to talk about something else, which is never

easy with Alister. Because he's a competitor, we've vowed not to talk about our work. Other forbidden topics include paparazzi, Andrew, curses, psychic objects, sleeping rough. As usual, it's quite a list.

Davina has some news of her own. She's off to New York as soon as the last design is done. I feel suddenly bereft, as if everything I rely on is giving way.

Meanwhile, Alister's offering her his apartment.

"I only offer it to friends," he says when she declines. "And it's better if it's not vacant. You'd be doing me a favour."

"Would I now?" She tilts her head and pleats her forehead. "Then I accept."

***

It's time for Alister to go. He offers to drive me to Makiki Heights, but I hastily say I'll take the bus.

"Let me know when you're leaving for Paris," he whispers with his usual peck in my hair. "We'll have a farewell drink."

I nod. "I can't thank you enough."

"My pleasure."

I watch him drive away.

Back in the living room, Davina inspects the dress. There's a tiny tear in one of the seams, and she repairs it by hand since I won't take it off.

"You won't be wearing it day in and day out, you know."

"Why not?" I'm only half joking. "It drip-dried pretty fast."

"It's just your reaction to losing it," she says. "You can't bear to be parted. But soon its effect on you will be the

shouting and swearing make me curl up in the foetal position. Is someone being murdered? The flashing lights from the bar are flooded out by emergency vehicles.

When everything finally flips to an eerie silence, I drop off and dream.

I'm running a seminar in a private house. Not my house. I'm in the living room, reading aloud from my notes, but each participant is in one of the many bedrooms, unable to hear me even when I shout. They keep calling out that they're not getting their money's worth, but when they finally start moving to the living room, a gatecrasher races through chased by two giant geckos. They're as big as lions and move with the same loping gait, their mouths gaping and their teeth dripping with saliva. The participants are screaming and scattering, and I'm presenting the seminar to an empty room.

***

When I move into Sylvie's it's so wonderful to climb into her big bed, I cry. The steady quacking from the bathroom will take some getting used to, but I remind myself it's soporific.

As I'm dozing off, expecting sweet dreams, a sudden crack and a loud pitter-patter wakes me with a jolt. The garden gecko is attacking a cockroach on the wall just above my head. The noise of it being bashed to death is so graphic and so close that I escape to the sofa, where I spend every night for the rest of the week. My graduation to professional couch-surfer is complete.

I book my flight and prepare to travel, trying not to think about the night between Sylvie's return and my departure. In spite of the nocturnal mayhem in her condo, the floor of my office isn't any more inviting, and there's always the danger of Derek finding out. I don't know how long Rupert is staying – surely no-one could have him for more than a week – so the boys' spare room may still be an option.

When Derek comes in early on Monday looking wall-eyed and sleep-deprived himself, I break the news about my travel plans.

"Paris," he says, yawning. "Has it got anything to do with a missing sailor, a silver spoon and a ruined lipstick?"

"Nothing to do with Gaston," I say, "but the spoon and the lipstick played their part. And my dream." I give him an outline of the man with the bucket. "The buildings looked French and the sign said Paris. Andrew promised to take me there for my thirtieth birthday, then I crossed him on some trifle. I don't remember what it was, but I refused to apologise. No apology, no Paris."

"Textbook troglodyte."

"Yeah. I found the strength to stand up to him, but it never occurred to me to go to Paris anyway. With this seminar offer, I'm getting the airfare as part of the package."

"Perfect." He's not yawning now. "When do we leave?"

What would I do without Derek?

I worry that he'll be abandoning Nigel to Rupert, but he says the man who can't stop talking will be gone by then, to another cousin, this one in California.

Derek stirs up my excitement. We're going to France. He thinks he can line up a writing gig with Lonely Planet, their new Loire Valley guide, and he happens to have a friend we can stay with somewhere along the famous river. More spare rooms – but it's the region where Séminaires Tours is located.

I look at the calendar. By the time we return, Myrna will

be almost ready to vacate my bed at Wanda's and my quest to return home will be done.

CHAPTER

Ten

My home life is so precarious that I can't create any new activities for Being Sleek. Instead I spend the week before we leave making a scrapbook of clippings about my mermaid adventure – something to show little Tyler when he grows up. Five nights with the geckos, and no alcohol to compensate, sends me slightly feral. And when I read in a magazine on Sylvie's coffee table that they're not even native to Hawaii – they're blow-ins just like me – the whole belonging thing gets rubbed in even more. I can't wait to escape all these symbols.

I do manage to write up several posts in advance for the Moonshine blog: How to Blend Curiosity Into Your Core Business and How Are New Customers Like Fresh Fish? Suddenly I'm full of the wisdom of seals.

The contract for signing over the house to Andrew for little more than pocket money arrives at Wanda's, and she calls into the office with it.

"A parcel from the charmless Andrew Tabrett. You're about to sign him out of your life, right?"

"A contract I'm not going to sign, you mean. Could you 'pickle it in aspic' or whatever it is you do to your fish?"

"You need a shredder, but I could custom-make a fish to send him." She gazes wistfully at the ceiling. "Razor-sharp teeth. Black. And a few imbedded prawn heads for some authentic halitosis. They'd smell for months."

We laugh until I open the parcel and read his 'headline': *Seal Siren goes Ape. Signs over House for Peanuts.*

That's when Wanda saves my sanity with a gift for my journey. As I open the handmade wrapping, a small resin fish leers at me with technicolour teeth.

"A magic mullet," she says. "To tie to the handle of your suitcase. I don't sell these, I give them away to the right people."

People she's kicked out of home?

"It'll keep you safe and prosperous, and help you remember your sense of humour."

***

Rupert has gone, so the boys can finally host their *kirtan* – but that means their house will be full of Nirvana-seekers for my final night in Honolulu. Many will be sleeping over, so Derek offers me the back seat of his car, parked in the garage where no-one will know. I'm ashamed by how desperate I've become, but his offer forces a bizarre twist. I tell him I can stay with Sylvie for one more night, but I make myself return to my office floor – to sharpen my resolve to leave Honolulu, the place that's been my home ever since I walked out on Andrew.

In spite of the heavy-handed signs that I'm passing through, it's a big thing to turn my back on my new life here, even for just a few weeks. Thank God Derek's coming with me, otherwise I'd be heading off into the unknown with only Being Sleek and the contents of my little red suitcase for company.

Derek and Nigel pick me up outside the office around midday. As we drive to the airport, I'm looking a little worse for wear but they don't comment. I've been trying to organise a farewell party in the departure lounge but Wanda can't make it, Davina has already left for New York, and then Alister calls to say he's got a meeting.

"We're always saying goodbye," he murmurs down the phone.

"Because we keep going in different directions."

"So let's start going the same way."

Not today.

"It's just the three of us for the farewell party," I tell the boys.

As we're stopped in traffic, my phone rings again. Maybe Alister can make it after all, but my peptic intuition says otherwise.

"Your father's been rushed to hospital," Stella says without preamble. "Chest pains."

"Oh my God. A heart attack?"

"What else? After the stress you've put him under."

"Me? What did I do?"

"You never phone him. He thinks you hate him. If you ever stop thinking about yourself, it will be a miracle." And I thought Stella might have mellowed towards me. "He's asking for you, in spite of everything. You've always been his favourite."

"Is he OK? I'm about to board a plane for Paris."

"I'll tell him you're busy then. A shopping spree. Why not pick up a little French number to wear to the funeral? Unless you're having too much fun to fly back."

Bloody hell. "I'm not going shopping, I'm doing a seminar tour."

"Cancel it."

"Is he going to die?"

But Stella's already gone.

The boys have heard everything. Derek's glancing at me in the rear-view mirror as I collapse on the back seat. Beside him, Nigel starts making calls. By the time we hit the airport, he's pulled some strings and rearranged our flights, booking me to Sydney and delaying Derek's departure for Paris by a week. He's even paid for the changes for both of us and I'm too broke to protest.

Derek parks, and we sit in the car while I pull myself together. I've never been close to Dad - he left my upbringing to Stella, and then disapproved of Andrew - but the thought of losing him now, before we can get to know each other, hits me like a missile out of nowhere. He's only sixty-five. Too young to abandon me to orphanhood. Or is this just my famous selfish streak in action? "It's always about you, isn't it?" Stella always says. She's right. Behind the sudden grief, there's an edge of anger. Dad and his heart attack are in the driver's seat of my life, just like Andrew.

Nigel's been waiting for the right moment. He hands me a paper bag with something heavy inside. "You might need this."

The rock I dug up in that midnight frenzy. He's washed off the dirt and its surface is gleaming.

"I was thinking you'd take it to France," he says, "find somewhere special to leave it. But maybe it's really for your dad. A peace offering, if you will."

I take it in my hands, its weight and coolness suddenly reassuring. Then I burst into tears. Nigel says nothing more as I shove the rock into the corner of my suitcase. He knows I'm hoping Dad will be alive to receive it, that I won't be putting it on his grave.

The three of us cluster in the departure lounge, drinking pina coladas. There's something particularly jarring about the jaunty angle of the little umbrella in my drink, as if it's poking fun at my sudden change of fortune. I pull the blank fortune cookie message out of my pocket and wave it.

"This seems significant."

Nigel nods. "It might be saying, *Wing it*."

"Or *Watch this space*," Derek adds.

"More like *Forget the plans, douchepants*."

I wonder what Davina would say. Because I ignored her entreaties about Sydney, has the universe conspired to intervene? But that would make me responsible for Dad's heart attack and make Stella right after all.

I push these thoughts away as Derek says, "It's a long flight to be alone with no news."

"My sister will keep in touch."

He nods. I can tell he wants to play guardian angel, but there are things you have to face on your own and your father's mortality is one of them.

When my flight is called, he's pushing send on his phone. "I've written a visualisation. To wrap you in a protective bubble. Not around your dad, but before you see Stella. Promise?"

***

It's only a few weeks since I left Sydney, after the birth of little Tyler. Dad picked me up from the airport that time, and the memory of his large hunched figure at the barrier causes me a pang. Back then, the summer was lingering but now the weather has turned. I arrive to an overcast sky and a strong wind off the sea. It feels like an omen.

I've checked my messages but there's no news from Gretel. Has he already gone?

Gretel knows which flight I'm on, not that I'm expecting her to be here. But when I walk through the arrivals door, I almost have a heart attack myself. Standing at the barrier is the figure I was just remembering - all broad shoulders and anxious eyes. Dad.

I stop and blink, thinking he's a spectre of my fear, then gasp as he rushes over and hugs me.

"I thought you might be dead," I say. Tears are falling. Relief tinged with something else. What the hell's going on? "You're not even in the hospital."

"False alarm," he says, looking sheepish. "Stella...overreacted."

Bloody hell.

"That's why I came to meet you myself. It's the least I could do, give you the news from the horse's mouth." Pause. "I'm touched that you wanted to fly to my bedside, Selkie."

Stella didn't give me much choice. Did she set this up? A little loyalty test would be just her style.

"It's what daughters do," I say, sounding as stiff as I feel. I can't find the words to tell him I love him. Do I? "There's no way I wouldn't have come, Dad."

He takes my suitcase and we walk towards the parking lot, but at the exit doors I stop.

"Now that I know you're well, I'll fly to Paris as soon as I can get a flight."

"Oh."

"It's where I was going when Stella called. I've got a seminar tour starting in a few days."

Surely Dad didn't think I'd play happy families? I did that a few weeks ago and it confirmed what I've always known: I'm the outsider in the family, the cuckoo in the nest, the daughter of Dad's union with Stella's crazy sister. Stella stepped in to mother me, and I know that in her misguided way she's wanted me to love her. But now that Gretel's given her a grandchild to dote on, she can finally give up on me. Until Dad threatened to die on us and called me back.

"You won't even stay overnight?" he asks. "Now that

you've come all this way?"

He knows a few hours with Stella will undo me, but he looks so hurt I soften.

"OK. I'll make a booking for tomorrow. Then I'll come back with you for a while. But I'll stay at a hotel tonight."

At the airline desk I can't get a flight for three days. I don't tell Dad. It's kinder if he thinks I'm leaving tomorrow.

Three days in a soulless hotel. I remind myself it's not my office floor, and that seminar presenters flit from hotel to hotel all the time, living out of a suitcase. It's freedom. But in the background, the small matter of unfinished business gnaws away at my resistance. Andrew and the house.

The drive to Seaforth in Sydney's north, to the house where I grew up, gives us time to talk.

"Tell me it wasn't heartburn," I say, remembering my 'peptic' intuition.

"Close, I'm afraid. A hiatus hernia. The symptoms can resemble a heart attack, apparently. And with my extra kilos and family history, Stella was sure I was finished. Ambulance, stretcher, the works. You don't take chances at my age. She did the right thing."

"She told me it was my fault. That you're stressed because I hate you."

"She said that?" He shakes his head. "That was just the worry talking."

We both know that's not true.

"Well," I say, "I'm glad you're not dead. I'm not ready to lose another parent."

It's as close as we'll get to discussing my mother.

"Why aren't you ready?" he asks. "Not that I'm planning to pop off any time soon. The doctor's got me on a diet. I might live till I'm a hundred."

"Because I don't know who you are, Dad. We should find out who our parents are, even if they're people of straw."

"Ouch."

"And you don't know me either. You've been content to buy the propaganda."

"I'm glad you're not pulling any punches just because I've been sick."

"I thought you were dead, remember? All the way to Sydney, I thought I could be coming to your funeral. Now I've got the chance to confront you, I'm not letting you off the hook."

Pause. "What do you want me to say?"

The question stops me in my tracks. All my life I've wanted him to apologise. For all his weaknesses and how they've impacted on me - as my mother's lover, as my hands-off father, as Stella's passive husband. But now, in a rush of something sharp and hot, I let it all go.

"I just want you to be real, Dad. A real person who's made mistakes. Stop hiding and be yourself. Is that so hard to live by?"

The traffic on Spit Road means he can keep his eyes ahead and be silent for a while.

"You're different since you ran away," he says. "You're strong. Outspoken. You've broken free from the propaganda, as you call it. Become your own person. Your mother was strong, but she had a knack for manipulating everyone and it made her selfish. You're not like that, Selkie, even though Stella can't see it - won't see it."

It's the first time he's criticised Stella and stood up for me - even if it's only in private. He's different too and it marks a small but breathtaking shift in our relationship. I look out the window with wet eyes, feeling what Davina would call *grand*.

***

Stella is waiting at the French doors. She pecks me stiffly on the cheek, but doesn't apologise for forcing my mercy dash across the globe. She doesn't do apologies.

I step into the dining room to find Gretel sitting there with Tyler at her breast.

"What kept you?" she asks, and winks. "I managed to get here last night."

She's played devil's advocate ever since we were kids and I was the big half-sister who never did anything right.

I bend to give her a hug and whisper, "You might have warned me Dad wasn't dead."

"He asked me not to tell you. He wanted to surprise you, and I knew you didn't have long to wait."

To look after his digestion Dad's got to graze throughout the day, so we sit around a table laid with cold meats and salads and bread and help ourselves. It's almost relaxing with Gretel and Tyler taking the focus away from me. A baby in the house brings out a soft side to Stella, a side I've never seen. I get a twinge of what I've missed all my life, but push it away.

When Gretel is ready to leave, I take my cue. She offers me a lift, and as we carry the baby and his gear to her car she's careful not to ask me where I'm going. Not in front of Stella.

"Are you going to take her past her old house?" Stella asks Gretel out of the blue.

"Why would she do that?" I ask.

"You know he's got himself a bimbo? It doesn't take

them long. Some little minx with too much cleavage and not enough morals."

She doesn't say 'just like your mother' but we all know that's who she means. I'm surprised Gretel's shown her photos of the voluptuous Juliet. Andrew hasn't blocked Gretel, so she's kept me up to date with his Facebook posts.

"Mum had a dream about your house," Gretel says, deflecting us away from bimbos.

"It doesn't mean anything," Stella's quick to add. She believes in dreams as much as she believes in apologies. "But it was...disturbing. Your house going up in flames and hundreds of cats jumping out the windows."

"Cats? Andrew hates cats." I don't like them either. I remember Myrna's cat sitting on my bed and shiver. "What made you think it was my house?"

It's a question I'm about to regret.

"If you must know...I saw you at the window. The pane was cracked and your face was a maze of jagged pieces."

"You didn't tell me that," Gretel says. "That's horrible."

"It was only a silly dream," Stella says. "Forget I mentioned it."

But I can't forget. Why tell Gretel the bare bones if she didn't mean her to tell me, and then save up the part about my fractured face at the window? I don't believe for a minute she had a dream. She made it up to unsettle me. About the house that was my home for eight years. About Andrew. And Juliet.

It's worked.

CHAPTER
Eleven

Dad's farewell hug makes up for the exchange with Stella. I flew halfway across the world in the wrong direction on a wild goose chase, but it's led to a new closeness with Dad. It's only after Gretel pulls away from the kerb that I remember I've still got the rock.

Gretel asks me where I'm going.

"Where can I rent a car around here?"

"Saturday afternoon – I don't like your chances. Do you want me to drive you to the airport?"

I pull out my phone and find a place at Manly Vale, but he hasn't got any sedans left, only one ute. When I say I'll take it, the guy agrees to wait.

"Utes are big in Hawaii," I tell Gretel. "Over there, they're called pickups."

"A good literal name," she says. "I reckon they name things with men in mind. So they know how to use them. Pickup. Like that cleaning stuff, Spray and Wipe." We laugh. "Women like a little more mystery in their names, don't you reckon?"

"Otherwise perfumes would be called Behind the Ears."

"And intimate deodorants? The mind boggles."

We carry on like this, avoiding the subject of why I want a car. Gretel knows when to mind her own business. Unlike yours truly. But she does ask about Dad.

"You had him to yourself for a while." She knows how rare that is with Stella on patrol. "How did you find him?"

"Alive, for a start. The heart attack scare gave us both a

fright and we inched a bit closer to an understanding."

"What does that look like?"

"For the first time, we can see each other."

It's something Nigel once said to me. Beyond liking or disliking, the ultimate act of acknowledgement is to see someone, without judgement.

Gretel nods her understanding. As Davina says, she's got a lot of wisdom, my sister.

***

The car rental guy sorts me out, and soon I'm driving my black tub ute and feeling like someone else – a woman with a ute. It's a powerful feeling, sitting behind the wheel, way above other vehicles. I just need a check shirt, elastic-sided boots and a little bit of country on my radio. It's a playful thought, but it hits me that without my memory of those two missing weeks I'm in a kind of identity warp.

I cruise down Pittwater Road towards Manly, avoiding the temptation to head up the hill past my old house. It would play into Stella's hands to go there on the strength of her 'dream', just to make sure the place hasn't burned down, and instead stumble upon Andrew and Juliet entertaining friends for drinks in the garden. The stalking ex-wife embarrassing everyone, especially herself.

I've already decided what to do: find a cheap hotel that's not near the beach. The seminar promoter has paid a small advance into my account so I'm no longer dead broke, but I don't want to blow it on hotel expenses. I might need it for something else. I find somewhere 'boutique' in a backstreet with parking underneath, and order toasted sandwiches from room service and a half bottle of red. Then I pull out Derek's visualisation. I forgot to use it with Stella and her poison got under my skin. I'm not going to forget tomorrow. With Andrew.

***

There's little traffic on Sunday morning, only early surfers with boards on roof-racks, as I take the road from Manly up the hill through Queenscliff to my old house. A Californian bungalow that Andrew and I bought eight years ago, just a few blocks from Harbord beach. We could almost afford it because it was a wreck.

"Not a house near the beach," I pleaded at the time.

"You're not getting your way this time," Andrew said. "I can surf before work."

"But what if I can hear the sea?"

"That's the general idea."

An image of the house comes into my mind. All the work I did to polish the floorboards, sand back the picture rails, paint every surface in a kind of frenzy, hoping to make it mine. Then there was the large neglected garden to tame. When I was inside, I couldn't hear the sea and the house became a kind of refuge from my marriage, a place I could channel energy into in a desperate attempt to make a home.

No-one knows what I'm up to this morning. My fear gives way to a strange sense of power as I sit behind the wheel of my ute. I'm counting on Juliet having stayed over, hoping her presence might smooth the way. I've even brought the rock that Nigel called a peace offering. Perhaps it was never meant for Dad. Otherwise I've got no game plan but to play it straight – knock on the door, present him with the rock, ask him to agree on a fair valuation. And avoid looking into his eyes.

It's early. Too early to arrive unannounced. I don't want

to aggravate him, and I don't want to catch Juliet in her PJs either. I park on the opposite side of the street where the kink in the road gives an uninterrupted view of the front door. While I settle in the seat to wait for Beach Road to wake up, I read Derek's visualisation again and smile. He's sent me a coating of pure white light to wrap me in its protective glow. And in my little black dress like silver armour, I'm ready to face Andrew. Davina would be proud.

The house is silent. In the early light it looks much the same: the 1920s weatherboard, the orange tile roof, the sandstone veranda. But in the brightening daylight, something's different. The house looks...abandoned. Just like when we bought it. What's happened to all the work I did, painting the woodwork, making a garden?

In a panic, I scan the front yard and see what Andrew's done. Nothing. Absolutely nothing. The garden is a tangle of untamed triffids. Overgrown shrubs are obscuring the windows, vines are climbing the walls, lifting the paint and invading the gutters, tentacles reaching out into the street, and weeds are obliterating the path. It's been a hot wet summer and through neglect he's coaxed the garden back to jungle, devaluing the property big time. And that's just the outside.

Clever. Until I decided to take a peep.

Suddenly it's all I can do not to storm up to the front door with phone camera blazing and catch Andrew Tabrett in the act of ripping off his ex-wife. Instead I take a swig of water. And remember I'm here to negotiate. But the evidence of his treachery revives my sense of power. I snap off photos until I remember not to exhaust the battery.

Six twenty-eight. I need a pee. There's an old-fashioned coffee lounge nearby, all chrome and Laminex, and it opens early. I'm about to start the engine, when a man appears on the kerb opposite Andrew's. Something about his body language makes me take the key out of the ignition.

It's Neville, my former neighbour. He picks up his newspaper, then scans the street. No-one's around and he doesn't notice me hunched behind the wheel of my rental. He turns as if to go back inside, but stops behind his front hedge. I've got a clear view of him from where I'm parked.

Another movement. Another man. Doug this time, from the house next to Neville's. He joins his neighbour behind the hedge. The two men are obviously hiding. And waiting. For no good reason I photograph them.

Now there's a movement across the street. A young woman is on the footpath. She's wearing a short pink bathrobe, polyester. It's tied at the waist and she's bulging out in all the right places, especially her boobs. Neville and Doug press their faces into the hedge at the same time as she bends to retrieve her newspaper. The action gives her breasts their chance and they escape like peeled melons spilling out of a basket. She doesn't seem to mind and lifts her head to look across the road, pausing while I photograph her display. Then, with less zoom, I catch both her and her audience.

At a leisurely pace, she stands up and tucks her boobs back in. They bounce up and down because the robe seems to be a couple of sizes too small. Neville and Doug are motionless. I can feel the tension from here. As she opens the robe and ties it again, I get another couple of shots.

Finally the woman turns and walks up the path, pausing to brush her hand across her backside. The hem of her robe rides up to reveal a long glimpse of bare buttocks. Then just as I'm thinking it's over and wishing I'd taken a video, she drops her paper and bends at the waist to retrieve it. Even from this distance, I hear the strangled cry as the men acknowledge her final gift.

She straightens, opens the front door and disappears into the house. Andrew's house. My house. I've just seen Juliet – almost all of her.

Neville and Doug have collapsed on the lawn, writhing like victims of snake bite. They look like they need resuscitation. I get another shot, then look at my watch. The whole peepshow has taken little more than a minute.

It's my turn to collapse. I must have tensed up and now I'm quivering.

Neville and Doug are composing themselves. They adjust their jeans, and exchange a few words before returning home – no doubt to serve breakfast in bed to their wives. Neville might get his kids out of the way by sending them next door. "Uncle Doug's invited you all in for breakfast," I imagine him saying. He was always the funny man of the pair.

***

Placido's Coffee Lounge is pumping out breakfast aromas to challenge the salt on the air. I use their loo, then over a mug of flat white coffee and thick slabs of raisin toast I scroll through the pictures I've taken. Like a silent movie, they trap the players in an endless dance. Juliet disporting herself in my front garden. Entertaining my neighbours. Entering my house. Straddling my husband. Ex. None of my business.

By nine o'clock, I'm standing on Andrew's doorstep clutching my rock, while he stands in the doorway blocking my way. The house might have changed but he's just the same. Blond curls tumbling into blue eyes and creases etched at the corners by sun and wind. His face is always tanned to walnut by the end of summer, but now his colour's started to fade. He's wrapped in a bath towel with arms folded and chin defiant, boring through my protective coating with a glare of abject hatred.

"Well, well, well. If it isn't the little Hawaiian mermaid, *Elkie with an S.*"

When I was sixteen, Stella and Andrew colluded to change the name my mother gave me to Elkie. It's what he's always called me. When I ran away, I took my birth name back.

"I won't keep you long, Andrew." Shit, I'm sounding apologetic. "I just flew in to talk through this property settlement. Face to face."

I proffer the rock but Andrew ignores it.

"Really? That would mean I'm willing to talk to you."

"It's the only reason I'm here, to come to an agreement. So we can both move on."

"Move on?" he says. "Move on? I can't believe this. You're still little Miss Manipulative, aren't you?"

"No." Shit.

"You think I don't know how you operate, Elkie, after all our years together? The way you twist me around your little finger? Except now you've gone too far. I'm in control for a change. No discussion and no access."

He starts to close the door.

"All I want is a fair settlement, Andrew. I've flown in from Honolulu, so you only have to give up five minutes of your weekend."

"I wish you could see yourself, Elkie. See what you've become. In your shiny dress and your stupid shell and your fuck-you haircut, trying to be someone you're not. It would be pathetic if it wasn't so...calculating. For reasons known only to yourself, you wreck our marriage, you humiliate me in front of our friends, you insult me when I try to get a settlement, then…just when I start to put my shattered life back together, you turn up on my doorstep thinking you can charm your way through the door and I'll submit to your cosy little chat. Well, it doesn't work that way. The only chat will be between my solicitor and yours."

It's the way he's always controlled me – tying me in knots with his double-speak – but something inside me rises up.

"I've seen the garden. It's not very honourable, deliberately devaluing the property. You disappoint me."

He laughs. "That's the general idea, *Elkie*. Now fuck off."

He slams the door in my face.

"I've still got a key," I shout through the keyhole.

He laughs from inside. "You think I haven't changed the locks?"

I'm still holding the bloody rock, suddenly a symbol of my impotence. I consider throwing it through a window. Instead, I stride down the side path, trying to regain some fake power, and photograph the backyard, as overgrown as the front.

Back in the ute, I rest my head on the steering wheel and sob. Derek's protective bubble has been breached and my essence is leaking from multiple punctures. In just a few words Andrew had me on the ropes. Why didn't I show him the photos of Juliet?

I touch the cowry shell, but it's as cold as it's silent and it feels like abandonment. I've got to talk to someone and it can only be Gretel. Even if she's been up with the baby all night.

"Your voice is so clear you could be in Sydney," she jokes.

I tell her about the fiasco that's just played out on Andrew's doorstep.

"You're never going to negotiate with him, Selkie. The man's a borderline psychopath. They never negotiate, they only enforce. After twenty years with him, you were naive to think he'd changed."

"I thought with his new woman, he might be thinking to the future."

"On the surface he's sporting his new teenage bimbo, but at his core he's the same old Andrew. And you humiliated him big time when you left like that, so the satisfaction of blocking your every move is way too sweet to resist."

Like letting his home crumble around him just to score a low valuation.

"But I can't move on while he's got me skewered on his barbed-wire thread."

"I think he gave you the answer without meaning to."

"Get a locksmith?"

"Get a *lawyer*."

Good old Gretel. Put the whole property settlement into the hands of an expert. Someone ruthless who knows how to negotiate. It's an elegant solution, and the reason I had to be here. If I can afford it.

"Once you're out of the picture, Selkie, there's a good chance he'll lose interest. Because if he keeps fighting, there's no payoff except a fat legal bill."

"I like it, Gretel. Thanks. I feel lighter already. Do you know anyone nasty enough?"

She laughs. "No." She thinks for a minute. "Today's Sunday, isn't it? I lose track of the days. Buy a good book, go back to your hotel and chill, then visit a couple of law firms tomorrow. You'll know when you meet the right person."

I close my eyes and visualise a sumo-wrestler in a sweaty barrister's wig and Behind the Ears cologne, pinning Andrew to the mat until he agrees to my terms. The image starts to plug up my leaks.

CHAPTER
Twelve

When the passenger door creaks, I jump. And open my eyes to see a plump expanse of décolletage above the zipper of a pink tracksuit.

"Go away," I yell. "Waggle your tits at someone else."

Juliet ignores me and climbs in. Close up she must be half my age, with a pretty face as plump as her body, and brown uncombed hair pulled back in a ponytail. It's the kind of beauty that could fade.

"You've been taking pictures," she says.

I shrug. How does she know?

"I came to talk to Andrew. He won't let me in."

"Course not. Trust me, the place is a tip."

"I thought so. Why do you stay?"

"None of your business. A bit like those pics you took."

"What about them?"

"Look, it's, like, over between you and Andrew, yeah?"

"So?"

"So what do you care? About what I, like, flip at the neighbours?"

Good question, but I don't owe her an answer.

"Do me a favour," she says.

"What?"

"You know." She holds out her hand for my phone.

"Sounds more like an order than a favour."

"Whatever."

It's clear she won't be leaving till I do. I open the photo gallery and pass her the phone. She could delete them but she doesn't.

Neville's and Doug's assault on the hedge amuses her.

"Look at 'em. Their wives must be, like, over it." Now she's studying the close-ups, boobs and buttocks bobbing. "They're good. Are you a photographer?"

"Not really. I didn't plan to take them. You just...popped up."

She giggles again. And suddenly I like her.

"How did you meet him?" I ask.

She shrugs. "Temping in his office, till I crack it in catalogue modelling. Plus size, you know? I've had experience. Anyway, we started working back late. Then doing it on his desk. Now I'm, like, *permanent*. Till I get bored."

"You could do better. He's selfish. And cruel."

"And *old*." She's still scrolling. "What are you gonna do with 'em?"

"I don't know." Although something spiteful appeals. "But you've got something in mind, haven't you?"

She grins. "Post 'em online. Get right up Andrew's nose."

For a moment I see Andrew with his hand across his face as Neville's and Doug's wives attack him with brooms, and camera crews vie for a glimpse. Then there's his reputation. A junior employee semi-naked in his garden, posing for the paparazzi, then regaling them with details of what they do on his desk after hours. If the partners get wind of it, he'll go straight onto the demotion list. Or worse. Not to mention his political aspirations. Perfect.

But just as quickly, I let it go. This pantomime is happening in a parallel universe, a universe I no longer inhabit.

"They're yours," I say to Juliet. "Email them to yourself.

Then delete them."

"Cool."

After it's done, there's nothing more to say. She hands me back my phone before getting out, then she leans through the open door and gives me one last look at her equipment.

"You're much more, like, chilled than I expected. Andrew goes, 'My ex, she's one desiccated bitch'. Like coconut, you know? All the juice squeezed out."

It's an adjective he's used about me before. The bastard.

"But he hasn't got a clue, has he? He's the one that's sucked you dry. And you're still letting him do it."

She walks down the hill, the tracksuit clinging to her backside. Women would call her plump, but men wouldn't. She's the opposite of desiccated. She's, like, succulent.

On the way to Placido's for another coffee I can't stop thinking about it. How Andrew controlled my life; how I let him suck my juice out, smear my essence on the walls. But Juliet's a free spirit. Not because she drops her robe for the neighbours, but because of what it represents. No-one's going to suck Juliet dry, not even an expert like Andrew. She's getting the juice out of life. All of it.

***

It's great to have a plan. Gretel's always got something wise to say, even when she's up to her eyeballs in sleep deprivation.

Back at my hotel I shower off Andrew's toxic energy. Then, on a whim, I make my way to the beachfront. The surf is subdued, along with my phobia. Since my disappearance, my fear of the sea has morphed into something else. An emptiness I don't understand.

Along the promenade, there's a market in full Sunday swing. I browse the handmade soaps and bamboo wind chimes and Nepalese beanies, catching gusts of that autumn chill as it ripples through the pines. Even though I've done nothing more than decide to find a lawyer, I feel strangely out of reach of Andrew's vengeful clutches. Someone is selling helium balloons, and I buy one just to let it go. It jerks higher and higher into the pale sky, taking my impotence with it.

When I check my messages, Juliet has sent a link. She hasn't wasted time posting the photos, captioned *Dance of the Disappearing Bathrobe*. She's left out the most explicit ones, but the viewer gets the picture. Andrew will be incandescent. Especially if he finds out who took them. I laugh and turn off my phone.

It's time for fish and chips wrapped in paper. I eat them off my lap on a beachfront seat and try to stare down the seagulls, with as much success as I had with Andrew. It reminds me there are no seagulls on Hawaii. But there are mutton-birds. Meteorites with wings. My kindred spirits, clumsy but focused. Always finding their way home.

While I'm trying not to obsess about the whole home thing, a man in a wheelchair rolls up and stops beside my seat. He's got a large black dog with him and I realise he's also blind. He opens a parcel of paper and starts on his own fish and chips.

"Your dog's obedient," I say. "He's not even ogling the chips." Then I'm embarrassed for mentioning something he can't see.

"She," he says. "Daisy. She's obedient. She also doesn't like chips."

We laugh.

"What's the sea like today?" he asks.

"Flat."

"You're a woman of few words."

"Sorry, I've got a bit of a sea phobia."

"Well, you're safe on this promenade unless there's a tsunami. And I can't see the view, so knock yourself out on a description."

His forthrightness reminds me of a girl I knew at uni. She was in a wheelchair with advanced MS and I was one of her helpers. She got away with being as cheeky as this guy.

"OK," I say, "here goes. The beach is wide...so the sky is big above us. It's stretching in layers of thin grey clouds all the way from heaven to the horizon."

Can he remember colours? But he's already closing his eyes and moving his head as if he's visualising the scene.

"And there's almost no swell so the horizon is...sharp."

Another beach, another horizon, moonlight spilling across the sea. I try to hold the image so I can follow it to where it took me, but again it slips away.

"The water is a dull grey," I say, "with few white caps. And the waves aren't rushing to the shore, they're...meandering diagonally and colliding with each other in a companionable way, then trickling the last distance and dwindling into nothing in the shallows."

Splashing in the shallows... Dancing on the shore... But it's what I've seen before.

"And the cliffs?" he asks.

Something about cliffs. But I already know that I took off my shoes and descended Bantry's Bluff. Then...?

"The cliff," I say, "is high and crumbly. Jagged layers of rough sandstone in cream and orange, creating a patchwork of light and shadow."

"A great place for fossils. When I was a boy I found a fossil of a lizard."

I want to give him more. I close my eyes and try to feel the cliff.

"Its claim on the space...reflects something primal and true, something secret that lives deep inside." Where did that come from? "It makes me want to weep with gratitude." Shit.

When I open my eyes, the man is smiling.

I've finished my fish and chips, but I stay while he eats his. He tells me his name is Keith and I tell him mine.

"Selkie," he says. "After the Celtic myth about seals."

"My mother's mad idea. I always have to spell it."

"Selkies are seals but they're also people. They have divided selves."

To avoid this observation I ask if he lives around here.

"I've got a ground-floor unit. Nice and flat. Daisy and I can do all our shopping and roll home. What about you? I sense you're just passing through."

Bloody hell. What is it with this guy?

"I'm on my way to Paris." I find myself telling him about leaving Andrew and coming back.

"Hawaii. Sydney. Paris," he says. "Which place is home?"

Instead of spilling any more to this stranger, I offer to buy us ice creams, fetching them from a milk bar opposite the seafront. Then it's time to part company and I watch Keith and Daisy roll away.

I wander along the Corso, the short road that connects the seashore with the harbour wharf across what was once a spit of sand. The whole world is doing the same – the Sunday pilgrimage from the ferry to the beach, even on a grey day like this. This precinct is my old teenage stamping ground: Saturday nights with the girls, strutting our stuff in tiny skirts and big shoes. Until Andrew exploited my awkward adolescence for himself. These days the Corso is lined with cafés spilling alfresco tables onto the pavement, and glittering shops offering everything from designer jewellery to tacky souvenirs. The old slogan still emblazons mugs and T-shirts: *Manly. Seven miles from Sydney, a thousand miles from care.*

I'm imagining dwelling in the heady space beyond care when a brass shingle between two shops catches my eye. *Judy Cartwright. Solicitor.* There's a door to the offices above. I was going to hit the city tomorrow, but maybe there's a lawyer right here.

***

It's Monday morning. Judy Cartwright's rooms are old and small, but the paint job is new and the north-facing windows let in lots of light. The receptionist consults her screen and tells me Judy can see me at ten thirty. Back on the street, I've got over an hour to kill. Should I interview another lawyer to give myself a choice? There's another shingle and another stairway. *Roach and Leggett.* Sounds suitably scurrilous.

As I start to climb the stairs, a suited man is coming down. We nod as we pass but when I reach the landing I hear a voice behind me.

"Aren't you Elkie Tabrett?"

"Selkie Moon." What's going on?

He laughs. "Ah, yes. Elkie with an S. Your hair's different from the photo."

"What photo?"

"Your ex thought you might be looking for a lawyer. He's put your photo around, warning everyone to show you the door. No-one's going to touch you, babe. He knows a lot of people."

Andrew's the in-house accountant for a big city law firm. This guy's right: through his networks, he'll have contacts everywhere.

"And you are?" I'm trying not to sound rattled. "Roach or Leggett?"

He smirks. "Neither."

While he's enjoying himself at my expense, I pull out my phone and snap his photo. "Just in case I have to make a complaint to the Law Society."

Now he's shouting and climbing the stairs, then stops. He was thinking of grabbing my phone but he doesn't want to risk an assault. And what can I do with the picture? There are no witnesses to our conversation, and I'm already locking myself in the toilet on the landing.

A few minutes later, the coast is clear and I return to the Corso for a coffee. Has Judy Cartwright got the message to leave me out in the cold? She's only a suburban solicitor, so even if she's happy to represent me, does she have the balls to face up to Andrew? Unless she's a hard-faced bottle-blonde who started her career as a prison guard. I wish.

I'm worrying away when Keith and Daisy roll right past my table.

"Hey, Keith." Daisy is sniffing my hand. "It's Selkie, we met yesterday, remember? Care to join me for a coffee?"

He laughs. "I'd never forget your name. Or your voice channelling the cliff. Order me a coffee and regale me with stories of the seashore."

As the coffees arrive, I'm telling him my seashore story, the one where I disappeared.

"Part of you hasn't come back from that beach," he says.

"Why do you say that? You've only just met me."

"Because you don't remember. You're in an amnesia

loop, Selkie, and it makes you vulnerable." Derek would love this guy. And Davina. "It's like post-traumatic stress. Those guys coming back from war zones. They keep reliving the horrors because part of them is trapped in the experience."

Rupert.

"Except I can't remember what happened."

"Flipside of the same thing. They've got the mental video running and they can't get out of the movie. You're still on that beach because you can't remember. In both cases, you've got to get the trapped part back so you can live fully in the present."

It's what I wondered myself.

"How do you know this stuff?"

"I work with traumatised people. I'm a psychotherapist."

"Now you tell me. No wonder I'm spilling my secrets. When you say 'regale me with stories' you're pressing the play button."

He laughs. "I seem to have that effect on people."

"Because you're not at all threatening, Keith."

"No. The blind guy in the wheelchair. It helps people open up."

Is he a war-zone casualty himself? That would give him serious cred with his clients. Something stops me from asking.

"OK, so how do I get myself back? And don't say five years of therapy."

"Sometimes it's as simple as a short visualisation."

Keith's whole world must be visualisation. On the other side of the table, he's fiddling with his smart phone. He's got an earpiece that must be guiding him with sounds.

"Close your eyes," he says. "Listen to this."

I don't know what I'm expecting, but what pours out into the darkness behind my eyelids is a bird carolling. Its slow rich song echoes in the dark, the notes flowing from high and clear to deep and mellow, piercing my heart. I'm transfixed by the perfect pitch as it carries me to a lonely moonlit night, poignant with feelings of longing.

When it's finished we're both silent.

Eventually Keith says, "The pied butcherbird. I've just come back from Uluru, and when I heard it calling across the outback, I knew I had to buy the app."

I don't know what to say, I'm almost in tears. We're sitting at an outdoor café in Manly and I'm connecting with a bird call on an app.

"Did something come back?" he asks.

"Yes, but I don't know what it means." The emptiness again.

He says no more and returns to his coffee.

After a while I ask, "Why did you go to Uluru?"

"A tribal elder invited me. I helped his son escape his mental horror movie and he wanted to thank me." He waits a moment before adding, "I spent a whole day in a secret cave."

A visceral jerk sideswipes me with thoughts of Andrew.

"Where only the initiated go?" I manage.

"Yes. They put me through a ceremony, then they carried me to the cave."

Because I'm a woman, he can only talk in general terms about the men's business he experienced – the sacred totem carved at the entrance that he touched with his fingers, how they sat in silence and allowed him to just be there, how he felt the air moving through the cave, the sun bouncing off the rocks as it travelled across the sky. After a while he heard distant chanting and imagined a sacred campfire with elders gathered around it. As it got louder, bouncing around the valley and playing on the wind, he asked where the ceremony was. "You hear singing?" the elder asked. Keith nodded but no explanation was given, and eventually the voices drifted away.

When we say goodbye, I return to my own mental message: *Turn the tables on the troglodyte.*

Keith's talk of secret caves has brought me right back to my mission.

Chapter
Thirteen

The woman who greets me is pushing sixty. Above her tailored navy suit, her face is lined and puffy. She's never been a beauty and age isn't doing her any favours. It never occurred to me that Judy Cartwright might be old. Then she smiles and her eyes meet mine with a sharp twinkle.

"Miss Moon," she says, ushering me through to her office and closing the door. She gestures towards a seat, then sits down beside me, ignoring the chair on the opposite side of the antique desk. "What can I do for you?"

Something about her manner makes me spill the whole story. From meeting Andrew as a sixteen year old to walking out on him a few months ago. It makes me sound pathetic, almost twenty years as his doormat, but I can't seem to spin it any other way.

Judy listens and doesn't interrupt, then looks at the photos of the house.

When I'm done and she still hasn't spoken, I ask, "You do family law, don't you?"

She laughs. "I hope so. Now that you've given me the life story."

"Sorry."

"Don't be."

"You didn't need to know all that."

"I did. Thanks for not making me prise it out of you with a crow bar. Some women are so ashamed, they can't even share it with their lawyer."

She gets up and stands with her back to the window.

"Now that I know the score, you need to hear me out and decide if I'm the person for you. That's why I don't charge for the first interview."

I like her already. Is that enough?

"What you've described was only a marriage under the law. In reality it was a union of unequals, where Mr Tabrett dished out all the power and forced you to eat it...cold. When you skipped out you turned the tables on him..."

The same words as my message.

"...and if he can't restore the old *un*equilibrium, he's going to watch you fry."

"Did you get all that from my story?"

"No." She sits down beside me again. "He's posted a warning not to represent you. With your photo attached."

"So you already know who I am."

"Correction: I know who he *wants* everyone to think you are. Elkie with an S. But it says more about Andrew Tabrett than it says about you."

We sit with this for a while.

"You need a good lawyer, Selkie. Someone who isn't intimidated by troglodytes."

Bloody hell.

Judy smiles. It's a confident smile. "If I become your advocate, I'll cut through Andrew's power plays. I'll insist that the house can't be sold to him or anyone else in its present state of disrepair. It's half your house, so if he stays obstructive we'll get a team to tidy the gardens and go through the interior to prepare it for sale. This will be expensive, but it will increase the value exponentially and we'll deduct the cost from the final settlement. Meaning he pays half. He'll try to block us, but in the end we'll win. And negotiating with me won't afford him much pleasure. I'm a tough old battleaxe and he won't be pleased you've found me.

"Once the house is restored to market value, he may suddenly cease to be interested in buying you out. While he could get it cheap, with you out of the way, he was looking at a nice capital gain - the icing on his revenge cake. But now that's no longer an option - you've cruelled it by flying over here to take a look - he'll want to *maximise* the value to sell to a third party. Followed by a fifty-fifty split."

It sounds so easy when Judy says it.

"How do I hire you?" I ask, smiling back.

She runs through her fee structure and it sounds like half that of a city firm. She gives me an estimate of the range of hours she predicts and asks for a retainer upfront to show good faith. Thank God for my advance from the seminar promoter.

When we're done, she puts her hand on my shoulder. "Go away and let me handle everything. That's my job. And stay away from Andrew. Email me any questions, but otherwise let me run with what we've discussed. I'll be in touch when I need instructions - and to share any good news. Your job is to let me to do my job."

"I'm not sure I know how to do that."

"You keep hoping Andrew will become reasonable. He won't. Leave him to me. Take a holiday. Don't go straight back to Hawaii, straight back to work. You're exhausted. You're so used to it you don't notice, but your ex has spent twenty years tapping your veins."

Not just a troglodyte, a vampire. Sucking me dry. It's what Davina said. And Juliet.

"Desiccated," I murmur. The truth is right there in his jibe.

***

In a state of euphoria about finding Judy, I collect my luggage from the hotel lobby and take the exit to the car park. The ute is where I parked it yesterday, but bliss flips to horror when I get up close. The windscreen is a mosaic of tiny fragments spiralling outwards from a caved-in blow. Someone smashed it with a hammer. It must have been last night.

An image of my own face frozen behind the glass as the hammer struck brings on a wave of nausea. Have I seen that image before? I lean my head against a pillar and try to calm my breathing, telling myself it's a random attack, there are plenty of passing vandals around here. But the venom behind it feels personal. Very personal.

"He's trying to get to you," Judy says when she takes my call.

"You think it's Andrew?"

I know it's Andrew.

"Easy to follow you down the hill and see where you're staying."

With me driving a distinctive black ute. I should have gone to the city, lost him in the Sunday traffic. But then I wouldn't have found Judy.

"We can't prove anything," she's saying, "unless they've got CCTV. But send me a photo and we'll put the incident in the file. And you'd better inform the police. Do you want me to deal with the rental company?"

"No, I'll do it. Hey!"

A woman has grabbed my suitcase from where I left it by the pillar and now she's running away with it.

I take off after her, across the car park and up the stairs to the street. In jeans and sweatshirt and running shoes she looks like any other local – only my red suitcase with its bobbing resin fish and the way she's dodging the passers-by prevents her from blending in.

She's had a head start and I'm losing her, but as she rushes past a rubbish bin it catches on the corner of the bag, bursting it open. The rock tumbles out in slow motion, carrying my little black dress with it. The thief turns and clutches the suitcase closed, before disappearing with it around a corner.

The dress is all I want, so I stop by the bin, where a woman with grey hair has picked it up.

"She stole my suitcase," I pant. "Why would she do that?"

"Was there anything precious in it, sweetie?"

"Only this," I say, as she hands over my dress still half wrapped around the rock that saved it. I press it to my chest, trying not to cry. "Thank you so much."

My few possessions were my remaining sense of home. And now they're gone.

As I wander in a daze towards the police station, clutching the rock and the dress like a life raft, I feel light-headed. A renewed wave of emptiness makes me stop and take some deep breaths. Then I call Judy again and break the latest news.

"A troubling coincidence," she says. Neither of us believes that. "Report the theft too."

***

When I show my passport as ID at the police station, the female officer gives me a funny look.

"We believe you can help us with our enquiries on another matter, Miss Moon."

"What other matter?"

"A complaint about trespass and property damage. A house in Harbord."

Shit.

"Be polite," Judy says when I phone her. "Don't say a word, and put me onto the officer."

It takes a while but she sorts it. Andrew's got a surveillance camera on the side of the house, which snapped me storming down the path carrying my rock. He told the police that someone smashed a window in the back shed where he keeps all his childhood sports trophies. Like the way 'someone' smashed my windscreen? The evidence shows it could only have been me, the vengeful ex-wife. A neighbour saw me taking photos.

"He's hired Reece Chapman from Roach and Leggett," Judy tells me, as I sit on a park bench and watch normal people going by.

The guy in the stairwell. He probably called Andrew right after I threatened him with the Law Society. The old boys' network closing ranks.

"Mr Chapman's been angling for an Apprehended Violence Order against you."

"What?"

"I've blocked it."

"This is getting scary, Judy."

"I know, and it's easy for me to say it's just intimidation, but that's all it is. Chapman told the police that you're the scary one, by the way. You're so jealous of Andrew's new girlfriend, you've been stalking the house and taking photos of her."

So Andrew knows I took those pictures – more fuel for his revenge pyre.

"He's doing all this because he's terrified of me. What a joke."

"Look, Selkie, I have to say this. It's possible that hiring me is making things worse. Reece Chapman and I have locked horns once before and I won. He's got a long memory, so I'll understand if you want to change lawyers."

"No way. Andrew smashed the windscreen before I hired you, remember? And you've stopped the AVO."

"That was easy. I showed the police the photo of your windscreen and said we'd apply for a counter AVO. They know a domestic beat-up when they see one, so they're not going to touch it. And that caper with your suitcase was a step too far."

My case was found in pieces in the bin outside the police station with all its contents slashed. Luckily my laptop was in my shoulder bag. Wanda's fish tag also survived so at least I won't be losing my sense of humour.

"It's got all the signs of retaliation," Judy continues. "He's at risk of overplaying his hand. You've got to get out of here, Selkie. Paying someone to snatch your bag and shred your clothes is petty, but it shows he's already getting creative. He's caused you the maximum inconvenience, but I'm worried about his next move."

"Is Paris far enough?" I tell her my plans, wishing my flight was today.

"Perfect. You've lost your luggage so take yourself on a shopping spree."

***

There are no surveillance cameras in the hotel car park, so Andrew's off the hook. Several hours of phone calls and insurance paperwork keep me distracted. By the time the windscreen has been repaired, it's a relief to return the ute and make plans to stay with Gretel.

When I phone her, I don't mention the windscreen or the bag snatch, but she adores my description of Judy.

"Sounds like your intuition's kicked in," she says.

Gretel's always believed Andrew stifled it, along with her own mother, Stella.

Before catching a bus to the city, I buy a few toiletries, a change of knickers and a cheap suitcase with wheels. It's bigger than I need for my remaining belongings and its emptiness reflects my own. I miss my little red suitcase already – the symbol of my bid for freedom ever since I ran away. But I've got the clothes I'm standing in, including my cowry shell. And my dress. A wave of gratitude overcomes me. They're all I need for now.

As I step into the street, the rock feels heavy in the new bag. It was the saviour of my dress, but it's also a reminder of my impotence with Andrew. The customs guys at Sydney airport were bemused when I declared it. They checked it over, then squirted it with disinfectant before sending me on my way with smirks and eye-rolls. I don't want to carry it to Paris.

Gretel would put it in her jungle of a garden, but that feels too ignominious. I've brought it all the way from Hawaii. Just like me, it needs a home.

Keith and Daisy are traversing the Corso. Derek would call this third sighting auspicious, but Manly's a compact place and Keith and Daisy are local identities. Keith's got a thermal bag perched on his lap so he's probably on his way home with some shopping.

I catch up to them, fall in step with the wheelchair and try not to cry as I tell him I've got a present for him.

"A rock?" he says.

"A Hawaiian rock." I tell him about the island custom of presenting a rock as a greeting. "I'd like to give it to you."

"I'm honoured. May I see it?"

He stops the wheelchair under a roadside Norfolk pine and rubs his fingers over the rock. Then he holds it out for Daisy to sniff.

"I like this crack," he says.

I don't want to admit that I haven't looked at it closely. But I don't remember a crack. It must have happened when it fell out of my suitcase.

"Cracks signify wonderful things," he adds.

"Imperfection?"

He laughs. "Openings, secrets, doorways to hidden places, chinks in our defences, entrances to inner caves. Don't get me started on cracks. I love them for another reason too. I can *feel* them. It's a very special gift, Selkie. Thank you."

"Great." I mean it. "Where will you put it?"

"Where I'll know exactly where to find it. Come on."

We continue along a backstreet to Keith's unit and leave his thermal bag in the shade inside his gate. Then we make our way to the promenade and turn in the direction of North Steyne. It's a long journey by motorised wheelchair and I worry that his battery won't make it, but Keith is enjoying himself and Daisy trots along beside us wagging her tail. I suspect they don't usually go this far.

At the northern end of the beach the promenade stops where a traffic bridge crosses the lagoon. The tide is out and the sand stretches right across to the cliff. I'd forgotten that the path doesn't go all the way.

"Where to now?" I ask.

"The cliff. It's just the right place for my rock."

"You won't get across the sand, Keith."

"I know. I'll send my emissaries. You and Daisy."

Something surges in my chest. I don't want to tell Keith

that I'm not up to the job, and the tide is so low that from the sand I'll hardly even see the water. Only the smell of it is all around us.

"What do you want us to do?" I ask.

"Find the right place and put the rock there, with a little ceremony to honour the moment. Then Daisy will know where it is if I ever need it."

It's ridiculous.

"What will the right place look like?"

"Feel like. Find the place that feels right."

He leans over and whispers in Daisy's ear, before facing his wheelchair towards the cliff.

Daisy and I set off on our quest, descending the few steps to the beach and starting across the sand. Daisy's loving it under her feet. She runs ahead, doubles back, wags her tail and circles me, before running forward again. Eventually we get to the channel that takes the low-flow water from the lagoon to the sea. It's narrow enough to jump over. Then we clamber over the rocks to the shelf at the base of the cliff.

Before I remember that he can't see us, I turn around and wave to Keith. To my astonishment he waves back. Bloody hell. Time to get this over with.

"OK, Daisy. Find us a place to put the rock."

I perch on a boulder as Daisy races backwards and forwards across the elevated rock shelf, sniffing at pools and cocking her leg at boulders. Then she circles me and sets off again. She's enjoying herself so much, I suspect she's forgotten her mission. Then I notice she keeps going back to the same point and disappearing for a moment before reappearing and bounding back. She's found something.

I get up and follow her, trying not to think about the sea, but we're a long way from where tiny waves are splashing onto the rock platform. Daisy slips behind a boulder. The fissure is tall and narrow, snaking its way from a chink at the base right up the cliff. There might even be a cave in there. It's impossible to tell how far in the opening goes, if it's inhabited by stray troglodytes.

Daisy wags her tail and sits. This is the place. Keith loves cracks. I'm relieved it's this simple as I hold out the Hawaiian rock and look at Daisy's expectant face. Her lolling tongue seems to be saying, "Time for a little ceremony."

That's when I feel it. Something profound. The crack cleaves open my heart, just like the call of the butcherbird, and lets in a sliver of light. Just for a moment I remember everything, then forget it. I'm full of knowing but empty. It's enough.

By instinct, I press my lips to my rock, place it in the chink at the foot of the cliff, and weep.

western suburbia when he could be making a fortune as a private specialist and living in luxury in the eastern suburbs.

Gretel unloads Tyler, who's still asleep, and takes him to his room. In her kitchen, I spoon portions of Thai into bowls. Gretel returns, and pours the wine.

"Have you remembered anything from your disappearing act?" she asks.

"Bits and pieces." I tell her about Tutu's mirror – the look I saw in my eyes.

"I noticed it when you arrived. It wasn't there a couple of weeks ago."

"How does it look to you?"

She grins. "The cat that's got the canary...meets Tyler while he feeds."

At the mention of his name, Tyler starts to yell. She goes into his room and returns with the baby and a bottle.

"But you were breastfeeding him the other day," I say.

"I expressed this earlier, so I can drink and you can have a turn." Before I can protest, she pops Tyler in my arms and puts the bottle between his lips. "He needs to learn to suck from a bottle so he's happy to feed both ways."

As I look down at the tiny person in my arms, Tyler's eyes are closed. Then he opens them, fixes me with a gaze as cavernous as the universe and I fall in.

With Tyler fed and back in bed, I tell Gretel about my Paris dream. "I was running away from a man with a bucket."

"Andrew?"

"No, but the bucket felt like a weapon. To catch my juice." I remind her that Andrew refused to take me to Paris, then we get to his latest pranks. I tell her about Juliet and show her the photos she's posted.

"Just the woman he deserves," she says. "And one

CHAPTER
Fourteen

As I sit at Central Station waiting for a train to Gretel's place, the glow of meeting Keith and Daisy and my moment at the base of the cliff fade. In their place is a growing fear that I haven't escaped Andrew. The bag, now adorned with Wanda's leering fish, is a constant reminder of the bag snatch. And my mind keeps seeing that hammer directed towards my head, the fragments of windscreen splintering my face. He found out where I was staying last night; he had someone follow me and steal my bag. Does he know where I'm going now?

It's over an hour to Blacktown. I keep an eye on the other travellers, but if I am being followed it could be anyone. Or no-one. I hate him for creating this unease.

Gretel picks me up with Tyler in his car capsule. If she notices my missing red suitcase she doesn't mention it. Barry's working late so we stop for some takeaway Thai.

"I was going to cook," she says. "I'm cooking better since I got some boobs."

She gives her breasts a gentle push up. Gretel's normally as flat-chested as Stella, while I inherited my mother's curves.

"How does that work?"

"Channelling Nigella Lawson."

It's wonderful to laugh.

We arrive at their humble cottage in a street of post-war boxes. Stella has never understood why Barry chooses to work in community medicine and subject Gretel to outer-

thing's obvious – she won't be threatened by a bucket. Now he knows you've ditched him for good, he's launched his pathetic vendetta. What a...*caveman* he is. What's the word?"

I catch my breath. "Troglodyte."

"Yeah. In his case, troglo-*dick*."

To my horror she picks up her phone.

"What are you doing?"

"Calling him."

"Don't!"

Gretel always loosens up after a glass of wine. "You're not the boss of me," she says, as she used to when we were little. She hums a nursery rhyme while she waits for him to pick up. "Andrew? It's your soon-to-be-ex-sister-in-law. I hear you've reverted to troglodyte."

Shit.

She rushes on and he must be too stunned to hang up. "Selkie's with me – but you probably know that already. A troglodyte with tentacles. If you had her followed, tell your spook there's a good curry house opposite the station, open late. But I wouldn't recommend the station toilets – or the bushes in the park for that matter. Too many troglodytes. Not that it would bother you. But that's not why I'm calling. Selkie is leaving Sydney tomorrow and she's not coming back. Nothing to do with your trog tactics. So you can call off your henchperson, go back into your cave, and save your money for the property settlement."

She bangs down the receiver and we crack up.

"How'd I do?" She's choking on her wine.

"Not bad." I can hardly speak. "You could have varied the insults a little."

"Too many trogs?"

I nod. "You've been wanting to give him a serve for

years, haven't you?"

"A serve? A serve?" Her voice escalates. "That wasn't a serve. That was a slap on the wrist with a limp lettuce leaf."

To my horror she calls him back.

"I've got a new baby in this house, Andrew. It makes me super jumpy. If I see any trogs lurking in my garden, I'll be straight onto Barry's uncle – the deputy commissioner of police."

***

After breakfast Gretel drops me at the station. My trip to the airport is uneventful but I still feel wary and tense. Last night insomnia fuelled my paranoia. By venting her anger, Gretel told Andrew too much. If he knows I'm flying out today he can probably find out where I'm going.

While I'm waiting for my flight, there's time to phone Derek.

"If only Stella hadn't called until your Dad's condition was assessed," he says. "And if only you hadn't gone to the house. But I don't see how Andrew can threaten you in France. The Paris apartment's booked in my name, then we're staying with Fabienne."

The Being Sleek seminar. Shit. If Andrew googles me, I'm all over the Séminaires Tours website, plus the ads on business blogs and Twitter. He doesn't need to have me followed; in just over two weeks he'll know exactly where I am. I can't believe I didn't think of it.

But bullying me on foreign soil would be a whole new ball game. Surely he won't risk doing anything illegal. No, he'll just do things to frighten me.

A three-word text from him confirms it: *Bon voyage, Elkie.*

***

When we touch down at Charles de Gaulle airport without having been hijacked to a war zone courtesy of Andrew's network, I can't quite believe it. For the next few weeks France is going to be my home, and the seminar tour will fill my bank account and restore my dignity. *Parfait.*

Even though I know he won't be arriving until tomorrow, I step into the terminal imagining Derek perched on a café stool, a croissant in one hand, a hot chocolate in the other, a beret on his head and a Gauloises between his lips. The apartment he's booked is off Boulevard Saint-Germain, right in the heart of Paris. I take the expensive option of a taxi, blowing most of what's left of the promoter's advance. It's paid for the changes to my flight and the retainer for Judy. Now all I've got to do is earn it – the one thing I can rely on.

The taxi drops me in the steep narrow street, and without any luggage to speak of I ignore the rickety old lift and take the spiral stairs to the top floor. Behind the heavy front door there are two bedrooms, a kitchen, a *salon* full of antique furniture and a terrace overlooking the city's skyline, including the Eiffel Tower. How did Derek find this place?

It's still daylight and I'm desperate to settle into this home away from home with its complimentary champagne and olives, but I make myself walk off the jetlag. I wander down the hill, feeling free from Andrew for a while. The surrounding three-storey buildings have tiny shops at street level selling all manner of quirky merchandise and I press my nose to the windows, mentally choosing gifts for everyone I can think of. The afternoon is sunny so the full-length windows of the apartments upstairs are open, and cats with enigmatic expressions manage to look comfortable as they perch on the wrought-iron railings.

On reaching a large intersection, I stop at an outdoor table in the sun and order a carafe of rosé. Around me, stylish couples meet on street corners, cigarettes bobbing as they chat. The women are slender and fabulously dressed, and the men have a rakish way of wearing casual jackets. The wine arrives with a basket of baguette slices and a bowl of olives, allowing me to sit and people-watch the rest of the day away. There's water on the table, but the wine is lighter than I'm used to and it slips down easily.

When the sun drops behind the magical skyline, I'm ready to crash but suddenly starving. I follow the crowd into a maze of crooked pedestrian alleyways between Boulevard Saint-Germain and the Seine. They're paved with cobblestones and lined with eateries of every nationality. The three-course menus on easels in every doorway are surprisingly cheap. I ignore the Greek, the Moroccan, the Lebanese, and choose a café offering French food. Mushrooms in garlic, duck a l'orange, crème caramel. Then I make it back up the hill to the apartment and bed.

The phone wakes me, and when I hear Nigel's voice my stomach does a somersault.

"Something's happened to DD," I wail.

"Just his toe," Nigel says. "Not too serious, more inconvenient. He's broken it. In four places."

My skin prickles. "How?"

"He was on the kitchen counter, changing a light bulb. When he climbed down he bumped the fruit bowl and it fell on his foot."

The heavy wooden fruit bowl I collected in my sleep. Shit.

"He's got to have surgery. And he won't be walking – or

travelling – for a few weeks."

I sigh. "Thanks, Nige. Send DD my love and commiserations. And ask him how many idiots does it take to change a light bulb." Then I get a thought. "He can't walk, I get that. But he can talk, can't he?" Derek can always talk. "Why didn't he phone me himself?"

Nigel hesitates. "He's...calling it an omen. It's one of your seven objects, so he thinks it jumped off the counter and crushed his toe...on purpose."

Bloody hell.

"And why would the bowl want to keep DD at home?"

Nigel sighs. "You know what he's like. He thinks that deep down you don't want him along on your quest."

What quest? The quest to get as far away as possible from Bantry's Bluff? The quest to fill my bank account and try to belong somewhere for five minutes?

"He's hurt because he thinks I pushed the bowl onto his foot? To exclude him from all the fun?"

"Not literally. Psychically."

"*He's* hurt? What about me, for being misjudged? I'd be pretty cruel to stop him visiting Paris. He'd adore it here."

"I know. He's being irrational."

"What do you think – about the psychic sabotage?"

"I don't know," Nigel says. "Your hunt for the objects showed a lot of intent...and we're guessing what any of those things means. You said the bowl represents a doorway-"

"Not literally. Psychically. You fill it with bad feelings and when you swirl it they disappear."

"Well, DD isn't going anywhere so the accident could be just that. An accident. It works for me."

"Thanks, Nige. Tell DD I miss him."

It's still early and I try to go back to sleep, but now that

I know Derek's not coming, I think I hear the call of the butcherbird. As I lie in my rented Parisian nest, it's singing my loneliness all the way from the Australian outback.

CHAPTER
Fifteen

I wander the streets of Paris feeling lost and alone. The city isn't the cause. It's everything I imagined – classic architecture down every narrow street, just like in my dream, covered passages hiding charming cafés and galleries, cosy restaurants tucked into corners and basements, outdoor markets with everything from pig snouts and duck eggs to vintage jewellery and espadrilles, fashion boutiques with window displays as quirky and confident as the Parisians themselves, tiny specialist shops dedicated to retro kitchen gadgets or millinery or a hundred kinds of cheese, and everywhere gardens and trellises and window boxes ablaze with spring flowers. No, it's not Paris that's wanting; it's me. With no-one to share its wonders, it seems to be mocking me.

As I sit on the tiered steps of a church one lunchtime, sharing a pocket of sunshine with laughing office workers, the language barrier exposes my isolation and the realisation hits me. It's the first time I've been alone. Really alone. In my life. From my teen years I was with Andrew, 'safe' in his control. When I took off to Hawaii, I lost that safety but not for long. Wanda was there, looking for a room-mate and a friend. Then Derek stepped out of the office next door and became my guardian angel. Even when I was missing for those two weeks, I wasn't alone. Wherever I was, there were 'others'. They were close enough to touch me.

Part of me wants to escape, back to Hawaii and Derek's bedside, but that's what I always do when things get tough.

Run. And on the practical side, I've spent the advance from the promoter. I'm trapped.

In my despair, I try to remember why I came to France. It was the only offer of a seminar tour – a way to earn serious money and give myself a base for a while. And the objects I collected pointed me to France. Not the bowl, but the spoon and the lipstick. And the dream. In it, I was trying to escape from the man with the bucket, turning away from the sign to Paris. Now I'm running away from Andrew, and I'm trapped in Paris. Has it all been a mistake? My so-called intuition kicking me in the guts? Was it warning me not to go to Sydney, not to come here, and in my desperation for money I misread the signs?

Davina's words come back: "There's somewhere else you're meant to go, to complete whatever you've started." What have I started? If I can't remember, I don't know. And now I'm stranded, a stranger in a foreign place.

Thrashing over the same old questions and the same old glimpses of the same old missing memories gets me nowhere, so I fill my days with distractions. Anything to mask my loneliness. Anything that's free.

I blow thirty cents on the weekly *Pariscope* guide and learn to ride the metro, travelling from one end of the urban sprawl to the other. But my predicament is the air I breathe; every experience is filtered through it. I'm not trapped in Paris; I'm trapped in my own mental malaise. One lunchtime I take in a free concert in a church not far from the Louvre. As I sit surrounded by a motley bunch of the less-sophisticated denizens of this city, an English soprano in a strapless gold dress fills the nave with lofty notes, while a male accompanist in ripped jeans and dreadlocks beats out a rhythm on a tea chest. The incongruity of the pair mirrors my alienation: an Australian woman with a Celtic name, called first to a Hawaiian beach, now in the centre of French culture. I'm like Nigel's cousin Rupert, leaving parts of my soul in distant places. Where do I belong?

***

Derek's silence continues, intensifying my sense of abandonment. Keith and I exchanged contact details at our last meeting, and I'm so needy that I Skype him almost straight away.

"How's the memory coming along?" he asks.

I should have predicted this–scratch a psychotherapist...

"I'm working on it," I lie. "Can we talk about something else?"

"Sure. Daisy sends a tail-wag and a tongue-slurp."

I manage to laugh. "Unconditional love."

"The only kind there is."

"How do you know they're for me?"

I'm not feeling very lovable.

"A confession. A little piece of your rock fell out of that crack when I rubbed it, and I kept it. Daisy sniffs it and licks it and bangs my chair with her tail. She remembers you."

"That's me – a chip off the old rock."

At that moment Daisy's smiling face fills the screen.

"The trip to the cliff was a big adventure for her," Keith says.

For both of us. That ceremony with the rock spoke to me. Spoke to my emptiness. But if I get into that with Keith I'll ruin everything by blubbering. For a guy who can't see, he sees way too much.

He remembers Paris from his youth and wants to hear about the concerts. I do my best to channel the music into words.

"What about Notre Dame?" he asks. "They do concerts."

"They also do queues around the block."

"That's to wander through, but they do music as part of their services. You have to gaze up at that ceiling, Selkie, and be serenaded by the voices of angels at least once before you die."

He was spot on about the butcherbird so I promise to give it a go.

The apartment is walking distance from Notre Dame, down the hill to the Seine and across a pedestrian bridge. The cathedral isn't just an architectural marvel to be admired by the lines of tourists snaking through the roped-off side aisles. It's also a working church and tonight, as part of vespers, there's Gregorian chant.

As I sit in a pew, dwarfed by the vast cavernous dome and surrounded by strangers, I wonder what I'm doing here. I don't need a reminder of how insignificant I am. In a hundred ways, the universe has shown me that. Then my thoughts are erased by voices - soft at first, then louder - as a procession of monks comes down the centre aisle behind me, chanting psalms. The humble beauty of their harmonies is so moving, I start to cry. As they echo through the soaring space above me, I feel something - and it overwhelms me. The depths of my own fragmentation, the loss of my absent parts, the pressing need to find home.

Afterwards, I return to my rooftop eyrie with a baguette, some brie and two bottles of cheap red. I pull on my little black dress and lie on the terrace, listening to the strains of the butcherbird over and over. I bought the app so I could wallow in the heartbreaking beauty of its solitary call, revelling in the feelings of longing that the poignant notes evoke, letting the tears flow. It's the longing I felt in the cathedral. Longing for something I've lost. Not the dress. That was buried, and now I've got to dig deeper. Something I can't remember. Something that started at Bantry's Bluff and followed me across the globe.

At dawn, I wake beside the two empty bottles, shivering under a layer of dew.

***

Derek finally gets in touch. His email tells me he's marooned on the sofa with his foot in a moon boot, but he's sent me a ticket. To the Moulin Rouge.

You've got to go, he says. *It's the prophecy of the lipstick.*

Is it? Like the prophecy of the bowl? Or is Derek trying to manipulate destiny from his sofa?

I want to be excited – the Moulin Rouge is the most famous spectacle in Paris – but when I see the ticket, the lipstick morphs into an omen. So far the objects I collected haven't formed any kind of pattern. The bowl, the mutton-bird and the rock all symbolised a journey. Done that. Twice. But Moulin Rouge is very specific and that spooks me. If I submit to the pull of Moulin Rouge, I fear I'll be tempting fate, setting in motion a chain of events that causes the other objects – the spoon, the sheet and the cryptic words – to deliver a tsunami of consequences.

Part of me wants to drink myself into numbness again, but another part descends to the street and catches the metro. To the Moulin Rouge.

It's a gorgeous night, and the old red windmill that houses the show is ablaze with an excess of glitz. People are forming queues at the entrance. I hover on the fringe, watching the crowd. There's still time to change my mind.

A tourist coach is unloading seniors, and as they trail up to the entrance I hear English conversation. It's enough. With a sudden rush I join them, and I'm inside and forgetting the consequences.

I'm ushered to a tiny elevated table with an uninterrupted view of the stage. Below me patrons are surging in to take their seats at long tables. A waiter rushes past and deposits champagne and glasses on my table with a thud. One bottle, two glasses. They seem symbolic. Only couples at other tables. But as I sip my champagne, my excitement mounts. I was never going to stay away.

A very camp MC called Augustine is warming up the crowd. Heavily made-up with glittered eyebrows and painted lips, he reminds me of Wanda's fish. He rushes from table to table, planting a pink kiss on bald heads and wrinkled cheeks, asking everyone to pronounce his name into a microphone: "Ow-gooss-teen". The patrons on the mezzanine are out of reach. I'm safe.

Behind me a man is chuckling. "It sounds like *langoustine* – to match the sea creature he looks like."

I know the voice. I open my mouth, then close it again as he sits down beside me. Alister Sloane.

"A *langoustine* is a shrimp," he says.

"Stop showing off your French and start telling me what the hell you're doing here." But I'm so elated to see him, I'm in danger of bursting into tears.

"Delighted to see you too," he says, pouring champagne into a glass for himself and topping up mine. "*Salut.*"

I've barely moved in case I do something stupid like throw my arms around his neck and ask him to marry me, but he clinks my glass and reminds me how impossible he is to discourage. We make a fine pair.

"Derek sent me his ticket," he says. "It's less than an

hour from London. I'll stay overnight and fly back tomorrow. I hear you've got a spare room." He winks.

Alister at my table after my week of abject despair is one thing, but not in my spare room. In my depleted condition I might not be responsible for my actions. But before I can say anything, the music heralds a fanfare of feathers and flesh. The show has begun.

Ninety minutes later we're on the street, making our way to the metro. Alister wants to show me a bar he knows somewhere in the Marais with an interior of 'art deco perfection'.

"What did you think of the show?" he asks.

I've been quiet. Because I'm still annoyed with Derek for keeping Alister a secret, but mainly because I hated the show.

I fend off the question. "It was definitely an experience. Not to be missed."

"That's what you tell Derek, Selkie. You tell me the truth."

"OK. Formulaic and soulless. Nothing like the Bollywood romp of Baz Luhrmann's film."

"Is that all?"

"The girls – they look like clones." Baring their fried-egg breasts so often it's boring.

"That's their job, to be identical. Slim and athletic. I've heard they have to weigh in every week or they're out."

"Yeah, so they can perform that robotic choreography night after night. Dancing should be wild and free."

Alister smiles and I realise I'm sounding hysterical. But who are these girls when they go home in the early hours? I imagine them stripped of their sequins and feathers, fighting off pawing suitors at the stage door, then returning to lonely attic bedsits up endless flights of narrow stairs, where they shun the daylight and sleep off the night before with a padlock on the fridge. But why do I care?

The metro arrives and we travel in silence. There are some strange travellers at this hour but I feel safe with Alister.

He tries another subject. "Tell me about Sydney. Derek said your dad's come through his ordeal. Which explains why you're here and not there."

"His *ordeal* turned out to be a digestive problem – one that looks like a heart attack if your name is Stella."

"Your stepmother?"

"Yep. She can still get me to jump through flaming hoops."

"Robotic choreography."

That makes me laugh. "Yeah, the family fandango. Not even a feather to hide behind. If I don't weigh in, I'm out. And with Stella, I'm way off the scales before I start."

"But you want to be out, don't you? If Sydney was never home."

He's back to the personal stuff. After we told each other too much last time.

"Wanting out of Sydney is only the beginning." I think of Andrew and feel a chill.

"A journey of a thousand steps," Alister says. "Unfinished business. First Honolulu. Then Sydney. Now Paris."

"You make me sound like a vagrant. There's unfinished business. But there's also...business."

Thank God for the seminar tour.

"And that's the only reason you're here, so soon after you disappeared? To introduce the French to Being Sleek?"

I'm about to joke that the French have got sleekness handled when the penny drops. Derek. He's ratted. The bowl stopped him from being here in person so he's sent a spy. It's why he didn't tell me in advance.

"What's DD told you? Whatever it is, it's none of your business."

"He had the spare ticket for tonight and he knew I was in London. He thought you might appreciate the company."

"I do appreciate it. But why? What did DD tell you...about Moulin Rouge?"

He sighs. He's too honourable to lie, even to be evasive. "He told me about the lipstick. Those things you gathered in your sleep."

"Shit."

"He sent me photos."

"Since when was my private life shareable, Alister? DD had no business sharing it - I'll be dealing with him. But you - you had no business colluding with him either."

"You're right. And I'm sorry. But before you explode, see it from our side. After you vanished on us, with no explanation, after we kept watch for two weeks, and you came back - thank God - but with amnesia, we *were* involved. Then, in your sleep, you go and gather those strange things and they're all pointing towards a journey - and you choose France, a place that's new to you. Of course we're going to...keep an eye on you."

My isolation flips - now it looks like freedom in a playpen. This is much more than Derek breaching a confidence; I've had a band of guardians ready to jump on the next plane.

We've arrived at the Marais, but I won't get off. Alister's little speech hasn't brought me round. I'm furious. On the way back to Boulevard Saint-Germain he tries to get me to talk, but I'm too angry, too ashamed that they all see me as vulnerable, as someone who needs a minder in case I 'lose myself' again.

Outside my building, I start to turn the key in the lock, then spin around and face him. "Is that why you went to London? So you were only an hour away – if I got into trouble?"

I've warned him before that I'm trouble with a capital T, but he's said it's the trouble that interests him. It would be funny now, if it wasn't the opposite.

"The London trip was planned months ago," he says. "That's the truth. The caper with the Moulin Rouge was Derek's idea, after he sensed you were...dancing on the edge."

What's wrong with that? Dancing should be wild and free.

"I know you're feeling humiliated and betrayed," he adds. "We made a mistake not confiding in you. But don't lose sight of the bigger picture. Our...love."

"I'm a big girl, Alister." I can get wasted on the terrace all by myself.

"You know I want to be part of your life," he says.

"Well, you're making a hash of it so far."

He looks grim. "What do you want me to do?"

"Treat me with respect. It's the one thing I've learned from Stella – respect is more important than love."

Unless it's a tail-wag and a tongue-lick.

I watch him walk down the hill.

CHAPTER
Sixteen

Derek tries the same arguments as Alister. "You make it sound like either/or – respect or love. What about going for both?"

"Love comes with strings, DD. Respect doesn't. When you respect someone, you don't collude behind their back. Such...treachery is impossible."

"Treachery's a strong word."

He's hurt, but also chastened. A few days ago he was accusing my subconscious of the same thing with the bowl.

"Call it tough love," I say.

He laughs. He knows we're through the hard stuff. As long as he doesn't send any more spies.

Flipping to a safer subject, I say, "I need some new shoes for my little black dress." He knows the other pair got ruined by the bag-snatcher.

"There's great shopping in Tours," he tells me. "Fabienne says they've got more shoe stores per square kilometre than any other place on earth."

"Tour?" I ask, copying him. "Where's Tour?"

"The city where Fabienne lives. On the Loire. About an hour from Paris by train. It's where you're doing your seminar, Selkie."

My seminar? Singular?

"Remember, the promoter's called Séminaires Tours?" he adds.

"Spell Tours." I feel sick.

He spells it. The 's' at the end is silent.

"I thought they offered seminar *tours*, as in more than one seminar. Now you tell me Tours is the place."

How could I be so unprofessional? I was in such a dizzy state surviving in Honolulu that I grabbed the French offer like a life raft and took all the dates as bookings rather than options. If I'd checked the schedule – as I do now – I would have seen it. One event. In Tours.

"I've been counting on doing a seminar tour," I say, trying to keep the panic from my voice. Thank God I'll be saving on living expenses at Fabienne's.

"Oops," Derek says. "Let's pray that you draw a crowd."

***

It's time to leave Paris – a place where I've grieved for my missing memory, a place that's highlighted my sense of belonging somewhere else. Wherever I'm going, this isn't it.

As if to mirror my inner journey, getting to Montparnasse to catch the train to Tours involves navigating a complicated maze of underground walkways. The wheels on my new suitcase get a workout as I try to keep pace with the crowd. On one set of stairs, an arrogant idiot lets go of his enormous bag and it flies down the steps, making everyone leap aside like skittles while he laughs. It just misses knocking me over. Another omen?

It's mid-afternoon when I get out of a cab in a narrow street lined with tightly parked cars. Fabienne's place is in the old centre of Tours, on a cobblestoned lane closed to traffic. This is the artisan quarter, a maze of alleys lined with cafés and bars and studios. I pass a violin maker and a textile artist as the wheels on my bag bump over the cobbles.

The building is old and half-timbered, leaning towards its neighbours as if confiding secrets from its past. Fabienne is a sculptor, with a studio at street level and an apartment above. She's away for a few days and has left a key with a neighbour, an old woman who nods blankly at my French. She unlocks the ancient wooden door and we enter a stairwell full of bicycles. The staircase is steep and narrow and I remind myself to check out the fire escape.

The old woman ushers me inside and leaves me with the keys. Feeling like a voyeur, I drop my things and explore. What will Fabienne's home tell me about her? The opposite of what my home-in-a-suitcase says about me?

The living room is dazzling in bold colours, and spring light bathes the mismatched furniture in gold. It looks onto a private garden framed by ancient stone walls and climbing roses. There's no balcony, just an ornate wrought-iron railing at knee level as I throw open the full-length windows to the sun.

What I assume are Fabienne's artworks occupy every surface. Unlike Wanda's homespun resin fish, her style is eclectic, using metal and pottery and glass and found objects. Some resemble animals, naive and elongated, reminiscent of prehistoric art. Others are more surreal, their flowing lines reminding me of Chagall. I take photos of everything for Wanda. A ghetto dedicated to artists, an apartment of quirky sculptures – she'll think I've gone to heaven.

The other rooms are compact and functional. A bedroom with a double futon, a tiny kitchen with a washing machine beside an ancient sink, a small walk-in pantry, a narrow hallway leading to a bathroom and separate toilet. Opposite the front door there's a central storeroom-cum-closet, where Fabienne's clothes are as flowing and vibrant as her art.

I'll be sleeping on the sofa bed in the living room –

another spare bed to taunt me. But I take in my colourful surroundings and swap the wave of emptiness for gratitude.

When I call the people at Séminaires Tours, they're pleased that I'm in town. They won't have to worry about a room full of attendees with their presenter stuck in a departure lounge somewhere. I ask for directions, then walk to their office overlooking the main boulevard.

We discuss the arrangements, and they're happy with the enrolment rate, inspired by my mermaid exposure. They'll continue with their promotion, hoping to fill the room to its capacity of two hundred people, mostly from the UK. Holding my breath, I ask about the chance of a second seminar. They're unlikely to get the numbers, they say. It's a blow. My earnings will pay for Judy and not much else. But if the property settlement isn't delayed, I should be able to stay afloat.

Afterwards, I cruise down Boulevard Béranger past the town hall - a magnificent specimen of classic French architecture overlooking a roundabout blooming with flowers - and stop outside the seminar venue, a jarring modern building called Vinci, after Leonardo da Vinci who had a connection with the region. Its roof soars like one of the sails of the Sydney Opera House. The seminar people told me there was quite a stir when it was commissioned from a famous architect, but its conference spaces are excellent.

***

With Fabienne away, I'm on my own. But there's Being Sleek to work on, and the thought of presenting it again is grounding me more than ever. I've only presented it as a trial once before, and it took me over in a kind of trance.

This time the seminar is a whole day in front of a much bigger audience and I can't rely on the muse hitting me like that again. I rack my brain trying to remember what happened during the trance, so I can take charge of shaping it this time around.

Derek thinks I'm trying too hard. "Relax," he tells me during a Skype session. "If you put it in a straightjacket, that's how it'll feel to the audience. Do an outline, then let the workshop flow on the day. It's what made it so magic last time."

Magic. That's easy for him to say. He wants me to recapture it by learning how to meditate.

"Cross your legs and close your eyes," he says. "After some practice your mind goes quiet."

He's not here to make me try, and I'm strangely resistant to doing it. Resistant and afraid. Since I cut myself loose from Andrew, my mind's gone quiet several times and amazing things have happened. So why won't I give it a go?

"You're afraid of losing control," Derek says.

He's right, but it's more than that. A fear that I've had before comes back. The fear of disappearing again. Going into a meditative state feels like a doorway into the unknown. Like stepping into a virtual bowl and spinning myself into oblivion. Until I remember where I was for those two weeks, I won't risk getting lost again.

Derek asks how I'm spending my time.

"Working on the seminar, DD. It's my job." And my sanity.

"But you're in France. They're masters at the art of balance." He rattles off a few recreation ideas then stops. "This is hard work. What do *you* want, Selkie?"

"To feel like I'm living here."

Meaning, not just...passing through. But how can I do

that with only one seminar?

"You want to feel a little French?"

"Yeah. Slim, sophisticated, confident –"

He laughs, saving me from having to get into the whole 'home' thing, which is what this is really about.

"This won't make you sophisticated," he says, "but Tours is the centre of French language. Enrol in a French course."

It's a mad idea but it resonates. Learn some French and be part of the rhythm of life.

I start with some brochures from the tourist office that I'd tossed in the corner, then go online. There are several language schools in Tours, but only two take casual enrolments.

I dial a number and the woman who picks up speaks French – and keeps speaking French even when I speak to her in English. We end up laughing, and she pronounces an address slowly down the phone.

The school takes up three storeys in an old building overlooking Place Plumereau, a buzzing square five minutes walk from Fabienne's apartment. I walk through the crowds sitting at outdoor tables shaded by enormous umbrellas, and find the entrance in a narrow lane. The woman I spoke to on the phone hands me a program outline in English. When we're done, I'm enrolled in a small class for two hours of French for the days I've nominated, starting on Monday. She sends me downstairs to the ATM and I withdraw the last of my cash reserve to pay for it. Only pocket money left.

Upstairs again, students are surging out of classrooms into the narrow corridors for morning break. There are a lot of Asian faces – Korean send Japanese. Then I hear an Australian accent.

"*Bonjour*," says a tanned blonde at my shoulder. News of my enrolment has travelled fast. "*Moi, c'est* Cherry," she giggles, and kisses me on both cheeks. "Although I get *chérie* around here, which is OK by me."

She's tall and slim, and in a few minutes over coffee from a vending machine I learn that she's been crewing with her boyfriend on a luxury yacht in the Mediterranean. But a few weeks ago she was accepted for the chorus line at the Moulin Rouge.

"Rouge is my colour," she jokes. "Cherry red."

She's been doing a crash course to improve her French and, as I dismiss the Moulin Rouge connection as coincidence, she invites me to join the school's excursion tomorrow afternoon.

"This week's a *château* and a panto. They like you to get a bit of culture with your grammar. With a name like yours, you must be into fairytales."

"Fairytales?"

"They're big on *son et lumière* around here – sound and light shows. Most of the *châteaux* do them. History for the tourists. But this one's a bit different – a French fairytale."

When Cherry repeats the word 'fairytale' I know I've got to go – with a name like mine, and a whole bunch of symbols creating a path across the globe like Hansel's and Gretel's crumbs through the forest.

As Cherry returns to class she points to the noticeboard, where I write my name on the list. The last place on the minibus is mine.

*****

I wake from a dark place where a single candle projects a vast shadowy being onto a wall. In the dream the troglodyte is passive, but when I open my eyes a sense of portent overcomes me.

There's been no word from Judy, which suddenly seems odd. I email her for an update and an automated message informs me she's at home with the flu. It's dated a week ago. No wonder she hasn't been in touch. Doesn't she get a vaccination? At her age? And who the hell's keeping tabs on Andrew?

It's Andrew's style to use silence as a weapon. Whenever I had the nerve to cross him, he'd freeze me out for weeks until I begged forgiveness just for existing. Now, like the shadowy figure in the dream, he's gone quiet, letting me think it's over. But it's never over with Andrew.

I thought the increase in my Twitter followers was due to the publicity for the seminar, but at some invisible signal they launch a cyber attack. Andrew's been gathering his online forces. Not only a troglodyte, the man I married is a troll. A very subversive troll.

The best part of her seminar-cum-circus? When Selkie the skinned seal balances a ball on her nose! A photoshopped picture of me illustrates.

Sleek rhymes with freak. And weak. Will the real Selkie come out of hiding in time for the show? The photo shows me cringing under a table at a party, terrified that the guys were going to throw me in the pool.

The French word for seal is phoque pronounced fock. Being Sleek is best described as...PHOQUED. For this one he's found a tasteless stock photo of copulating elephant seals.

Over a drunken evening of 'Elkie' bashing, all his mates must have brainstormed a hundred abusive tweets, while Andrew's gone through our old photo files and pulled out anything ugly. As the taunts invade my stream, it's clear they've been programmed to tweet every few seconds, rotating from a dozen fake identities. I stare at the screen in a state of advanced desiccation. In a flash the tweets have sucked me dry and Andrew's bucket is brimming. I reach for my cowry shell, hoping for an antidote, but it's too late. I'm fading away.

Derek phones. He's been spying on me.

"I've got no idea what to do," I sob down the phone.

He laughs. He's been on the couch so long he's itching for action. "Let's turn the tables on the trolls," he roars.

Nigel alerts Twitter to the bombardment, while Derek whips up a press release. *Seminar Siren Attacked by Cyber Trolls* his headline screams.

My juice is back. I call Séminaires Tours, who start tweeting a counter-offensive using images from my mermaid moment. *Jealous competitor attacks #BeingSleek seminar. Turn the tables on the troll. Enrol now.*

Tweets in support flood my stream, and on the Séminaires Tours website the enrolment 'thermometer' rises rapidly. Then my phone starts running hot.

"I don't know who could be doing this," I say in each thirteen-second grab, "but professional jealousy just spreads the word about my seminar. And while the trolls choke on their tweets, I'm...Being Sleek."

If Andrew wanted to promote me on the international seminar circuit, he couldn't have done a better job. It's morning here, late afternoon Sydney time. He'll be witnessing the collapse of his campaign in real time.

A text comes through from Alister. He's in London, watching it unfold.

The trolls are hoisted with their own petards. Well done you.

I'm about to reply that it's really been everyone else, when a wave of emotion hits me. I've barely thought about Alister since we parted in Paris under a cloud. He's still keeping his eye on me, and I should be angry but I'm not – because it's attention with plenty of space? His offer of a room in London comes to mind and I think about hiding there, hiding from all this notoriety. Is that what I was doing when I was missing – hiding? But hiding would turn me into a troglodyte too. I send him a smiley face because I don't know what to say.

On the other side of the world, Derek has opened a bottle of bubbly. "Here's to your seminar *tour*," he says. But I've got to stay sober for the calls.

When the tweets from the trolls suddenly stop, the US is just waking up. The wave continues and people start enrolling from New York. Séminaires Tours adds another seminar to my schedule, and another, using the dates we originally canvassed. They'll keep filling seminars until it's over, but I'm done. In spite of the ordeal, I'm energised by beating Andrew and he's not going to spoil my excursion to the *château*. I look at my watch. There's just enough time for a shower.

CHAPTER
Seventeen

The bus leaves the Friday traffic in Tours and soon we're hurtling along narrow country roads that wind through hilly farmland and tiny picturesque villages. Cherry and I sit together.

"Why the Moulin Rouge?" I hear myself ask. The thought of her as a robot dancer doesn't fit with her bubbly individuality.

"It's been my dream ever since I was a precocious little princess in Brisbane, all pink leotards and my hair in a bun. I even gave myself a stage name, Cherry Tart. The show-girl-in-waiting, aged five."

"I saw the show in Paris. It looks like...a lot of hard work."

"Yeah. That's the point. If you haven't got the drive to learn the routines like clockwork – and bare your boobs and parade in a headdress five nights a week – forget it."

"The vamp keeps the hours of the vampire?"

She nods and laughs.

"Where will you live?"

"Home will be the Moulin Rouge – that's where my heart is. I still can't believe I've cracked it."

Her words have a powerful effect on me. She's about to drop herself into a whole new milieu and surround herself with strangers, but she's going to make it home. Where her heart is. For the first time I wonder where my heart is. And where was it when I was missing?

"For sleeping," Cherry continues, "I'll be slumming it

for a while, till I get trained and into the bigger money. For now I've got a furnished attic studio in the eleventh arrondissement. Not glamorous. Cheap."

Just like I imagined. "Up how many flights of stairs?"

She laughs again. "Five. One of those rickety old French staircases. I'll have to stoop all the way. The bathroom's on the floor below, sharing with five students."

"And a padlock on the fridge?"

"Yep. You can't gain more than a kilo. Are you psychic?"

I realise I've been confusing all my nights on spare beds with my sense of homelessness, but they're just places to sleep. Home is something else, and Cherry agrees with Davina: it's a place to dance.

But without going back to Bantry's Bluff what do I do with the insight?

***

The *château* is at Loches, a charming town nestled in the surrounding hills. In the car park, our small group climbs out of the bus and walks across a drawbridge, the teeth of a huge portcullis rolled up above us. On the other side of the archway, we make our way along the stone blocks of the outer wall towards an enormous turreted fortress. It's the perfect place to stage a fairytale, and hard to believe people lived here.

Our teacher shows us through a heavy oak door and into vast rooms furnished with enormous dining tables or four-poster beds, each with a fireplace that must have consumed whole trees in one evening, and walls adorned with great tapestries of a trillion stitches. A steep stone staircase spirals upwards into a tower, leading us into a darkened hall. Ushers guide us to long wooden benches opposite a tableau of wax figures shrouded in shadow. It must be cold in here because I shiver. We scan our laminated guide-sheets and put on headphones for an English soundtrack.

"It's one of Perrault's tales," Cherry whispers.

"Perrault?" I ask.

"The guy who invented fairytales. He published a book of folk stories way back – in the 1700s – but he called them fairytales. Cinderella, Sleeping Beauty, Little Red Riding Hood, Puss in Boots – all the ones you know, they're all straight from Perrault."

"I've never heard of this one."

"Me neither. Creepy, isn't it? Donkey Skin."

As the title leaves her lips, something happens to my blood flow – a current races through my veins. If I was standing, I'd probably swoon. But before I can wonder, the audience goes quiet and the show begins.

The story is told in a series of vignettes, with spotlights illuminating each group of characters in turn and sound effects accompanying the narration. The king's wife has died, and to fulfil her wish that he marry a woman as beautiful as her, the king chooses his own daughter. The princess must escape this incestuous proposal, so she consults a fairy godmother – an old woman with gleaming eyes, who lives in a cave. The girl then sets her father a series of impossible demands, hoping to thwart his intentions. The king must produce a gown for her as stunning as the sky, then the moon, then the sun. Each time the king threatens his seamstresses with death, so one after another they produce a gown of exceptional splendour, as the lightshow demonstrates.

The tension in the music escalates as the girl becomes

desperate. The fairy godmother instructs her to demand the skin of the king's favourite animal – a donkey that excretes gold. The princess is sure it's a demand too far – the donkey is the source of the kingdom's wealth – but, to her horror, her father kills the animal and presents her with its skin. Now her only option is to run.

The audience gasps as the lighting effects show the princess cloaked in the donkey's filthy pelt, its head hiding her true identity. She wanders far from home and takes a job in a lowly kitchen, only removing the skin when alone in her room. The lights switch between her private beauty and her ugly outer persona. One day a prince visits the kitchen and spies her radiance through a keyhole. He asks who the beauty is but the kitchen staff laugh. "She's no beauty, she's Donkey Skin."

When Donkey Skin makes a cake for the royal table, her ring slips into the mixture and the prince makes every woman in the kingdom try it on until he tracks her down. Now Donkey Skin can shed her dirty false cloak and fulfil her destiny to marry the prince and be a queen.

Afterwards, as we descend the stone staircase, I lean against the wall for support. I'm trying to make sense of my reaction. Elements of the story are so familiar – the gowns, the animal skin, the whole identity thing, the girl's need to escape and her resulting homeless state – yet I've never heard the tale before. And when the fairy godmother appeared inside her shell-lined grotto, the lighting giving her eyes a sharp knowing look, it was as if I was looking at myself in Tutu's mirror.

Our little group walks through the maze of narrow lanes inside the castle walls. The evening light is making long shadows.

"I couldn't take my eyes off those gowns," Cherry says.

"But that donkey skin - God, how revolting."

I'm admiring the precision of the stone work, trying to pretend nothing strange just happened.

"The story's like Cinderella in a way," Cherry goes on. "The princess working in the kitchen, all the women in the land trying on the ring instead of the slipper."

"Yeah."

"And Beauty and the Beast in reverse - she can only show her ugly disguise in public, until the prince sees her beauty and breaks the spell."

"Hmmm."

"And what did you make of the fairy godmother? Her advice sucked, if you ask me. All those demands. Why didn't the girl use her own wits? Or just leave?"

"She was trapped. And afraid. That can make you...impotent." Sometimes for years.

"Impotent," she says. "Like the old man *wasn't*, the randy bugger. So hot for his own daughter he kills a donkey that craps gold. And all because the fairy godmother stirred him up."

"But Donkey Skin's father had all the power," I say, "and those demands exposed how ruthless he was. He was never going to let her go. The demands forced her to face the truth - that her only option was to run."

"OK. I get that. Sounds like you liked the old woman."

"I don't know. When they dimmed the lights, she was in that grotto surrounded by shadows, her eyes glowing. It felt -"

"Creepy."

That's not what I was going to say.

***

It's a matter of life and death. I'm running, running, running from something I cannot see. If only I can cross the sea, I'll be safe.

Just as panic is tightening my chest, a bridge appears like a rainbow, but a troll lives under the bridge, and if I try to cross he'll eat me. I rack my brain for three clever questions. If the troll can't answer one of them, I'll be free to cross.

"What colour is the sky?" I ask in wonky French. "*Bleu,*" says the troll.

"What colour is the sun?" I ask. "*Orange,*" says the troll.

Now I'm desperate. I've only got one question left.

"What colour is Selkie Moon?"

"*Gris,*" says the troll, baring his teeth. *Grey.* He thinks he's won but the answer is silver.

"Silver," I scream, but I don't know the word in French. It doesn't matter. He's going to eat me anyway.

Then something dark descends and I'm wrapped in eerie looming shadows. I think it's a pursuer, but then I'm crossing the bridge unseen. On the other side, relief flips to horror, then despair. The donkey skin saved me, but now it's stuck fast and I can't get it off.

Chapter
Eighteen

It's Saturday morning, so I shake off the dream and hit the *brocante* market just a stone's throw from Fabienne's apartment. With a seminar tour ahead of me, I should be working on Being Sleek, but after yesterday's emotional rollercoaster – and the dream – I need a cultural antidote.

Place de la Victoire is abuzz with stalls and patrons. Trestles and car boots and rugs on the ground display all manner of second-hand goods. Old gramophones and broken tools, vintage hand basins and costume jewellery, books and vinyl records stacked in boxes, and old clothes mounded on tables. Stallholders chat with their neighbours over cigarettes, ignoring the customers. It's their negotiation strategy – feigned indifference.

I'm cruising the improvised displays looking for jewellery and scarves – gifts to mail to Gretel and Wanda and Davina, even to Judy if she ever gets off her sick bed and deals with Andrew. At one table I get into a kind of conversation with an old lady who's fingering trinkets tangled in a box. "*Une bonne présentation,*" she says to me and chuckles. I'm thrilled because I understand. She's being ironic – dumped in a box is hardly 'well-presented' – but I can only laugh and reply, "*Oui.*"

As she moves away, I see the ducks: a set of six, each a tiny silver stand that sits beside a table-setting for your cutlery to rest on. I'll buy them for Nigel and call them mutton-birds. I begin to bargain in my best French but the stallholder lapses into English. We agree on twenty euros, which seems a fair price to me – until the man beams and I'm sure I've just been ripped off.

That's when a movement catches my eye – a woman turning away. A scarf covers her hair, but the face I glimpse behind the sunglasses is ringing a bell. She strides across the square and disappears down the alley towards the artisan quarter. It's her figure that makes me recognise her. Just like when I photographed her leaving my office. Genevieve.

The man is wrapping my parcel and I won't leave without it, so it's an excruciating sixty seconds before I can make chase. I take off across the square and dive into the alley she went down, running all the way to Place Plumereau and looking right and left down each narrow lane. Not a trace of her.

As I hobble on a twisted ankle back to Fabienne's, I remember that I've got form when it comes to being stalked by phantom women. My mind must be turning any French connections into visual tricks. But why am I thinking about Genevieve?

Over a baguette and coffee at the kitchen table, I open the parcel to look at Nigel's ducks. They're charming. After I collected his silver spoon that night, he told me about his soft spot for *brocante*. I rub my fingers over each one, admiring their simple shape and hoping he likes them. Then I drop one as if it's hot. It's not a duck. With trembling hands I pick it up and confirm that I'm not imagining it. On my palm is a tiny silver donkey.

The guy in the market must have put it there. Why? He was one duck short and slipped the donkey into the parcel when I was distracted by the phantom of Genevieve? But when I count the ducks there are six. And the donkey makes one more. Seven.

I pace for a while, then Skype Derek. He'll tell me it's

spooky, that seven is a magic number, that it isn't a coincidence – and he'll be right. It's got something to do with me. I'm the one who found the bloody ducks and bought them. I'm the one who felt compelled to go to see Donkey Skin and related to her plight. Or am I doing what Stella always accuses me of – imagining it's all about me?

Derek listens to the story of Donkey Skin and makes no comment about the seventh 'duck'. He's either sick or he's up to something. He limps away from the screen and returns with a torn and taped-together photograph. When he holds it up, I see a donkey.

"Why are you showing me this?"

He smirks. "Guess."

He's been doing this ever since Davina pronounced I've got 'psychic powers'. But my flashes of intuition don't come with a guide-sheet.

"Stop trying to make connections where there aren't any," I say in desperation. But after another look at the donkey pic, a word leaps out of my mouth. "Shit."

Derek grins. "Pony up."

"You mean 'donkey up'. It's the picture I tore up, isn't it? Of the mutton-bird?"

He nods. "The donkey was on the back." He remembered it from when he taped the mutton-bird back together.

"So it wasn't the mutton-bird I was collecting. It was the donkey."

"Looks that way." He makes his smug expression worse by adding, "Isn't this fun?"

We don't have Davina on tap, but Nigel's at home. Derek's in his element summarising the Donkey Skin tale for him. But when he starts to expound on the symbolism in the story, Nigel interrupts. "Selkie's turn."

I sigh. "Well, the only fairytale I know anything about is the selkie story. And Donkey Skin seems to be about the same thing."

"How?"

"They're both about identity theft. And escape." They listen as I think aloud. "In the selkie story, the man steals her sealskin so the selkie must live with him as his wife. Without her true identity, she's living in another skin – as a woman instead of a seal."

Just like the girl called Elkie was trapped in her marriage to Andrew.

"Makes sense," Nigel says.

"In Donkey Skin," I continue, "the king wants his daughter for his wife, but that's not who she is. It would be another form of imprisonment. And abuse. She tries to stop him with impossible gowns, but when he kills his precious donkey at her demand she's got no choice but to run."

In last night's dream, I was trapped in the skin that didn't fit – a mirror of my years with a family who couldn't 'see' me, who called me Elkie.

"The donkey skin is a false coat," Derek says, "but in the selkie story the sealskin is her true self."

"Yeah," I say. "I like that twist."

"It's the job of every offspring to leave home, to not be clones of their parents," Derek says. "That's what the story means."

But my mind keeps worrying away at the fairy godmother in the grotto. I tell myself that the look in her eyes was just a trick of the light. Light that threw shadows like my troglodyte dream.

"The donkey's one of the seven symbols," Derek continues. "You're on a journey, Selkie, and you're ticking them off one by one. The fruit bowl to keep me out of it, the rock you left behind in Sydney, the Moulin Rouge in Paris. Now Donkey Skin in the Loire."

"The Moulin Rouge wasn't destiny, DD. That was you, buying a ticket."

But Cherry gave me a fresh perspective on home. And the donkey image was in the seven symbols, I just wasn't aware of it. Its discovery now – after seeing the sound and light show – seems to confirm what DD wants to believe. That I am on some kind of quest, doggedly following the prophecy of my own subconscious even though I have no idea what it is.

***

It's time to get back to the seminar – something I've got control over. But first I check my inbox and find an email. From Genevieve.

I know you saw me. I'm not following you. I'll explain. Meet me at 3 at the Irish pub in Rue Colbert.

The Irish pub is hard to miss. Its garish facade of shamrocks wraps around the corner of a side street in the pedestrian precinct of Rue Colbert. I get there early, grab an outdoor table and order a beer and a bowl of *cacahuètes*. As I wait for three o'clock to arrive, thoughts about Genevieve swirl. She really is in Tours. I'm not psychic, just observant. But relief morphs into worry. In her email she made a point of saying she isn't following me, so what the hell is she doing here, in the very town where I'm running my seminar? It must be more than coincidence, bumping into her in the market like that. And why did she take off when I spotted her? She's had time to come up with a story.

Into my second beer, she arrives, wearing the same dress as this morning, but the scarf has slipped to her neck. She waves when she sees me, and signals to the waiter for a drink.

"I must have given you a fright," she says when she sits down.

"Only because you bolted. You looked familiar, but when you took off I recognised you." Or what I took for her phantom.

She picks at the peanuts in the bowl. She's got some explaining to do and I'm not going to make it easy. The waiter puts her drink on the table, and fishes the change from his pouch.

"I'm looking for Tony," she says. "I think he came back to France and I'm going to find him."

"OK." Meaning 'bad idea'. "But France is a big place."

What she tells me is strange. After losing Alister and hearing about my disappearance, she decided to get serious about looking for Gaston.

"I found a blog called On the Luce. It's a joke he used to use about himself, before he married me. I think the blogger is him."

"Is Luce an unusual name in France?"

"Not really."

"It could be anyone, Genevieve. It's an obvious play on words."

And the blogger could live anywhere. Why Tours?

"There's more. Tony loved to mix French and English. Goofy poems using both languages – *franglais*. He was good at it, made people laugh. The On the Luce blogger does it too."

She pulls out a tablet and opens a blog entry. It might be none of my business, but Gaston's story is nibbling at my edges like a jellyfish. What if he disappeared like I did, but woke up somewhere else and didn't remember who he was?

Just a name on a photocopied passport? Another victim of 'the curse of Bantry's Bluff'? "Amnesia only happens in bad movies," Derek said. But it happens. It's happened to me.

I shade the screen with my hand. The blogger calls On the Luce a *bloglo*, which I assume is a French word for blog. I read a few entries in the *franglais* Genevieve's talking about. Then I read them again.

A fenêtre and a lune, fenestrating one true trou, oh grand air.

Pain in my heart. Pain at my door. Baguettes à la porte. Any port in this orage. O'rage against my cage.

I don't understand the poetry but the emotion behind the words is palpable. I close my eyes, trying to zone in on the feelings, and a wave of revulsion envelops me, followed by paralysis. Suddenly I'm rigid in my chair.

Genevieve's voice brings me back. "Are you OK, Selkie?"

"Fine. Just exhausted. I've had a busy couple of days."

But as I take a slurp of beer, the message is clear. There's something unhealthy emanating from this *bloglo*. Is it foreboding...death?

Genevieve resumes her story. "I went through the things Tony left behind. I'd looked before but I wasn't thinking straight then – I just threw all his stuff in a box. This time I had a proper look and I found a postcard, from someone called Hugo. He never mentioned Hugo to me, and the message is smudged. But the postmark on the card...is Tours."

A postmark on a postcard and she dropped everything and rushed to Tours. Poor Genevieve. If Gaston really is alive, has he got any idea how much she loves him?

"That just means someone called Hugo was passing through Tours and sent him a postcard," I say. "It doesn't mean Gaston's here."

"You're here."

Bloody hell. She thinks I'm going to lead her to Gaston. She's gone a bit loopy since she found out we both disappeared from that beach but when a man's involved, any woman can lose her common sense. And Genevieve's got a big stake in the outcome.

"I can't help you," I tell her. "His disappearance has got nothing to do with me."

"I know that. It's just another...coincidence."

Something makes me look up and see what I missed behind the shamrocks - the name of this pub. Bantry's Bar. Shit.

"You chose this place on purpose," I say.

She nods. "I saw it on my way to the market. Then I saw you. It seemed...propitious."

This revelation calls for another drink. I signal the waiter and consider my predicament. I'm sitting at a table outside Bantry's Bar talking to Alister's ex about a string of coincidences linking me to her missing French husband. How did this happen?

"You said you weren't following me."

"I wasn't. I really didn't know you were even in France."

"It's all over my website."

"Yeah, I saw that when I went looking for your email address. It's why I ran off this morning. When I saw you in the market, I got one hell of a fright." She laughs. "You'll think I'm mad, but I thought you were a ghost."

She hasn't asked for my help. She's content that she's in the right place - that all the coincidences have lined up to put her in Tours. I don't tell her that my own convoluted journey indicates things are never that simple.

"What have you done with the twins?" I ask.

"With my sister. She's out of rehab so she's looking

after them, for a change."

Rehab from what? Alister was concerned about Genevieve's emotional state, so I hope her sister is more stable than she sounds. Five-year-old twins are a handful for anyone, but it's really none of my business.

"I've taken a month off work," she adds.

This is one serious agenda.

"What will you do now?" I ask.

"I've already looked in the phone book. There's no Gaston Luce, but there's someone called Hugo Luce. He's got a *brocante* business – vintage jewellery. That's why I was at the market this morning. I thought he might have a stall."

"Call him," I say. "You've got nothing to lose."

She shakes her head. "My French is terrible. What would I say?"

"Ask him if he's related to Gaston. I'll do it. Even I can understand *oui* or *non*."

I pull out my phone, but she stops me. She's desperate to find her man, but she's also afraid. The last five years – and the last few weeks – have taken their toll on her.

"It might be another coincidence," she says. "The wrong Hugo."

"So you're just going to hang around the markets, hoping to chance on his van?"

"Don't look at me like that. This is my mystery, not yours. I'm going to wait. It's how I want to play it. For now."

Her passiveness is reeling me in and I repeat her warning to myself: her mystery, not mine.

We kiss each other on both cheeks and wish each other luck. Then we walk down Rue Colbert in opposite directions.

Chapter
Nineteen

The undercover market is still open and I go mad over bread and cheese and wine and spring fruit. The raspberries are to die for. When I've unloaded it all in Fabienne's kitchen, I look at the time. Too early to start on a bottle. And I feel a bit queasy after too much beer in the sun. Instead I open my laptop, planning to review the latest activity for Being Sleek - but my fingers wander to On the Luce.

I peruse the entries over the last week, trying to make some sense of them. Being immersed in the local language helps a little - I recognise a few words. Then I get Fabienne's dictionary.

A fenêtre and a lune, fenestrating one true trou, oh grand air.

This feels poetic and wistful. A window and a moon making a hole in the air.

Pain in my heart. Pain at my door. Baguettes a la porte. Any port in this orage. O'rage against my cage.

'Pain' means 'bread' in French, which leads to *baguettes*. From *porte* meaning 'door' he moves to a port in a storm: *orage*. From *orage* he makes 'rage'. But what's his cage?

The more I read, the more the emotions behind the words get to me - not dread this time, but waves of sadness.

It's almost dark and I'm exhausted. There's some serious baggage emanating from these entries and I'm repelled, but also hooked. I turn on a lamp to dispel the unease, but what I need is some fresh air. As I walk the lanes of the artisan quarter, the lighted windows of my neighbours remind me of the fairy godmother's grotto. Glowing private spaces that give me secret glimpses into the places that other people call 'home'.

***

On Sunday Judy finally gets in touch.

"Sorry to call on the weekend but I'm trying to catch up. I've been nailed to my bed for eleven days." She laughs a gallows laugh that ends in a cough. "That's how the French put it – *clouée au lit*. It's the closest I've ever been to death."

She's oblivious to Andrew's Twitter attack.

"Another manoeuvre we can't nail him for," she says, sounding a little defeated. "He'll be sure to have covered his tracks."

"I keep worrying he's going to turn up here."

"I doubt it. He's the kind of coward who won't expose himself. But he'll be digging for dirt. Something to use against you in court."

"It's a no-fault divorce."

"Sure, but there's the property settlement. He can try to manipulate that."

Bloody hell. The troglodyte who won't die. I've turned the tables on him more than once. How many times have I got to do it? And what will he do to me next?

"He's let the house run down," I say. "Isn't that enough?"

"It's hard to think like a troglodyte, but I'm doing my best." She laughs with some of her old fire. "He could challenge a fifty-fifty split. Convince the court that you shouldn't get half, that your financial position is better than his."

"As if. On his salary and super."

We leave it there, agreeing to keep in touch, and I return to the *bloglo*. Against my better judgement. The deeper meaning of the words eludes me and that's part of the allure. But today's post confronts me with a word I wish I hadn't seen, and it's too late to avert my eyes.

Une prison troglodytique, une vie monastique. O bored of the precipice. O bored of this ennui.

The word *troglodytique* almost makes me faint. I read on. The blogger is talking about troglodytes and caverns and grottos.

May I tomber to my tomb? Sans hésitation? Mais mon courage m'abandonne.

The clue is I am cloué to ma caverne, to ma grotte.

Diminué I am, émasculé I am not.

The word *clouer* – to nail – is the word Judy just used. Trying to take account of the plays on words, I come up with a translation:

A troglodytic prison, a monastic life. On the edge of the precipice. Bored with this ennui.

May I fall to my tomb? Without hesitation? But my courage abandons me.

The clue is I am nailed to my cave, to my grotto.

I am diminished, I am not emasculated.

The English lacks the poetry of the *franglais*, but as I read it again an image comes into mind, an image I'll never forget. A replica from Michelangelo's Prisoner series, on display in Sydney's Central Station. I was crossing the concourse with my head down when an enormous lump of rock blocked my path. I looked up and saw above me a male figure trapped – half-sculptured and half-encased – in the stone. His predicament, his struggle to break free of his prison, was so palpable it moved me to tears. Tears for him, and for me, trapped as I was in my marriage.

The author of On the Luce is trapped in some way too. Desperation emanates from this poem and it speaks to me, because I'm still struggling to escape Andrew. And, on the flipside, I'm still struggling to discover where I belong.

***

The troglodyte returns in another dream. This time, I see more than his vast shadow flickering in the candlelight. It's clear by the deliberate movements of his arm that he's painting a wall, but no matter how I twist and turn I can't see what he's painting. By the morning I'm exhausted by the effort.

***

Judy steps up her pressure on Andrew and his lawyer, Reece Chapman. She sets a deadline for Andrew to get the house ready for market, or else an army of gardeners and cleaners and decorators will descend on Beach Road. Chapman is defiant, but Judy assures me that's standard. It will happen in the end, because Andrew won't want to relinquish control – or be humiliated in front of the neighbours.

I've befriended Juliet on social media, and although she rarely mentions Andrew – her independence is so refreshing – her photos provide occasional insights. In one he's wedging a trap beside the fridge, because he swears he's seen a mouse. *Try* in *the fridge*, Juliet writes. *Like, under the mouldy food.* Andrew – who used to shower twice a day and insist on a fresh towel every time – has stooped to this, all in the name of shafting me. What an inspiration I've turned out to be.

Keith and I keep in touch. He's back at work with his

war veterans, but his time with the elders has changed him.

"I keep going back to that cave and hearing the voices," he tells me. His own troglodytic moment. "I'd love to be able to look in a mirror, see if my eyes are different."

Like my eyes?

"What do you think you'd see?" I ask.

"A lighted window, into the heart of my experience. My eyes would look –" He casts around for the word.

"Replete?" I say. Where did that come from?

"Good word. Like Jung says, the cave...is now inside me."

I'm trying not to think about caves when he asks, "Are you back from that beach yet?"

"Not my memory, no. It looks like it may never come back."

"It will. You can't keep a lid on something like that. If you don't tease away at it gently, it'll knock you over like a tsunami."

"That's not very original, Keith – not with a name like mine."

"So stop avoiding it," he says.

***

The troglodyte with the paintbrush gives me restless nights, painting a message I'm not getting. After Donkey Skin I'm wary of the school's cultural experiences but I hear myself asking a teacher who speaks English, "There are lots of caves around here, aren't there?" She nods. "Could we visit some?"

"Sure. You're spoilt for choice in the Loire Valley, so name your *troglo*."

She suggests an excursion to a *château* with another

château buried underneath, and then a wine cellar in the tunnels where they harvested stone for the castles.

When the minibus heads off on Friday afternoon, I'm full of expectation that one of them will trigger an insight into my dream. But as I try to pick up vibes in the labyrinth of caves beneath the Château de Brézé I feel nothing but interest. And when we shuffle along the dark tunnels where champagne is aged, the automatic lights throw creepy shadows, but that's all.

"You might be dreaming of another kind of cave," Derek says when I share my disappointment.

"I've given up on caves, DD. I'm lucky I didn't bump into any troglodytes."

"But the caveman in your dream is painting something and France is full of prehistoric cave art. Remember Lascaux."

Some of Fabienne's sculptures remind me of cave art.

"I'll think about it."

"You've forgotten the rule of three," he adds.

Not the rule of seven, thank God. Otherwise I'd have to take out speleology insurance.

"Get a crystal and a map."

"What?"

"You know," Derek says. "Dangle the crystal over the map, when it starts vibrating you'll know which cave you're meant to visit."

The odd 'psychic twinge' might hit me, but I leave Derek to don't dabble in the downright ridiculous.

I thank him, and get back to cleaning the apartment and stocking the fridge. Fabienne is due back on Monday.

One of the language students gave me directions to the Asian supermarket and I take the bus there and fill my bag with ingredients for a stir-fry – the closest I can get to cooking Fabienne some Australian cuisine.

It's when I'm taking the rubbish downstairs that I glance into her studio and decide to take a peek. It's the biggest key on the key ring and I haven't been inside – it's felt too intrusive. Now I'm drawn to the enormous oak door and the cave-like space behind.

The tiny area is lit by a window from the alley. Shelves and floor are crammed with art materials and sculptures in various stages of completion, and there are canvasses stacked in a corner. But it's the sculptures that attract me and I move around touching them, enjoying the textures of wood and metal and glass, the pleasing angles of line and shape, the humour she's created as the materials collide.

One work-in-progress stops me – an enormous creation fashioned out of spoons. Dozens of spoons, exactly like Nigel's spoon – antique and silver. She's collected them one at a time by the look of the different designs – maybe from the *brocante* market. Several unused spoons lie in a box, waiting to join the others. I sit on the stool and gaze at the flowing lines of the sculpture. The spoons overlap in several threads that almost leap towards the ceiling, reminding me of seaweed. And there's something about it... Not just the spoons. Something else.

Grabbing an unused spoon and a length of fine chain from another box, I lock the studio and return to the apartment. Fabienne's got a laminated map of France on the kitchen wall. I lift it down and lay it on the floor. Then I tie the chain to the spoon handle. Derek said to use a crystal but I don't have one – and a spoon was on my list of seven. Trying to remember what he said, I hold the chain very still, letting the spoon dangle over the map. It's almost how I chose Hawaii after I won the green card, except then I used a blindfold and a pin.

I wait. Nothing happens.

"What's supposed to happen?" I yell.

No answer.

The spoon hangs like a dead weight and I feel myself relax - what's to fear from the divination qualities of spoons? I start at the top of the map and gradually move my hand horizontally from west to east, each sweep moving further south. As my hand passes the Dordogne region, the spoon starts to spin.

"Are you twirling it?" I say, like a sceptic at a séance.

No answer.

I move it away to the east, where it hangs still. When I move it back, it starts spinning again. Bloody hell.

I push my face into the map and read a place name: *Vézère Valley*. I peer closer and find dozens of red dots.

The Vézère Valley is a region full of caves and prehistoric art, Google tells me. The word 'art' sets my skin on fire. I need a map of the Vézère. Do spoons work over screens?

Within minutes, I'm advancing the map across the screen with my left hand, as the spoon in my right starts going crazy. I move it away and back again just to be sure, then I read out the name. Rouffignac.

CHAPTER
Twenty

After my French lessons, I catch the bus to the airport to meet Fabienne. I recognise her immediately from a photo on her shelf. Blonde, tanned, beautiful. She's wearing a turquoise midriff top with splashes of white over orange jeans and crocs. Her stride across the terminal shows she's comfortable with herself, like the rest of her nation. Is she older than me? Probably by ten years, but who cares? She's tall and lithe like a dancer and she's got skin that will carry her into old age with grace. I read somewhere that French woman regard each other as rivals, but I'm the one feeling jealous. Not of her beauty, of her poise.

She picks me out in the sparse crowd, no doubt for the opposite reason. "Selkie?" she says, before greeting me with kisses on both cheeks.

As I help her with her bags, she bombards me with accented questions. What have I been doing? Has her apartment been comfortable? Do I adore France?

On the bus, she knocks me over with her next question. "Why do you want to go to the Rouffignac?"

"What?"

She laughs at my confusion. "You have changed your mind?"

"No. I don't know." If she's psychic, I'll move out immediately. "How did you know?"

"You do not remember? You sent me a text last night. You asked me how do you get to Rouffignac."

No, I don't remember, but I pretend I do. She'll hardly

want to share her home with a somnambulant amnesiac. But it's about to come out anyway. I start with the spoon, and how Derek inspired me with his talk of crystals.

"Derek," she laughs. "He's a black donkey, yes?"

Shit. Did I text her about the donkey too? But Fabienne means something else. It takes a minute to work it out.

"A dark horse, is it?" she says.

I can't help laughing. "Yes, we do say that. But I wouldn't call Derek a dark horse."

"No?"

"He's more like...an open book."

She thinks she understands as I explain how predictable Derek can be. They know each other through an old boyfriend of Fabienne's who went to school with Derek, back in the days before Derek embraced the new-age with such gusto.

"So this thing with the spoon, this *divination* – is it the same word in English?" I nod. "Derek, he does it before?"

"I don't know. And I was the one who did it. But Derek believes in that kind of thing – that you can hold an object and get a message."

"It's special, this spoon?" she asks. "In your country?"

"No." I can hear Stella choking at the very thought. "I used an old French spoon."

Her hand goes to her mouth. "*Mon dieu*. Where did you get it?"

I tell her about the objects I collected, then how I borrowed a similar spoon from her studio. She's genuinely intrigued, so I describe the seven things and what's happened to them so far. She quizzes me about each one and counts them off on her fingers. The spoon is number five.

"Old spoons, they have long *histoires*," she says.

"Histories. Secrets. And they have the shape of a woman. That is why I am collecting them, for the sculpture I make – the Seven Sisters." She promises to explain later. "Only the holes in the sheet and the message are left. What did this lipstick say?"

"Nonsense words. Nothing that made sense." But I realise I haven't looked at the message again since that night.

She presses me about Rouffignac and I tell her about my latest dream.

"You see a caveman painting, but you cannot see what he paints? It is a mystery. It drives you crazy. And you think the answer is in Rouffignac?"

"The spoon thinks so."

We fall silent for a while, then I ask her about Tuscany, where she's been showing her work.

"It is good for the ego to be invited to exhibit, and I love to mix with the other artists. The camaraderie, it is very...easy. We understand each other."

I feel a 'but' coming.

"But...it does not pay the rent."

"Your sculptures are amazing, Fabienne. Doesn't everyone want to own one?"

"Sometimes, yes. But mostly they just like to...visit them."

That's when she tells me that to make ends meet she moonlights at the Vinci conference centre. She'll be on the team looking after the refreshments for my seminar.

***

"That nails it," Derek says when he hears about the spoon. "You've got to get into that cave."

"It's in the Dordogne, DD." Too hard to get there on my own. "I've gone online and seen what's on the walls in Rouffignac - horses, mammoths, bison." No donkeys. "What I don't know is what's on the walls in my dream."

"The Buddhists say, 'The finger that points to the moon is not the moon'. So photos of cave paintings aren't the same as the real thing, Selkie. No ambience. Or perspective. Rouffignac has stirred up a sleeping beast, and you won't know what the dream's about until you beard the lion in its den."

Derek does make me laugh. "Great metaphor, DD."

I'm not afraid of lions. Or mammoths. What am I afraid of?

***

Being Sleek is more than ready, so I turn my focus to the minute-by-minute details. Last time the seminar was an ecstatic experience - I abandoned my notes and dropped into a trance. This time I'm in charge of the program and, as the day approaches, my confidence grows that the participants will be blown away and I'll be awake to watch.

When the day arrives Fabienne leaves early to help set up the seminar room, and as I fold away my sofa bed, the old pang hits me. Each evening I pull out the sofa bed and each morning I fold it up again, as if my presence here never existed. As if the crack that's always beneath my feet swallows me up over and over.

Reminding myself it's only a place to sleep, I refocus my thoughts on the seminar, but a new word has taken root. *Impermanence.* I'm like the mandala that the Buddhists create only to destroy it - to demonstrate that even beauty doesn't last. But Being Sleek is my antidote. Security amidst all the uncertainty. Instead of taking the bus, I walk to the Vinci centre, savouring the firm ground underfoot.

Séminaires Tours runs a very slick operation. I wave to Fabienne and take in the classy venue, perfect to boast about on my website. The sweet and savoury refreshments on a side table are worth the flight on their own. I've arrived on the seminar circuit at last; it's a privilege to just turn up and teach.

This first audience is largely from the UK and, as I arrange my notes, I look up to see another person who's flown over from London. Alister Sloane. The one person I wasn't expecting. What's he doing here? He's been giving me the space I wanted – for weeks, what a saint – but now, in one action, he's cramping my style. I don't want him hovering around with a judgemental twinkle in his eye. Or worse – an admiring one. I'll just have to ignore him, and he's professional enough not to make contact before I begin. With a bit of luck, he's only here to discuss the prospects for his own seminars. Business is business.

My notes are impeccable, and each activity flows as planned. My anecdotes are well-timed and my jokes arouse some titters. The audience is attentive enough, but after morning tea the numbers dwindle slightly; then after lunch less than half the participants remain. I try not to take it personally, given their attendance is a ruse for a holiday in the Loire Valley. But I was sure I'd inspire them to soar.

When the remaining attendees leave at the end of the day with barely a thanks in my direction, instead of being on a high I'm drained with exhaustion. The juice-bucket comes to mind and I've got no idea how it happened.

I look up and see Alister's face. He hasn't even bothered to pin on a smile to hide his feelings. Disappointment. It strikes me like a blow in the gut.

The seminar was nothing special, and a word pops into my mind. *Ordinary.* It's the word Genevieve struck me with. The word I've shunned ever since my troubled childhood and marriage. The word that's kept me dancing into the spotlight in a desperate attempt not to be. There was nothing wrong with my performance. The seminar was well-planned and well-executed – the audience won't feel cheated – but it was ordinary. Along with its presenter.

My legs wobble and I grab the lectern. Alister does his Errol Flynn impersonation, flying across the room to steady me.

"You looked like you were going to faint," he says.

My mouth's gone dry. Not with a hankering for Alister, whose proximity usually has that effect, but with the shame of my lacklustre performance. Humiliation is sticking to my soul like French dog shit on a different sole. There's something very exposing about humiliation. Like being caught in the middle of the road without a stitch on: everyone stops to goggle and you're suddenly aware of their judgement. Can Alister see on my face that I know what's behind his eyes? Something close to pity.

Desperate to escape his strained expression, I plead a headache and hurry away. Past the charming cafés and bars where I don't belong. Back to Fabienne's living room where a surge of emptiness cleaves me open. Being Sleek is the one thing I was counting on – when I lost my home, when I lost my belongings, when I travelled across the world alone on a quest I didn't understand. Now it's abandoned me. And thanks to Andrew and his troll attack, I've got to present it three more times.

I collapse on the sofa and sob myself to sleep.

CHAPTER
Twenty-One

On Sunday morning I drag myself out of bed and mask my pallor with some makeup. Then I sneak out before Fabienne's had time to emerge. I don't want to bump into her. She was there yesterday. She saw it all.

The French don't do early, so I'm alone on the street. The empty lanes and alleys confirm my isolation. The isolation that's always there just below the surface. The maze of paths mock Coral's pronouncement: *ala* - a path to oblivion.

My desire to feel a little bit French comes back like a cruel joke. After yesterday's performance, I'm not even a little bit *me*.

Grabbing a *pain au chocolat* from the Sunday bakery, I walk through a deserted Place Plumereau to the American café - the only place that's always open and does coffee in takeaway mugs. It's a bitter brew but it's caffeinated.

Today's the day of the huge monthly *brocante* market that stretches the length of Boulevard Béranger. Numb to my surroundings, I wander down the hill in time to see over a kilometre of stalls being set up out of vans. On a bench in front of the town hall, amidst gardens of spring flowers, I try to empty my mind of soul-crushing thoughts.

I've got no idea what went wrong yesterday. Being Sleek is a signature seminar with a great message - to align business thinking with the wisdom of seals. It's about curiosity and focus and innovation and risk. I've got a drawer full of testimonials from the first time, and I'm still the same polished performer. And I couldn't have been more prepared. So how the hell did I plummet into ordinary? And why is the word so painful?

I hear Derek whispering, "Not enough magic." The spring sun warms my face, but inside I'm succumbing to an old rage. Everyone wants to tell me how to be.

Yeah, says the voice in my head, *they should just let you be ordinary.*

Enough.

I get up and wander through the market, now open for business. Stalls line each side of the broad central pedestrian area, offering a caning service for old chairs, tables of odd glassware and whole canteens of vintage cutlery, toys, sundry bric-a-brac, mirrors and hat stands, leather bellows, posters and illustrated pages from books. Some stalls specialise in *bijoux* – jewellery – with glass cases divided into tiny segments. Others have pinned their brooches and rings and fob-watch chains to velvet cushions. I'm on a mission to find a pendant or a pair of earrings that aren't ordinary. Maybe I'll see some spoons for Fabienne.

I spend ages going from stall to stall, hoping for something to catch my eye. And around me the market fills with patrons doing the same. It's when I'm poring over a cushion of unusual silver bangles that I hear a woman's voice behind me.

"Tony!"

I stiffen, and stop myself turning around.

The guy behind the stall ignores the woman, and I cautiously examine him without lifting my head. Not very tall and rather stocky, good-looking in that devil-may-care French way – like the fuzzy photo on the wall of the Bay Bar?

"I knew I'd find you," the woman says. "It's been five

years, Tony. The least you can do is speak to me."

Again the man doesn't respond. He continues to groom his stall as if no-one has addressed him, his body language relaxed, a cigarette in the corner of his mouth. The scene is so bizarre, it could be one of my trances but the woman behind me is real. I turn around and face her.

Fifteen minutes later, I'm sitting with Genevieve in a café on Avenue de Grammont. The guy never once opened his mouth, even – or especially – when she spoke to him in halting French. I've ordered two glasses of *vin rouge* and a bowl of *cacahuètes*. It might not be midday yet but they serve wine all day around here – even for breakfast – and we both need a drink.

Genevieve's in bad shape. "I know it's him," she keeps repeating. "His hair's greyer, he's a little heavier...but I know my own *husband*."

I sigh. After five years of wondering what happened to him, no-one would blame her for pouncing on the first unsuspecting look-a-like.

"He doesn't know you," I say. "Even when you told him your name back there, his face was completely blank, as if he was sure you were mad."

"Amnesia," she says.

Now I understand why Derek called it convenient. Up till now I've also wondered if Gaston had lost his memory, but the word rings a false note. For Gaston and for me. It's a moment of realisation that I'll have to examine later.

"Amnesia only happens in bad movies," I say. But she's not going to let it go until we come up with another explanation. "Tell me what happened this morning. Before you stopped at that stall."

She sips her wine. It seems to be taking the edge off her agitation. "I got up early. I knew it was the monthly market with all the *brocante* dealers, and I thought Hugo Luce was sure to be there. I wanted to look at the vans, and I saw it – his van. His business name from the phone book is painted on the side: Cuillères en Troglo."

I'm focused on the man himself. "Did you see Hugo?"

"No. I hung around the van but he'd already unloaded. So I started looking at the *bijoux* stalls. Then I saw Tony."

It seems like a no-brainer now.

"Hugo. You saw Hugo, but you got confused when he looked like Gaston. They've got the same name, they look the same – they must be brothers. Maybe even twins. Your boys are twins, so Gaston could be one too."

This seems compelling, but Genevieve says, "He never told me he had a brother."

"You said he never talked about his past. He might have lots of siblings."

"So why didn't he say something when I said Tony's name?"

I think about this. "Because he's got a brother called Gaston. Tony is his American name, isn't it?"

She nods.

"Tony sounds nothing like Gaston, especially with an American accent. He probably thought you were just another loud-mouthed tourist trying to get something cheap."

She starts to cry. "And now I've blown my chances to ask him about Tony."

I don't know what to say, because she's right. After that scene, Hugo Luce will be sure to stonewall her if Genevieve tries to approach him again.

"He's still in the market," she says. "You could speak to him."

I should have seen this coming. I sip my wine to give

myself time to think. I could prepare a sentence in French that tells him I'm looking for Gaston. But he probably wouldn't tell me if Gaston is still alive, and he's not going to give me his phone number.

I explain this to Genevieve, then add, "We've already guessed that they're related. We just don't know if Gaston's living around here. And I don't think Hugo will tell us."

She pulls out a tissue and blows her nose. We finish our wine in silence. Then I notice a change in her posture. She's had an idea.

"What are you going to do?" I ask, wondering if I want to know.

"Follow him," she says.

***

Fabienne isn't home so I've got space to reflect on my revelation about the amnesia. I pull sandwich ingredients out of the fridge and put them inside a baguette. If I haven't got amnesia, why can't I remember where I was those two weeks?

I munch on my sandwich and the answer comes: I don't want to remember.

That's a shock. Why? Surely the need to remember has focused my mind ever since I turned up on the beach?

I usually avoid what Davina calls 'delving into the murky depths', but it seems that's no longer an option. My memory loss has made me afraid. Afraid of losing myself again. It's driven me out of my home and halfway across the world, following subconscious clues. Clues that will retrieve my missing parts, solve the mystery of where I was for two weeks.

Or have I been running away from the clues and they're

the ones chasing me? I don't want to remember because…I don't want to confront that truth. The truth would draw me back to where it happened. To Bantry's Bluff, the beach with the curse.

Just the thought of returning to that beach brings back my fear of disappearing again. The path to oblivion.

What if next time I don't come back?

***

I'm not surprised when Alister sends a text suggesting dinner. I'm still feeling mortified about yesterday's performance, but the heat's going out of it. Somehow settling for ordinary seems easier than unpacking what went wrong. This acquiescence surprises me, but I don't want to unpack that either. The encounter with Genevieve has given me something else to think about. A secret. Do I share it with Alister?

We meet for a drink in the square. Alister doesn't mention the seminar, probably because he senses how fragile I am. He's used to capricious success gurus and I'm getting the kid-glove treatment. Until the gloves come off.

He asks where I want to eat, so, in accordance with our last meal, I take him to the humblest place I can think of – Tours' answer to the Pearl. We sit outside at a tiny folding table and try to make sense of the Chinese menu in French. When we've finally made our selections, the distractions are over.

"What would you like to talk about?" he asks.

I start one of my mental lists of forbidden topics. I'm dreaming about caves. I've divined a cave to visit using an antique spoon. I keep turning the tables on Andrew but I fear further revenge. My seminar was dull with a capital 'D'.

The next one will be the same unless something gives. Genevieve's in Tours. She's abandoned the twins to her rehabbed sister while she follows a guy who looks like her ex.

"Have you signed up any female gurus yet?" I say instead.

The question surprises us both. He wanted to sign me up, but I found good reasons to refuse. Do I really want to know that he's found someone else? Someone who isn't ordinary?

"I'm always looking for new talent," he says, "so I attend local seminars wherever I go."

"And?"

"Why do you want to know?"

"Professional interest."

"Well, I've seen a potential success guru but she wasn't very good. Her seminar was –"

"Don't say it."

He puts down his wine. "If you won't listen to the truth, Selkie, then your career's already on the skids."

Bloody hell.

"Yesterday's seminar was downright forgettable. Those participants won't be buzzing on social media, so your word-of-mouth will be zip. If you keep boring your audience with your perfect-but-lifeless delivery, you'll be a has-been before you've begun."

I feel like I've been slapped. My face goes red and I think I'm going to cry. It's not supposed to be like this. Alister's supposed to admire me from afar and I'm supposed to feel sceptical about it.

"What charmed everyone the first time," he continues, "was your wild unpredictability, your fresh take on tired principles, your ability to read the room and inject the audience with inspiration. Yesterday the only thing you were inspiring was a rush for the exits, and the only thing you were reading was your notes. For the next one I challenge you to tear up the cheat-sheet and...wing it."

Alister doesn't take his eyes off me. He's giving me tough love and I hate it. I'm thinking of making a run for it, but the food arrives. The waiter is blocking my exit so I do the next best thing – slurp too much wine and stuff my face with comfort food.

Alister does the same but with much more finesse. My table antics have amused him in the past, but tonight he's playing hardball. He's not going to walk me home until I've said something in response. Just as well this place does a great Beijing-style *bombe alaska*. We're going to be here for a while.

"Genevieve's in Tours," I blurt. "I saw her at the *brocante* market."

I can tell he's shocked, but he's not going to let me off the hook. "Has that got anything to do with what I just said?"

"No." That's the point.

"What are you afraid of?"

"Losing control." It just pops out.

"That's a relief."

"What?"

"The truth. Now we've got something to talk about. All presenters are afraid of losing control. It's a fear you've got to move beyond. You lost control in your very first seminar – with powerful results – and now you're trying to claw it back. Wrong move."

But I'm remembering my missing memory. During my first seminar I disappeared into Being Sleek and I still don't remember what happened. It's why I wanted to control it this time. So I didn't get lost again. If I keep losing parts of myself every time I run a seminar, it will be worse than my missing two weeks. Eventually there'll be nothing left.

Alister's got more to say about letting go – about how a great seminar always has elements of surprise. He's dishing out the kind of talk I usually dish out to him, so we're even. It's the only thing we are even on, since he's a big-shot millionaire and I'm still a pretender in a power suit, but it's an imbalance I'm used to. I start to relax.

"Will you be there on Wednesday?" I ask. My next seminar.

"Wouldn't miss it for all the *bombe alaska* in Beijing."

It's not the answer I wanted, but if he's there I'll have to accept his challenge. He knows that and so do I.

"Great," I say.

"And you'll take up my challenge for what reason?"

"Because I hate you."

"And?"

"Because I want it. For myself."

It's the right answer and I mean it. If I present another seminar like yesterday I'll disappear for a different reason – into the pit called ordinary.

We order a dessert wine and when it's in the glasses, Alister pulls a small parcel out of his pocket and pushes it across the table.

"I saw this at the *brocante* market. Something quirky that made me think of you."

I don't know what to say. He's never given me a gift and I'm not sure how I feel – about being 'quirky' or what it implies about our relationship.

"I don't know, Alister. It's not a peace offering, is it? After the shit sandwich?"

"Shit sandwiches don't come with peace offerings."

"Good. But I still feel awkward about accepting it."

"It doesn't have to mean anything big, Selkie. It reminded me of you so I bought it. For ten euros."

The low value clinches it. No diamonds. And no gift wrapping.

I rip open the brown paper bag and what's inside makes me gasp. It's a silver bangle fashioned from a French spoon, flattened and curved to go around the wrist. It's what the guy we think was Hugo was selling on his stall. I'd just realised his bangles were spoons when Genevieve's voice interrupted.

I blink down at it, remembering all the crazy connections that have followed me across the world. Does Alister remember there was a spoon in my collection of seven? But he's reaching across and slipping the bangle over my hand. His touch feels good and I don't pull away.

"The jeweller makes them himself," he says, "from old coffee spoons. It's solid silver. And very French."

I look down at my wrist and fall in love with it. I can deal with the premonitions later.

"Thank you, Alister. It's very special." In more ways than he knows.

He pours us both more wine. "Now tell me about Genevieve."

When he hears what I've got to say, he's furious and I regret telling him. Then, in trying to make him understand her motivation, I describe the incident at the bangle stall and only make things worse.

"Her French is terrible," he says. "And that guy with the bangles had trouble understanding mine. He's got no English. He isn't Gaston."

I don't tell him about Hugo. It's Genevieve's story and I've already said too much.

"How do you know all this?" he asks.

"We went for a drink. Genevieve was pretty upset."

"I'm not happy about this, Selkie. Gennie's trying to involve you in this mad scheme to find Gaston and it's none of your business. Or mine."

"It's just a coincidence that we bumped into each other."

"Is it? Does she know where you're staying?"

"I don't think so."

"She'll be able to find you at the seminar venue. Make sure she doesn't follow you home. Don't stop at your front door until you're sure the coast is clear."

He's remembering how she waited outside my office, but he's overreacting. Genevieve isn't going to cause me trouble.

***

My fears about the next seminar give me sleepless nights. Winging it is something you can't prepare for. You have to live in the moment – and jump. But the whole losing control thing is bigger than I thought. Why am I so afraid? I'm not going to disappear like I did at Bantry's Bluff – not in a seminar room in France in front of two hundred people. But the snippets of my missing memory haunt my dreams – the moonlight, the dancing, the caress of rough fingers. It's what Keith called an amnesia loop: my fear of the truth is keeping me endlessly circling through what I already know. Like Rupert. Then there's the troglodyte and his shadow – forever hiding from me what he's painting on the wall.

By Tuesday night I've worked myself up into such a phobia about going to sleep that I do something I've never done before. I buy some sleeping pills. They work.

After a deep sleep, I open my eyes to see a note on my pillow. The handwriting is elegant. It's signed by Fabienne.

> *I hear your alarm. You do not wake up. I make a drum with a saucepan. I slap your face. You open your eyes then close them. Three times. Mais ne paniques pas – I look after them till you arrive. A warm-upping for your seminar.*

What?

The clock on the wall says it all. Ten o'clock. Being Sleek started an hour ago. I fall out of bed.

After the shortest shower in history, I throw on my red suit and hit the pedestrian precinct, repeating her words like a mantra: *ne paniques pas.* Don't panic.

By the time I've downed a coffee en route and walked the brisk fifteen minutes to the Vinci centre, my head has cleared. I can only imagine what went through Fabienne's mind when she couldn't wake me up. I didn't need a stomach pump but I did need another couple of hours. And she's given me that with her warm-up. Part of me is so grateful for the rescue that I want to cry, but the other part is hating her for being so bloody versatile. Artistic, beautiful, French. Is there anything she isn't good at?

Before I enter the seminar room, I rearrange my face to look like this morning was planned. People are sitting at tables spread with art materials and Fabienne is moving around making encouraging noises. I walk up to her and we kiss on both cheeks.

"You're a superstar," I whisper.

"*De rien,*" she says. No worries.

I wander from table to table, introducing myself and finding out what people are doing. The exercise is to mind-map – using whatever materials inspire them – their aspirations for the workshop and beyond. It will flow beautifully into Being Sleek, however it plays out. After this stunning start, I just hope I can bury my fear of letting go and follow through.

"Ten minutes more," Fabienne says in her gorgeous accented English. "Then we hear what you are all making."

What a package she is. Her energy is relaxed and again I notice the way she moves, her lithe grace. I look at Alister, who's been doing the exercise with everyone else, and catch an admiring expression on his face. He used to look at me that way.

When the ten minutes are up, she nods at me to take over. I introduce myself and call for volunteers to share what they've created. Hands go up, but one participant gets to his feet uninvited. I don't recognise him at first - even though his photo is still on my phone - but I do recognise his nametag. Reece.

Shit.

"I didn't fly all the way from Australia," he says, as my legs start to wobble, "to play with...crayons."

The room that was buzzing a moment ago is stunned into silence.

"We were promised a seminar from a business guru – a 'success siren' if you believe all the hype – but instead we get a childish drawing exercise from a...retired clown."

The room lets out a collective gasp.

Fabienne's background is news to me, but he's obviously spent the last hour googling her. The bastard. He flew over with the intention of shafting me in front of my audience, and by sleeping in and needing a rescue I've played right into his hands.

The audience is a frozen tableau, waiting for my response. Reece Chapman has folded his arms and fixed a smirk on his face - sticking to what he's good at.

It's the moment of truth for me – to prove my mettle in front of a group I've only just met – but my mind is blank. Was Fabienne ever a clown? To make ends meet? Andrew's image of me with a ball on my nose flies past. Nothing I do now can make anything worse. It's time to take up Alister's challenge. I jump.

"Mr Chapman." By using his surname I hope that some will realise I know this joker. *He's my ex-husband's lawyer*, I want to scream. "You've reminded the group that if anyone is unhappy with the workshop, they may leave at any time and have their fee refunded. No questions asked. But your critical comments – about the mind-mapping and Fabienne herself – require a response to everyone here. I'd appreciate it if you'd stay and hear me out."

He'd be churlish not to agree, undermining his chance to take half the room with him, which is no doubt his plan. I've got him where I want him, but how do I retrieve the situation? He's confident I can't. Too confident. It infuses me with courage.

"Firstly, I'd like to remind you all that Being Sleek is a blue-sky workshop and the mind-mapping is designed to help you think creatively about your business life. 'Outside the box' is a cliché but it does explain why you're here. You want more than old thinking can give you – you want to give more and get more back. If you're not sure about this morning's exercise, remember that the money-back guarantee applies if you're still not satisfied at the end of the workshop. You've booked your flights, paid your accommodation – all tax deductible – why not keep an open mind and see the workshop through? In Mr Chapman's case, he'll receive a double refund to cover his return airfares to Australia. Fair enough, Mr Chapman?"

The audience visibly settles, while Reece glares at me.

"Doesn't change the fact that you misrepresented who'd be running the workshop," he says. "In my country that's *fraud.*"

"I'm coming to that. Fabienne, please tell us why Mr Chapman called you a clown just now."

First rule of negotiation – never ask a question you don't know the answer to. It's a big risk, but I've already jumped.

"Of course," Fabienne says. She turns to the room and lifts her chin. "It is ten years I am a member of the Cirque de Soleil. First as an acrobat, on the high wire, then as a movement coach and body artist."

Bloody hell. Something warm rushes through my veins as I pretend I knew the answer all along.

"Ladies and gentlemen, you've just spent an hour with a guru. Fabienne Bouchard has a demonstrated history of," I tick off my fingers, "dedication, focus, balance and flexibility." They laugh. "She performed at the highest level and without a hitch over and over again – a model to emulate in any business. It's essential to learn from experts outside our field, and that's why Fabienne is here. She's a living example of Being Sleek. These days she's an artist by invitation from the city of Tours. She's just returned from an invitation-only exhibition in Tuscany. So you've also spent the morning with an expert in creative thinking."

I turn to Reece Chapman. "This is obviously not the right workshop for you, Mr Chapman." *You're the clown*, I whisper under my breath. "You owe Fabienne an apology."

As he storms out alone, the oppressive atmosphere lifts and hands go up wanting to share their mind-maps. Thanks to Reece Chapman, I've been winging it with panache.

I look across at Alister and suspect he's just stopped holding his breath.

Fabienne stays and Being Sleek flows. My planning is at my fingertips, but my knuckles are no longer white. Not only do I witness what magic means, but my fear dissolves as I hear the voice that Nigel once told me to listen for – a shushing whisper that guides me with a wordless touch.

By the end of the day, it's caressed me into a sense of profound belonging. My memory hasn't returned in a cataclysmic flash, but the knowingness in my bones is back. Something about creativity. Something about home. Something about...bliss.

CHAPTER
Twenty-Two

It's time to celebrate and Fabienne suggests the *guinguette* – performance stages and bars along the riverbank that provide entertainment until the early hours. For the first time in weeks I'm on a high. There's nothing to think about but being here.

My little black dress is about to get its first night out on the town, so I pick up some strappy heels at Fabienne's favourite store. Aptly named the Shoe Cave, it even makes me laugh. There'd be worse places in the world for a girl to turn *troglodytique*. Then, just in case the symbolism of my outfit isn't enough, I add the cowry shell and the spoon bangle. My hair needs a trim, but Jerome's in Honolulu and he's the only one I trust to cut it, so I do my best with the product he gave me called 'seaweed'. Another reminder of the beach.

While we're waiting for Alister to meet us on the riverbank, Fabienne and I chat about the day we've shared. I want her to open the next seminar and she can't believe it. From 'retired clown' to success guru in one morning. We discuss payment for today, but she doesn't expect it. She's now got the experience to create her own workshops, and Séminaires Tours has seen her in action.

As Alister arrives, the dusk is making the water glow silver and the buzz at the *guinguette* is just beginning. We move from bar to bar and stage to stage, trying out different styles of music. The rock fusion is a favourite, and after a few drinks with some of Fabienne's friends Alister asks me to dance. He turns out to be quite a dancer, twirling me with such skill I respond. Since moving to Hawaii I've done some wild dancing myself – alone and in bare feet – and after the day I've had, I've got nothing to lose.

He takes me in his arms and we move like old partners as a crowd begins to form. They clap us on while we lose ourselves in the rhythm, our movements getting way too sensual for a public display. Alister and I have been waiting too long for this moment – to be this close, to explore the chemistry that's always there – and eventually he pulls me away from the spotlight into the shadows of the riverbank and plants a deep kiss on my lips. It's the first time we've kissed and my body responds like a schoolgirl's, tingles of heat rushing to my toes and other places.

We melt into each other in a way that's so new and so out of control that, just like a schoolgirl out of her depth, I freak out and pull away. He tries to hold me but I'm already running. Past the music and the lights, past the tables of laughing people, all the way back to the apartment. By the time I reach the front door of the building, I've stopped crying. I don't understand what went wrong. A kiss is just a kiss. Even if it leads me to his bed, it doesn't have to mean anything.

Except it is going to mean something with him. The depth of his ardour still frightens me. And now the depth of my response. He's after the right woman – a soul mate, someone to love again after his long-ago loss – and he thinks that woman is me. It feels like way too much responsibility – to be as special as Fleur was, as special as he thinks I am.

I'm just mixed up and selfish, I remind myself, with an act that fools everyone. Except me.

***

I'm inserting the enormous key into the lock of the front door when someone tugs my sleeve. A woman has stepped out of the shadows. Alister's warning to watch out for Genevieve has caught me too late.

"I found him," she says simply.

It's better than thinking about that kiss, so I walk with her to the end of the lane, to a bar with outdoor tables.

As we wait for glasses of wine, she says, "We can go there tonight. If you see him, you'll know I'm not mad."

"I don't think you're mad, but it doesn't matter what I think. How do you know it's him? Have you spoken to him?"

"No."

My heart sinks. "Is it the guy in the market?"

"No."

"You were sure he was Gaston."

"I followed him. He's not Tony. This time I'm sure."

Her answers are strangely elusive and her demeanour has changed since Sunday. She was angry after the encounter in the market. Now she's...sad. There's a mystery here and it's making me uneasy.

"It explains everything," she says. "Why he left, why his blog is so...depressed."

I'll never forget the melancholy – and something darker – oozing from the *bloglo*.

"He's the author of On the Luce?" I ask.

She nods, but how can she be sure? She hasn't even spoken to him.

"We can go there now," she says again. "You need to see him."

"Go where? How will I see him?"

I imagine peering through a keyhole, spying on a man I don't know.

"Through the window of his *troglo*," she says, making my skin prickle.

"He lives...in a cave?"

It's enough. We leave our drinks and walk to her car and I let her drive me out of Tours.

We take a road to the west, towards the town of Chinon. It sits on the banks of the Vienne River, a tributary of the Loire, and in the cliffs above the town, silhouetted against the night sky, are the ruins of another *château*. Genevieve drives past the darkened shops and parks on the outskirts of town, then we walk along a narrow road that snakes up the high walls of the river valley, not towards the castle but in the other direction. All along the lane there are *troglos* carved into the cliff. Squats and abandoned spaces mostly, with holes cut for windows and doors that never existed. Peering out at us with unseeing eyes like ghosts.

I shiver, grateful for the occasional street light. Here and there, a cave has been turned into a dwelling with stunning views of the deep valley below. It's a long climb and I wonder if it's a wild goose chase, almost hoping not to see what I'm going to see. Is Gaston the troglodyte in my dream?

There's no traffic in the lane, although we pass a few parked cars. Vines dangle from the cliff above as the pavement narrows. Genevieve's pace slows - we're both puffed from the steady climb - then just before the road ends in a turning space, she pulls me back and puts her finger to her lips.

We shuffle towards the lighted window of a cave dug deep into the cliff, and perch on the wall opposite, hidden by the shadow beyond the window. The living space within is bright but empty and I wonder what I'm doing here. Then something flickers through an inner doorway and a figure appears. He's quite visible to us, sitting outside in the dark. He could be the man in the market. The hair and face are the same, but one thing's different. The wheelchair.

I remember the line from the *bloglo* that freaked me out: *une prison troglodytique, une vie monastique.* A life trapped like a hermit – in a cave and a wheelchair.

The tale of Beauty and the Beast comes to mind, more famous than Donkey Skin. Of the prince cursed by his beastly appearance to hide his humanity from the world. It's another view of the troglodyte – the outcast shunned and alone, and only the love of a woman can set him free.

Despite his limited movements, the man throws shadows on the wall, but they don't conjure images from my dream. The light's too steady, his shadow's too compact, the room's too...civilised. No wall art. He may be the man who disappeared from Bantry's Bluff, he may write the *bloglo en franglais* that intrigues me, he may have a brother who works with silver spoons, but he's not my troglodyte.

My thoughts turn to Genevieve, silent beside me. After all these years of wondering, and then seeing what's become of him, what kind of shape is she in?

She signals that it's time to go and I'm relieved. She's not planning a house call. It's after eleven o'clock and the guy's disabled, even if he is her runaway husband long overdue with an explanation.

"He looks like the guy in the market," I concede once we're some distance away.

"They're twins," she says. "I saw them together this afternoon. I've been following Hugo's van around and today he parked it at the end of this lane. It explains the name of his business: Cuillères en Troglo – Spoons in a Cave. The van gave me somewhere to hide so I could watch."

"The wheelchair...must have been a shock." An

accident?

She doesn't reply straight away and I realise she's crying.

"Tony was an ocean sailor, Selkie. He was so proud of his strength, his body. It...explains why he's never contacted me."

"He'd never want you to see him like this?"

She nods. "In one way it's a relief. He wasn't cruel, he was compassionate. But, call me selfish, I thought if I found him, he might...come back. Now I know he's not going anywhere."

It's a strange story and I'm tangled up in it. Connected by a series of coincidences, the final one a silver spoon.

"Well, you've seen his situation," I say. "That gives you time to think. To decide what you want to do."

"I have decided." She's stopped crying, and her conviction makes me wonder if she's going to walk out of his life again. No-one would blame her. "I expect he'll refuse to see me, but I want him to know I'm here."

"If you knock on his door, he can hardly refuse." He's not going anywhere.

"I've been thinking about that – how he'll react. He'll be appalled that I've tracked him down. Angry to be exposed...after he's hidden himself so well. Humiliated that I'm seeing him like this. If he feels any of those things and he won't talk to me...then it's over."

Gaston also doesn't know about the twins. Whatever his reasons for leaving her – and ending up in a wheelchair, wanting to kill himself – she won't want to risk being sent away before she can tell him about his sons.

"Write him a note," I say. "Push it under his door."

"Then he'll know I've seen him and his reaction will be the same."

"Send Hugo a text – you've got his number. Address it

to Gaston Luce."

She shakes her head. "He'd probably talk to a friend of mine – someone he doesn't know."

"Who?" The penny drops. "No way."

We've reached her car and we face each other.

"I saw you down by the Loire tonight," she says. "With Alister."

If she's been following me too, then she saw me run away. It explains how she turned up at my door.

"He's crazy about you," she says. "He'll never come back to me and the boys."

"That doesn't mean I should get involved in your unfinished business, Genevieve. You need to find a way to speak to Gaston yourself."

I wish Gretel was here to murmur some sense in my ear, because I can feel myself wavering. Genevieve's next remark clinches it.

"Don't you want to find out if Tony's disappearance can throw any light on your own?"

Chapter
Twenty-Three

My next seminar is on Saturday, so I've got a two-day window to speak to Gaston. My intuition says to do it tomorrow. If there are repercussions, I've got Friday to recover. I may be being fanciful, but there's a secret here, a deep secret. It sends my mind back to the beach. If I'm right about the reason for my memory loss, it's a secret I don't want to remember. And my meeting with Gaston might give me the clue that will unravel it all.

Even though I'm long overdue for bed, I pick up the phone and catch Judy over her breakfast. She doesn't know about the latest sortie from the Reece/Andrew sabotage unit and is appalled but not surprised by Reece's appearance at my seminar. Even though she's dealt with some tough customers in her time, these two are plumbing new depths when it comes to intransigence and retribution.

"Their deadline to make the house presentable is imminent," she says. "I'll drive by after work and see if they've started. I'm not hopeful."

"They're trying to inflict as much pain on me as possible – emotional and financial."

"Giving in to the emotional pressure is optional, Selkie, so stay strong. You can recover the renovation costs from the settlement. As soon as they miss their deadline, our decorating team goes in."

As I hang up, I check for messages from Alister. Nothing. Either he's giving me space or he's furious that I ran from his kiss.

***

Genevieve is sitting on a bench at the end of Fabienne's lane, munching on a croissant. She pulls one out of the paper bag for me. We decided last night that she'll drive me to Chinon and wait in the village until I call. It's not fair on Gaston if she's waiting too close. He has to decide to see her without pressure. We walk towards Les Halles - the covered market - where she's squeezed her car into a space that would be illegal in any other country. We negotiate the one-way streets out of Tours, and she drops me at the bottom of Gaston's lane before driving to a café to wait.

The climb on foot to his *troglo* gives me time to reflect on my folly. This is a man who's clearly depressed by his condition. I've read his blog posts and there's only one word for them: dark. How will he respond to a stranger - an Australian, a so-called friend of his ex-wife - knocking on his door?

I stand at the wall where we sat last night, looking down to the river. It reminds me of my own journey over the edge, down to the beach. I was afraid of the cliff, but I didn't fall. *May I tomber to my tomb?* Gaston wrote. If he fell, he'd certainly die. But first he'd have to get over the wall.

Except for its location, the *troglo* isn't private. Just like last night, I can see right into the living room. The rough walls are lined with odd-shaped bookshelves and narrow tables, leaving the central space for his chair. On a desk there's a laptop and the lamp that lit the room last night. On a side table several spoon bangles lie beside a polishing cloth. Luckily Gaston isn't visible. It feels less intrusive to bring him from the other room when I knock. Then I worry that he might still be in bed, that he might need someone to help him get up and dressed. I look around but the lane is silent.

I knock. No answer. I knock again.

I open the door a crack and call out, "*Bonjour.*" I haven't prepared what to say, whether to start in fumbling French or English, whether to mention Genevieve straight off and be sent away for my trouble. Better to get in the door if I can.

"My name's Selkie. I'm hoping you're the blogger of On the Luce. I've been reading your posts." Not a total misrepresentation.

I hear a sound from within. Then a voice. "Wait."

A minute later he's coming through the archway from an interior room, looking unkempt.

"You make some coffee," he says, pointing to a Nespresso machine through an arch at one end of the room.

I step inside and do as he says while he watches me. I hope he's got milk.

"I don't get visitors," he says. "Especially pretty visitors with funny accents."

"Australian," I say. "I'm running some business seminars in Tours."

"And playing the detective with underground bloggers."

"Only one."

"Why?"

Good question. I thought he'd be curious about how I found him, but this monastic state has probably inspired introspection. Time to come clean.

"I live in Hawaii. I know your ex-wife. Genevieve thought if I found you, you might talk to me. About why you left."

"Ah."

He doesn't seem angry. More resigned. As if he

expected she might track him down one day. Instead, it's her accomplice.

I pass him his coffee and start making one for myself. He can hold the mug but only with effort. His movements remind me of the girl at uni, the one with MS. I helped her by taking notes. Sometimes I took her to the toilet and wiped her bum.

"She is a friend of yours?" Gaston asks, bringing me back to Genevieve.

"Not really. I've met her...a few times. I wouldn't call us friends."

"I didn't want her to know. About this. This disease. I wanted her to be free, so I left. Tell her that."

He's a guy who gets to the point.

"She took it hard," I say. "She was humiliated. For five years she's wondered if you're still alive. It would be good...if you could tell her yourself."

He shrugs. "I wouldn't insult her by making a phone call after what I've done."

"You don't have to. She's here, in France. She's staying in Tours."

"*Merde*." Shit. His eyes flash with anger. But it doesn't last. It's as if he saves the fire for his blog posts and can barely get a spark going any more.

"She saw Hugo in the market. She thought he was you."

He starts to laugh, but ends up coughing, then wheezing. "He told me about a mad woman, how she yelled at him. He doesn't know about Gennie. I never thought it could be her." Then he says, "If she thinks she wants to see me, she makes a mistake."

I tell him how she followed Hugo, how she's already seen him through the window. "She still wants to speak to you."

"The last thing I want is her pity."

It's my turn to be angry. His exile has made him selfish.

"Don't jump to conclusions. If you meet her, what's the worst that can happen? You might...be surprised." By the twins. But that's Genevieve's news to break.

"Pah."

Does that mean he'll do it? I don't have any tactics up my sleeve, so we sip our coffee in silence. The next move is up to him.

"You say you're not Gennie's friend, but you came here to sweet-talk the broken old troglodyte for her. I don't believe it."

"There is something else. It might be a shock."

"So make me another coffee. Then you can shock me."

When he's got his fingers around the fresh mug, I tell him my story, how I vanished from the same beach as he did.

"The curse of Bantry's Bluff," he says. "You believe that?"

"No. But I was gone for two weeks. Then I turned up again without a scratch. And I don't remember any of it."

"You think this makes us soul mates, *n'est-ce pas?*"

"I hope not." It just slips out.

He laughs, then coughs. "I take it back. About the sweet talk." He lifts his mug and sips the coffee. Something in his manner shifts. "Gennie didn't know," he says. "About this. This MS. It's why I gave up sailing. I couldn't hold the ropes."

"You didn't tell her before you married her?"

"I kept hoping it would be slow. When I knew it was the aggressive kind, I tried to drown myself, but a boat picked me up. They saved a man who didn't want to be saved. I had no plan if I didn't die. I came back to France and the disease did its worst."

"Nothing to do with curses. Nothing to do with me."

"A curse of a different kind. A genetic curse."

Shit. What about the twins?

"MS killed my mother," he continues, "and my uncle. So I got a genetic test. Then a vasectomy. Then it got me."

My God, a vasectomy. The twins aren't his. It's a moment before I can ask, "Did Genevieve know?"

"That I...fire blanks? Then I would have to tell her everything. I couldn't. We were happy. I didn't want to...burst the bubble."

Genevieve must have had a lover before Gaston disappeared. Otherwise how did she pass the boys off as his? As I get up to leave, his secret and her lie are tying me in knots.

"Come back again," he says. "You do not...what's the word? ...simper. And you are *sympa*." He laughs at his play on words. "But phone first."

He gives me his number.

"And Genevieve?" But I've lost my commitment to her agenda.

He sighs. "Tell her I'm sorry. It's too late."

***

Outside the *troglo*, I phone Genevieve. She gives me directions to the café but doesn't ask what's happened. It reminds me how good she is at waiting.

I walk through the cobbled streets, weighing up what to do with what I know. Above me, at upstairs windows, duvets are draped over window sills to catch the sun. They mirror how I feel after the revelations – hung out to dry.

The café is easy to find in the tiny town centre, and

when I've joined Genevieve under an umbrella I give her the news she's expecting.

"That's all he said? Sorry but it's too late? After everything I've been through?"

I'm finding it hard to play my part, knowing what I know. But it's another secret that's not mine to share.

"He's worried you'll pity him," I say. "I told him to give you a chance. Then he told me about his disease." I repeat his story, leaving out the vasectomy. "He says it's why he left, so you'd be free."

"Still married to a missing man isn't free." She stares into space with a look of utter despair, while I wonder about her integrity. "I thought I'd steeled myself for him to reject me, but now that it's happened... I can't bear it. Not again."

There's nothing I can say.

She looks back at me. "Thank you for trying. But I can't accept that I'm this close and still so far away. I'm not giving up."

"What are you going to do?"

I'm dreading the answer – that she'll want me to tell him about the twins, try to woo him with her fake offspring. I'd have to come clean about what I know.

"Wait," she says. "I'm going to wait. I've got time. He knows I'm here, so there's a chance he'll change his mind."

Short of barging in there and demanding an audience, it's all she's got.

As we drive in silence back to Tours, I push Genevieve's quest from my mind and think about my own. Gaston didn't share any secrets, but I replay the clues that led me to his door – the strange confluence of the troglodyte messages and the spoon. The old Hawaiian word comes back: *ho'ohihi*. Interconnectedness. It's what guided me to the cemetery and the beach at Bantry's Bluff – all the psychic clues that seemed so bizarre and unrelated converged inevitably at the cliff.

The clues that led me to Gaston also point in another direction, to another cave: Rouffignac. But I've ignored them.

CHAPTER
Twenty-Four

I watch through the studio window as Fabienne works with a drill. I want to ask her about Rouffignac but I won't disturb her. As I start to move away, she notices me and waves. She pulls up her face mask and comes to the door.

"You make a visit to the Seven Sisters?" she asks. "I have not told you the story, I think."

"I want to ask you about Rouffignac," I say. "How to get there. But now that I'm here, I'd love to watch you work."

We go inside and I sit on the stool. She's added more spoons to the sculpture since I first saw it. After her handiwork with the drill, some of them have holes right through their bowls.

"It is almost finished," she says. "There are seven sisters, so I make seven holes. To match the pattern of the stars. You know it, the Pleiades? The seven stars?"

I shake my head.

"I don't know the word in English. For stars when they make a group."

"Constellation."

"*Bien sûr.* The Pleiades, it is a constellation." She looks down at a printout that shows the position of each star. "I make one more hole. Then I tell you the story."

She puts a dot in the bowl of one of the spoons, picks up the drill and creates a large hole, then brushes away the shavings. She uses sandpaper to smooth the edges, before standing back to look and sanding it a little more. Finally she wipes the sculpture over with a silver cloth so that

chosen surfaces shine and create extra depth under the overhead light.

The sculpture is sitting on the workbench on its own wooden base. When Fabienne's satisfied, she moves it to a table in front of the window.

"It is the best view of the constellation," she says, "with the light at the back."

We stand in front of it, allowing the work to speak for itself. My eyes move over the shapes the spoons make, almost woman-like in their curves. She's created movement, as if the seven sisters are leaping upwards with arms outstretched. Then my eyes take in the holes illuminated by the daylight streaming through the window. There's a pattern to them – the constellation called the Pleiades – a pattern I've seen before.

Fabienne hears my intake of breath, but says nothing as I move to the printout she's been working from. I have to be sure, and the image on the paper confirms it. I move back to the sculpture. The light is turning the holes into stars – just like a black satin sheet on a white tiled floor.

"The sisters, they disturb you?" Fabienne asks.

"I know this constellation. It's the pattern I created in my sleep." I remind her about it. Clue number six.

"*Mon dieu*," she says. "I make the sculpture in Tours and you dream about it in Honolulu. You think you read my mind?"

"No." I hadn't even heard of Fabienne when I collected those things. "Tell me the story of the Pleiades," I whisper, as I drop back onto the stool.

Fabienne leans against her workbench looking as unnerved as I feel. "There are many stories from many cultures," she says. "You have one in your country. The Australian Aborigines, they tell the story of the Pleiades. I

research all the stories. They are not very different from the other. They always tell about the seven sisters and how they run away from an evil man. Run away and jump into the sky."

I think about the story and how it resonates with my own predicament - trying to escape from Andrew. Am I like the seven sisters, forever running away from the man who would possess me? A chilling thought.

We're both spooked by the psychic connection. Did the holes in the sheet connect me with Fabienne, or did they predict the connection that Derek was going to make between us? Without the ability to explain it, we switch to other things.

Fabienne's got enough works for a small exhibition now that the Seven Sisters is done. But, like most artists, she's not very good at selling her work and she doesn't have money to spend on promotion.

Then we get to my original reason for disturbing her: La Grotte de Rouffignac. It's in the Dordonne, east of Bordeaux, and Fabienne tells me the nearest big town is Périgueux, a couple of hours drive on the motorway south. She's seen the cave herself, and suggests that I stay nearby because I'll have to get there early in the morning. There's always a queue wanting to see the prehistoric art and they limit the number of visitors. Or I could join a group tour. She has a friend who'd lend me a car, but I thank her and say I'd rather be independent. Being Sleek has finally given me some spending money.

It's in the space between us that it was one of her spoons that directed me to Rouffignac - the spoons she collected to make the Seven Sisters - but we've had enough psychic connections for one day.

I go upstairs to draft Fabienne's contract for Being

Sleek. It's a relief to have something to focus on. She still doesn't want to be a paid partner, saying the experience is enough, but experience works both ways - her involvement has encouraged me to let the program flow beyond my planning. Because of her - and Reece Chapman - I'm into the rhythm of winging it and I want to thank her with an appropriate share. And if I use the mind-mapping in future seminars, she needs a royalty clause too.

I'm immersed in the contract when there's a knock on the door. My first thought is Genevieve, since she knows where I live, but when I open up I'm face to face with Alister. The first thing I notice is his lips. Because they were the last connection between us? No. Because he's got one thing on his mind.

He pushes me inside and presses me against the nearest wall. Our lips connect again and this time I've got nowhere to run. It's a long hungry kiss that reels me in and doesn't let go. The next thing I know we're on the sofa.

Who knows what might have happened if Fabienne hadn't come upstairs carrying a huge bucket of flowers. The bunch is so big she doesn't see past them to what she's interrupted.

"I cannot resist," she's saying. "A man, he comes down the lane with a cart. Freesias, irises, roses, poppies."

She puts them on the coffee table and starts tweaking the arrangement before she sees our startled faces blinking at her from the sofa.

"*Desolée.*" Sorry. She rushes out the front door.

The moment has been doused and we sit up breathlessly and giggle.

"Just checking it wasn't permanent," Alister says.

"What?"

"Your abhorrence of my kiss."

I stop giggling. "You kiss OK, Alister, but don't ever barge in on me like that again."

"No problem, I've proved my point." He gets up and walks to door, rearranging his clothes. "Next time it'll be my place."

What a nerve.

"Don't count on it," I yell after him.

What I don't say is that last night's trepidation has vanished and I loved every juicy moment. I might have gone further given half a chance. Fabienne saved me from that big mistake. But Alister won't have any trouble reading that kiss.

***

I finish the contract and start planning the trip to Rouffignac. Early next week when there's less traffic than on a weekend. The thought of driving all that way – on the right-hand side of the road and alone – feels like an ordeal. Just like a fairy tale, it must be one of the obstacles I have to overcome to get to the end of my journey.

With a hire car and accommodation booked it's time to face the clue I've been avoiding. The seventh clue from my nocturnal collection. After the discovery of the Pleiades, I can't ignore it any longer. With a mix of excitement and apprehension I peer at the image that needs more than ticking off the list; it needs deciphering.

Glo tro on air quee

Shot shoe key zard lay shay share

The words make no sense, except for one...if I read it backwards. *Glo tro* becomes *troglo*. Shit. Is it the clue to the troglodyte of my dreams?

"Sometimes you have to look at things backwards to see

the truth," Davina said. *Turn the tables.*

On a piece of paper I transcribe the other lines backwards:

Quee air on tro glo

Share shay lay zard key shoe shot

Bloody hell. It reminds me of Gaston's *franglais.* Was I channelling one of his poems that night? Another psychic connection with someone in France I hadn't yet met?

I don't want to believe it, but I do believe he could translate this in a flash. That would mean seeing him again. Getting to Chinon somehow, and dealing with the depths of his despair. The alternative is to struggle through the translation on my own.

I sigh and try the first line. *Quee air on troglo.* Queer is right. Then I look again and correct myself. *Quee air.* As soon as I say it aloud, I recognise the French. *Quee air* must be *cuillère.* Spoon. *Cuillères en Troglo* - Spoons in a Cave, the name of Hugo's business.

Without thinking about how on earth I knew this when I was in Hawaii, I go to the next line and get success with the first word. *Share shay* must be *cherchez,* as in *cherchez la femme.* This is exciting. *Cherchez la femme* - look for the woman - points to the motivation behind many a man's actions. What must I look for? Something that's behind my actions. *Cherchez lay zard.*

It must be '*les zards*' as in 'the zards' but here my search stalls. There is no 'zard' in either French or English, even when I replace 'z' with 's'. I think about what I know of French. The 's' on the end of *les* might be sounding at the beginning of 'zard' - '*layz ard*' - meaning the word I'm looking for is 'ard'. Still nothing. Except aardvark. I've already got a donkey. If I've got to cosy up to an aardvark, I'm out of here.

The word 'key' makes me shiver. A key was one of the clues that led me to Bantry's Bluff – I kept dreaming about a key that cried tears of blood. In a flash that comes and goes just as fast, I see myself standing on the beach, holding the wet key in my hand. What happened then? I opened something.

Sure that I'm getting somewhere now, I go to the last two words: 'shoe' and 'shot'. The English meanings are implausible. A *chou* is a cabbage, which describes the state of my brain, but I toss that into the cast-off pile with aardvark. Beyond that my French isn't good enough to play with the sounds. I'm stumped. With Gaston's poems there was something to go on – a hint from each language that made the meaning clear – but my message seems to be in code.

I stare at the whole second line, frustration mounting to bursting point. I wrote these words in the middle of the night for a good reason. What? I rummaged in my makeup purse until I found a lipstick called Moulin Rouge and then I scrawled these words on a white tiled floor. Why?

Gaston answers the phone and says he'll be happy to see me again on Sunday. I don't tell him I'm bringing some strange words for him to translate, and he doesn't mention Genevieve. He does tell me about the train from Tours to Chinon, perhaps so I can be independent. Good. I won't be telling her about my visit.

CHAPTER
Twenty-Five

Being Sleek is tomorrow, so I get an early night. Without the aid of medication. Fabienne is going to kick things off again, but this time I want to be there.

When I arrive at the Vinci centre, Alister is already waiting. Hasn't he seen enough? I winged it last time, didn't I?

The sight of him sets my senses aflutter. I really am a schoolgirl around him – running away one minute, swooning the next. After that second kiss, I'm worried he's going to pull me behind the nearest damask curtain and I'll abandon the workshop to join in. I've never felt like this before – this interconnectedness on a carnal level. It's like a kind of music caressing my skin until it burns. It was never like this with Andrew. When I was sixteen he seduced me with his will, conned me that control was love. He cryovacked my schoolgirl heart and now it's starting to thaw.

It makes me think of another schoolgirl – Fleur. The one who's cryovacked forever. Is that why Alister is attracted to me? My lack of sophistication reminds him of her? It's enough to ring the alarm bells again. But how do I turn back from here?

Being Sleek has an extra edge to it today, inspired by my awareness of the man at the back of the room. The participants pick up on the buzz, and at the end of the day no-one wants to go. While they stay, I don't have to face Alister, so I call for wine and canapés. By the time everyone leaves – including Fabienne, who makes a discreet exit – it's late. Just the staff remain, doing a final tidy up.

Alister has said nothing all day. Now he walks up and takes my elbow, then steers me towards the stairs and onto the street. I don't know where he's staying, but I'm about to find out. Unless something happens to change the course of history.

It does.

Its name is Andrew.

I shouldn't have answered the phone. But when I see it's Judy, I do.

"Thank God, Selkie," she says. "I thought I mightn't get you." Her voice is strange. Husky and desperate.

"What? What's he done?"

"There's been...a fire."

"I don't understand."

Beside me, Alister's face has gone from passionate to pissed off to perturbed. My legs have gone shaky so he's pulled me onto a street bench.

"It's gone, Selkie. The Beach Road house. It's...a pile of ash."

"But it's been there for a hundred years. Why would it...burn down now?'

"Old weatherboard – it happens. The police are investigating, but it could be as simple as an electrical fault."

Something fizzes in my brain. "We had the house rewired."

"Something else then. I'm sorry, Selkie. It's not my preferred way to solve a property settlement."

"There's...still the block of land," I stammer.

"Yes. And less to quibble over, so he shouldn't object to fifty-fifty. Plus the insurance."

The insurance. It's happening too fast and my head is spinning. She suggests I call the insurance company, but it's not yet daytime in Sydney.

"Where was he...when the fire broke out?"

"Far away."

"Of course."

"Fire investigators will go over it, Selkie. With a fine toothcomb. The insurance won't pay until they're satisfied. If they've got questions and they don't pay, then you've lost your equity in the house."

"And I get to visit Andrew in prison."

We haven't said it yet, but we both know. Me, because I'm psychic and my skin's been prickling with heat all day. Judy, because she's got a nose for ex-husbands with a penchant for revenge. It's Andrew's final act of retribution. He only ever wanted a house near the beach, any house; but I was the one who slaved my guts out trying to turn it into a home. Destroying what I created makes for the ultimate payback. If he can get away with it.

Alister walks me to Fabienne's, knowing our evening has gone up in smoke. Fabienne is staying with a friend, so he pours two glasses of wine and finds bread and cheese in the fridge. I haven't got the stomach for it. I keep remembering the heat on my skin all day, how I thought it was Alister. Judy's call has created a greater sense of loss than the pile of cinders that used to be my home.

I know he'll go if I ask him to, but I need his company. When I fall asleep on the sofa, he covers me with a blanket and makes a bed for himself on the other couch – as I discover when I wake around midnight after a disturbing dream.

A cat was on fire. It raced along the top of a paling fence, turned its blazing eyes on me, then disappeared. I've never liked cats, but I know someone who adores them. Juliet's been posting images of the tiny kittens she's been hiding under Andrew's floorboards. The dream makes me check in with her on Facebook, but she hasn't posted anything since the fire.

I look at the clock, then call the insurer in Sydney. I keep things like policy numbers in my Dropbox files, but when I give them the number I find Andrew's got the drop on me.

"He's cancelled our joint policy and taken out a new one in his name only," I tell Judy when I call her back.

Something in her voice changes - the suspicion she was suppressing for my sake. "Did he now? Did they say when?"

"They wouldn't tell me any more because I'm not on the policy."

"Clever," she says. "When the fire's deemed an accident, the insurer will pay him the full amount."

"But it's my house too."

"You'll have to sue him for it."

***

When daylight steals into the room, neither of us is very good company. We've spent our first night together on separate sofas, fully clothed, and with Andrew haunting the space between us - a wraith with ash on his face.

Without a word Alister scrambles eggs, while I keep seeing the pile of embers where my house used to be. The ultimate symbol of my homelessness. I'd already said goodbye to it when I won the green card and ran away, but its destruction - and my suspicions - have rekindled the emotion of giving it up. This morning it feels like Andrew has finally claimed victory over me.

After a silent breakfast, I see Alister to the door.

"Please don't leave town without telling me," he says,

giving me a platonic hug.

"I'm not going anywhere till the seminars are over."

Another week. Then what?

"I thought you might jump on the next plane to Sydney."

"No. What about you? When do you go back to London?"

"I'm finished in London. With business. Pleasure is another matter."

His apartment. The one with two bedrooms. Perfect to consolidate our new sleeping arrangements.

"Or there's New York," he says. "Davina flies out in a day or two."

It might have been fun, a few days together in either city. But the fire has burnt our fingers.

Derek phones. When I tell him the news, he's in no doubt about who's been playing with matches. "Torching the house - that's ruthless even for a troglodyte like him. But it's hard to disguise arson. Those investigators know all the tricks."

"Judy was talking about an electrical fault, but all the cabling's new." And something about that's bothering me.

"They'll find where it started - which room, which piece of furniture. Then they'll know." He pauses before adding, "It's tough that the house is gone, Selkie, but...it cuts another cord with Andrew, doesn't it?"

"Burning down my house and pocketing all the insurance money? Yep, he's cut the cord all right and set me adrift with nothing, DD. Nothing to show for eighteen years of oppression."

"I know, but sometimes bad things have a good side, that's all I'm saying."

I say goodbye to Derek, and cry until I'm done. I no

longer own a house with Andrew Tabrett. It's hard to walk out on all those years with someone, even if he's destroying you. I got away from him, but the house where I never belonged was shackling me to Andrew. Because the walls were smeared with my essence?

Until we reached a property settlement, it was always there, mocking my search for home. Burning it down was the final card up his sleeve, but Derek's right. He's set me free. Haggling over insurance money and a vacant block of land might keep me dangling on his leash, but for me there's no emotion any more. Now it's just about money.

CHAPTER
Twenty-Six

The day is warm and it's a long walk from the station. I'm sweating by the time I reach Gaston's door. Before I knock, I take another look over the edge to the river. It's a vertigo-inducing drop and again it takes me back to Bantry's Bluff. There was something that couldn't be seen from the top of the cliff...the reason I disappeared. It could only be seen from the beach. But if I've got to overcome my fear and go back to find the answer, why did the symbols bring me to France?

My mind returns to the lipstick message burning a hole in my pocket. My little collection of objects didn't start a tsunami, but it did start a slow chain reaction. With the final clue ending in Chinon.

I turn away from the precipice and knock on the now familiar door. Gaston appears in the archway and signals me in.

"I don't see too well these days," he says, "especially with the light behind. But I know it's you, Selkie from Oz. You're the only visitor who doesn't have to duck."

The *troglo* is a kind of hobbit house with a tiny front door, but inside the curved ceilings allow most people to stand at full height. I remember Hugo as a typical Frenchman, stocky, not tall. Once he's through the door, he'd be able to move around easily. Is he the person who comes each morning to get his brother out of bed?

"Let me guess," Gaston says. "You have not come back because I'm...fascinating."

I laugh. "Not totally true. Your poems fascinate me – how you write them, what they mean. And your poetry is why I'm here. I need your help with a translation."

"Nothing to do with Gennie?"

"No."

"You told her my answer and she's gone?"

I hesitate. After the news about the twins, Genevieve's quest is her own. But Gaston needs an answer. "She's waiting around for a while. In case you change your mind."

"*Merde.* What does she want with a cripple? If she thinks she still loves me, I'm in trouble. There's nothing to stop her knocking on my door."

Time to change the subject, but when I put the message on the table Gaston says, "Coffee."

Holding his coffee carefully, he peers at the reversed message under the strong lamp. It's such a cruel disease, MS. The girl at uni told me how she once went into remission. For three weeks she could walk and see, with no symptoms at all. She partied like there was no tomorrow, until the morning when she woke to find all her disabilities had returned in one hit. No gradual decline this time. She was utterly confronted with her helpless state and wished she'd used the remission to end it all, because now she'd lost the ability to do it.

"*Quee air on tro glo,*" Gaston reads. "That's Hugo's business."

"And yours?"

"I polish the bangles after he makes them. It's one thing I can still do." He points at the message. "Where did it come from, this *franglais*?"

I hadn't planned to tell him but of course he needs to know. He listens to the drama I wreaked on Nigel's kitchen floor.

"I'm not fascinating," he says, "but you are, Selkie from Oz."

"Only mixed up and selfish," I hear myself say.

"Pah." He returns to the words on the paper. "I can tell you what this says, but I can't tell you what it means. You understand?"

I nod. "I'm the only one who can work out the meaning. Because it's personal."

"If the story you told me is true, about how you wrote it in your sleep."

"It's true."

"And you want me to translate?"

"Yes."

"A favour?"

"Yes." I swallow, fearing what's coming.

"Then I ask a favour back."

"What?" The word pops out before I can soften it. In spite of my misgivings, I can't refuse a return favour for a blind man in a wheelchair. I think of Keith. Did I meet him to prepare me for this encounter? "Sorry. A favour for a favour. If it's...legal."

He laughs, then coughs, and signals for me to bring a glass of water.

"You are good at finding people," he says, when he gets his breath back. "I need you to find an old friend. He doesn't know about this." He points to himself with a shaky finger. "I was too...ashamed so I hid. I need you to find him...and tell him."

I'm so relieved it's not a pillow over his face that I agree instantly. "I'll do my best. I need his name and everything you know about him. Where does he live?"

"You don't ask why?"

"You want to find an old friend. The reason is none of

my business."

"I tell you anyway. I'm going to ask him to kill me."

While I'm reeling from too much information – and my own prescience – Gaston returns to my message. A favour for a favour. I've been desperate to know what the words say, but now I want to make a run for it. Do I have the right to deny him contact with his old friend? Even when I know the agenda?

Gaston hums while he thinks, enjoying the mental task. Perhaps he's also enjoying the company of the girl with the funny accent, a break in his hermit-like monotony.

He's finished as quickly as I predicted and dictates the words for me to write.

"Look for..." he begins, "Gaston's friend." He laughs at his joke. "No, no, but this says you must look for something. It knows you're good at looking, *n'est-ce pas?*" He continues, "*Cherchez* the lizard – *lézard* is lizard. Look for the lizard that...whispers."

The lizard that whispers. I've had seals, I've had donkeys and butcherbirds, now lizards. At least it's not a bloody aardvark. I think of Sylvie, but her geckos didn't whisper, far from it. Just like Coral in the bus shelter, just like a fortune cookie, the message is cryptic, leaving me to figure out what it means.

I should be feeling elated that I've got something tangible to work with, but the animal clue has reminded me of Donkey Skin, the bargain she made. Gaston has fulfilled his part of the bargain and now it's my turn to find his friend. Donkey Skin didn't know how her story would end, but she kept faith with the discomfort until destiny took over. I'm about to do the same.

***

On the train back to Tours, my promise to Gaston focuses my mind. I ran from death when I thought someone was trying to kill me, but I'm not confined to a wheelchair and facing a slow lonely decline. Miguel Sanchez must be special – a true friend with a rare courage – if Gaston thinks he'll help him die.

How will I find him? I'm about to start with Google, when I remember that Genevieve mentioned Miguel drinking at the Bay Bar. I can't ask her about this, but Gaston used to drink there too, used to poke fun at Nigel's kayak. Maybe Nigel knows Miguel.

I send Nigel a text and he surprises me by calling straight back.

"I've just finished a shift. You want to know about Miguel Sanchez – the captain of *Déesse de Mer?*"

"Yeah. I've met Gaston – Tony Luce – here in Tours."

Nigel whistles. "The missing man."

"It's a long story. He's trying to get in touch with Miguel."

"Miguel's still sailing the Pacific. He comes into the Bay Bar now and then. A big guy with a big black moustache."

While I wait, he texts the barman. Within minutes, he's got Miguel's contact details and I forward them to Gaston.

"Awesome, Nige. Thanks."

I think. Because it's done, just like that. Another secret I can't share.

Derek's listening in, so I update them both on the lipstick message. Derek's miffed that he didn't even know about Gaston, but he's somewhat mollified when I read out his translation.

"I would have got most of this," he sniffs, "if I'd thought to reverse the words. Spoons in a Cave."

The last time we Skyped, he noticed Alister's gift on my

wrist and said another spoon on the scene made the hairs on his arms stand up.

"*Cherchez*," he continues. "That's easy. Even you would have got that, Nige." He works his way through the rest. "*Lézard*, 'lizard'. OK. Is it masculine or feminine? It doesn't say. 'Key' must be *qui*, according to Gaston the guru. Meaning 'who' or 'that'. Makes sense. And 'shoe shot' is *chuchote*, 'whisper'. Look for the lizard that whispers. It reminds me of that new French restaurant in downtown Honolulu – *Au Lapin qui Fume*. I'm down to write a review but the name puts me off – At the Smoking Rabbit's. While I'm tucking into my *escargots*? Pass."

"At least you know where that rabbit is," I say. "The lizard that whispers is still at large."

I wonder if there are lizards in France. Talking lizards. Or if I'm meant to return to Hawaii and spend another night with the geckos. There are blue-tongue lizards in Sydney. Tongues whisper. But I refuse to go back to Sydney. With my luck, when I find the reptile he'll whisper the truth in Swahili.

"Your messages use a lot of animal symbols," Derek says. "That donkey on the back of the mutton-bird was a sleeper, until you started bumping into donkeys wherever you went. Are you going to start tripping over lizards now?"

***

The cobbled lane across from the station goes all the way to Rue Colbert. I cross the boulevard and walk past the Vinci centre, then past the park opposite the chocolate shop. Families are pushing strollers between the spring garden beds but I don't stop to smell the roses. At Gaston's we only drank coffee and I'm starving. It's Sunday, so many of the eateries are closed. Except for Bantry's Bar – 'pass' – and the Italian café on the other side of the square. I take a table with a view of the sauntering crowds and order a goat's cheese tart and a glass of rosé.

While I'm waiting, I send a text to Sylvie about the whispering lizard, without expecting an answer until tomorrow. Then I google *whispering lizard*, knowing the message can't be literal. There's a winery with that name in Margaret River, Western Australia – thousands of kilometres from Sydney and Andrew. There's a cautionary tale repeated on several religious sites about the red lizard that whispers lustful thoughts that must be resisted. I refuse to think about Alister. This lizard might be red, but so are herrings.

The food is taking its time. Around me, everyone is doing what the French do so well – passing time in convivial company over a glass or two. I can't even eavesdrop on their conversations. I think about calling Gretel, even dial her number, but hang up when I remember it's the middle of the night over there. Then my phone rings and it's her.

"Watch out, Gret. You might be turning psychic."

She laughs. "Only with missed calls. We keep the oddest hours – me, Tyler and my phone. What's the latest on Tabrett the Troglodyte?"

I glimpse the man who casts a shadow in my dreams. He's still at large. Has he been Andrew all along? Backlit by a house on fire?

"That's what I was going to ask you," I say.

Gretel's been linked into Andrew's social network since I ran away. It's how he broke the news about Juliet, letting me know he wasn't pining for his runaway wife. Not pining, plotting.

"He blocked me after my outburst on the phone," she

says. "You know what they say about truth – the supply exceeds the demand."

"He's burnt the house down."

"What?"

When I bring her up to date, Gretel whistles. "If he's capable of this, Selkie, he's capable of anything. Including hurting you physically. He's always been a psychopath, but this is a whole new level. You're staying away, aren't you?"

"Yeah."

But if he wants to get me he only has to do what his lawyer did. Catch a plane.

As Gretel rings off, a woman emerges from a doorway opposite the square and walks briskly towards town. Genevieve.

After she's out of sight, curiosity makes me abandon my table and walk to the doorway she emerged from. It's an ancient entrance to the floor above, framed by huge oak pillars. Over the door, a plaque pronounces something about Joan of Arc. If Joan was once here, I doubt she'd be impressed by the milliner and the artisan jeweller who've set up shop downstairs. I push against the door, which surprises me by opening, then climb the wooden staircase to the rooms above. On the landing there are three doors– two apartments and one office. Tours is a student town so there are lots of furnished digs to rent short-term. This must be where Genevieve's staying.

I'm turning back to the stairs when the sign above the office door catches my eye. *Sandrine Echinard. Avocat.*

Without thinking, I try the lawyer's door. It's unlocked. On a Sunday. Shit.

I'm backing away, when the door opens. A woman – early fifties and impeccably groomed in a tailored suit – looks at me quizzically, and I murmur an apology which makes her laugh.

"It's my day for *anglophones*," she says. "First an American. And now – let me guess – you are Irish?"

"Sure, sure, sure," I say in a parody of Davina, wondering why Genevieve is visiting a lawyer.

"How can I help?" she asks. "You are lucky to find me here on a Sunday, but a client had urgent business."

The French guard their weekends so Genevieve's business must have been very urgent. I remember that it's none of my business, then try to think of a way to find out more.

"Genevieve Luce is my friend. I thought she said to meet her here, but it looks like I've missed her."

"Madame Luce left a few minutes ago." She starts to close the door.

"Gennie needs a good lawyer, to be sure. It's grand that you can help her."

She smiles. "French law is complex, especially for foreigners. It is good that she has consulted me before she takes any action."

What action?

"For the children's sake," I improvise.

It's a remark too far and she raises a suspicious eyebrow.

Luckily my phone chimes.

I glance at the screen and exclaim, "Gennie. Waiting at the American café."

I wish Madame Echinard a *bon weekend* and almost fall down the stairs. If she asks her client about her Irish friend, I'm hoping Genevieve won't think of me.

The text is from Keith proposing we Skype. I text back that I'm going away for a few days, and let him know that he might get a call as I gave his number to Gaston.

Back at my table in the square, the waiter pulls a face

but brings my order. Genevieve and her cuckoo twins. An urgent appointment. French law. I had some friends who tried to buy a farmhouse in the Bourgogne but decided against it because of French law. I've forgotten the details, but one word stuck. It pops into my mind before I can call it back.

Inheritance.

CHAPTER
Twenty-Seven

It's the day I'm going to Rouffignac – another collision of caves and spoons. The excursion feels both arduous and portentous, and the troglodyte who haunts my dreams keeps me tossing and turning all night. Then, at the crack of dawn, a call from Judy puts everything in perspective. At the sound of her voice, something curdles inside me.

"Are you sitting down, Selkie? Things just got...complicated."

"Arson?" The burning cat comes to mind.

"Still too hot to investigate. No, a policeman I know is keeping me informed off the record. He just called. This morning, two neighbours spoke to a fireman guarding the site. They said that a young woman stays with Andrew most weekends and they were wondering where she is."

Neville and Doug, missing their peepshow. I swallow.

"The firemen were sure there was no-one in the house. No...bodies. The police were called. They walked around the ruins and were leaving when they heard a muffled cry. From underneath."

Bloody hell. She was with the kittens.

"She was trapped under the floorboards. Andrew's girlfriend, Julia Saunders."

"Juliet."

"You know her?"

I start to cry. "Yes. Is she OK?"

"Not in great shape. She was down there for over forty hours. She's suffering from smoke inhalation, dehydration, slight concussion, a broken finger and sundry grazes. And shock. But she's alive."

Juliet could have died down there. Under my house. The tears flow as I imagine the cheeky woman I remember hearing the fire and trying to open the trapdoor above her head. Falling back, huddling alone in the dark, covered in filth, fearing she was going to be buried alive, then being trapped for days with no-one hearing her calls.

"There was some cat food apparently," Judy says. "She ate that. A saucer of milk. No water. It took them a while to get her out –"

"– because there's only the trapdoor in the dining room floor. The foundations are bricked in."

"Yes, too hot and too much rubble to get to her from above, so they had to smash a hole in the foundations with a sledgehammer. Have you been down there?"

"Yeah." The image of a trapped Juliet comes back. "It's dark, a bit damp. Only space to crouch. I tried growing mushrooms once."

"Well, the dampness saved her life. And the tiled floor. The tiles stopped the flames penetrating the underfloor. And not much smoke either."

The tiles I imported from Italy against Andrew's wishes. They saved her life. And without the peeping toms across the road, she might still be trapped down there, slowly starving to death.

"Didn't anyone else notice she was missing?" Like Andrew?

"She's been staying with Andrew at weekends," Judy says. "Her mother assumed they were together."

"Why weren't they?"

"The police want to know that. They're checking Andrew's account of events, and waiting to interview Juliet.

Andrew's 'a person of interest' until the matter of arson is resolved. It's complicated," she says again, "because if it's arson, this could be…attempted murder."

***

When I pick up my hire car late morning, I'm already exhausted after the news about Juliet. It's probably why it takes me an hour to navigate my way out of Tours. There are roadworks and detours and one-way streets, and the GPS directs me onto a road that ends at the railway line with barely room to turn around. Fabienne's mud map saves the day and I'm suddenly entering a motorway. But my relief is short-lived when I see a sign to Paris. I'm going in the wrong direction. It feels symbolic as I exit and find the opposite entrance.

Motorways are easy. No obstacles. Just keep going till you get there, then stop. Until the exit, when overconfidence at the first roundabout leads me to look the wrong way. Cars bear down from the left and, in a fluster, I take a turning onto a narrow industrial road, only to be tailgated by an enormous logging truck. At last there's somewhere to pull over, and I return to the roundabout and take a provincial road with little traffic. Phew.

I stop too long at a restaurant frequented by vans with ladders – a sure sign, according to Fabienne, of a good lunch for a good price, including a glass of wine – which means I hit Périgueux in the middle of the afternoon peak hour. Again the GPS is out of its depth in the maze of narrow streets. I see a hotel sign, pull into its parking lot and burst into tears. I've already paid for a room above a brasserie and was looking forward to some local food and ambience downstairs. But finding it will be impossible. I stare at the modern ugliness of the hotel I've chanced upon. Ugly and expensive. At least there'll be a good bathroom.

As evening falls, I'm wandering through a pedestrian precinct of crooked lanes and old buildings, congratulating myself for getting here and gazing at menus in lighted windows. La Grotte Illustrée catches my eye – The Illustrated Cave. How could I go any further?

The interior walls press in on me with clumsy *trompe l'oeil* murals – modern scenes, no prehistoric knock-offs. There's not another soul in the place but the food is good enough. Only the wall art gives me indigestion. Or it's my expectations buzzing fit to burst. In a few hours I'll find out why I had to go through the ordeal of getting here. Tomorrow it's the real thing. La Grotte de Rouffignac.

***

Underground, we were all dumbstruck with awe, but as our group emerges, the bright sun on our faces turns one of my companions on like a tap.

"They had to be in some sort of trance," he says in an English accent to no-one in particular. "A shamanic journey to the centre of the unconscious, channelling the spirits of the animals they were in harmony with. Look at the way the paintings are floating on the walls. They're akin to *gods*."

We're all moving towards the parking lot.

"One thing's certain," the guy continues, "they never lived down there. So they had to have a bloody good reason for going right down into the darkest most hidden corners of the deepest caves, with only hand-held flames for light, crawling, squeezing through cracks, lying on their backs in those narrow spaces and transforming the walls into what amounts to...prehistoric *prayers*."

Their tourist coach has blocked in my car. I'll have to wait till they leave.

"The perspective gives it away," he says, as his companions line up at the coach door. "How did they paint the animals in the right proportions like that, while their noses were pressed to the surface of the rock? They had to be *channelling*."

No-one else has spoken. The tour guide starts counting heads.

"They would have used chanting and ecstatic dancing to put themselves under and lose their fear. Then, when they reached the darkest recesses, the painting would have been a ritualistic connection with the divine. When they came back to the surface, it was like returning from the centre of the *soul*." He pauses. "You know what Picasso said when he saw the cave paintings at Lascaux?"

Everyone ignores him, but he goes on anyway.

"We've learnt nothing, that's what he said. In the thirty thousand years since the cave painters, we've become modern and sophisticated, we've invented logic and science, we've separated our conscious minds from our unconscious...but we've learnt nothing – *nothing* – about art."

"Those paintings," a woman says, "made me feel...alive."

At this observation, the talker shuts up.

As the group starts to board, another guy murmurs to his neighbour, "I was going to say I liked the horses more than the mammoths, but I've changed my mind."

His neighbour chuckles. "What he said was probably right. But for gawd's sake let us have some thoughts of our own."

When the coach drives off, I get into my car and rest my head on the steering wheel. Like the man said, Rouffignac is a profound experience. I wouldn't have missed any of it – getting up before dawn so I was sure to get a ticket, hugging the right-hand side of the narrow road in the early light, shivering with cold as the little open-top train carried our group deeper and deeper into the cave, seeing the scratches on the walls made by cave bears long before the painters came, standing in the dark in the groove cut for the train where the painters had to lie on their backs, turning on our head torches and looking up at the Great Ceiling in hushed silence, admiring the majesty of over sixty animals above us, feeling a strange sense of connection to those ancient people who felt inspired to create such art.

None of that is why I'm hunched over the steering wheel, gazing into my empty heart.

The spoon guided me to Rouffignac, and the message said to find the whispering lizard. I was sure those two symbols were going to collide here. *Ho'ohihi.* I was counting on it. I scanned the Great Ceiling looking for anything that could represent a reptile, but the animals in Rouffignac are all large beasts. In desperation I even looked for a donkey. But it was like the painting in my dream – something I want to see but can't.

This morning's experience was profound on many levels, but as far as a deeper insight goes, some blinding flash about the symbols that brought me here, I'm with Pablo. After all the expectations about Rouffignac, I've learnt nothing, nothing at all.

It's late when I return the car in Tours and catch the bus to the artisan quarter. I'm relieved that Fabienne isn't home. I don't want her to ask about my communion with the troglodytes of Rouffignac, not until I feel up to telling her the truth.

I check my messages and find that Sylvie has scoffed at my enquiry about whispering lizards.

My geckos are my best friends, she writes. *And I love their chatter. But haven't gone 'lolo' enough to think they're chattering to me.*

A shower does its best to wash off the day's despair. Then I wander downstairs with the *guinguette* in mind – a drink or two and some music to transport me beyond my troubles. But on the street, Genevieve steps out of the shadows.

"What?" I ask, not breaking my stride.

"I need to talk to you," she says.

"And I need to be alone."

"What's wrong? You know you're my only friend in Tours."

"Some friend. You sent me to talk to Gaston without telling me the truth."

"That's why we need to talk."

I keep walking and she follows me. We cross the road to the riverbank where the evening's hubbub has barely begun. I choose a stage with African drummers – percussion to resonate with my mood. I get a glass of wine and take a table. Genevieve joins me.

"I've got things on my mind, Genevieve. Private things." I gaze into the mirrored water and ignore her.

"I've seen a lawyer," she says, hoping to snare me.

"Sandrine Echinard," I say.

She starts to ask how I know, then stops.

"Let me guess," I say. "You're thinking about the twins' inheritance."

"How did you know?"

"Just psychic."

"Look, Selkie, I don't know what I've done, but I need to talk to you. About the lawyer."

I put down my glass and face her. "Gaston's got MS. His mother died from it. His uncle died from it. So he got a genetic test, then the *snip*." It's brutal but I want her to go. "Before he met you."

As expected she's looking shell-shocked.

"I know the twins aren't his," I continue. "So whatever you've been saying to the lawyer, I don't want to know. OK? I've heard enough secrets that are none of my business."

She's silent for a while. "Does Tony know? About the twins?"

"I didn't tell him."

She looks relieved. "You need to hear the truth."

"It's too late for that. Just go."

"The twins aren't mine either."

Bloody hell. She knows how to get my attention.

I sigh. "I know I'm going to regret this. Tell me everything."

"It's very simple," she says. "The twins are my nephews, my sister's boys. Clementine's been in and out of rehab for years. Heroin mostly, but she's not fussy. She got pregnant to some guy she didn't remember, then couldn't look after them. I stepped in."

The link with my own childhood surfaces. Stella stepping in and mothering her niece. Me.

"You let Alister think they're yours."

Why do I care?

"Don't look at me like that. I didn't plan it. We met at a charity fundraiser, and the twins were with me. Alister thought they were mine. I let people think that – for their sake – and they've been calling me 'Ma' since they could talk. Alister and I started seeing each other and...it became too late to tell him."

She'd found a man who'd love them and father them – until he met me. It could be true.

"So why do you need a French lawyer?" I ask.

"To get a divorce."

"But you must know he'll be dead soon."

Sooner than she thinks if Miguel comes good.

"That's the point. I've read Tony's blog, I've seen how he is. The boys aren't his, but when he dies they'll get his property."

"Why?"

"It's complicated. Sandrine says that because I adopted the boys while Tony and I were married, French law considers them his children. Even divorce won't change that, and neither will changing his will. In this country it's almost impossible to disinherit your children. Tony's got to declare that Joel and Jake are not his. The vasectomy helps... I didn't know." Her voice catches, but she's saving her emotions for later. "He's got to prepare a legal document with attachments like his vasectomy date, their birth dates, when he left me – and then leave his estate to someone else."

"And he doesn't know any of this because he's refused

to see you."

She nods. "Sandrine rang him this morning, but he hung up on her."

"Maybe it doesn't matter if the boys get his money."

Except to his family. That would be a shock.

"It's not what I want." I remember that she didn't want Alister's money either. "And there's something else. Clementine will try to get it. She loves money more than anything. She let me adopt her sons - that's how close she is to them - but she'll try to get her hands on their inheritance, even if it means I lose my house and we end up on the street."

Another image that resonates. She's pushing all my buttons.

Of course I agree to speak to Gaston. As a favour to him more than anything.

Genevieve's relieved. This is a relationship of convenience and we both know it. Her glass is empty and she's just about to go, when I remember Alister's plans to put money in trust for the twins.

"You've got to tell Alister about this, Genevieve. So his money for the twins' education is somewhere Clementine can't get it."

"OK, but Tony's urgent. Alister...can wait."

"No, he can't. He's still in Tours. I know it's going to be hard to tell him, but you've got to do it. Before I talk to Gaston. Otherwise no deal."

She looks like it's an emotional bridge too far, but agrees to do it tomorrow. When she leaves, I get another glass of wine and a plate of *frites*. Sometimes a girl's got to eat *frites* and now is one of those times.

When my head hits the pillow a few hours later, it doesn't surprise me that the troglodyte of my dreams has abandoned me.

***

Keith does his Skyping after work, which is early morning here. The screen opens to his craggy face and Daisy looking eager on her chair beside him. Keith's been talking to Gaston, and thanks me for the referral.

"I'm surprised he got in touch," I say. "Counselling seems like the last thing Gaston would go for."

Not while a bullet's a live option. Because Miguel Sanchez sounds like a gunslinger with his big black moustache and a belt of ammo over his shoulder. A fanciful thought, but if he's not going to shoot Gaston, how's he going to do it without being a murderer? The question is doing my head in.

"We've got a lot in common," Keith is saying. "It gave us a connection from the start."

"That's what I thought. What did you talk about?"

"Can't tell you that, Selkie. He's a client."

"Oh." But I want to know. "OK. If I was a client, what would *we* talk about?"

"Your memory loss. What you're blocking. We'd peek under a few rocks, tease open a few cracks, slip into some dark recesses and light a few virtual candles."

It's poetic coming from a blind guy, but candles in the dark throw spooky shadows and I don't want to think about my troglodyte dream.

"That way we might uncover what you've forgotten and why," he adds.

"Has Gaston forgotten something?"

He sighs. "No comment. And why do you want to know? He might be your friend but his psychology is none of your business."

Not quite true, but I'm not going to tell Keith about Miguel. There's a code of friendship too. I can't help wondering if a session with Keith has made Gaston change his mind about ending it all. Keith seems to bring a lot of people back from the brink. Which takes me right back to the cliff. In my case, I went over.

"How do you know him?" Keith asks.

I tell him the saga of Alister and Genevieve, how meeting Alister started a relationship tsunami that swept around the world and washed me up on Gaston's doorstep. Then I tell him about Gaston's *bloglo* and my own reverse *franglais* in lipstick on the kitchen floor. It's an amazing tale and he's hooked. And Daisy's eyes are dancing as if she's followed every word. I remind myself they liked me before they knew my story.

"Moulin Rouge," Keith says. "Red's my favourite colour. It's the only colour I can hear."

I laugh. "How does that work?"

"The emotion behind it...lingers like a love song. It's dramatic. Intense. And...true."

"Like the call of the butcherbird."

I tell him I bought the app and grab my phone. Soon the call fills the French air with the sounds that match the description on the app: *Slow, rich, mellow, with liquid notes that seem perfectly chosen to reflect the loneliness of moonlit nights in the outback.* Afterwards we sit in silence. Not your usual Skype behaviour, but it reminds me how important companionship is. Just being with someone you're close to – even if they're on the other side of the world. Even if they can't see you. Breathing together is enough.

I think of Gaston alone in his *troglo* and remember my promise to visit him today.

Keith is the first to speak. "The sound of red," he says. "Thank you. I'll treasure it."

"But you can listen any time."

"You've given me a new experience of it. And if I play it too often, it spoils the magic. Better to savour it. Like the Buddhists who only see the outside world through a crack. A crack that amplifies the experience."

"That's not my philosophy," I say, always one to overdo things. "I play it over and over and it still gets me here." He can't see me tap my chest. "Every time."

"Why?"

He's good at what he does, and I want to tell him. Not as a counsellor, as a friend.

"OK. First there's...the longing. Those long soaring notes, they're so...sad. And ecstatic. It's a paradox. And it arouses all the emotions in-between. Longing...fulfilled."

"Is that why it touches you?"

"It's what I saw in the mirror after Derek found me on the beach. My eyes were glowing. They seemed to say that whatever happened to me, it wasn't traumatic. Not like a war zone, where amnesia makes sense. Something amazing happened out there."

"You want to get the ecstasy back."

"Yes."

The realisation takes my breath away. I was so sure I was blocking it.

"That's why you can't remember, Selkie. It won't come back by wanting it. It comes back by...not wanting it."

Another bloody paradox.

"I'll remember it when I'm doing the dishes?" Except Fabienne's got a dishwasher.

"Something like that. When you're fully in the moment doing something that consumes your attention."

It's what Nigel said once about aura-reading. And spoon-bending. Bloody spoons. These things only happen when you're focused on something else. When you don't care if they happen or not.

"So wanting to go back there and solve the mystery," I say, "is like worrying away at a problem and getting nowhere. All the effort is actually counterproductive."

"You've got a lot of wisdom, Selkie. Listen to it."

Or listen to a whispering lizard.

"How do I listen without trying too hard?"

Is that why I missed the power of Rouffignac? So busy trying to find the clue, and getting caught up in my frustration, that it went right by me?

"You've already done it. You were listening when you collected those objects and wrote those words backwards in lipstick."

"I was asleep."

"Your subconscious was awake. It was creating a picture of something beyond your conscious knowing. Beyond your desire to know. It was neutral. It just *was*. And you've been following the clues in a haphazard way that feels right. Keep doing that – following your gut."

My peptic intuition getting another workout.

Keith is chuckling. "I call it thinking crookedly – the opposite of thinking straight. That's how the meaning of the words will come to you. They'll make sense in a flash one day, when you're looking the other way."

He's very convincing. Something's got to pop. I just hope it isn't me.

"Here was I thinking I'd have to wear a raincoat and loiter in reptile parks with boiled ants in my pocket instead of sweets."

He laughs.

But there's something creepy about a lizard that whispers - hiding in the shadows, catching you unawares. Not like the gecko catching the cockroach on Sylvie's wall - that's survival. A lizard that whispers is sinister, murmuring things you don't want to hear. A donkey skin is creepy too, but at least it doesn't talk.

"I found a winery called Whispering Lizard," I say. "Maybe it's telling me to drink more."

Keith laughs. "Alcohol can be useful, especially the first glass. After that the benefit declines with the quantity consumed. Eventually your intuition is totally impaired."

My usual state of 'wisdom'.

"The other thing that works," he says, "is art. Playing with art materials stimulates the subconscious."

Davina would love this guy. If only she was here. Then I remember Fabienne. I've got an art therapist on tap and I haven't noticed. She can help me mind-map the message. Better still, I can join in the exercise in my next seminar. I've been so busy helping everyone else think crookedly, I've overlooked myself.

I start to laugh and Keith joins in. "Why are we laughing?" he asks and I tell him about Fabienne.

"Not all artists are good at guiding others," he says. "Some are stuck in their own creative impasse. They demand perfection - from themselves and their students - and that inhibits crooked thinking."

"I've seen Fabienne in action and she's very crooked. She personifies *sleek*. She's helped a lot of people get out of a mental rut. And she's French. Just her accent loosens you up."

Keith is laughing again. "You make me laugh, Selkie. Not many people can do that. It's a gift."

***

So far I haven't made Gaston laugh, but while he's breathing there's still hope. But telling him Genevieve's inheritance news won't be funny.

After Keith signs off, I try Gaston and he accepts the call.

"You have spoken to Miguel," he says.

"No. I'm ringing to see if I can visit you."

"We had a deal. I translated your *franglais* –"

"– and I got you Miguel's address." Then I remember he wanted me to tell Miguel about his condition so he wouldn't have to do it himself. Shit. "I forgot about the other part, Gaston. Sorry."

"Do it."

Looks like the laughing is on hold for the moment. For both of us.

I hover over a blank email. Am I responsible for what happens next? It's the relationship tsunami all over again – my knack for creating a swathe of consequences wherever I go. I keep telling myself that what happens between Miguel and Gaston is none of my business, but part of me isn't buying it.

I try to do what Keith said – listen to my own wisdom – and in the end I can't deny Gaston the right to be in touch with his friend.

I tell Miguel how I know Gaston, then inform him about his disease. I say that his friend would like to hear from him 'for old times' sake'. I sign off and hit send.

"It's done," I tell Gaston over the phone. "I said to ring you or Skype you, because reading emails is getting hard."

"You've done me a big favour, bigger than the translation."

That's what I'm afraid of. But now it's out of my hands.

I take out the pushbike Fabienne has lent me and ride to a bakery on the other side of Tours. It's a family-run affair with the wife behind the counter, being patient with my French, and her husband in the background, covered in flour. I've been here a couple of times, because I love to ride like the wind back to the artisan quarter with a pannier full of baguettes. Like a local. The tourists who take my photo are fooled. Little do they know that I'm only passing through, that they're snapping an Australian girl with a Celtic name and a Hawaiian haircut who's eating her way into French culture until she discovers where she belongs.

Back at the apartment, I sink my teeth into heavenly bread lashed with butter and jam. I can't trust Genevieve to keep her promise, so I send Alister a text – getting mixed up in his business again.

Has Genevieve been in touch?

Are you involved in this?

Long story. Can we meet?

He's already at an outdoor table in Place Plumereau when I get there. His report on their meeting is brief.

"She lied to me about the boys, but I've still been the man in their lives for a year. A good influence, I hope. She won't let me see them, but I'm not going to abandon them."

"I know."

"Why did Gennie come clean with you?"

So she didn't say any more than she had to. I tell him what she told me about French inheritance law.

"She wants you to talk to Gaston? About his estate? Why did you agree to that?"

"We've developed a kind of...friendship."

"You and Gennie?"

"Me and Gaston."

If I want Alister to come with me – to convince Gaston that the twins exist – then I've got to tell him the rest.

"A vasectomy," he says. "A tough decision for him, but not telling Gennie..." He shakes his head.

"He's very disabled now."

"All this inheritance stuff might not be true," Alister says. "Gennie might have another agenda. Have you considered that?"

He's still got a low opinion of her. Her lie about the boys hasn't helped.

"I know. I'm just going to alert Gaston to the possible issue, then he can talk to his own lawyer if he wants to. But he's got to be reassured that the boys exist. That it's not just Genevieve trying to connect with him. That's where you come in."

Alister has a car, so after I've let Gaston know I'm bringing a friend, we drive to Chinon. The day has turned overcast and there's a strong breeze scouring the river valley. I haven't brought a jacket and Alister puts his arm around me as we climb the lane to the *troglo*. It's a gesture of protection, and it feels good to lean into him and share his warmth.

Gaston welcomes us. He seems to be enjoying the attention of strangers since I came into his life. I make coffee and put out the pastries we've brought, while Alister explains who he is.

"You used to date Gennie and now you date Selkie? And you're all staying in the same region as Gennie's runaway husband, all at the same time." He thinks for a minute. "What's the word?"

"Cosy?" I suggest.

"Incestuous," he says.

Wait till he hears the rest of the story. He might have to write a poem.

As I tell Gaston what Genevieve told me, Alister pulls out his phone and finds a good close-up of what used to be the happy family unit. Until I came along.

Gaston peers at the screen for a long time. "You know this sister?" he asks.

"No," Alister says.

"Pah. She didn't come to our wedding."

Neither did Hugo. But I thought this might happen, so I did some research in the car.

"She got busted a while back and it was in the local paper. I've found it online." I read out the brief report and her name: Clementine Davenport.

Gaston confirms it's Genevieve's maiden name. "I'll think about it," he says. "A lawyer is coming soon. I'll ask him."

He was already getting his house in order, before Miguel arrives. If Genevieve hadn't come looking for him, what would have happened to his estate? I wonder if this is one tsunami that's going to wash up a better outcome.

I step outside and text Genevieve to let her know it's done. When I return, Gaston floors me.

"You are both invited to my party," he says.

A party? "When?" Why?

"Miguel's idea. He rang me right after he got your email. He'll be here in a few days, then we'll make the date."

A party. After years of hiding away. Apparently, *Déesse de Mer* is back for a refit and the whole crew is coming to the party. As he talks about it, Gaston's mood is so much brighter that I update my image of Miguel Sanchez. Not a gunslinger. Or a murderer. The captain of *Déesse de Mer* is a miracle-worker.

***

In Makiki Heights, Derek's been busy. After the Donkey Skin incident he ordered a book. An analysis of French fairytales.

"To help me unpack the symbolism," he says. "After dabbling in Bruno Bettelheim and *The Uses of Enchantment* I'm hooked."

The girl at uni with MS was studying children's literature. I summarised several chapters of Bettelheim for her, so I know what I'm in for. And Derek's book has arrived just in time to stir some extra red herrings into my cauldron of clues. He reads me extracts from the analysis of the Donkey Skin story.

"Wait a minute, DD. I get that Donkey Skin's three gowns symbolise the different aspects of her character that she needs to discover, that they help her dig deep to find the power to escape her father and direct her own future. Then wearing the donkey skin and running away reflect a transformation, with a lot of ordeals she has to undergo so she can grow up and become independent. But the fairy godmother, are you saying she isn't some kind of *kahuna?*"

I want the fairy godmother to be like Coral, and her cave to be as benign as a bus shelter. But I can't forget the look in the old woman's eyes, just like my own in Wanda's mirror. While the light was throwing her shadow onto the wall just like in my dream.

"The grotto is lined with mother-of-pearl because it's a

sanctuary for Donkey Skin," Derek says. "She goes there for some time out to view her problem and explore her options. And the godmother is a symbol of Donkey Skin herself, of her own inner wisdom."

"But that...turns the tables on the troglodyte." Shit. "What does that say about the troglodyte in my dream? If the fairy godmother isn't an oracle like Coral, if she's the knowing part of Donkey Skin's own mind, then I could be dreaming about –"

"Your own inner cave."

Keith's words come back, about the cave near Uluru: "Like Jung says, the cave is now inside me."

"Then why can't I see what's on the walls?" I ask. "At least Donkey Skin got some clear instructions. I'm working blind."

"You're being literal, Selkie. The dream is playing out beyond your conscious mind. Like the objects you collected."

I'm thinking about the fiasco that was Rouffignac, about me doing my literal best to spot a lizard sporting a speech bubble.

"If the troglodyte is documenting the mood of my own subconscious," I growl, "it must be scrawling obscenities."

It's not Derek's fault and he can tell that I've had enough. After we hang up I pace for a minute, then hit the stairs. It's time to talk to Fabienne.

***

She's sitting at her studio window, playing with a design on paper. We've barely seen each other lately, and while she puts the kettle on I tell her about the translation of my message, about Rouffignac and the lizard.

She frowns at all the dead ends, but her face lights up when I tell her Keith's idea about the art. She puts down her mug and starts opening drawers and putting materials in a box.

"We go upstairs," she says. "More *liberté*. Not so much the air of another artist."

"I didn't mean now, Fabienne. I'll do a mind-map at the seminar." When I've got used to the idea.

"When is the best time to plant a tree?" she asks.

I shrug.

"Ten years ago. When is the second-best time? Now."

She shoves a box in my arms and picks up another. Then she pushes me out the door and locks up.

Upstairs she points me to a chair, and shoves yarn and knitting needles into my hands. "Knit."

I can't help laughing. "What am I going to knit? A mind-map?"

"I do not answer stupid questions. Knit. Until it is time to stop."

This is a side she hasn't shown in the seminars. She's adapting her style to suit her pupil. She knows that I need a firm hand.

I start casting on stitches the way I learnt years ago, when Stella sent me to the Girl Guides. I didn't last as a Guide - too hard to tame - but I did learn how to knit. Today I knit crazily, inspired by the atmosphere Fabienne is creating as she rushes about, opening the windows onto the garden, putting on a Vivaldi CD, filling the living room with light. There's something very soothing about the rhythm of my fingers and I stop thinking about everything but the yarn around the needles.

After a while she puts a large piece of art paper on the coffee table. It must be time to stop knitting. I sit cross-legged in front of the table where she's opened paint pots in vibrant colours.

"Painting with the fingers," she says.

The knitting has numbed my will to resist. I dip my fingers into as many tubs as possible at once and start pushing delicious blobs around the paper. There's a texture in the surface and I explore it, smearing the colours in satisfying streaks and making fingerprints here and there. Then I go for black and make stripes of various shapes and sizes, twisting my fingers to make lines that are thin or fat.

She keeps replacing the paper and I become mesmerised by the paint. Panels of thick colour appear, with patterns over the top. Squiggles emerge as I experiment with different parts of my hand. Then I pick up sticks and other objects to use as tools and apply the paint in quirky ways. I'm beyond conscious thought as I immerse myself in the colours and the shapes and the lines.

The next thing I know I'm wiping my fingers on a cloth and Fabienne is handing me a pencil. She's put a vase of flowers on a side table and tells me to draw it.

"Do not lift the pencil and do not look at the paper."

Her tone is very persuasive and I follow the instructions without question. It feels strange at first, working 'blind', but the finger painting has loosened me up and dissolved any need for perfection. I look directly at the flowers as the pencil makes confident lines. Before I'm tempted to look at the drawing, Fabienne takes it away and replaces the paper. This time there's a teapot to draw, then a bowl of fruit. Next she instructs me to find a corner of the room to draw, again without lowering my eyes to the page, then it's the window and the rooftops beyond.

The shadows outside are getting long as the light slips into that delicious time of day – the gloaming. An Irish word. For a moment I think of Davina and wonder where she is.

Fabienne is spreading all my creations across the floor and asks me to choose three to describe in haiku poems. The concept doesn't faze me and the words flow.

Next I combine the pencil and the paint.

"Make lines that please you," she says, "then use the light inside and outside to make shapes in the paint. Do not think about colour, think about tone. Light and dark."

If I was mesmerised before, I go way beyond that now to total immersion. I'm adoring the view from inside to outside, making lines for the objects in the room, now in shadow, then the doorway, the windows, the folds of the curtains, the curls of the iron rail, the patterns of the rough stone walls beyond. Because I'm not going for accuracy, it's easy just to draw my impressions. But when I pick up the paintbrush, I find it's the light that's whispering to me - the way the room has darkened with the dusk, and a ribbon of late sunlight between the buildings is stealing obliquely through the open window with a final flourish. I leave slashes of white paper to render the light and make panels of blues and purples for the darkening interior.

When I'm done, the room is dark. I've been working in the dark for I don't know how long. I look up to see Fabienne sitting in an easy chair with a glass in her hand, watching me. Beside her is a tea-light candle. It's the only light in the room.

"You are an artist," she says.

"A beginner."

"A beginner, a novice, a *débutante*. You are still an artist. Artists, they are born."

"You haven't seen what I've painted." I don't even know myself what I've painted.

"I see *how* you paint. With your whole being. Without light to see. You paint with your heart. It is enough."

I look down at my work, but it's hard to recognise what it is. Only the slash of white shows, lit by the twilight coming from the garden. Fabienne gets up and brings over the tea-light in its holder. She puts it beside my painting, then returns to her chair.

The flame throws a soft flickering light over the picture. I can see the whole image, but my eyes are immediately drawn to the crack of white paper slashing it in two. It's dramatic. Eloquent. It says something about light in dark places.

A snatch of music comes, then slips away.

Fabienne brings me a glass of champagne and turns on a lamp. She spreads out everything I've created.

"You paint like you knit," she says, "loose."

I laugh. "It's why I failed the Girl Guides. Knitting too loose." To match my character, according to Stella.

Fabienne pulls a face. "Many artists, they die as children, die in their hearts. But you paint with the fingers of a child. You dream on the paper. This is rare, good."

"Just like your mother," I hear Stella say. "Stop daydreaming and do something useful."

"And your blind drawings, they are...beautiful."

She's right. I can see the beauty. The lines are strong but loose. The overlapping shapes suggest the original objects in a way that looks like art.

"And what about this?" I ask, pointing to my final work.

"What does it say to you?"

"I can't take my eyes away from the light. It's sharp like a knife and it feels like it's cutting through something. My resistance."

I didn't know I was going to say that.

She nods. "What is it that you resist?"

"Death."

Bloody hell. Am I channelling Gaston? Or there's something in this champagne.

Fabienne doesn't think it's odd. "Art is a kind of death," she says. "Real art, it is painted in blood."

She says no more and gives me a large folder for my creations. Then we go downstairs to the Lebanese café at the end of the lane. The creative process has made us hungry and we each order a huge plate of shawarma. After the art therapy there's a new closeness between us, and I thank her for guiding me through it.

"When an artist is creating," she says, "it is a precious thing to breathe the same air."

On our way home, I realise I'm still no closer to decoding the message. My knitting was scaly enough, but it didn't resemble a lizard. My finger paintings conjured up nature – jungles, waterfalls, things that inspired my haikus – but no lizards. The message urges me to search him out, so if that indicates he's hard to find, it's matching my experience. But the art was supposed to stimulate my subconscious. "Tease open a few cracks" as Keith put it. It did that, but cracks I wasn't expecting. Fissures. Resisting death...where did that come from?

A text arrives from Alister: *Thinking of you. Sleep tight.*

I text him back a smile and get into my pyjamas. He's a considerate guy. A sexy guy. A rich guy. He wants me. So what's my problem?

My girlfriends would tell me to grab him and savour the ride, but that's what drove me into Andrew's arms. Alister reminds me of Andrew in one crucial way – not only his blue eyes, but what's behind them. His intensity. Andrew wanted me with a passion. His motivation might have been different – to possess me – but Alister's devotion feels as deep and unexplored as the fissure in my painting.

Davina phones from New York. We've been so focused on our own projects, we've hardly been in touch. But it's one of those friendships that doesn't need constant input. Gretel's got a term for it: foul-weather friends. "If they need help, I'm here," she says. "If they need maintenance, I'm out of here."

"Selkie Moon," Davina coos. "It's wonderful to hear your accent, girl."

"Yours too. Alister told me you were leaving about now. Has the fashion shoot been huge?"

"Insane. Those photographers finally respect me – the eejits – just as the shoot is done and dusted. After treating my ideas like rubbish."

"Your take on tribal chic might be out of their comfort zones."

"That surprised me. Not the arrogance – they're fashion photographers with egos as big as zoom lenses – but behind it, you know, they're stuck in their ways. Even *avant garde* loses its edge and becomes another cliché. And what about you? Has your memory come back? My plane's delayed so I've got time to talk.

Where to start? The word 'backwards' pops into my mind. Things aren't so shocking when you tell them backwards: each consequence precedes the action that caused it. Juliet under the floor, then the fire. Rouffignac, then the divining over the map. The lizard that whispers followed by the Gaston encounter.

"I know what you're thinking, Selkie, but just because you're at the centre of these connections doesn't mean you caused them."

"If I hadn't walked out on Andrew, Juliet wouldn't have got trapped down there. What if she'd died? I can't stop thinking about it...the ripple effect of my actions. I may have to move into a convent. Where I can't hurt anyone but God."

She snorts. "Convents are rubbish. Get out and live. And you're wrong about cause and effect. It's not as linear as it seems. Sure you're part of the mix, but the happenings have their own momentum."

"You mean Juliet had to have a brush with death?"

"If it's in her cards. If she's one of those stars that burn brightly then snuff out early. She didn't die under your floorboards, but she might be dead soon enough."

I shiver. "Isn't it possible to defy fate? To take a different path and miss the lightning bolt?"

She hesitates. "Sometimes. For a while. If you get an early message and take evasive action. But the signs are cryptic. Read them the wrong way and destiny wins. And the experiment's impossible to prove, because you can't go back and try the second path."

"How do you know this stuff?"

"Haven't I told you? My mother was a witch."

No, she hasn't told me and I want to know more. But she goes back to the fire.

"It didn't come out of the blue, this fire."

As I bring her up to date on Andrew's vendetta - the smashed windscreen, the bag theft, the Twitter trolling, Reece's attempt to ruin my seminar - I remember it was Davina who was so insistent that confronting Andrew would expose him as a coward, turn him to jelly and set me free.

"I know what you're thinking," she says.

"I stood up to Andrew and look what's happened."

"If you'd stayed away it would have been better, is that it?"

"I'd still have a *house*."

"A house that gave Andrew power over you. Now the tables are turned."

Really? She's trying to justify her advice to confront him.

"Every one of his actions has intimidated me, Davina. And confirmed just how powerless I am."

"Are you sure about that? Your little black dress escaped the bag snatch, didn't it?"

"Yes."

"So he didn't get control of your mythical pelt. And the Twitter attack – who won that round?"

"I did."

"Leading to extra seminars and more money in your pocket. And that lawyer of his, he stormed out with nothing but a refund."

"You're telling me his vendetta's been good." It's what Derek said, that the fire has cut the cord with Andrew, but I'm not letting Davina off the hook. "What's good about a pile of ash instead of a house? And an expensive legal battle to claim the insurance money?"

"You don't know that yet, but so-called bad things can be leading to something grand. Good and bad are two sides of the same coin. Like thinking backwards."

Davina's admitted she's not infallible – if her secret past is anything to go by. But it was my father's 'heart attack' that drew me to Sydney, not Davina. So whether the outcome's good or bad, I have to take responsibility for confronting

Andrew.

She likes the sound of Judy. "If you've got to have a lawyer, make sure they're as hard as hobnails. A woman, for sure. If all this chaos is anyone's fault, it's Judy's - scaring poor Andrew back into his bully suit."

That makes me laugh.

"Now tell me again about the seven clues, and where they've taken you." She's fascinated by the way each one has led to something unpredictable. "See what I mean about cryptic? Anyone would say a spoon is about food, not jewellery or stars. And the words on the floor - you've translated them but your memory's still in fog?"

"Keith says to keep thinking crookedly and one day it'll pop."

"I like this Keith. Is he Irish?"

"Australian."

"Irish ancestors, I'd say. Like you."

"He also said that art would stimulate my subconscious."

"I like him even more."

I tell her about my art session. That nothing's popped yet.

"You always were too impatient, girl. The universe does not jig to your fiddle, you know."

It makes me see the lighter side. And realise how much I miss her.

"Come to France, Davina. Join me on the crooked trail."

"The lizard that whispers," she says. I hear her sniffing the air the way she does - she's clairvoyant, but she's also 'clairolfactorant'. "There's something out of kilter about this lizard."

"I've wondered that too, but I wrote 'lay zard' on the

floor. Gaston translated it straight off."

"*Lézar*," she says. "The 'd' is silent. A whispering lizard might be too literal. Keep thinking crookedly."

"OK. But you need a holiday, and the weather here is perfect. Alister's around, and you'll adore Fabienne. If your flight's delayed, they'll let you change it."

"I won't fly into Paris."

"But you can jump straight on a train to Tours. You don't even have to leave the terminal."

"Not Paris," she says. "I'm not even sure I should come back to France."

"Why not? You're scaring me. What happened when you were here before?"

"Bordeaux," she says, ignoring me. "If I can get a flight into Bordeaux, I'll come."

After I hang up I get a terrible sense of portent. Miguel is coming. Davina might be coming. Alister is already here. They're presence in Tours is tangled up with me. Is it too late to leave town? If I slip away now, it might change what's already in play. But where would I go?

"Destiny has its own momentum," Davina said. So do tsunamis.

It brings me back to my reasons for being here. I dreamt about Paris, which led me to France, where I saw Donkey Skin and the fairy godmother, stayed with Fabienne and discovered the Pleiades, met Gaston who translated my *franglais* – but I wasn't in France when I disappeared. Unless I astral-travelled – thank God Derek hasn't suggested that – I was near Oahu's windward shore. What if the lizard that whispers is a cryptic name for a Hawaiian place? A place near Bantry's Bluff? What if France has spilled all its secrets and now, with the last clue, it's time to go back?

I push away thoughts of disappearing again as I pull up

a map of Oahu's coastline. In spite of Keith's opinion to let the answer creep up on me, the lipstick message entreated me to *cherchez* – to take action. I start searching place names combining 'lizard' and 'whisper'. It seems to be going nowhere when I make my first discovery. The Mokuluas, the two islands in Kailua Bay where Nigel communes with mutton-birds, are so named because the word means 'twins'. Genevieve's boys are twins, Gaston's a twin, the Mokuluas are twins. Derek would call it the rule of three.

I sit with my dodgy intuition and decide that if it's significant, it's separate.

But thinking of Derek reminds me how endless his patience is. And if the answer to my conundrum is drawing close he won't want to miss a moment.

"I thought the lizard that whispers might be a place," I say, when he answers my Skype call. "A rock that looks like a lizard...somewhere on the coast where the sea whispers...or the wind?"

"A real place that's taken on a mythical name," he says, already in his element. "There might be a legend."

Another legend? But with a name like mine, I might have got tangled up in a Hawaiian legend.

"I haven't found anything yet," I say.

"It might be a local name," he says. "Like Bantry's Bluff."

Named by a homesick Irishman and only known by word-of-mouth. I've never tried to google it. Until now.

"DD," I scream. "You're a genius. Bantry's Bluff gets one mention – on a scuba-diving blog. They saw a monk seal in an underwater cave in the cliffs offshore...they frolicked with it." I read the entry aloud: "*Our final dive was the icing on the cake. We saw a sponge-crab, two green turtles, a white-tipped reef-shark – then a critically endangered monk seal was lounging in the Bluff Cave. It was awesome to hang out with him for a while. He wanted to play.*

"So you do get monk seals around Bantry's Bluff," I say, remembering the dead one that washed ashore at the same time I disappeared.

"Yeah," Derek says, creasing his forehead, "I've heard that. But...what's it got to do with...lizards?"

I flop back in my chair. "Nothing."

Is there any wine in the fridge? A glass of speedy access to my subconscious.

"My turn," Derek says, and starts thinking aloud. "It's got to be a Hawaiian lizard. What about those geckos you house-sat?"

"Sylvie didn't think so." And I'm with her. "They're not native to Hawaii either."

Within minutes Derek's pulled up some new connections. The Hawaiian lizard from legend is called Mo'o and it's an *aumakua*, one of the shape-shifting spirit guides that take animal form. In Hawaiian folklore you can have an animal as a totem and it looks out for you, keeps you safe. I had a brush with the concept of *aumakua* before I disappeared – one of Coral's pronouncements.

Derek starts reading out the myth, and after a minute or two he says, *"Mo'o connects the Earth and the stars by reflecting the night sky in his jewelled eye. Attracting Mo'o means you have a connection with the Pleiades."*

I squeal, and remember I haven't told Derek about Fabienne's spoon sculpture. He's annoyed, then amazed. He starts typing in the other six clues from the kitchen floor, while I find an almost finished bottle of red and squeeze out half a glass. Roll on wisdom.

Before long he's reached another dead end.

"I thought there might be a red-lipped lizard," he says,

"to link up with the lipstick. I did find a red-lipped batfish."

"DD…"

"I know, I know, that's what happens on Google. There's such a thing as a donkey fish, but it's only found in the Atlantic."

"Enough."

I've felt connected to the other clues, even if I've done my best to ignore them, but the lizard that whispers is a stranger to me. As I reflect on my journey so far, I wonder if I'm running towards the lizard or in the opposite direction.

***

Needing a serious distraction from a path with too many blind corners, I text Alister to meet me downstairs. The idea's been brewing for a while – a surprise for Fabienne. At the cabinet in her kitchen I put every wine glass she owns in a box. They don't look valuable, and we can replace any breakages from the *brocante* market.

When I get to her studio, Fabienne is just locking up.

"It is champagne o'clock, *n'est-ce pas?*" She's expanding her vocabulary with my favourite drinking phrases.

"*Da!*" As I agree, she notices the box of glasses. I pull some euros out of my purse, feeling great that my seminar earnings mean I can do this for her. "A case of champagne. Cold."

"I do not understand."

"It's a surprise. Get the bubbly and you'll see."

There's a wine shop around the corner, and by the time she's unloading bottles from the bags on her pushbike I've rigged up a makeshift sandwich board in the lane. In my best *franglais*, it says *Pop-up Exposition – Vide Atelier. Entrée Libre*. I learnt the last phrase in Paris – free entry – when sussing out concerts in churches.

"*Vide Atelier*," she reads. "Empty Studio. I am selling my art?" I nod. "This is wonderful, Selkie, but what does it mean, 'pop-up'?"

"You'll see."

Inside, Alister has already set up an impromptu bar. Within minutes a crowd is spilling into and out of the studio, waving glasses of champagne.

"It's working." He winks at me and I get a tingle I should only get from the bubbly.

"This pop-up," Fabienne says, "it is the same as a piss-up?"

Oops. She'd better lose that one from the lexicon. I explain the difference.

It's a tiny space and people are jammed together, hardly able to view the works. In one corner several are arguing over a sculpture I can't see, their passion lubricated by the bubbly. Alister leaves me at the bar and starts a Dutch auction, taking written bids.

Fabienne's eyes are dancing as she leaves him to it and makes her way towards me. "It is crazy, Selkie. And fun, I think."

"You don't do this kind of thing?"

"Never. I am a serious artist." She laughs at herself. "I put my sculptures in a bar in the square but no-one buys. But these 'pop-uppers', they come for the free champagne and they pay too much for something they do not understand. Then tomorrow they are sorry."

"But they own a work of beauty, so does it matter?"

"Of course."

"This is just another kind of art, Fabienne. It's called marketing."

She nods.

"The trick is to get them to buy while the bubbly has made them happy but hasn't impaired their judgement." I'm channelling Keith. "Then they'll adore your sculpture forever."

"Already I feel better, but I cannot watch. You and Alister can make me rich – and the buyers happy – while I turn my back."

Alister has sold one sculpture and moved onto another, but when I see what's happening I push my way through the crowd. "Not for sale," I shout. "*Pas disponible.*"

Alister nods and slaps a red dot on it just in time. The Seven Sisters already has a buyer. Me.

CHAPTER
Thirty-One

"We have learnt something about pop-ups, I think," Fabienne says as we stumble upstairs, more than a little worse for wear. Alister has given her a wad of cash and slipped away.

"You make all the sales over the first glass," I say, "when people who love the art reach for their wallets." Including me. "Then the rest of the crowd...drinks you dry."

She laughs as she gets her front door open. "At least they do not buy it by mistake. And I am happy that you buy the Seven Sisters."

"Me too. But you won't be able to see them any more."

We go into the kitchen and sit down.

"You take home a little part of me," she says. "Of my soul. So I sprinkle myself into places where I am loved. Hawaii. The Sisters will breathe the ocean air. If my work can breathe, I can breathe too and keep making art. It is the meaning of life."

"You were worried if your work isn't loved, it can't breathe. What happens then?"

"Then I must call myself back. And the work, it loses its soul, it is an empty shell, a fake. Worse than fake, an...impostor. Because it has my name on it."

An empty shell with her name on it. I think of Wanda and her fish creations. Her relationship with each one is ephemeral: she makes them with an intense passion, gives them a face only a tourist could love, then lets them go. And the letting go puts a roof over her head and food on the table. Is that less authentic than Fabienne's experience? Or just different?

We talk more about leaving a part of yourself in each work of art, and I tell her about the Chinese phrase for a memory – 'old friend from far away'.

"Calling yourself back from artworks that aren't loved reminds me of facing up to memories and bringing them home." I wish.

"Old friend from far away," she repeats. "I make a French translation."

"And there's a bird in Australia that seems to sing about the same thing. About longing for things lost. And calling them back."

"About love, I think. That is love."

I play her the butcherbird's call.

"Your mind is inside your heart, Selkie. That is why you can make art. Heart and art – they rhyme in English – later, I make a haiku about it. It is why you find the connections between Chinese phrases and Australian birds." She laughs. "And seals."

***

Gretel calls, wanting to talk about Stella.

"The night before you got to Sydney," she says, "Mum had a dream. Remember? At the time I put it down to all the worry about Dad giving her nightmares. She was pretty uptight. In the dream she saw your house – it was on fire and cats were jumping out the windows."

I remember. "Shit."

"Yeah, that's what I thought."

"I thought she made it up – wishful thinking. It's got to be a coincidence."

"Well, I've just remembered something else. You asked her why she thought it was your house."

I feel a sudden chill. "She saw my face at the window."

"And the glass was all crazed and cracked. Your face was...in pieces."

The smashed windscreen. Bloody hell. Stella saw it. I'm shocked into silence and Gretel asks if I'm still on the line.

"Still here. But not in good shape. You're thinking about the hammer through the windscreen? Her dream could match what Andrew had in his mind when he wielded the blow." And Stella dreamed it before it happened. Along with the fire and the cats.

"Both visions together seem to be beyond coincidence, don't you reckon?" Gretel says. "One could be chance, but not two."

I feel sick.

An email from Judy continues the theme. Juliet's still in hospital but she's been able to talk to the police. As I imagine her propped up on pillows, with her hair pulled back and her ordeal behind her, a rush of emotion hits me. I remember the message I took from our brief encounter – never to be desiccated again. It feels selfish to be thinking about her gift to me, when it was the vacuum I created by Andrew's side that led to her brush with death, but I'm determined to honour the insight.

Judy reports that Andrew was at a bucks party in a Bondi bar the night of the fire, so there's no chance he was near the house. I'm relieved. He's not an arsonist. A scheming vindictive troglodyte without a scintilla of empathy is enough. Juliet was invited to the hens gathering the same night, but she didn't show. One girl sent her a text but then got too drunk to wonder why she didn't reply. It seems it was all an accident, so why doesn't it feel like that?

Something keeps creating a random spark just beyond my vision.

I turn away from the screen and look onto the walled garden alive with spring flowers, remembering where I am. There's no planning to be done for the remaining seminars. Winging it comes with freedom. I forget about Andrew. The rest of the day is mine.

Fabienne texts suggesting an excursion – to a vast warehouse where worn-once designer fashions are sold for ten euros a piece. It seems that French women are great recyclers of hardly worn clothes. It's a system called *dépôt-vente* – second-hand goods sold on consignment. If Davina arrives in time, she can join us. She and Fabienne will get on like a house on...

Even my clichés won't leave it alone.

***

We walk to Rue National to wait for a tram.

"How can you work with the studio still in a mess from last night?" I ask.

I offered to clean up after the pop-up, but Fabienne refused.

"The energy of the mess, it inspires me. I call it After the Party."

"A sculpture? I can't imagine what that looks like."

"No, you can't."

We laugh.

Davina texts that she's arrived at Tours airport and has found her way to the tram. The same tram we're about to catch. I text her to stay on board, hoping she's travelling light and isn't too tired.

A dépôt-vente warehouse? she texts back. *I must be in*

heaven. Or France : -)

We find her in the front carriage. I give her a hug and introduce her to Fabienne. Love at first sight might have been too much to expect, but their reaction to each other is cool.

"*Enchantée,*" they say stiffly, barely pecking each other's cheeks.

I try to get a conversation going but they both look out the window, and when we alight in Avenue de Grammont, Davina says she'll take a cab to her hotel. What's happened to being in heaven?

"Hôtel d'Univers," she says, reading my mind. "To match my orbit." She smiles and tosses her red curls, but the comment sounds forced and a touch competitive.

We leave her to hail a cab and cross the road.

"Hôtel d'Univers is just around the corner," Fabienne says, pointing towards the town hall.

"Is it?" I turn towards Davina but she's already in a cab going the other way. "Why didn't you tell her? The taxi might take her...for a ride."

Does Fabienne know the double meaning?

She shrugs. "She goes in a hurry. She has...baggage."

Sounds like she knows the double meaning of that one.

"Why did she want to get away?" I ask.

Fabienne doesn't hesitate. "I saw her before. In Paris."

"She used to study in Paris. Fashion design. She's just won an award with *Vogue.*"

As artists, I thought they'd be discussing this themselves.

"Before," Fabienne says again. "I saw her before."

"Before?"

"Before she calls herself...Davina."

We walk in silence. I'm feeling protective of my Irish

friend. Fabienne's a friend too – a warm woman who's taught me a lot – but I knew Davina first. True, Davina's only hinted about her past. Our friendship has sprung from our psychic connection, from who we are now, not who we were before. And Fabienne doesn't know it, but I've changed my name too.

I decide it's none of my business who Davina used to be. If it's even true. It's years ago that Davina was in Paris, and people change as they age. Fabienne sounds certain, but a look-a-like would explain it. Everyone's got a double somewhere. Then I remember how rattled Davina was at the sight of Fabienne.

The *dépôt-vente* warehouse is in an ugly street close to the railway yards, surrounded by humble residences opening straight off the pavement. You'd miss the place if you didn't know it was here. The dominant colour is grey. Judging by the people we pass, it's an area for immigrants and students. A woman in a shabby skirt hunches on a concrete step beside the warehouse's front door. Fabienne throws a coin into the paper cup she's holding, so I do the same and she flashes us a toothless smile.

The narrow front window facing the street is full of second-hand shoes, but when we step inside the space stretches back into an enormous barn, every wall covered with hanging rails to the ceiling. In spite of the Davina incident, the shopping is a bonding experience. We start at one end, and soon we're holding up quirky garments to show each other.

"This is you," Fabienne says, holding up something sheer and white with an Eiffel Tower outlined in rhinestones. "You do not want English, I think."

She's right. It seems that funky styling around here includes English words, just like we English-speakers adore anything French.

We fill our arms and take turns at the change rooms. It's getting on towards eight when we're struggling back to the tram stop, laden with half a dozen things each. I think about going to find Davina, but decide to let her sleep off her jetlag – and her shock at seeing Fabienne.

Back at the apartment, we hunt in the fridge for leftovers. After we've got through a meal and a bottle, Fabienne returns to Davina.

"This Davina, she is your friend?"

"Yes. She's helped me through some tough times."

"Then you must trust your instincts," she says.

"Why do you say that?"

"She is a chameleon, I think. You understand the word?"

I nod. "They change their colour to...suit the situation."

"It is not bad. It is not good. But when someone is your friend, it is...something to know."

It's late. We stack the dishwasher and say goodnight. When I'm lying in bed I make the connection. A chameleon is a...lizard.

***

I ride my borrowed pushbike to the Hôtel d'Univers, hoping to catch Davina over breakfast. I've hardly slept for wondering if she's the lizard. And if she is, why we both had to come to France. Just so we could meet Fabienne? It's exhausting just thinking about the wild ride my subconscious has contrived for me. Has the real clue to my disappearance been in Hawaii all along?

But Davina has already left. Checked out. Gone. She didn't even stay overnight. I stand at reception on the verge of tears, feeling utterly abandoned.

The girl behind the counter checks who I am, then hands over a note. As I read Davina's words I hear her voice, as if she's standing beside me. Whispering.

Selkie, you're looking for answers and I've flown the coop. I'm so sorry. I can't stay in France. Seeing Fabienne was a shock and a gift. Your gift – I'll not be forgetting that. I knew I had to run like the wind and hope that the old cloak of invisibility hasn't lost its magic. If I'm still in my refuge when you get back, I'll tell all. Trust me if you can. Because I have a gift for you: Not everything that whispers, breathes.

I read the note over and over, trying to peer through the cracks between the words, trying to get more than what I've already pieced together. It's why she changed her name – she's been on the run from something. Her refuge has been Kailua, and she's running back there in fear of her life. Her 'cloak of invisibility' conjures up Donkey Skin. To save her skin, Davina is hiding under a false skin. Her name.

Trust me if you can.

Or trust her parting gift. Because it's about the lizard. Am I sure it isn't Davina? The chameleon. An image of her with bulging eyes haunted my dreams. And now she's whispered a clue.

Not everything that whispers, breathes.

After a text from Genevieve, I'm sitting outside Bantry's Bar sipping a lime and soda. I've pushed Davina to the back of my mind. It's the only thing I can do. Her Delphic clue is one clue too far. It's made me decide to ditch the psychic revolving door and flip to practical investigations. Starting with Gaston. He'll see me later today, but I'll hear from Genevieve first.

She arrives looking like she's just stepped out of a beauty salon. Hair immaculate, makeup perfect. She's lost weight, and her gold and white sundress shows off her figure and her tan.

"You look fabulous," I say. "Who's the man?"

That was thoughtless but she doesn't notice.

"Tony," she says. "It's his favourite dress."

An alarm bell rings. "Has he agreed to see you?"

She hesitates. "I have to see him, Selkie. Time's running out. I've got to go back to the twins. And Tony...who knows how long he'll be...around?"

She doesn't know about Miguel and I can't tell her.

"What happened with the lawyer?" I ask.

"I don't know. Sandrine's heard nothing so we're in the dark. I'm good at waiting but it's...wearing me down." She's about to cry, but stops.

"You've done your best to inform him," I say.

"With your help."

Another bell. "You can't do any more."

"Except see him."

I look up sharply from my drink. "No."

"Don't look at me like that. You could take me with you. I'd wait outside while you-"

"No."

"Put yourself in my shoes, Selkie. Trying to get up the courage to knock on his door, running through endless dialogues in my head that might get me over his threshold, that might get him to at least speak to me. Meanwhile, you visit Tony whenever you want. He likes you, doesn't he? My husband. And Alister, he can't get enough of you. But I'm like the wallflower at the prom. Sitting on the sidelines waiting, while you charm away...both my men."

She makes me sound manipulative and I start to defend myself, then stop. I haven't charmed anyone, but she knows that. The word has achieved what she wanted. I'm in her shoes and the view is different.

"Look, I can see how it is for you. You're going through hell. But my decision isn't about you. It's about Gaston. I can't betray his trust like that. If I take you there to wait outside his door, it would put intolerable pressure on him. He's made his position clear, and, as painful as it is, you have to honour it."

"Did he tell you how he disappeared?"

"Briefly. But it's not my story to tell. I'm sorry."

She doesn't wait for more. She walks off, without looking back.

***

It's too hot to walk from Chinon station, so I take a taxi. When I get to his door, Gaston is in the living room. He invites me in and for the first time I see it, against the whitewashed walls of the *troglo*. His aura. I've never seen an aura before but I know what it means. His former robust self is circling him like an invisible skin. He's dying. Not quickly. Slowly.

Tears prickle my eyes and I brush them away. Then I grab a tissue from the table and blow my nose. "This hay fever," I say.

The aura has faded, and I notice that his human skin is washed and groomed. In his sleeveless T-shirt, his muscles have a memory of the sailor he used to be.

"My carers just left," he says. "Two big guys come in twice a week so I can wallow in the bath like a wounded orca. It's a pleasure I never miss."

It reminds me of Genevieve's own beauty treatment and I feel like weeping all over again. If only they could get together, the old spark might dissolve the emotions that are keeping them apart.

Over our Nespressos, I tell Gaston why I'm here. Another favour. Nothing to do with lizards.

"You used to swim at Bantry's Bluff."

He nods. "Every day. I was stronger in the water. I thought it might slow down the disease. And I enjoyed it."

I nod. "So you knew that cove pretty well."

"And the cemetery. It isn't haunted, if you're asking about that again."

"No. I thought you might have some ideas about where I might have gone when I was missing."

"You were wearing scuba gear?"

"I don't even swim."

"There used to be a hut on the cliff," he says. "It got blown into the sea in a gale. A woman was hiding there from her lover. She drowned."

"No."

"Another example of the curse, if you believe the locals.

Are you sure someone didn't kidnap you? Put chloroform over your mouth and take you away?"

It's an explanation that feels impossible, but it's good to cross it off my mental list. I'm just asking him about local place names that might include a lizard, when a shadow crosses the windows of the *troglo* and a woman opens the door. The light's behind her but I saw that gold dress this morning.

She steps inside. "I won't stay away any longer, Tony."

"Gennie."

He starts to back his wheelchair away, but she's the woman I first met, determined after her long wait. She walks up to him and puts her hands on his shoulders, then kisses him on both cheeks.

She turns to me, "More coffee, please, Selkie."

I scurry into the kitchenette and clatter the mugs as loudly as I can. Their voices are only a murmur and I take my time. When I put the mugs on the table, Genevieve has pulled up a chair beside him. They're holding hands and they both look like they've been crying. Whatever's happened, their grooming no longer matters.

"I'm outside if you need me," I say.

I wait for a while, but there's no shade at all, and the abandoned caves nearby, with their weeds and empty bottles, don't invite trespassers. Many of them have graffiti on their walls – a reminder of my dream.

I send Genevieve a text to let them know I'm leaving. At the bottom of the lane, I keep to the shady side of the street and walk to the centre of Chinon. A stall selling *sandwichs* overlooks the fountain in the square, so I buy a baguette filled with brie and chicken and tomato and eat it on a bench. Then I wander down to the riverbank and lean over the rail, catching some breeze as the Vienne flows by.

Will Gaston tell her about Miguel? If he doesn't, she may believe she's got more time with him than she has. After their new connection, he may decide to wait. Or it may happen before she goes back to Hawaii, which could be the cruellest thing he's ever done to her. Let her have her last week, then exit. I remind myself that it's none of my business – the maxim I'm having trouble living by.

They slipped so quickly into being together again. If he was angry that she invaded his hideaway, he moved through it to something else. Love? A wave of sadness hits me when I think about what they've both been through. In the name of protecting themselves. From what? Another person loving them, even when they're broken?

It makes me realise that I know nothing about love. My mother's love fizzled out when I became an unhappy toddler. Dad couldn't get past his shame to show me he cared. Stella only loved me if I pulled on my Elkie-skin and left the real Selkie to be glimpsed through a keyhole. And Andrew – to him I was a mannequin, draped in garments of his choosing, to be paraded on his arm.

Is that why I can't love Alister? Part of me wants to let his love in and try it on for size – the part that thinks crookedly and gets sideswiped by stray emotions when I'm stacking dirty dishes. But I'm working without a script. It's like the seminar – I've got to wing it. What if I...bomb?

Alister chooses that moment to send a text. *Bombe alaska?* It makes me laugh out loud.

As well as reading my mind, he's proposing dinner at 'our' Chinese café. It's our first date since my house burned down. He's playing a long game.

I accept.

CHAPTER
Thirty-Three

We sit at the same outside table and order a bottle of Pouilly-Fumé. The last time we were here Alister gave me a serve about my seminar performance and I came close to making a run for it. Tonight is a date. An even better reason to make a run for it, but so far I'm sitting at the folding table on the folding chair, sipping wine and deciphering the menu, while my companion does the same.

I tell him about Genevieve and Gaston.

"Congratulations," he says.

"I didn't do anything, Alister. Genevieve barged in. Gaston couldn't run away. The rest is history."

"You did everything. You made the contact that made the barging possible. I tried to talk you out of it, remember? But you ignored me as usual. And you were right. You should start respecting your intuition."

"It wasn't intuition. I had my own reasons for wanting to speak to Gaston. I thought he might have some insights into my disappearance. In the end he didn't, but he did a translation for me." Which has caused me no end of trouble.

"You reminded him he's still a man. That's important to any guy, especially a guy like him. That's why he didn't send Gennie away. By the time he'd spent time with you – an attractive woman who didn't mind his company, who brought him pastries and greeted him with a kiss on the cheeks – he was ready to allow Gennie in."

"But she's his wife."

"And he's hurt her badly. All the more reason for him to cut her dead. You'd softened him up enough to let that first moment pass."

"I hadn't thought of it like that."

"You never give yourself credit."

"Can we talk about something else? Listing my finer qualities is my least favourite subject."

"I've noticed. What would you like to talk about?"

It's the old question and I laugh. I dodge the forbidden things - such as the imminent arrival of Miguel - and tell him about Davina.

"I've always thought there's something secretive about her," he says. "She's vibrant but she holds something back."

"Her real identity by the sound of it. Fabienne thinks I should be wary of her, but she hasn't told me what she knows."

I don't mention the whole chameleon-lizard connection. It's too bizarre, even for me.

"It depends on what Davina's hiding," he says. "Her real name, her true identity, but why? You and I have changed our names and our reasons aren't sinister."

His professional name is Lester. Long story.

"Speak for yourself."

He laughs. "What do you think about Davina? She's your friend."

"So I'm giving her the benefit of the doubt." Something I learnt from Gretel when she stood up for me as a child. "Davina said she'll tell me the whole story when I get back." If she's still there.

The entrées arrive. Spicy French-style dim sums that only look Chinese.

"I've got something to tell you," Alister says. "I'm leaving town before Gaston's party."

"You can't. He's invited you. I don't think he knows many people. You've got to come."

"It wouldn't be fair on Gennie. I won't cramp her style."

"What about my style? I promised Gaston I'd be there, and I won't know anyone else besides Genevieve."

"I've made up my mind."

"But I've only just told you about Genevieve and Gaston. You'd already decided."

"I'd decided to leave soon. I just hadn't decided when."

"So this is a farewell dinner."

"In a way. I'm going to Honolulu, so I'll see you when you get back."

So casual. He's cooled off. I've been getting up the courage to kiss him again – maybe even tonight – then see where it leads after a glass or two of Dutch courage. But he's had enough. Taking that phone call from Judy a few days ago, when we were on a trajectory to his boudoir, was one obstacle too far. The long game I thought he was playing just got short. Very short.

Shit.

He's watching the emotions flitting across my face. I know I've got one of those readable faces. Where's that donkey skin now? Ugly would be better than transparent. I take a sip of wine to give my thoughts some space to do an editorial loop. Space… He's given me the space I asked for, and now he doesn't want me any more. But I want him.

In a kind of trance, I hide my hands under the table and slip off my spoon bangle. When the soup arrives, Alister has a word to the waiter and I drop the bangle into his bowl. It's stupid to think a fairytale is going to be the blueprint for my future, but I'm cutting my intuition some slack.

He finds it, of course. It's not hiding coyly at the bottom of the bowl like Donkey Skin's ring. It's wallowing there like an anchor in a bathtub.

He laughs. "How did this get here? Are you giving it back?" He's not supposed to be laughing. "Sounds final."

"It's just a fairytale thing," I say. "Like the slipper or the ring. You find it and you're so obsessed you have to track down the woman who fits it."

"Then marry her and make her my queen."

I blush. "Now I feel like an idiot." Again. So much for intuition.

I try to grab the bangle back, but he's wiping it on his napkin. "I know who it fits. So I'll keep it until I find her."

"Too deep for me," I say. "And you can't keep it. I need it back."

"Why?"

He hasn't remembered that a spoon was one of my clues.

"It's my talisman. Like my dress."

"Good. I'd love to know how it works. And you can have it back. But I liked the idea of trying it on the wrist of every maiden in the land. I might have met someone...legendary."

Clever. "OK. I deserved that."

He slips it onto my wrist and keeps hold of my hand. "What did you think just now, when I said I was returning to Hawaii?"

"Your soup's getting cold."

"Have you ever studied psychology, Selkie?"

"Yes."

"Then you'll remember the concept of 'fact' and 'frame'."

"Remind me."

"A fact is just a fact. I'm returning to Honolulu. The frame is the meaning another person attributes to the fact. For example, someone might think I'm leaving...because I don't love them any more."

Shit.

"But that 'frame' isn't correct."

I swallow. "So why are you leaving?"

He pauses and I notice his eyes. Bright. He's almost in tears. "A private investigator thinks he's found Deshi. My son might be living in Honolulu."

"Wow. That's huge." But a word has popped into my head. *No.* As if my intuition knows it isn't him. I push it aside and say instead, "You've been looking for him for a long time."

He nods. "I tried on my own at first. That was hopeless. I was grieving for Fleur and my desperation only closed doors. Everywhere I turned, her relatives in San Francisco shut me out. Fleur's cousin was the only one who'd talk to me. He told me to back off, but he put me onto a Chinese PI. As soon as I could afford it, he started the search. It's why I couldn't come to the airport when you left Honolulu. We had a meeting. He had some promising leads."

The word 'labyrinth' comes to mind.

"We thought we'd found him about five years ago..."

I mentally finish the sentence: *But it wasn't him.* Maybe there's a queue of young Eurasian guys wanting to be Alister's son. Looking for a long-lost daddy. Or an inheritance. I wish him luck and mean it.

To celebrate our last night together, we go for the *'bombes* Beijings' – renamed by mutual wit and too much wine. Then the evening is over. We both know I won't be going back to his place, so he walks me home. A quick tumble on his rented bed the night before he leaves town isn't going to be how it happens. And the space between us that I'd tried to smother with my insecurities has been filled by the living spectre of Deshi.

Our kiss on Fabienne's doorstep takes its cue from the end of an old movie – romantic, lingering, sweet. Full of promise.

***

Neither Genevieve nor Gaston gets in touch. It's a good sign. They've forgotten about me. I check Gaston's *bloglo* but there's no new entry. I'm guessing she's moved in and they're getting to know each other all over again. A bittersweet time. Five missing years to catch up on over a few days, then...wham, she's back where she was before, without her man. I remember the remission of the girl at uni with MS. Is the suffering easier for having had that one brief glimpse of joy?

Judy calls with the news we were both expecting. The fire assessors have ruled an electrical fault, not arson. It confirms what Andrew's alibi showed.

She summarises from the report. "It started in the kitchen, under the fridge. It seems that one of its back feet was standing on the cord."

Already I'm on alert. "So why didn't the fridge wobble?"

"They don't comment on that. But over time the sharp metal edge of the foot must have frayed the cable right through, causing a spark. There was some shredded paper behind the fridge. A mouse nest, according to Andrew."

The mousetrap. A smokescreen. Smoke and mirrors, to overdo the puns. Because I've remembered what's been bothering me.

"It's a setup."

"How can you say that?"

"It's exactly what happened to Andrew's uncle – how his factory burnt down."

I tell her about the bar fridge in his uncle's office, how the foot was on the cord and how it wore right through the insulation until one night it sparked.

"OK," Judy says. "I believe you. But how could Andrew manipulate that? He wouldn't know when the fire was going to happen."

"No. That's what's so perfect about it. Fray the cord a little to get it started and wait."

"But it might never cause a fire, and he was living in the house. Those old weatherboards went up like a bonfire."

"I'll bet he's installed smoke alarms recently. And the main bedroom's a long way from the kitchen, with new double doors opening onto the stone veranda."

Judy's quiet for a few minutes. "There's nothing you can do, Selkie. The uncle's fire isn't evidence. Even if you tell the assessors, they can't prove any of it. The frayed cord looks like an accident. Andrew's even got a photo of the mousetrap, of him pushing it behind the fridge."

Thanks to Juliet. Thank God he didn't kill her.

Judy's right: there's nothing I can do. Except wait for her next email outlining the costs involved in suing him for half the insurance money. I hang up feeling the rage and impotence that Andrew always inspires.

For the first time, I present Being Sleek without some kind of support network. It's the final seminar in my series and I'm on my own. Alister's gone, and Fabienne has a previous commitment. Something about it feels significant. Making it. Arriving. But they're words from a success manual. This is...something else.

The audience is small – the last enrolments from the Twitter troll attack – making it an intimate experience. Mind-mapping is now part of the program, and I leave the front of the room and join in. With art materials again at my fingertips, I drop into a creative trance.

When I stand back to see what I've done, the first thing I think of is the collage. Davina got me to make it not long before I descended to the beach at Bantry's Bluff. But the mind-map in front of me is more cryptic. Instead of using images cut from magazines, I've created them myself. The most striking feature is the slash of white between solid areas of black, twisting down the page and cutting it almost in two. It's nearly identical to the one I painted with Fabienne. On either side of it, primitive scribbles – like cave art – collide and overlap like my blind drawings, representing the collection from Nigel's floor. A bowl and a spoon, seven stars, a four-legged creature and a lump-like shape that must be the donkey and the rock. Haphazard letters are scrawled in red and, with a start, I see a grouping that spells *lay zard*. The lizard might elude me, but it's firmly planted in my mind. The whole combination has a disturbing quality – and an embarrassing sense of exposure – but I've got nothing to lose by sharing it with the group.

"Those things you've drawn," one guy says, "it's hard to tell what they are."

"A bunch of things that have been turning up in my life," I explain. "Each one in an unexpected – and significant – way."

"Something to do with your future direction?" a woman asks.

"The past and the future are linked," the first guy says. "Who you are now is a direct result of your past experience. You might cut your ties, but their influence hangs around. Like a noose."

Everyone laughs, but I think of Andrew.

"No seals," another woman says. "I thought you'd draw seals, but there's only that horse." She means the donkey. "And that lizard."

What? "Where's the lizard?"

She leaves her seat and points to the slash of white. "This looks like a lizard from where I'm sitting."

Others agree.

I prop it up on the whiteboard and stand further back. The way it twists, the slash could be a snake, but blobs of paint look like legs.

"You've used colours for everything else," another guy says. "All that red for the letters. But the lizard shape is white against black. Like a candle flame."

A flame in the dark. If the lizard is the candle lighting my dream...is that a cryptic meaning for 'whisper'? *Not everything that whispers, breathes.*

When they start discussing the red graffiti, I'm too disturbed and move them on to sharing their own mind-maps. But mine inspires comments throughout the day.

Then we're wrapping up and discussing what we've learned from seals.

"The shamans up where I come from," says a guy called René in a Canadian accent, "used to take advice from orcas." He's got everyone's attention. "A shaman would go down to the shore and wait for an orca to come close, so he could channel its wisdom and take it back to the tribe. Is that how you got the activities for this workshop...by channelling seals?"

My first response is to laugh, but the faces around me are taking him seriously. To give myself thinking time, I bat the question back. "Why do you think Being Sleek is more than a marketing gimmick?"

"It's a great gimmick, don't get me wrong. It's why I'm here. When I heard about the seal connection I remembered those damn orcas and thought I'd fly over, see what the fuss was about. But it's more than a gimmick. It's something else, this workshop."

Others are nodding.

"I'll be truthful, René. I don't know where the activities came from. Every time I run the seminar, the activities...create themselves."

"But you've been talking to seals, right?"

"Not that I know of."

Bloody hell. Is there any chance I was doing the shaman thing? Evading discovery and talking to seals? Talking about what?

"How did they do it, the shamans?" I'm keeping the question lighter than I feel. "Did they swim with the orcas? Did they go into some kind of...altered state?" For days at a time?

He shrugs. "No-one knows how they did it. It stayed with them – their secret. But the messages from the orcas brought harmony to the tribe, so I've heard."

The seminar is over. People thank me on their way out. René hangs back, and although I'm grateful for his contribution - it lent extra depth to people's perception of their experience - I'm hoping he doesn't want to carry on. But he's in a hurry.

He shakes my hand and leans in to murmur, "You're a whisperer and you don't know it." Then he's gone.

I want to dismiss it all, but it gets me hovering over Google. Not 'shaman' or 'orca' - they're someone else's reality. In the end I type in 'seal whisperer' and laugh at what comes up. It's the scuba-diving blog from Hawaii, the one that described frolicking with the monk seal in the Bluff Cave. The scuba-divers think of themselves as seal whisperers. It's a wonderful image, swimming with the seals and learning their secrets. I envy their freedom. But I can't see how it solves my memory problem.

***

Gaston leaves me a voice message: "Miguel is here." After the days of silence its implications bring a sudden chill.

Then Genevieve rings. We haven't spoken since I left her with Gaston and she brings me up to date.

"I can't believe how happy I am. You'd think I'd be angry or sad or bitter or something, but those old feelings vanished as soon as Tony looked at me and I saw that he still loves me. His body's a train wreck, but in spite of the disease and what it means, I'm...happy. Explain that. It's a cliché, but love is enough. You helped bring us together, Selkie. Sorry I haven't called till now."

"I guessed you two were...catching up." It's all I'm going to say about love. "That's much more important than calling me. And I've been busy. So what's this party about? I hear Miguel's arrived."

"And half Tony's old crew. They've descended on some rooms over a bar here in Chinon. Getting their land legs and warming themselves up for the party."

Gaston mentioned the party before Genevieve walked in on him, so it's not a celebration of their reunion.

"What's the occasion?" I ask. "Is it Gaston's birthday?"

"No. He's come out of hiding, and his wife and friends are here. It's just a celebration of...living."

After blogging forever about the opposite. I let it go and ask how I can help.

"We need music. The woman you're staying with, she might know someone. I saw her talking to some musicians...at the *guinguette*."

The night Genevieve was following me, and I was spinning around the dance floor with Alister, then running from his kiss. He hasn't been in touch since he left to chase a phantom called Deshi.

Genevieve gives me the details. They're hiring a bus and taking the partygoers to the beach at St Malo. It's on the coast beyond Rennes, a spectacular walled town with pirate history. Probably the perfect location for Miguel and his crew.

"Tony wants to smell the sea," she says.

I promise to ask Fabienne. Perhaps she knows a band that would be prepared to travel – and subject their instruments to the salt air.

She's in her studio, wrapping the Seven Sisters for their next journey across the sky – to Honolulu. I can't gaze at them any more. They're already hidden under layers of bubble wrap.

"I put them inside this box," she's saying, "then I put

this box inside a bigger box. It makes the room to…dance."

She winks at me and I feel a surge of affection for her and her sculpture. How amazing it is that we've met. She senses it too, because we give each other a spontaneous hug, then brush away a tear or two.

She says she'll speak to her musician friend about playing at Gaston's party.

***

Keith and I Skype one last time before I leave Tours for St Malo. While we try to talk, Daisy sits up on her usual chair and barks at the screen.

"She's trying to tell you where we went today," Keith says. "All the way to North Steyne. I waited by the rail while Daisy raced across the sand to the cliff. And before you ask, I could hear her barks fading at speed."

"Why did you go back there?"

"Daisy was insistent. She's been jumpy for days, running away from my chair and coming back. I knew she wanted to get something. From the cliff."

"What?"

"She'll show you."

Daisy has disappeared from view, but I can hear her happy growls as she returns. She comes right up to the screen to show me what she found. Dangling from her jaw is a lizard. Large and brown with a broad blunt face. A blue-tongue lizard. An icon of Sydney's fauna, just like the ones I brought home as a child to torment Stella.

"It's alive," Keith is saying. "Daisy carried it gently in her mouth all the way across the sand and put it in my lap." He laughs. "I nearly passed out when I put my hand on it."

I'm trying not to do the same.

"A young guy came back with her. He was walking on the rock shelf and saw Daisy sticking her head through a long vertical crack in the cliff and coming out with the lizard. He was fascinated to know where she was going with it."

The long vertical crack where we put the Hawaiian rock. Daisy must have seen the lizard hiding inside the opening. But that was weeks ago. Why did she want to get it now?

"It's now living in our garden, with Daisy keeping an eye on it."

I'm feeling queasy. Daisy is reading my clues. She knew where to put the rock. She knew where to find the lizard. I thought meeting Keith was significant, but maybe it's been Daisy all along. Has the lizard been whispering to her? How can I find out what the hell it said?

"Does Daisy talk to you?" I ask Keith, feeling sure he won't find the question bizarre.

"Not in words."

"But you know what she's thinking?"

"A lot of the time. We share thoughts with each other. Telepathically."

So Daisy's a telepath. She's been reading my thoughts about the lizard. Davina says I'm a telepath. We should be able to 'talk'.

"Could I try?" I ask.

"Sure. Be my guest."

Keith doesn't pry into my reasons, and he obviously trusts that I'm not after the password to his bank account. As he moves his chair back, Daisy's shiny black face fills the screen, the lizard in her jaws like an offering. She stands very still and looks straight at me. I do the same, pushing all thoughts from my mind. If I'm sceptical, it's not going to happen.

Nothing does happen.

I gaze into Daisy's eyes for what seems like an age before I notice how rigid I am. Rigid with expectation. I start to curse that I'm not fit to be a telepath's armpit, when a thought cracks me in two. Without words to shape it, I know it and I don't know it all at the same time. It's something about the dark, something about the light, something about dying, loving, listening, turning, something about...being. Sleek.

The name of my seminar. It's as if the words have been translated through several languages, like Chinese whispers, and finally been translated back with a whole new meaning. I'm blinking fast, but Daisy's eyes have closed. Her mind is quiet.

That's when I see that the lizard has opened its eyes. It's looking at me with a reptilian stare that's holding mine without blinking. The thought didn't come from Daisy. Did it come from the lizard?

After Keith signs off without asking what happened, I'm exhausted. Did the telepathy really happen? And if the lizard's message is the final clue from the lipstick words, does it mean there's more for me to discover? From Being Sleek?

My seminar has accompanied me across the world. It's anchored me while it's taught me about letting go. It's connected me on a creative level with Fabienne, and it's been the means for me to turn the tables on Andrew. Is there something else?

CHAPTER
Thirty-Five

The band has a van. I'm travelling to St Malo with them, while Gaston and Genevieve will travel with the crew in a hired minibus direct from Chinon. The spring weather is warm and clear and it promises to be a perfect night. A night on the beach.

The old combo of fear and excitement grips my chest as I pull my little black dress out of the suitcase and lay it on the sofa. It isn't very practical but of course I'm going to wear it. Made for me by Davina - the chameleon but not the lizard. I didn't want that blue-tongue lizard to be whispering to me from Sydney - whispering something cryptic - but it's a relief that it isn't Davina.

The dress is as precious as ever, shimmering black then silver, like something alive. It's the closest I get to a seal pelt and the mythology around my name - along with the spoon bangle. And the cowry shell.

The dress goes back into the suitcase for later, but I put on the jewellery now. The cords of the cowry go around my neck, and the tiny shells at their ends clink against my spine. It's the only sound it makes, mute since my unexplained absence. Its silence over all these weeks suddenly feels...eloquent.

As I slip the bangle around my wrist, my thoughts go to Alister. It's not a coincidence that he found Hugo's stall and connected me with a silver spoon. Not because he's psychic, because he's...attuned. He's similar to Andrew in only the most superficial ways - blue eyes and a passion for me. Like me, Andrew was a mannequin in our marriage, his fear of emotion maintaining a brittle shell. He kept me under control so I'd never discover his core of clay. But Alister's search for Deshi shows he's soft on the outside, vulnerable to joys and hurts, while his inner core doesn't need protection because it's strong. It's a way of being I'd like to emulate.

The bangle also makes me think of Hugo. Will he be there tonight? I wonder if he's met Genevieve and accepted her into the family? And if Gaston has any other siblings, and if they've also been struck down by MS?

A jacket over my shoulder and I'm ready to head down to the car park overlooking the Loire. Fabienne and I have said our goodbyes. I'll go straight to Paris after the party. She told me the colours of the band's van – black and silver. To match my dress. And their name: Fous de Foudre, Mad about Lightning. Clever for a group of precision drummers with the occasional clash of cymbals and flurry of flutes. It's also a play on words, rhyming with *coup de foudre* – a bolt of lightning of the emotional kind, as in love at first sight. Something I find impossible to imagine.

I spot the van easily. The band leader is a guy with ebony skin and a big white smile, while the two women in the group are as blonde as he is dark. I introduce myself in my best French, trying to remember everyone's names. They all welcome me and we pile in. The journey to the sea has begun.

The van is an old rattler and the noise, combined with my limited French, makes conversation impossible. We laugh and give up. The familiar landscape of farms, punctuated by church spires and nestling villages, flies past. In a field I see a donkey and think of its symbolism in the Donkey Skin tale: both ignorant and wise, according to

Derek's book. Just like me. Then we're on an *autoroute* and I doze.

When the van slows I wake. Soon we're pulling into the guesthouse where the whole party is staying tonight. The women in the band are sharing, but I've got a room to myself, up an old staircase at the back in what was probably the maid's quarters, with a tiny triangular bathroom retrofitted into a corner. I change into my little black dress and rub some 'seaweed' through my wild hair. In the mirror I see myself and the blue-tongue lizard's thought comes back: *Being sleek*. Just like the name of my seminar, it's got nothing to do with body shape and everything to do with that look in my eyes.

The reception area is lavishly furnished in red and gold. I descend to find Gaston surrounded by guys who could only be sailors, with sun-bleached hair, weathered faces and various degrees of stubble on their chins.

"Selkie from Oz," Gaston cries, splashing his drink onto his Aloha shirt. "The other woman in my life." I bend to greet him and he throws his arms around my neck and kisses me on each cheek. "Miguel, here she is. Didn't I tell you she'd make your dreams come true? *Quelle robe magnifique*. What a dress."

Gaston's gone from taciturn to garrulous in a matter of days. Because of his reunion with Genevieve or the alcohol or both? I'm doing my schoolgirl blush and wishing I'd stayed in jeans and T-shirt as a chunky guy with a big black moustache peels himself away from the bar. If I came across Miguel in an alley, I'd be making for the nearest exit. He's exactly how I imagined, with all the features that go with his name, but then I'd seen his photo in the Bay Bar without noting it, as well as a description from Nigel.

"You are the one who wrote to me," he says, his

expression serious. "The mermaid that Tony raves about, his friend when he needs one. And you come to his party before you go back to Hawaii. This is good."

I tell him that I got his contact details from Nigel Shaw. He remembers the big guy with the kayak.

"He goes to the twin islands to be with the birds, then comes back looking like he has seen...God." He crosses himself and I see the crucifix at his neck. "The boys say he keeps a bottle of whisky in that canoe, but I say he doesn't need it."

Genevieve comes down the stairs in a dress as impractical as mine – full-length and strapless. She's radiant and the sailors whistle. She gives me a hug, then introduces me to the crew, who all want to buy me a drink.

Everyone's in good spirits, but Gaston wants to watch the sunset over the water – something he hasn't seen for a while – so we finish our drinks and pile into the vehicles. Two big sailors lift Gaston into the minibus and stash his wheelchair in the back. Then we drive the short distance to the beach.

It's a fairytale scene, with the tide way out and the sun low over the broad bay. Behind us the masts of boats in the marina crowd the eastern skyline. If I was hoping the beach might kickstart my memory, it's nothing like Bantry's Bluff – no narrow cliffs, no moody atmosphere.

The crew start carrying coolers from the bus down a ramp to the sand. There's an almost fantasy view back to the ramparts of the walled city, and to the west two islands are connected to the shore by a wide stretch of sand. Fabienne warned me about the racing tide that floods the shallows and brings the sea right up to the city walls. In rough weather waves even invade the seafront buildings and city cellars. But now the water is a long way off and all is calm –

except for the fluttering in my chest. The setting might be nothing like Bantry's Bluff, but the clues to my memory are circling. Just out of reach.

The two big sailors carry Gaston down the ramp and onto a chair. Genevieve and I unload party food onto folding tables. The crew members push bamboo lanterns into the sand ready to be lit at sunset.

"A Hawaiian touch," Genevieve says. "Tony wants to have a foot in both places tonight."

She's smiling but there's sadness behind her words, and something else I'm not quite getting. She's happy to have her man back, no matter what shape he's in, but her time to leave is close so I guess the old emotions must be seeping back.

Fous de Foudre have set up their gear in a flash that matches their name. Within minutes we're into a party mood as the air fills with their rhythms. I'm the only available woman so I've got no shortage of dance partners. I kick off my shoes and feel the sand between my toes, a sensation that's so familiar I close my eyes. But the collision of recollections doesn't come.

All the time I'm dancing, Genevieve stays at Gaston's side. She nods when I come over to chat to him.

"The sea," he shouts. "I can smell the sea. It takes me back to Hawaii."

His mood is getting wilder. He's clapping out of time with the music. I wonder what he's taking – a cocktail of medications no doubt, now mixed with alcohol.

"Selkie from Oz, before I forget." I bend down so he doesn't have to keep shouting. "Read my *bloglo*. I have written something today."

"A poem?"

"Of course. It's the best poem I've ever written."

"Great. I'd love to read it." I grab my phone from my bag, but he stops me.

"After," he says. "After...tonight."

"OK. Any hints?"

"I stole a word from your *franglais*."

I laugh. "No need to steal it, Gaston, you can have it. You can have the whole bloody poem. Which word?" But I already know.

"*La lézarde*," he says. "Your lizard whispered the word I needed."

The blue-tongue has been busy if it's been sending words to Gaston as well. I haven't told anyone about that encounter. Only Keith and Daisy know. And Gaston it seems. Has his disease given him a sixth sense? It's possible. Like Keith can read Daisy's mind.

Miguel interrupts my thoughts. He's just come back from the bus and on his outstretched arms he's holding a bowl. A large wooden bowl, hand-carved and identical to Nigel's. Its appearance makes me hyper-alert as he puts it down on the table and the sailors form a circle around it. There's a fabric bag in the bowl, tied at the end with a cord and full of a powder that's formed a ball. There's liquid in the bowl too – sand-coloured – and Miguel starts swirling the bag around in it.

He looks up at me and Genevieve and grins. "In the islands the young women chew the kava root, to mix it with the saliva, make it strong. But just two women, your jaws get tired." He winks. "So tonight we use the powder."

Under the light of the bamboo lamps, Miguel begins squeezing the bag over and over with both hands and clouds invade the golden liquid, making it darker. I look at Gaston and see that the rhythm has mesmerised him.

Miguel brings the bowl over to Gaston and says to the

assembled group, "The special Hawaiian *hiwa* brings with it a prayer. For our old friend, Tony Luce."

He holds the bowl for Gaston to sip from it, then passes it to Genevieve, who also drinks. The bowl goes around the circle, each person sipping from its lip, until it finally gets to me. I hesitate. I've heard of kava but I've never tried it and I know nothing about its effects. My drug of choice has always been alcohol. But I collected a bowl in my sleep just like this one.

"Drink," Miguel says. "For Tony. Tonight we celebrate with him."

I gaze into the bowl and push every objection from my mind. I close my eyes and sip. The taste matches the colour and I pull a face, making everyone laugh. Then the bowl goes back to Gaston, who gulps a mouthful, and around the circle again. Miguel tops up the water and keeps squeezing the bag.

After a while we notice that the Fous have stopped playing. They're intrigued by the ritual, so Miguel takes the bowl over and they all take a sip before starting up again.

What happens next is a blur. Some time after they sample the kava, the band starts playing a haunting rhythm and my body begins to move. As I pull away from the circle, I look over my shoulder and see the full moon rising above the masts. The spots on my cowry shell are pulsing against my chest, resonating with the rhythm, and before I know it I'm dancing on my own. But instead of feeling self-conscious I'm feeling the opposite. Introspective. It's the kind of focused inattention that Keith talked about. If Hugo was here, I could bend all his spoons. And my senses are heightened by the potency of the dance, making insights rush into my mind.

I collected the bowl...just for this moment. It's about

leaving.

Someone is leaving.

Someone is going home.

***

When I wake, the light is silver. The moon has risen over the ramparts above me. Some distance off, people are shouting and I try to move, but I'm trapped, curled up in a crevice in the sea wall. I'm shivering. There's a chill seeping through my back from the stone and a strong breeze is coming off the sea. I look around to see the tide rushing in. It won't be long before it reaches the wall.

Panic isn't far off as I imagine the sea consuming us all. I leap out of my tiny *troglo*, grazing my shoulder, and race across the beach towards the confusion of people. The sand makes me fall over, but I get up and keep running.

The party is over. The instruments and tables and lanterns are gone. The sea is lapping the place where I was dancing and everyone is shouting. In the middle of the melee, Gaston is slumped in his chair. The alcohol and the kava have been too much and he's crashed. When I get to his side, I hear what the shouting's about. The big sailors want to carry him to safety, but Miguel has other ideas.

"Wait," he shouts. "The sea must touch his feet. Then we move him."

I'm confused. My head is fuzzy. Why must Gaston's feet get wet? Why was I curled up in a crack in the wall? And why is Genevieve crying?

Everyone goes into freeze-frame and it happens as Miguel instructs. The sea rushes up the sand. Just as it splashes around Gaston's bare toes, the sailors lift him up still in his chair and race up the beach to the ramp. Seconds after we all stumble into the car park, the first waves start lapping the wall.

I'm on my knees, sobbing. My body is shaking with cold and shock. A blanket is thrown over my shoulders and someone helps me to my feet. Genevieve is under a blanket too, wrapped in Miguel's arms.

Gaston hasn't stirred. There's a blanket around his shoulders, and everyone stands in a circle around him, but the kava bowl is gone. The crew doctor is taking his pulse. He nods at Miguel, who instructs the sailors to lift him into the bus. The band's van has gone, so I get into the bus too.

Back at the guesthouse, Gaston is carried up to his room. A subdued version of the party starts up again in the bar, with Genevieve at its centre, but I'm exhausted. I've lost my shoes, and the sand on the soles of my feet is distracting me like hot coals. My brain won't unscramble what's happened, what I've seen, what I know.

I'm grateful for my private room, where I stand under the shower until every grain of sand is gone, then I crawl into bed and cry myself to sleep.

CHAPTER
Thirty-Six

I'm meditating in a dream. I'm sitting cross-legged in front of a piece of paper. It's white, but with the paintbrush in my hand I begin painting it black. Long overlapping stripes of black. I work fast and rhythmically, it's part of the meditation. Like Buddhists create their mandalas in a state of mindfulness, I'm building up layers and layers of black. Each time I lay down the stripes there's one spot I miss. A narrow slit, a crack, a fissure. The white shows through and as the layers get darker, the crack seems to get brighter. I keep going with the stripes. Part of me can see the slit and wants to cover it over, but that part is impotent and the part that's controlling the brush ignores it.

Eventually my hand stops painting. I pick up the paper and press it against a window. The light through the slit is blinding. I rock back and sit very still. I seem to be waiting, and sure enough there's a movement behind the slit. At first it's a far-away dot, but the dot is growing bigger and bigger. It gets to a size that matches the width of the slit and slips through to the other side. My side. It continues to grow, and as it gets closer I see that it's round and hidden by a hood of raven hair.

Shock stabs me through the heart when it starts to turn. It's a head. A human head. A disembodied head. Someone has lost their head. The thought makes me giggle, until I see an ear, then the skin of a cheek. I know who it is but I'm confused. It isn't Gaston, it's someone else. My mother.

I don't want her to see me, but my legs are crossed and I

can't move. At first she's looking down, but when her head stops rotating, she lifts her eyes and looks at me. The emotion that's blazing out from them is another shock – she's looking at me with an expression of infinite regret.

For several long seconds we're caught in the embrace of this look. Then, as if to a silent signal, her hair falls from her head, crumbling to the ground like dust. She's totally bald but her look doesn't waver, then she drops her eyes and turns. I watch her head speed away, back through the crack, and become just a dot. Then nothing. In front of my crossed legs, a tiny pile of raven sprinkles is all that's left of her visit.

I stumble around the unfamiliar room until I find a light. She's visited me tonight, after all these years of silence. Why? To bring me a message, sealed with that look – a look of regret I'll never forget. As much as I've dismissed her as shallow and selfish, we're connected. Forever. A three-way connection. With Dad.

There's no answer at the Seaforth house, and Stella refuses to carry a mobile phone. The tension in my body mounts towards dread, until I finally get through to Gretel.

"I was just about to call," she says. "He's breathing again. We thought we'd lost him. He was gone for a couple of minutes. He's covered in tubes but he's alive." She realises my call is strange. "How did you know?"

"A dream."

"What is it with you and Mum and your dreams? Dad and Mum were at our place and Mum suddenly made Barry get his stethoscope. He listened to Dad's heart and called the ambulance straight away. Dad was inside it when his heart stopped. The paramedics brought him back."

His heart stopped. Stella saved him. Dad isn't dead, but he was. For a couple of minutes he was dead. And I know the exact moment. My mother sent me a message.

***

My emotions are in overdrive so I don't expect to go back to sleep, but when I wake much later, daylight is streaming through the window. Then outside my door, another death confronts me.

Men in dark suits are manoeuvring a stretcher down the back stairs. It's draped in a sheet, but I know who it is. Last night Gaston died too, and he's not coming back.

There's a hush in the dining room. Everyone's at different stages of breakfast. I shouldn't be hungry at a time like this but I'm starving. I ate nothing last night, which might explain my behaviour - and the dream. More insights inspired by my gut.

Genevieve's sitting over an untouched plate, her eyes puffy from crying. The band must have left, and last night's kava-swilling seamen are talking in murmurs. I spot the crew's doctor and imagine him signing the death certificate. No suspicious death to investigate after a spiked drink on a public beach. Instead they brought Gaston back to die in his bed from natural causes. The man had a terminal condition, he was on a lot of medication, he drank too much. He died. The local undertakers would handle the rest.

At the buffet I pour myself a strong coffee and fill my plate with pastries, before taking a seat by myself. I'm the outsider here and I feel it. They all know what happened - including Genevieve, I'm sure of it - but I'll only ever have my suspicions.

The near-death message has left me raw - seeing my mother and nearly losing Dad. And now there's my grief for Gaston. It means I'm not in a fit state to know how I feel about anything. Did Gaston know when he called for Miguel that he'd give him a peaceful death? There must be ports around the Pacific where a substance for such a purpose can be obtained. Perhaps Miguel keeps something under lock and key for 'emergencies'. Because that's what it was, peaceful. Not the cruel decline that MS promises. Out with a bang, surrounded by friends and mementos of the islands, dipping his toes in the ocean to signal his final farewell.

I realise I'm crying. Gaston told me Miguel would kill him - inside knowledge for the stranger - but I played the part of the bystander. There was a risk for anyone who colluded in his death. That's why Hugo wasn't there. But with *Déesse de Mer* back for a refit, the whole crew provided a smokescreen, everyone drinking from the kava bowl.

Should I go to Genevieve? She's the one doing it the toughest. For the crew, Gaston was a colleague long gone. They were here for the ritual, and it's over. Genevieve might have been in the know, but now she's got to deal with the aftermath. After their brief reunion she's alone with her love and her grief. How many times has she lost him now?

But when I look across the room at the circle that's protecting her, I see that she's at the centre. Sitting beside Miguel. A phrase from Cherry about Beauty and the Beast comes back - *only the love of a woman could set him free*. And the truth hits me. Miguel supplied the means, but Genevieve loved Gaston more than anyone else. Loved him enough...to kill him.

***

Back in my room, I'm pleased to have something else to focus on - my escape to Paris. A taxi to St Malo station, then a train to Montparnasse.

There's a knock on my door and Miguel asks if he can come in. I hope he isn't here to insult me with a lame explanation. He isn't.

"You stay for Tony's funeral?"

"No."

"In Hawaii then."

"The funeral's in Hawaii?"

"We scatter the ashes. At Bantry's Bluff."

All paths lead back to Bantry's Bluff.

"I won't intrude on a private ceremony, Miguel. That's for his family and friends."

"You are his friend. He does not suffer because of you."

"I didn't do anything."

He walks to the door and turns. "Sometimes there is a powerful person who makes things happen. They are not at the front. They are...in the shadows."

As I go down the stairs to the taxi, I can't stop thinking about it. The person in the shadows is the fairy godmother in the grotto, the troglodyte in my dream. There's something about that shadow that's calling me home.

Is that what Hawaii is? But I had to come all the way to France to know it?

CHAPTER
Thirty-Seven

In Paris, I've got two days until my flight to Honolulu. The acute loneliness of my previous visit is replaced by a numb emptiness. I speak to Dad, who assures me that after surgery he'll be good as new and there's no need for me to fly back. I don't tell him about the dream. Any mention of my mother's wandering spirit could give him a relapse.

I send Keith a message about Gaston's death, then I call Fabienne for a final goodbye. She met up with Fous de Foudre after their gig and she tells me something strange.

"They all drink from the bowl of wood at your party. It is like tasting the earth, I think. After, they play the music they never play before. At St Malo they all know the rhythm, they play like *fous*. But when they try to play it again last night at the *guinguette*, no-one can remember how to play."

Because of the kava itself, conjuring up a rhythm from a far-away shore? Or because there was a powerful person dancing her heart out in the shadows?

***

Davina surprises me at Honolulu airport. I hide my tears of relief with a joke.

"Your invisibility cloak isn't working. I can see you."

She laughs. "It's working fine. So far. I'm still here."

Thank God.

We walk to her car.

"I was pretty pissed off when you left, Davina. Thanks for the note, but it didn't answer any of my questions."

"I know. I owe you an explanation, girl. But now's not the time."

"About why you changed your name? Fabienne told me."

She flashes her green eyes. "She had no business telling you that. She knows nothing about it."

"She just said it was something to know, but to trust my intuition about you."

"That's not so bad then."

We get onto the freeway and off again, then up the mountain to Makiki Heights where Derek is expecting me.

"When will you move back to Wanda's?" she asks.

"Soon. Her cousin will be out in a couple of weeks."

"So you're still looking for home."

I nod and fight back sudden tears. The rush of emotions I was expecting when the plane landed – a *coup de foudre* that this is where I belong – hasn't happened. It's a blow. After everything I've been through, I'm back where I started. Homeless and confused.

"I've been around the world, Davina, and I'm no closer to finding it."

"Don't be so sure about that."

I need to unload about Gaston.

"Well, well, well," she says. "It's not every day you get to dance at a euthanasia party."

"How did you know I danced?"

"In my mind you're always dancing. What happened?"

I tell her about waking up in the crack in the wall, about running across the sand as the tide rushed in.

"What do you think it means?" she asks.

"Means? While Gaston was dying, I was hallucinating.

After the kava, I danced like a wild exhibitionist, then I crawled into a hole to hide. Then the sea nearly claimed me. It's a metaphor for my life, Davina."

"I wouldn't dismiss it like that. *In vino veritas est.* Kava's like wine – it brings out the truth."

Derek's been waiting at the window. He's walking with a stick when he comes out to the car.

"Aloha, Selkie. It's been too long"

We hug.

"You're back on your feet," I say.

"Yeah. I was almost sorry to lose the *mo'o* boot."

"Mo'o boot? Isn't it a moon boot?" Not that I need any moon metaphors.

"It's that lizard I told you about, Mo'o. I got reading about his legendary exploits: *He connects heaven and earth with his crystal eye.* The boot was keeping me off my feet and horizontal like a lizard, so I renamed it a *mo'o* boot. It made my accident feel more...spiritual."

Good grief. I don't want to get into lizards. And is he still harbouring a grudge about the bowl?

We carry my things inside and Derek brings out homemade lemonade. As we sit at the kitchen counter, he shows Davina the wooden bowl. It's cracked where it hit the floor.

"You were both injured," Davina says. "Your toe and the bowl."

"Both cracked," he says. "My toe in four places, but it's healed. The bowl's worse off. It'll never make kava again."

"Kava?" I almost choke on my lemonade and avoid eye contact with Davina.

"We used to do kava with our *kirtan* group. To put us in the mood to chant."

A kava bowl. I didn't know that when I collected it. Or

my conscious mind didn't. My subconscious knows way too much.

Davina leaves, and I eat some leftovers. Then I go to the boys' spare room and sleep for twelve hours.

When I wake up Alister is in the kitchen. Along with Derek and Nigel. The old team back together. The new-age tragic, the dementia nurse and the seminar tycoon. An unlikely trio. All devoted to me in their own ways. Devoted and overprotective.

Being on my own pushed me to navigate my own path, haphazard as it was. But being back feels important. And scary. How will the journey end?

We catch up over coffee and I present Nigel with the French cutlery rests.

"Mutton-birds," I say.

He laughs. "Yeah, they could be mutton-birds. They're perfect, Selkie. Just right for my *brocante* collection. I'll keep them with that spoon." He winks.

Then Nigel nudges Derek and they make a discreet exit. Alister and I have got things to tell each other. Alister can't take his eyes off me, but his body language indicates his state of mind: depressed. I was right about his son. The DNA test showed that the latest candidate isn't Deshi.

"How do the investigators choose who to test?" I ask.

"Date of birth. Fleur's parents probably re-registered his birth in China. They wouldn't have used his real birthday in case I tracked him down that way, but they couldn't have fudged his age very much. Deshi's birthday was very close to Fleur's, so I've been betting that's the date they used. It's what they'd do – remember Fleur and claim Deshi all in the one action."

I think about the number of people in China. "A needle in a haystack."

"Better odds than that. We advertise in every Chinese newspaper worldwide and investigate everyone who replies. There's a reward for information. This guy ticked the extra boxes – he looks part-Caucasian and his parents recently admitted he's adopted."

"He's looking for his parents too."

Alister nods. "If he was telling the truth. The reward also attracts fortune-hunters, but the DNA test frightens them off. This guy even had a birthmark on the back of his thigh like Deshi. A clue we don't advertise. That's why the PI got in touch and I flew back. If this was Deshi, I didn't want to delay our reunion."

Reunion. A big word. Genevieve and Gaston had a reunion. Then Gaston had a reunion with the hereafter. And I had one of sorts, with my mother in my dream.

There's nothing more to say about Alister's long-lost son, so I tell him that Gaston's dead. As soon as I describe the events at St Malo, he guesses what happened. But he makes no judgements. He saw Gaston's physical condition, and now Gaston's at peace. It's hard to argue with that outcome.

I don't reveal my suspicions about Genevieve's role, but he wonders how she's taking it and when she'll return to the twins. Perhaps he's realised he misjudged her. Then it's back to me and my issues.

"Has the trip answered your question about where home is?" he asks. "Forgive my hidden agenda."

"Still looking. I became a little bit French, but..."

"Perhaps you've been looking in all the wrong places."

"Story of my life. But where's the right place?"

"Here."

"Your hidden agenda is showing."

"Here meaning 'where you are'. Home is more than a

location, Selkie, it's a sense you can carry with you."

CHAPTER
Thirty-Eight

Now that I'm back with Derek and Nigel, a rhythm returns to my life. But a cataclysm is building – I can feel it. Keith's warning about my lost memory hovers like a prophecy: "If you don't tease away at it gently, it'll knock you over like a tsunami." Any kind of tsunami terrifies me – real or metaphoric – but now that I'm back from chasing clues across the world, the right combo of action and detachment is eluding me. It's doing my head in.

Jerome cuts my hair with his usual flourish of scissors and psychology, and although I adore the way the spiky style has become my own look, it pushes me closer to the edge. His haircuts are a paradox – grounding me and unbalancing me all at the same time.

If it wasn't for Being Sleek, I'd be losing it completely. Participants from Tours have spread the word and the demand is growing beyond the mermaid publicity. Invitations come in from Canada, the UK, the US, even Ireland. After learning to relinquish control and let my creativity flow, the seminar has become mine in a different way – the magic will be there when I need it. And after the extra seminars, I've got a tidy sum in my bank account. More than enough to take the pressure off until I sort out my 'home life'. The cliché taunts me.

Dad is recovering from major heart surgery and we talk every few days on the phone. There's a new peace between us, as if that look of regret included him too. My mother's disembodied head looks sorry in a dream, so I forgive Dad.

Whatever.

Gretel keeps me up to date with the rest of the family. She insists that Stella is a changed person since she saved Dad's life. "Her premonitions freaked us out at first, but I reckon you two could find common ground."

"The jury's still out on that one," I say. A psychic Stella is something I can't cope with.

Talking of juries, there's a decision to make about Andrew. Suing him won't be cheap, but we're talking about half of a lot of insurance money. And there are good reasons not to walk away – practical and symbolic. I can invest the money in my future – if I ever find out what it is – and the energy I poured into that house needs to flow back to me as cash. Judy also gives my decision a nudge. She's on the verge of retirement, so if I wait too long to decide I'll have to find another lawyer. I tell her to go ahead.

Juliet's back online with her old *joie de vivre*. As well as losing her phone in the fire she also lost weight from her ordeal. With her new device, she's documenting every step in putting the kilos back on. Reading her blog makes me hungry. There's no mention of Andrew, who's now as homeless as I am. Wherever he's living, Juliet isn't a fixture. Because she's got suspicions of her own? Or because he forgot to visit her in hospital? He used to hide in his trophy shed whenever I was sick.

A parcel arrives from Keith. It's a rock. His handwritten message is short: *Greetings from my garden. Daisy found it and slurped on it.*

A rock from Manly, my teenage stamping ground. I hold it in my hand and feel the love from Keith and Daisy, sending a symbol of a lost part of Selkie Moon...home.

When the Seven Sisters arrive, I'm out for a run. A rare event, but all those baguettes had to go somewhere – and pounding the pavement keeps the demons at bay. I return to find Derek hovering over the enormous box. Nigel's already left for work, with a dire warning to Derek to keep his curiosity in check. I make him wait while I take a shower, then consider opening it in my room, until he threatens to hide the scissors. Half an hour later the sculpture is revealed in all its quirky splendour.

"This is what I call art," Derek says, appraising it from different angles. "It needs an arty name. The Pleiades – no, too obtuse. The Seven Sisters – a tad suburban." He pulls a face. "I know. Spoon-bending For Star-seekers."

Shit. It's a thought I had in France, then forgot. The sculpture brings two of the objects together. After Coral announced *ala*, I treated the objects as sequential things, leading me one at a time along a path. But now I remember that they might all be part of the same clue. Interconnectedness. *Ho'ohihi.* By landing in Hawaii, have the Seven Sisters brought the answer with them?

A message from Genevieve interrupts – inviting me to scatter Gaston's ashes in the waters off Bantry's Bluff. I'm honoured she's asked me but I have to decline. Just the thought of viewing that stretch of sand from a bobbing boat makes me seasick. She replies that she understands, that she's doing OK, that she'll meet me in her lunch hour soon.

Our exchange reminds me that I was in such a state after Gaston's death, I never did read his last blog post. The one he didn't want me to read until...after.

It's another work of art.

La lézarde chante, un moment poignant

Une nocturne éternelle ma vie longue rappele

This profound mare of night attend à la mer profonde

Ma trajectoire aux étoiles est près, and too the time to pray

La lézarde chante, la lumière blanche émettante

Mon époque dans le roc commence, un espace où je dance
J'adore la mort. Mon dieu. Adieu.
No more.

The process of translating keeps my tears at bay. He's played with both languages to create rhymes, but they disappear in the translation.

The lizard chants, a poignant moment
A timeless night-song recalls my long life
This profound nightmare awaits the depths of the sea
My trajectory to the stars is near, and too the time to pray
The lizard chants, emitting a white light
My time in the rock begins, a space where I dance
I adore death. My God. Farewell.
No more.

I'm sobbing by the time I finish. Each image is a metaphor for death, for the afterlife, eternity. The song, the sea, the stars, the light, the space. A space where Gaston is no longer wheelchair-bound, where he can dance. Home.

I keep rereading it, stumbling over the one thing that jars – the lizard. The lizard isn't whispering, it's singing. What's it got to do with Gaston's last moments? I try to recall what he said on the beach, before Miguel cracked open the kava.

"Your lizard whispered the word I needed – *la lézarde*."

Bloody hell. I see it. Letting out a scream, I fumble for the photo of my lipstick message and read it backwards. *Lay zard*. Derek had the right idea – "it doesn't show whether it's masculine or feminine". Suddenly that says it all.

I flick through the pages of my pocket dictionary, trying not to rip the paper. *Lay zard*, if translated directly back into real French, is *le lézard* – the lizard. But Davina said it's pronounced *layzar* – silent 'd'. On the St Malo beach Gaston said *la lézarde* with the 'd' sounded. And there it is in the poem.

With shaking hands I blink at the dictionary entry: *la lézarde* – the crack.

With an 'e' on the end, *le lézard* becomes *la lézarde*. Two different words. Two different meanings. When Gaston looked at my lipstick message his knowledge of French made him translate it as 'lizard': *lézard* with no 'e'. But any native English speaker seeing the words *lay zard* would sound the 'd'. If the word I scrawled meant lizard, I would have written *lay zar*. The word in lipstick means a crack. A crevice. A fissure. Like the one I've been painting and dreaming about for weeks.

The room is spinning and I collapse on the bed. If there never was a lizard what about the blue-tongue? Did that pantomime with the telepathic message really happen? It's a moment before I can think straight. Daisy was the 'telepath', not me. She'd heard me talking to Keith and getting wound up about the lizard. Either with her doggy sixth-sense or her understanding of our conversation she knew I was looking for a lizard, so she brought me one. Another symbol of her unconditional love. There was no message. Being Sleek – the name of my seminar. I didn't read the lizard's mind, I read my own.

The code is finally cracked and I should be elated, but what's really cracked is my composure. Suddenly I'm surrounded by cracks. And it's too much. After all these weeks of mystery, the answer sideswipes me.

The crack in the fruit bowl means there's not a drop of kava in the house. Joke. I'll have to numb myself from the overwhelm of too much truth in the time-honoured fashion.

With a glass in my hand, I correct my translation.

The crack chants, a poignant moment
A timeless night-song recalls my long life

This profound nightmare awaits the depths of the sea
My trajectory to the stars is near, and too the time to pray
The crack chants, emitting a white light
My time in the rock begins, a space where I dance
I adore death. My God. Farewell.
No more.

As the alcohol does its thing, I play the call of the pied butcherbird. Just like on the lonely terrace overlooking the Paris skyline, the music washes over me with its notes of joy and longing. The old emotions keep me captive all over again, until something about the phrasing sends me back to Gaston's verse.

It fits. Every single line of *franglais* matches the rhythm of the bird's fluting notes. The confluence blows me away. Is it chance? Or a dying man's hyper-connection to the other realm? Or did he simply hear about the app from Keith and write the poem to match it?

The reason becomes irrelevant as the poem and the music combine. Soon I'm forgetting about the crack that sings and focusing on the white light. I painted that too. Beaming through the crack, bringing my mother with it, taking her back. The light signifies a path. A path...to the other side.

***

When I wake, I'm in bed – this time with a crack in my head. It's so bad I can't open my eyes. I roll over and through the crack between my eyelids – bloody hell – I see water and fizzy pills on my bedside table. Bless the boys. This might not be home but it's a bloody good substitute.

When I wake again, my eyes open with less meaning and the throbbing in my head has morphed into a dull ache. That's when I see the box. While I've been knocked out, Derek's been mind-reading.

Before I got immersed in Gaston's poem and the phantom lizard, I was putting all the objects together to see how they fit. The bowl and the Seven Sisters are already on the floor. I open the box and spread the other things beside them – the spoon, the ruined lipstick and a printout of its message, the taped-together photo of a donkey. The rock is missing, perched in yet another crack in the North Steyne cliff, so I replace it with the rock from Keith.

Now that the crack has been exposed, the objects should be dripping with nuance, dropping hints and willing me to intuit their secrets. Instead they mock me with how ordinary they look – except for the Seven Sisters, which looms above them like something alien.

The tiny silver donkey is in my bag. I put it with the collection, but there's a question to be answered. Why did I tear up the donkey photo? The taped-together image forms a puzzle, and it's made up of seven pieces. Both elements match my quest. As I stare at the torn edges, they communicate one word. Cracks.

When Keith found a crack in the rock I gave him, he had a lot to say about cracks – openings, secrets, doorways to hidden places, chinks in our defences, entrances to inner caves. I add some of my own: flaws, fracture points, insights, glimpses, weaknesses. Cracks appear suddenly, just like I appeared on the beach. Did my appearance signify a crack? A crack in time?

I read the lipstick message, replacing the whispering lizard with the crack:

Glo tro on air quee
Shot shoe key zard lay shay share
Spoons in a cave

Look for the crack that whispers

Not only a crack...a whispering crack. It's no less cryptic than a whispering lizard, but it brings back Davina's message: *Not everything that whispers, breathes.*

Something makes me grab my cowry shell and look at its crack of a mouth. It doesn't breathe, but it doesn't whisper either. I remember how it used to serenade me and infuse me with strength, but since my disappearance, not a peep. For the first time, I realise that the cowry shell was with me the whole time I was missing. It was *there*. A witness. What does it know that it's not sharing? Something that made it mute.

Through the remnants of my hangover, I look at the seven things and try to employ Keith's advice. Think crookedly. I sort some washing and fold some clothes, hoping the answer is so close that it will pop while I'm inattentive. Nothing.

Over several days, I leave the objects grouped together and glance at them sideways. Still nothing.

I spread them around the house, and jump each time I spy one of them at an odd moment. Nothing.

Racking my brain hasn't done it. Crooked thinking hasn't done it. I've been across the world and that hasn't done it. There's only one thing left, one place I haven't been. The most obvious place and the most confronting. The place with the curse.

Bantry's Bluff.

When I get off the bus a couple of blocks behind Waikiki Beach, Coral and her floral *muu-muu* are nestled in the corner of the bus shelter. I give her a wave on my way to Wanda's flat. I'm about to stash a month's rent in Wanda's version of a safe – an envelope taped inside Doris the dummy's armpit – just in case I need to reserve my bed against intruders waving cash. I haven't seen Wanda since I got back, but we've kept in touch via text message.

She forgot to remind me about the cat. It's sitting on my bed as if it owns it, flaunting its comfort and my homelessness. Shrugging off its unblinking stare, I remove the sunhat from my Shona sculpture. Shona might be silent, but her closed eyes and sense of peace remind me of the last thing Alister said. Shona isn't confused about home. She's grounded wherever she is.

In the doorway to the bathroom I pause, getting the courage to confront Tutu's mirror. The mirror where spirits can be glimpsed passing through the crack between worlds – the same crack my mother used to visit my dream.

Taking a deep breath, I walk up to the mirror and look at my reflection. No spirits, thank God, but my eyes are there, looking back. They're just the same. Did they glimpse something through a crack while I was missing? Like Donkey Skin was glimpsed through a keyhole? Something so shocking that it gave me this otherworldly look?

At Hi-Fibes in the basement I buy a big bag of mixed nuts and dried fruit. Coral beams as she stuffs my offering in her pocket. She's going to tell me something I don't want to hear, but I won't go anywhere without her counsel. I've worn shorts so she can press her feet against my bare thighs.

After a couple of minutes she opens her eyes and speaks. "*Moana.*"

Back on the bus, her two words of advice come together. *Ala Moana* - famous in Honolulu as the name of a boulevard, a shopping centre and a beach. Does that mean if I'd waited for Coral's second pronouncement, I'd have known the answer was here all the time? It seems obvious now, but also unbelievable that I might never have raced off to France.

I text Wanda the two words and she texts back the translation: *Path to the sea.*

It fits with what I know in my gut. It's time to take the path down the cliff. To the place where it all started.

*****

Derek is happy to lend me his camping gear, but he can't help me carry it down the cliff, not until his foot is in better shape. But I have to go now, before I lose my nerve.

Nigel steps in, and we're about to set off when Derek produces an envelope.

"It fell out of the box with the sculpture," he says, "when I was flattening it for the trash. I saved it for a special moment," he adds, before I can scold him.

A card from Fabienne. To read when I'm alone.

Derek waves a handkerchief at the window, making a big deal of being left behind. I'm leaving the objects behind too, because their physical form obscures their message. There's a physical element to my disappearance - I was *somewhere* for two weeks - but the reason I was missing must go beyond the physical.

On the road to the windward shore, Nigel updates me on Rupert. "My cousin in California breeds dogs. When Rupert arrived there, he fell in love with one of them."

"A *coup de foudre*," I say. "Love at first sight."

He nods. "It's early days, but when he's around the dog Rupert comes home, if you will. Stops talking about the war. I've seen it at the dementia unit. With a dog you can't keep hiding in the lost place – it makes you live in the present moment."

I'm thinking about my own 'lost place'. "Why did you call it coming home?"

Nigel thinks about this. "Parts of Rupert were out in the cold. All that war talk created a refuge, a place where his fractured psyche could hide. Coming home is when you call all your lost parts back together."

It's what Davina said. A refuge isn't the same as a home.

We're on our way to Davina's place now, because she's picked up some news about the curse.

"It's all local tittle-tattle," she says over glasses of fruit juice. "When you start asking, everybody's got a story about the curse of Bantry's Bluff. I winkled out some gossip down at the Bay Bar, from a couple of old-timers with some drink under their belts. They say there's a moaning sound that comes from that cove. Years ago, people walking on the beach at sunset heard it – moaning like a ghost. There's a story about a woman running from her drunken husband – Irish of course, and full of Guinness – and she fell to her death on those rocks. Others say she leapt into the sky and became a star, but at the full moon she always returns. To moan."

It resonates with the Seven Sisters, and the story Gaston told about the woman who hid in the hut. It was the full moon when I disappeared. I shiver and wonder what I saw.

"Then I tried Google," Davina says, "and stumbled across a scuba-diving blog."

"Monk seals in the Bluff Cave? It's the only reference online to Bantry's Bluff."

"Sure, that was there. But listen to this, Selkie. At the exact moment you set foot on Hawaiian soil again," she fixes me with a knowing look, "they posted a new piece. About the curse."

The hairs on my arms are standing up. Miguel's words come back: the powerful person in the shadows. It looks like he was right.

"What did the blog say?" I swallow. "Has anyone else...disappeared?"

Davina snorts. "The blog's not believing in any curses, girl. There's a sea cave called the Moaning Cave, in the cliffs below the cemetery. They think that's where the story of the curse comes from."

Nigel's been silent till now. "Sometimes scuba-divers name these places themselves."

Davina is nodding. "They've got some grand theories. I've printed the blog post so you can read them, Selkie. Monk seals moan, you know, and they used to visit Bantry's Bluff in big numbers, so that could be the source of the moaning. But another theory made me think of Derek."

"He only moans when he doesn't get his own way," I joke, trying to ease the tightness in my chest.

"He named his moon boot a *mo'o* boot," Davina says.

"He's on a renaming spree."

"There's a legend about Mo'o the lizard," she continues. "He's called a water spirit – it's all in the blog. The divers think the Moaning Cave was once called the Mo'o Cave, that the name got corrupted."

"Why's the cave named after Mo'o?" Nigel asks.

Davina laughs and gives me a knowing look. "Because there's a great big crack in that cliff, shaped like a lizard."

The revelation almost knocks me over. A *lézarde* shaped like a *lézard*. Just like my mind-map. The collision of clues has begun.

***

We park outside the cemetery gates.

"I'll carry the heavy stuff down the cliff," Nigel says. "Then help in reverse when you're ready to come back."

So he's not afraid that I'll disappear.

"Thanks, Nige. I don't know...how long I'll be."

"DD's packed rations for an army, so don't rush it. It's been a long journey. Now might be when the real patience begins."

"I won't get at the truth by wanting it?"

He grins. "The old spoon-bending trick. It only happens when you don't care either way."

Nigel's a spoon-bender from way back, but I look down at the bent spoon on my wrist and think of Alister. Now that it's too late for him to stop me, I send him a text.

His reply is a shock: *Ho'i mai! Return!*

My fear of disappearing rises up, but I whisper Alister's words like a charm.

We enter the garden of gravestones, silent except for waves pounding the cliff. It's a sound that squeezes my chest, but today it's changed. Last time I thought I was going to die. This time I'm afraid in a different way. But I need to face what happened, so I can live.

Nigel gives me space as I kneel in front of my mother's grave. She was only thirty-five when she died, and I don't know what killed her. Something dramatic. It was the way she lived; it must have been the way she died. Last time I was here I heard a voice, but today she's silent. She's gone. When her wild raven hair crumbled to dust in my dream, she was shedding the remnants of her earthly persona. She was saying goodbye.

I pick a star fruit from the tree that grows on her grave. For later.

I put my ballet flats on the edge of the cliff. To wait for me.

Then I signal to Nigel and, with our gear on our backs, we scramble down the path to the beach.

***

It's several nights until the full moon. After Nigel's helped me set up the tent and left, I sit on the beach. And wait. Something I've learnt from Genevieve. The power of waiting.

I'm alone. After my time in Paris, I know about alone. There, I was confused by my sense of abandonment. But alone isn't the same as lonely. Lonely is an emotion that longs for something else. Alone is a state of being that embraces the present moment. Even the song of the butcherbird sounds different now. Does that mean I'm ready to face the truth?

There have been so many symbols visiting my consciousness these last weeks. Symbols that are implicated in the final outcome. I've brought the blog post about the curse and the scrapbook of clippings about my disappearance. I read, trying not to attach myself to anything. The French article that got scrambled in translation gives me a jolt.

When a girl disappears from the back of a seal, it is mysterious, then goes again two weeks later, we ask a Hawaiian empty beach, a crack did she swallow her?

Swallowed by a crack. A crack in time?

As my fear of disappearing threatens to take over again, I let it go. Detachment. Thinking crookedly. Focused inattention. Allowing the puzzle pieces to align themselves beyond my will.

If I analyse what I'm doing, I'd say I'm *lolo*. Crazy. Taunting the gods to recreate something I don't understand. But I've collected the objects, I've gone on the journey, I've come back to the place where it all began. Isn't this the hero's path – to undertake a great quest, to overcome obstacles and return with wisdom? *Ho'i mai! Return!* But I'm still waiting for the wisdom and I don't feel like a hero.

I watch the outcrop of rocks where Alister found my dress. Buried, like my memory. Another symbol. Something happened here. Something big. Something so big I had to bury it. The forgetting feels like the key. It was something that challenged everything I believe. Something about home. Leaving home. Finding home. But I danced on this beach in the moonlight. Home is a place to dance.

The word about whispering comes back: *chuchoter*. To whisper. Whispering has a quality about it, not necessarily sinister. I've been confusing the 'frame' with the 'fact'. Whispering is just a rush of air. A secret. Something to be shared with someone special. Whether it's a lizard or a crack or a crack shaped like a lizard, when it whispers its message is for me.

Or I'm the whisperer – and I don't know it.

As the sun sets each evening, I pull on a sweatshirt and listen. How will the whispering manifest itself? As a kind of moaning from the ghost of the woman who haunts these shores? I don't believe in ghosts, but I've experienced a lot of things I don't believe in since I landed in these islands. They've been very real. If the moaning happens each full moon, I'll hear it.

One afternoon, a boat appears offshore and a spray of dust takes flight from its stern. Gaston is going home. I say goodbye to him. A troubled man. A selfish man. A brave man. And, to the end, just a man. I remember his horror at the thought we might be soul mates and laugh through my tears. But the objects led me across the world to meet him, so he could mistranslate my message and get me digging deeper. So he and Genevieve could teach me something profound. About love.

***

Derek packed a solar phone charger for me, but I'm letting my battery go flat. Before it does, I turn on the app to listen to the pied butcherbird one last time. The familiar flute-like notes resonate with my reasons for being here – longing fulfilled. I'm being transported by the poignant melody, when I hear something I haven't noticed before. The distant reply of another bird, almost beyond my hearing. There are two birds on this recording, a long way apart but responding to each other. Their connection brings up the hairs on my arms.

Just before my phone dies there's a text from Keith: *When you get the message, hang up the phone!* It's so timely and ridiculous, I laugh.

I'm saving the special things until the full moon. Fabienne's card, Keith's rock. My little black dress and my cowry shell. The full moon is when it will happen. The symbols colliding in this place.

When the afternoon arrives, a storm is brewing. Clouds are building over the sea and the oppressiveness makes it hard to breathe. The cataclysm is almost upon me and the tension is too much. It transforms my excitement and my fear into a new emotion. Dread. I try to drop into a state of calm, but after so many weeks of wondering the waiting has become unbearable. What if the storm comes so late that I miss the full moon?

I throw my hands into the air and shout at the sky, willing the storm to break and crack open my tension, to fill the heavens with thunder claps and lightning bolts, to drench me with a downpour. But there's nothing I can do. The universe doesn't jig to my fiddle. It takes its own good time.

My job is to do what I planned. So, with deliberate movements, I eat the star fruit and drink a lot of water. Then I change into my little black dress and tie the cowry shell around my neck. The blank slip from the fortune cookie goes into my secret pocket, and my fingers find a key hidden there. A reminder about doorways. A crack is a doorway...

Late in the afternoon, it happens. The heavens open. I imagined myself channelling some *fous de foudre*, bounding across the sand and savouring the deluge, but the power of the storm sends me into the tent. Taking refuge in a temporary shelter – another symbol. But the rain pounding the nylon fabric just above my head calms me. I know about tropical storms. This too will pass, as the Buddhists say.

I open Fabienne's card. Between two sheets of cardboard there's a tiny blob of red glass hanging from a black ribbon. A pendant. And with it a haiku. She promised to write one.

The heart shape I blow
Runs away on legs of glass
Making a dancer

Under the steady rhythm of the rain, her words make me laugh with joy. They match the tiny work of art in my hand and remind me of what she said, how 'heart' holds the word 'art'. A beautiful image. Behind her English I hear her accent. And her love. She's made this for me with her own hands, and I spin the tiny runaway heart on its ribbon and laugh as my thoughts form their own haiku:

Hanging by a thread
My heart of glass dances
Finding its way home

I want to tie it around my neck, but I'm already wearing the cowry shell. And the spoon bangle is already on my wrist. I put the heart back into its cardboard covering and slip it into my secret pocket.

The rain stops. When I emerge, the clouds have disappeared and I'm stepping into a fresh new world, with a fresh new view.

I look up. Fabienne didn't mention the Seven Sisters. She's already let them go, and they've made their own *trajectoire* across the sky, carrying a little of her soul with them. I think of my essence smeared forever on Andrew's walls and frown. Like Rupert, parts of my soul are imprisoned in a war zone. But those walls have gone up in smoke! Davina was right about bad things flipping to good. The fire has released my essence, allowing it to leap into the sky like the seven sisters, where I'll know just where to find it.

The scene I've been viewing for days looks new too. The whole time I've been sitting on this beach, I've been aware of the Moaning Cave, its crack of an entrance snaking up the cliff like a lizard, its tail dipping into the crashing waves. It's a lava tube, the scuba blog says, formed when a river of lava flowed over the very tip of the point and into the sea, leaving a tunnel at its core. It's only accessible from the sea, but now the tide is out. Way out. A rare event, according to the blog. It means that at this moment the bottom of the crack is exposed.

Down the sand I race, clutching Keith's rock. I have to get to Mo'o before the sun sets, before the moon rises. Mo'o rhymes with *lolo* – crazy! Because there are huge boulders to clamber over in bare feet and wearing my little black dress.

Mo'o looks down on me as the boulders form a kind of path and, after much scrambling, I'm standing underneath his tail. I look up at the crack that's also a lizard, a dark slash in the face of the cliff. And hear the moaning. The lava tube is moaning through the crack. Or is it the ghost of the woman?

The thought cracks open my mind. Not the woman. My mother. In this moment I know that the woman escaping a drunken man and washed into the sea was her. Always stupid with men, starting with my dad. Tears are flowing. She's gone and I'll never know her. But the rumours about her ghost and the curse that she inspired have brought me back to this place.

It's impossible to climb up the cliff to the crack, but I do it anyway. I roll the skirt of my dress up to my waist with Keith's rock inside. Then, one step at a time, I climb from one toehold to the next, up to the base of Mo'o's tail. Not really the lizard of legend, just a crack that looks like him from a distance. Up close, I see its true identity. A crack that moans as the wind whistles through. And the wind has started to blow.

My hand has grabbed a hold in the base of the crack.

With strength fuelled by impatience, I pull myself up until I get my foot into the crack, then lever myself upwards until my whole body is aligned with it.

Then I laugh. My communication with the blue-tongue lizard might have been one of my figments, but the lizard knew what it was talking about. It's all about...being sleek. I've run off the baguettes and the croissants for just this moment.

I push Keith's rock through the crack and, with a squeeze and a slither, I'm through.

CHAPTER
Forty

Inside is a revelation. I've slithered into a vertical space that broadens into the lava tube. Where the lava twisted on its way to the sea, it formed a platform. A cave. A *troglo*.

The first things I notice are the walls. They're covered in art – sea creatures and shells and coral, a whole kingdom under the sea. An artist has lived here, painting the walls from the pots of powdered paints in the corner.

I wander around in a state of *déja vu*, seeing a shelf made of planks, cans of food, a box of candles, a mug, a bowl and a spoon. There's a fireplace and a stack of driftwood, a pile of blankets in a cosy corner, and an old cracked mirror stuck to the wall. Against the cliff, a spring is bubbling – water for drinking and washing and painting – and beside it a bucket, a *silver* bucket. In the roof beyond the living space, a rope hangs from a hole where an artist craving a secret space must have lowered things from the very tip of the cliff. Around the hole, other tiny holes are dripping from the rain and letting in sprinkles of light.

The sun is getting low and soon it will be dark. By instinct, I find the candle stuck to a broken plate. And the matches. I light the candle, knowing I've done this before. The flame flickers, throwing a shadow against the wall. The shadow of a figure. The troglodyte in my dream.

Memories are bombarding my consciousness. The painting. The silver bucket. The paintbrush in my dream. Other artists have been here, made a home away from home, but it was my turn and I painted my essence onto these walls for two weeks, documented my ancestral affinity with the sea. I may never overcome my fear to swim with seals, but they're my namesakes. I reach out and touch their images. Their lithe shapes, their whiskered faces, their *eyes.*

Grabbing the candle, I race to the mirror. That's what I see in my eyes. The eyes I've painted on the cave walls look like my own. Deep. *Replete.*

No wonder I don't remember. For two weeks I lived here in a state of bliss so profound, it was beyond my conscious memory. But my eyes carried the knowledge – *the look of someone who knows.* I wouldn't believe it, except it's happened before. The first time I presented Being Sleek, everyone was blown away by the magic while I remembered nothing.

I explore my paintings, trying to connect with their deeper meaning, to find the 'heart' in my 'art'. Just like in the Rouffignac cave, the creatures are lifelike but also naive. I focus on the seals, remembering the shamans and their orcas, remembering my sense of the 'others', my sense that I wasn't alone. A description of the artists of Rouffignac comes back: "A shamanic journey to the centre of the unconscious, channelling the spirits of the animals they were in harmony with." Does that explain who the 'others' were – the spirits of the seals? "You're a whisperer and you don't know it," René, the Canadian said. Is this the truth I've been running from?

I sit with my paintings, waiting for an answer. It's possible that the monk seals visited the end of the lava tube, and that when one of them died it reminded me that they were here, but it feels utterly fanciful that I channelled their wisdom.

Whose wisdom then?

As soon as I ask the question, two things happen.

The wind rushes through the crack and begins to whisper. I'm laughing. It moans on the outside, it whispers on the inside. I had to come *inside* to hear it whisper, and it's caressing my skin like long fingers.

Now the holes on opposite sides of the vaulted roof illuminate, one with gold from the setting sun, the other with silver from the rising moon. A brief moment of connection. As their light collides, the walls become iridescent, bathing the paintings in mother of pearl. Just like the fairy godmother's grotto.

Whose wisdom? My wisdom. I had to come inside. Into my inner cave.

I'm on my knees as more memories flood back, hungry to capture every insight, before the whispering stops and the iridescence is lost as the sun and moon go their separate ways.

The 'others' were my disparate selves, clamouring for attention, trying to come home. The parts that I'd kept in protective custody needed a place that was safe and warm, away from the world. Just like Donkey Skin. A space where my emotional wounds could stop bleeding and heal. A *troglo* where I could be the troglodyte. Home.

I spent two weeks of my life in here, but the clues were scattered across the world like crumbs through a forest. Just like the hero's journey, they've guided me back. My house burned down, my life became one spare bed after another, my father almost died and gave me a taste of orphanhood, my mother said her last goodbye. After the long hard journey, I look around the cave loving every familiar corner, knowing I've come home.

I'm crying. This is what I've been fearing – and longing for. To disappear again forever – into my own bliss.

Ho'i mai! Return!

Alister's words slice me open and something pours out onto the *troglo* floor. I fear it's my essence, another man draining me dry, but it's something else. Something I refuse to name. I've remembered my dress. I wasn't wearing it, because it was buried. How could I become whole without my mythical pelt? I left this haven to find it. But I didn't find it. Alister did.

That's the moment when the moon beams right through the crack and bathes my dress in silver. The seals are my namesakes. So is the moon! It brings back the night I descended to the beach, the path the moon made across the sea, how the tide was low, very low. Mesmerised by the selkie myth, my ears full of singing, I took off my dress and danced – along the moonlit path towards the retreating tide, and up to the crack in the cliff. I disappeared into a space of inner consciousness. A private place where my fragmented core could become strong. But when I returned to the world, I forgot.

Now I've remembered. Forgetting and remembering are two sides of the same coin. I've remembered why I didn't need my dress. I've been confusing it with a protective coating, but it's my vulnerable outer skin. The skin I need to be in the world. Susceptible to joys and hurts. I left the cave to look for it. But Alister was the one to find it.

When you get the message, hang up the phone!

I've got the message. I'm strong on the inside and soft on the outside. My time here is done.

I spin around and take in every corner of the *troglo*, the source of my inner strength. "Every place has a spirit," Keith said. That's what I'm channelling. My eyes show that I'm carrying the spirit with me.

I untie my cowry shell and hang it around the mirror. It brought me here the first time, and it's been silent because its job is done. Fabienne's dancing heart goes round my neck, my talisman for going forwards and thinking backwards. *Heart is where the home is.*

Before I blow out the candle, I pull out the slip from the fortune cookie and set it alight, letting my expectations about the future take off through the holes in the roof.

Dipping my fingers into the silver bucket, I use one drop of water to extinguish the candle. Then, by the moonlight streaming through the crack, I walk to the doorway that has taken me in both directions. I won't be disappearing again. From my secret pocket I take the key and toss it out to sea.

Before I lower myself down the cliff, there's one last thing to do. I press Keith's rock to my lips, then place it at the base of the crack. All the symbols of my journey together in one place, where I'll know just where to find them.

***

The gloaming has descended on Bantry's Bluff. The scramble down the cliff makes me laugh out loud – about the power of turning the tables, doing things backwards.

Back on the beach, I dance across the sand in the opposite direction to last time. Taking the second path. Wearing my pelt of vulnerability. Carrying my home in my heart.

Moonlight bounces off my spoon bangle, and Alister's words split me open all over again. *Ho'i mai! Return!*

The emotion spilling from my chest amazes me.

This time I name it.

Love.

When a voice wakes you up in the middle of the night and tells you to write a mystery series what's a writer to do? That's how Virginia King came to create Selkie Moon, after a massage from a strange woman with gifted hands was followed by this nocturnal message. Virginia sat down at the keyboard until Selkie Moon turned up. *All she had to do was jump*, the first sentence said. Soon Virginia was hooked, exploring far-flung places full of secrets where Selkie delves into psychological clues tangled up in the local mythology.

Before Selkie Moon invaded her life, Virginia had been a teacher, an unemployed ex-teacher, the author of over 50 children's books, an audio-book producer, a workshop presenter and a prize-winning publisher. These days she lives in the Blue Mountains west of Sydney with her husband, where she disappears each day into Selkie Moon's latest mystery. Bliss.